The Other Side of Silence

Also by André Brink

The Ambassador
Looking on Darkness
An Instant in the Wind
Rumours of Rain
A Dry White Season
A Chain of Voices
The Wall of the Plague
States of Emergency
An Act of Terror
The First Life of Adamastor
On the Contrary
Imaginings of Sand
Devil's Valley
The Rights of Desire

Mapmakers (*essays*)
A Land Apart (A South African
Reader, *with* J. M. Coetzee)
Reinventing a Continent (*essays*)

The Other Side of Silence

André Brink

Secker & Warburg
LONDON

Published by Secker & Warburg 2002

2 4 6 8 10 9 7 5 3 1

Copyright © André Brink 2002

André Brink has asserted his right under the Copyright, Designs
and Patents Act 1988 to be identified as the author of this work

First published in Great Britain in 2002 by
Secker & Warburg
Random House, 20 Vauxhall Bridge Road,
London SW1V 2SA

Random House Australia (Pty) Limited
20 Alfred Street, Milsons Point, Sydney,
New South Wales 2061, Australia

Random House New Zealand Limited
18 Poland Road, Glenfield,
Auckland 10, New Zealand

Random House South Africa (Pty) Limited
Endulini, 5A Jubilee Road, Parktown 2193, South Africa

The Random House Group Limited Reg. No. 954009
www.randomhouse.co.uk

A CIP catalogue record for this book is available from the British Library

ISBN 0 436 20592 0
ISBN 0 436 20600 5 (South African edition)

Papers used by The Random House Group Limited are natural,
recyclable products made from wood grown in sustainable forests;
the manufacturing processes conform to the environmental
regulations of the country of origin

Typeset by Palimpsest Book Production Limited,
Polmont, Stirlingshire

Printed and bound in Great Britain
by Clays Ltd, St Ives plc

TO EVA

who over the years has provided friendship, comfort, care, support, advice, help, insight, a place to rest, a view on the lake, a car to the Rigi, asparagus in many forms, breakfast at dawn, lunch on the terrace, items of clothing, and abundant love.

If we had a keen vision and feeling of all ordinary human life, it would be like hearing the grass grow and the squirrel's heart beat, and we should die of that roar which lies on the other side of silence

– George Eliot

One

1

SHE HASN'T ALWAYS looked like this. There was a time, there must have been a time, when the face looking back from the mirror was different. Diffidence, yes, always. Abjection, fear. Pain, often. Terror, perhaps. But a difference still – and not only because once her hair was long and, people said, beautiful, but a difference that went beyond the obvious, hovering behind the cracked and mottled surface. She goes on staring, as if she is expecting something else and something more. Surely blood should leave a stain? She has washed her hands, of course. Her whole body in fact. Washed and washed and scrubbed enough to draw new blood from under the skin; but there may be something else that shows in ways the eyes are indifferent to. Does death not show? Murder? The ghost stares back, still inscrutable. And yet there must have been another face, once. Not a matter of age: even as a child she was old, they used to say. But that was in the Time Before, and it was another country. There was greenness there, a green intense enough to darken the eyes, unlike the hard flat solid light of this land, its hills and outcrops and dunes, its sky drained of colour, a landscape too old for memory. The Time Before was green and grey and wet, and it was permeated by the booming of bells. Here is only silence, a silence of distance and of space, too deep even for terror, too everywhere, and marked only, at night, by the scurrilous laughter of jackals, the forlorn whoops of a stray hyena. Or, more immediately, by the whimperings and hysterical rantings of the women withdrawn into their rooms. This is the Time After. Untrodden territory. And no weapon of attack or defence to face it with, no protection at all. Only this feral knowledge: *I have not always looked like this.*

The candle flickers and smokes in an invisible draught; nothing can keep out the night. This is a special kind of darkness. So dark, so palpable, it closes in from all sides on the meagre flame. There is no radiation of light from it at all, just the shape of the flame, no halo, no hope. As if the surrounding darkness is rolling in, like a slow wave unfurling, to spill itself into the small blackness in the heart of the flame; the night outside reaching inward to the darkness in herself. (From those early days in the Little Children of Jesus come the voices of the pious women chanting like crows in the gathering night: *The light shines in the dark and the dark understands it not*.) So one cannot be sure of anything one sees. The eyes are tricked as her face dissolves in the ultimate dark, the dark beyond individuality and identity, beyond any name.

2

THE NAME WAS what first intrigued me. Hanna X. Again and again I worked through the documents in newspaper offices, contemporary reports, archives, all those dreary lists, all the names, each as tentative as the title of a poem, promises withheld. In typescript, shorthand, Gothic print, copperplate, italics, blotted scrawls. Christa Backmann – Rosa Fricke – Anna Köchel – Elly Freulich – Paula Plath – Babette Weber – Ilse Renard – Margarete Mancke – Frida Scholl – Johanna Koch – Olga Gessner – Elsa Maier – Dora Deutscher – Helena Hirner – Charlotte Böckmann – Marie Reissmann – Clara Gebhardt – Martha Hainbach – Christa Hofstätter – Gertrud Müller – and on and on and on, without any sense of alphabet or rhyme or reason, in that interminable shuttle of correspondence between Europe and Africa (in Berlin, Herr Johann Albrecht, Herzog zu Mecklenburg and his formidable sidekick Frau Charlotte Sprandel at the Deutsche Kolonialgesellschaft; in Windhoek, the Kaiserliche Gouverneur von Deutsch-Südwestafrika) concerning – and deciding – the fate of the many hundreds of women and girls shipped from Hamburg to the remote African colony in the years between 1900 and 1914 or thereabouts to assuage the need of men desperate for matrimony, procreation or an uncomplicated fuck. Thekla Dressel – Lydia Stillhammer – Josephine Miller – Hedwig Sohn – Emilie Marschall – names and names and names, each with its surname and its place of origin – Hannover or Holleben, Bremen or Berlin, Leutkirch or Lübeck, Stuttgart or Saarbrücken. Among all of them that solitary first name unattached to a surname. Hanna X. Town of origin, Bremen. That much was known, but no more. Later, true, after her arrival at Swakopmund and her confinement in the secular nunnery of Frauenstein somewhere in the desert, the name of Hanna X recurs once or twice in the odd dispatch or letter. In *Afrika Post* it surfaces in connection with a trial that was to have taken place late in 1906 but was cancelled before it could come to court, as a result of the suicide of an army officer, Hauptmann Böhlke, reputedly involved in the matter. After which, it seems, official intervention very effectively put a lid on it, no doubt to save the reputation of His Imperial Majesty's army. With that, she disappears once again into silence, still stripped of a surname, still fiercely, pathetically (or 'obdurately', as the report on the aborted trial had it) silent.

Hanna X.

Initially, it seems, the mystery might have been caused quite simply by a blotted scrawl in one of the lists compiled by Frau Charlotte Sprandel's secretary which her correspondents, either unable or too hurried and harried to decipher, replaced with the provisional, convenient, all-purpose X. And after that, most likely, no one could be bothered. Why should they be? What's in a name?

When nearly a century later I went to Bremen myself in a last-ditch attempt to return to sources, it only too predictably brought me up against the blank of the War. Almost nothing had survived that destruction: no records, no registers, no letters; and it was too late for the memories of survivors. I had no date of birth, no names of parents, to go by. At the time of her passage to Africa on the *Hans Woermann* in January 1902 she might have been twenty, or twenty-five, or even thirty (presumably not older, as one of the prerequisites for selection was to be of child-bearing age in order to be of use to the Colony); even if there had been town and district records left since 1875 or thereabouts, where would I start without a surname to guide me? As in practically all the other towns I'd visited whole blocks bore the sobering legend, *1945 Total zerstört. Wiederaufbau 1949.* But if buildings could be rebuilt or restored, this did not apply to printed records. Gone, all gone: census details, public accounts, lists of domicile, registers of births or marriages, particulars about the inmates of orphanages or poorhouses, even of brothels. Here was, had been, no Hanna X. Or, perhaps, too many. *Total zerstört.*

Maybe it was my disappointment with my wild-goose chase which on that rainy morning during my visit to Bremen had made me particularly receptive to the paintings of Paula Modersohn-Becker in the Roselius Collection: those glimpses of humanity, of femininity, those solitary and deprived figures, images of almost terrifying isolation, and yet of defiance, a universe of melancholy and understatement and muted colours behind which one sensed a forever unexpressed secret world the onlooker could only guess at, never gain access to. Suggesting, it seemed to me, the male spectator, the heart of being woman, the pathos of being irredeemably young, or irredeemably old, two stages of femininity here remarkably collapsed into each other.

I can recall, from that visit to Germany, only one other painting that marked me so deeply: a large canvas in the Neue Pinakothek in Munich called *Feierabend* by an artist whose name I jotted down on a piece of paper and have since lost. A very young girl seated at a kitchen table with a middle-aged peasant suitor who has his back turned to the observer. One large blunt paw rests on her thigh. His whole body, his ill-fitting jacket, the back of his narrow head, everything defines him as a loser – a mean-spirited, violent, hard-drinking, abusive loser. She, too, is evidently poor. But she is young, her thin body can barely contain the rage and resentment that seethe in her against this moment which will decide the rest of her life. In the debilitating knowledge that he is the very last man she wants, yet the only one she may ever be allowed to lay claim to.

Behind the gallery in Bremen where I spent the whole morning, Modersohn-Becker's melancholy drawn across my shoulders like a threadbare blanket, lies the Rathausplatz with its post-war sculpture representing the Musicians of Bremen – the decrepit old Rocinante of a horse, the mangy dog, the scraggy cat, the dilapidated rooster from the Grimms' tale, their cacophony eternally petrified; but one could still imagine, turning away from the square, with what hellish abandon, given half a chance on a winter's night, they might once again break into braying and barking and mewing and cockadoodledooing to blast the fear of everlasting damnation into robbers and honest burghers alike.

From the Platz, too, came, at night – and that has become for me the defining memory of Bremen – the sound of bells invading the entire Hotel Uebersee in which I was lodged. It would continue for minutes on end, feeling like hours, a summoning of uneasy minds to heaven or to hell. Bells obviously of various shapes and sizes, at least one of which, judging from the sound, must be enormous, reverberating with a deep, unearthly boom that conjured up the image of a giant sculptor giving form and dimension to chaos, creating from it an entire town and its people and its dark history, ringing and ringing through all the centuries of crawling, teeming human life, and hope, and despair, and suffering, and suffering, and suffering.

From this Bremen, from this sound, from the memory of those throwaway musicians, came Hanna X. Into a life marked by her own several deaths. The first of these must have occurred even before she was dumped, more dead than alive, on the doorstep of the Little Children of Jesus on the Hutfilterstrasse. And then twice during the years in the orphanage. Once, we do know, on the *Hans Woermann* ploughing through darker than wine-dark seas on its way from Hamburg, past Madeira, and Tenerife, and Grand Bassa, down the coast of Africa. And then, of course, any number of times in German South-West Africa, now Namibia. Each of these the shedding of an old skin, a death, a new beginning, like a menstrual cycle. A little mourning, a little celebration. Life does go on. And each of these might be the starting point of a story; each, like the sound of the giant bell in Bremen, the shaping of a person, of people, of memories, of a history.

For me, for reasons too dark to unravel, that moment when Hanna X's life breaks into story comes – not the moment of death, but in between deaths – in the lugubrious building of Frauenstein, as it strains against the night sky like a huge ship marooned in the heart of the desert: she is staring by the light of a dripping candle into a cracked mirror on the landing where her image has been caught, in passing, like a ghost. It is the first time since she has been brought here, the first time in three years, seven months, thirteen days, that she faces herself in a mirror.

She does not flinch. The reason is that the reflection is so alien, there is no memory to set beside it. (She hasn't always looked like this.) This may as well be a ghost, one of the innumerable shadows that steal through Frauenstein at night, sometimes even by day. She studies it, detached, unmoved, as if it is a curious large pale moth suspended in the glass. Not scary, because it is not alive. The tufts of blonde or greying hair, hacked off unevenly with a kitchen knife, surrounding the face like ectoplasm. Part of the right ear missing, a dark hole set in a kind of mushroom growth. Only half an eyebrow on the left, trailing off into a twisted line of scar tissue. The eye below it protruding slightly, as if it has been removed and carelessly thrust back. The bony nose crooked. The entire surface of the face criss-crossed with scars, some white, others purplish. Most startling is the grimace that widens the thin-lipped mouth, itself more scar than orifice: it opens across part of the right jaw, below the cheekbone, so that the broken teeth are visible, stuck unevenly into the jaw. A face already partly resolved into skull. Perhaps she is, or slowly becomes, as she stands and stares, fascinated by the image after all. Raising the candle an inch or two, she opens her mouth. She makes a sound. Ahhhhhh. There is no tongue. Only a small black stub, far back. Ahhhhh.

This must be she. This must be what they see, when they face her. But usually of course they look away.

Now she sees. It has come to this. Tonight she has killed a man. She alone is awake in this dark rambling house.

3

THE HOUSE. MORE an outcrop of the earth than a house. Set in an
Old Testament landscape, a moonscape, a dreamscape. To the women
transported here the days and weeks by mule-cart or ox-wagon must
have seemed not so much a journey through geographic and geological
space as the traversal of a region of the mind, an abandonment of
uncomplicated time, and undoubtedly of hope; the arrival an entry
into a peculiar mentality, an emotional state, warped most likely.
Kilometres and kilometres and days of arid earth with tentative patches
of brittle grass, or scrub, small flinty koppies or ridges, flat sheets of
scaly rock showing through the unrelenting ground like blackened
bones through the skin of a massive primordial animal left to the
ravages of sun and wind. Then the gradual sloping upward to the high
tumulus of eroded rocks which especially at sunset or by moonlight
would appear like a congregation of petrified figures. (*There were giants
in the earth in those days.*) Dominated by what to half-crazed sex-starved
men from the desert might seem like a giant woman, a figurehead on
the prow of an absent ancient ship, face turned up, breasts exposed, a
grotesque parody perhaps of the Victory of Samothrace. The strayed
wife of a Biblical Lot. The Frauenstein, the Woman Rock.

Just beyond the Woman looms the house, improbable even in the
full glare of daylight. No one knows its origins. 'It's always been
there,' people say if you ask. It certainly bears little resemblance to
the early colonial buildings of Swakopmund or Windhoek. Those not
inclined to ascribe its foundations to some lost tribe, black, brown
or white, 'from the north', with obscure connections to the vanished
Monomotapa, Mapungubwe or Great Zimbabwe, if not to Solomon

and the Queen of Sheba, or to the inhabitants of a sunken Atlantis, advance theories about early Scandinavian whalers, or possibly crew members who jumped ship when Bartolomeu Diaz first set foot in Africa at Angra Pequeña. Historical reality is likely to be much less fanciful. It may well have been begun somewhere in the eighteenth or nineteenth century by a band of explorers or adventurers, including in their midst someone with delusions of architectural grandeur and bribing or coercing indigenous people into their service.

From the early days of German settlement, over a period of several decades, that much we know, it was extensively rebuilt into its present shape; but its purpose has remained obscure. A country residence for some fabulously rich retired dignitary or general from Bismarck's army (or even the Iron Chancellor himself!)? A grandiose fortress against enemies real or imaginary? A vast prison for Hereros, Ovambos, Damaras or Namas captured in the colony's neverending wars and raids, or even for invaders from elsewhere in Africa or abroad? A hunting lodge for huge parties disembarking from the Reich to decimate the fauna of the interior on a scale not even the British could match? A religious retreat and sanctuary? A house of sexual extravagance? Or did whoever embarked upon it simply lose himself (it could only have been a 'he') in the crazy excess of the act of building for its own sake? An outrageous statement that *I was here*, even though no one remembers any longer who that I could have been?

In one way or another, at some time or other, it may have served all those purposes, perhaps several of them simultaneously. Its magnificence lies in the fact that it has no reason to be there at all. Frauenstein exists, dream or nightmare, a phantasmagoric Schloss, not on the Rhine or in Bavaria but in the African desert. And from the turn of the last century, it found a new designation as asylum to those women transported to the colony for the support or delectation of its menfolk, and then turned down.

Upon the arrival of a female shipment in the bay of Swakopmund, after a journey of thirty days along the west coast of Africa, hundreds of men, consumed by the fires of lust unslaked by native women or domestic animals, would throng and wrestle and clamour on the quayside. Some of them had registered their written requests and requirements weeks or months before; many others came purely on the off-chance, or just to ogle and cheer before drinking themselves into a stupor in the taverns of the teeming town. Then followed the four-day train journey to Windhoek, a seething and brawling sleepless rage in which women were tried out and passed on and exchanged or reclaimed among battling suitors. Men died on those journeys. Sometimes women too. But generally, after four days and nights, the majority would have settled into bleary-eyed couples; and the churches were in business.

Invariably, however, some of the women would remain unclaimed. And these, the ultimately rejected, found unworthy by even the most disreputable of men, were candidates for Frauenstein. In their latter-day tumbrels they were driven through streets of jeering males forming a guard of dishonour baring their backsides or shaking their veined pricks at their rejected quarry; and carted off into the interminable silence of the desert.

And so to Frauenstein, colossal against the shimmering black sky (arrival always seemed to occur at night). Prison, convent, madhouse, poorhouse, brothel, ossuary, a promontory of hell; but also asylum, retreat and final haven. Into which, at long intervals, bedraggled individuals or bands of marauding soldiers, hunters, *smouse* or remittance men from distant mines would stumble in search of shelter or refreshment. And under cover of darkness the most intrepid, or drunk, or desperate of these would find among the inmates some not too utterly irredeemable with whom to disport themselves; and if even then a face would appear too repulsive the act could be performed from behind, as must be the wont of men more used to quadrupeds anyway.

Not all the women were flotsam from the fatherland washed up in search of employment or matrimony. But they had in common the fact that they were all rejects of society, whether through widowhood, indigence, moral turpitude or disability of one kind or another, and that no one else could or would be burdened with the care of them.

The place was overseen by a small flock of females resembling nothing so much as an aviary, birds of all shapes and sizes and dispositions, but all of a feather. Some of them had drifted there to escape from various fates all worse than death, or had been attracted by misplaced missionary zeal; others had presumably been recruited – but by whom? Various churches, it would seem, were involved in one capacity or another, in a rage of righteousness to prove through good works and divers acts of dour charity their Christian worthiness as a step towards everlasting reward and grace. The colonial authorities also had a hand in maintaining the institution: the women incarcerated there had after all been shipped out under a governmental scheme, and the turning of a blind eye might be frowned upon from distant Berlin.

Not that anyone compelled the inmates to remain within those forbidding walls. They were never locked up, not even at night. It was as much by their own choice as by a decision of the provincial authorities that they remained there. But of course, there was also the consideration that even if someone might *wish* to escape, the surrounding desert was more effective than any lock or barrel-bolt. Twice in the early days of Hanna X's sojourn a woman did abscond. On both occasions the skeleton was later found, half-buried in the ever drifting sand.

There were also, barely a year ago, the girls Gertrud and Katja: two young sisters from Windhoek, fifteen or sixteen years old, orphaned by the war in the north, their parents slaughtered by Hereros on the run from the terror perpetrated by the colonial armed forces of Generalleutnant Lothar von Trotha. Placed in the care of a series of foster-parents, the girls had been detained several times for running away and loitering in the streets; held in prison cells or army barracks for a while, reprimanded and punished, all without effect; and then, as a measure of desperation until a decision about repatriation could be taken in Berlin, transported to Frauenstein. There they seemed meek and obedient enough, but only until the doughty woman in charge, Frau Knesebeck, believing all was well, began to relax her vigil; and then they ran away. After a week the older girl, Katja, returned, a dishevelled and emaciated rag doll with half its stuffing torn out; Gertrud had died in the desert. What remained of her after the vultures, the jackals and hyenas had done their bit, was brought back to Frauenstein in a hessian bag and buried with little ceremony in the quietly expanding cemetery beyond the pumpkin patch. After that Katja was like a dispirited puppy broken by too many beatings, whimpering as she wandered through the halls and passages and empty spaces like one of the many ghosts that haunted the place.

The only person to whom she appeared to react was Hanna X; at night the girl slipped into the woman's room to find comfort in the dark they both feared. No one could fathom the reason for this attempted closeness; no one cared. And as time went by they became almost inseparable.

Katja could be silent for days on end, a silence interrupted suddenly and unpredictably by bouts of uncontrollable chattering. It was not necessary for Hanna to respond much, which was just as well, as without a tongue she could of course not speak. But from dark recesses in her memory she began to retrieve snatches of the sign language she'd had to learn at a time she looked after an angry deaf old man and his angry deaf young daughter; this she taught to Katja, in fits and starts, and the girl was a ready learner. Where she couldn't recall the original signs she made up new ones. They even had fun – in that grim place – devising these together: a clenched fist for *man*, an open hand for *woman*, thumb and forefinger opened and closed for *bird*, a hand cupped in a crescent shape for *moon*, a hand with fingers spread wide for *sun*, a rippling motion for *water*, easy and obvious gestures to indicate walking, running, sleeping, while body parts were simply pointed out.

Soon Katja was the only person in Frauenstein with whom Hanna could, in a way, communicate; and Hanna the only one to whom Katja cared to talk. This sealed the unusual bond between them. As it was frowned upon by Frau Knesebeck and her staff, they tried as best they could to keep it secret. But most nights Katja would come tiptoeing from her room to Hanna's and creep into her bed with her. Which sometimes stirred painful memories of another girl, another woman, in her mind: but these she resolutely repressed. That was a territory sealed within her, where no one would readily be allowed to obtrude. And if there was, in the occasional unguarded moment, a fleeting memory of the arcane yearnings and urges a body was capable of, it would be denied almost before it could be acknowledged. If anything, Hanna's reaction to Katja was maternal, not carnal. And this made it possible, for both, to survive between the barren walls of the great building surrounded by the desert, swept by the wind.

Frauenstein was too vast for its inhabitants. Rooms on some floors had not been opened or entered in years. By the time Hanna X was dumped there parts of the ground floor had already been invaded by desert sand, blown in through broken shutters and shattered windows and gaping holes where doors had been hacked up for firewood; sand accumulating in corners and against walls, as very slowly the desert began to reclaim the space that once was part of it. Even the inhabited rooms were subjected to the long inexorable process of decay: erstwhile ballrooms and refectories, kitchens with gaping furnaces, cavernous halls and lobbies with ornate ceilings; or the smaller rooms and cells and cubicles where the inmates slept or spent their days staring and mumbling, shuffling, masturbating, moving restlessly to and fro, doing useless embroidery, making patchwork quilts or curtains or tablecloths or shifts for imaginary trousseaux, or just sitting, or preening in front of real or non-existent mirrors, or slicing patterns into their skin, using knives and forks and shards of glass or scraps of rusty tin.

The more enterprising ventured outside into the garden, wearing outsized kappies they had made with the same studious care and lack of skill that marked their other endeavours; and with grim Teutonic determination persuaded the earth to bring forth thirty-, sixty- or hundred-fold. Pumpkins and carrots and leeks, potatoes and gnarled sweet potatoes, even tomatoes, cabbages, beans, peas, gooseberries. This is the secret of Frauenstein: that high up against the rocky promontory, behind the statue of the Woman sculpted by the wind, there is a magic fountain. Invisible unless you accidentally stumble across it, it bursts white and rapid from a fissure in the rocks, courses briefly among the boulders and then disappears underground again as if it has never been there at all, except in a febrile dream.

4

THE WHOLE SHIPWRECKED house is straining against the cables that creak and tense to keep it anchored in the shifting sands. Suppose at a given moment they can hold it no longer. Suppose it takes off, and sails into the pitch-dark sky, sailing through space, moonless starless space, back to beginnings. Like a stream returning to its fountainhead.

5

THE FOUNTAIN IS where Hanna X buried the dead man. The event will still be with her as she scrutinises her naked face in the mirror, all of its history folded into itself as if it were a single moment. Because this is where her whole life converges: what has happened until now, what is waiting yet to happen. A death, a birth.

The sound of the man's head as she descends the staircase, dragging the body down, the two heavy boots tucked under her armpits. Thud thud thud. With a curious jerk of the head at every thud, as if he is still alive, nodding in approval, or perhaps convulsed in silent laughter. A muted sound, for she has swathed the head in a sheet to stanch the blood. Thud thud thud. The girl Katja is not with her. She must still be crouching in her room, on the stripped bed, against the wall, naked as a small plucked chicken, the pillow crumpled against her insignificant breasts, stricken eyes staring. It is a long way down, two storeys, but Hanna is not aware of it. All thought is suspended. Attending to the matter at hand as she would otherwise concentrate on washing flagstones, emptying a bucket of nightsoil, working her way through a pile of dishes, washing a bundle of dirty laundry, slitting a chicken's throat. For now, this is the only necessary action, descending step by step, as if all her life she has been waiting for this moment. Thud thud thud.

She stops only at the bends to check for leaking blood. The man is as messy as a slaughtered pig. But a trickle or a smear here or there need not be a cause for concern. It is that time of the month in Frauenstein. Her own sheet had been stained even before she tore it from the bed to wind around the man's pulped head. All the inmates have tuned in to the same rhythm. Which made it a less than propitious time for the visiting garrison earlier in the day – no doubt the reason why the encounters between officers and women were so much more violent than usual. Little Katja must have been the only one not in flow; her bleeding has been very irregular since she came stumbling from the desert that day under the spiralling vultures. Poor thing. Now this. Thud thud thud.

It used to be the same in the girls' orphanage when Hanna was a child. All of them in unison with the dark rhythms of the moon, under the forbidding eyes of the women in charge: *That time again. Now the bread won't rise, the milk will turn, the meat will go off in the cool-room, the knives will become blunt, the mirrors will tarnish*. The curse, the curse. Except that tonight she has turned it against a man, this pink bloated pig. He is outlandishly heavy. It is hard work. But she is strong. It has always been her one commendable virtue. *Hanna is as strong as an ox*. They would add: *And as thick-skinned*. Or: *As stupid*. Anything heavy to lug from one room to another, to carry the groceries from the market or the joint of meat from the butcher's or the shit bucket to the pit at the bottom of the garden, call Hanna. She's strong, and she doesn't mind. Thud thud thud.

Tonight the mirrors won't tarnish, the bread will rise, the knives will remain sharp, exhilaratingly and exquisitely sharp. It is the celebration of the blood. For once she has not flinched. (There was that other time, on the train. But that was different. God, how different that was.) Thud.

She opens the front door. Behind her the great house groans and murmurs in its sleep. Outside there is wind. It has been blowing all day, in long sweeps and waves interspersed with shorter, angrier gusts, drowning out the possibility of other sounds, confirming the fearsome solitude of the house below the outcrop on the plains. She drags the body after her, returns to shut the door, closing off behind her a dimension of existence, something that can never return to her or be returned to. Like a mule yoked to a plough, bent double into the wind, every muscle of her awkward body strained, she moves on, hearing now only the hiss of the thing behind her as it is dragged over bare earth and patches of scrub and ridges of stone. She knows that what marks there may be will be obliterated by the wind in no time.

In a wide curve past the vegetable garden and the graveyard. Up the incline towards the rocks from which the spring erupts. In the silence of the wind she can already hear its subterranean liquid libidinal sound. A smoothness embroidered with a delicate sibilant tracery. She moans in response, a deep low sound from her guts, up through her heaving chest, into the wet darkness of her throat, past the miserable brief stump of a missing tongue, through parched lips. Without waiting, except for a brief moment to stretch her back, she proceeds to strip the clothes from the body. There is no moon, though the stars are strewn recklessly through the sky, almost within reach. By their disinterested light the bare body seems faintly luminescent, a pale anonymous lump which she drags across the boulders and through the icy water to heave it into the black hole from which the stream comes gushing. Infinitely patient, tireless, she labours to lug and carry stones from lower down back to the source where she rolls them into the hole. She works with admirable economy. This, too, seems to have been prepared and rehearsed for a long time, a lifetime; not in the mind but in the very body, the body that is right now ridding itself of another fruitless waiting and an accumulation of unnecessary blood as it prepares for a new beginning.

The clothes, wrapped in the stained sheet, she carries back with her to the outside baking oven behind the kitchen wall. There she meticulously tears all the brass studs and buttons from the uniform before she opens the half-round metal door of the oven. Using twigs and dried grass from the firewood boxes beside the woodpiles she soon coaxes new flames from embers still smouldering inside from the afternoon's baking. She adds one piece of wood after another until the fire is burning with impressive vigour. Giving it time to settle, she picks up the brassware stripped from the now anonymous uniform and goes down the footpath to the latrine pit where she can dispose of it. By the time she returns to the back of the house the blaze in the oven is so fierce that it singes her hair and eyebrows. But she adds even more wood, stands back for a few minutes, contemplating the flames with the intensity of a meerkat waiting for a snake to move; at last, with a small grunt of satisfaction, she hurls into the fire the uniform jacket, the trousers, the jackboots, the helmet, the soiled sheet in which she'd wrapped the officer's head. A brief glance reassures her that there is no sign of human or animal life around. She tears the long dark-stained shift, which is all she is wearing, from her body and adds it to the raging fire in the oven.

From a safe distance, bent over to peer into the flames, she surveys for another few minutes the burning clothes, and then, swiftly now, she flits like a shadow around the house and pushes open the heavy front door. Back inside, she listens warily in the great dark entrance hall, then steals, naked, upstairs to Katja's room. The girl is sleeping now. Fitfully, and whimpering, but bludgeoned into oblivion by exhaustion. So let her be. With a nod of satisfaction, perhaps relief, Hanna returns downstairs. In the kitchen she fills a large basin with water from the tub beside the stove which is gleaming at her with the eye of a wicked cat in a robber's house; and although the water sends a shock of cold through all her limbs she begins to wash and scrub and scrub herself, from head to toe, with a controlled rage that is at odds with her seeming placidity. Then dries herself with clean kitchen towels from the bottom drawer of the sternly formal dresser. Still naked, but mostly invisible, gleaming only briefly, palely, as she passes the windows on the landings, every movement of her ungainly long limbs soundless, she returns to her room.

It is when she comes past the large mottled mirror on the second landing that she catches sight of herself. And goes to fetch a candle from her room, and returns to stare, for the first time in three years, seven months and thirteen days. At her face. Then at the rest of her body, all the way down. Everything *they* have seen and she must now dare to look at. What has happened has finally set her free to look.

6

THIS IS WHAT has happened. It is late that night when she hears the scream from Katja's room, across the landing from her own. She sits up in her bed. No one will come. Many inmates scream or cry in the night. And Katja, everyone knows, has nightmares since she came stumbling back from the desert on bleeding feet. But this scream, Hanna recognises immediately, is not provoked by any dream. She knows the child; she knows nightmares. She knows screaming. One does not need a tongue for that.

Clothed only in her shift, and not bothering to cover her face, as she has the habit of doing, with her voluminous kappie, Hanna moves across the floor on bare feet to open her door. One leg drags after her, but she has long become used to it and moves swiftly. Tense, pressing her forehead against the jamb, she waits. There is a second scream, followed by what may be a blow, or a body falling, and then more muffled sounds, a man's voice raised in anger. She reaches Katja's door and pushes against it. It is not bolted.

As she bursts across the threshold she has a heavy brass candlestick in her hand. How it came there she doesn't know. It happens. Once before, soon after her arrival at Frauenstein, she was walking in the veld far from the house, when she put her foot down right beside a bloated beautiful brown-and-yellow puff-adder. As the snake struck she jumped up to get away and when she came down she had a rock in her hand. Only after she had killed the puff-adder did it occur to her to wonder about the rock. The earth was bare and sandy there, no stones lying about. But she didn't stop to tease the thought for long. Such things happen. And this time she has the candlestick. The man is standing beside the narrow bed with its striped grey blanket. It is the officer from this afternoon. She recognises the uniform even though he is wearing only the khaki jacket with the fancy golden braid. The helmet lies discarded on the bed. His trousers are crumpled on the floor. His buttocks show up very white through coarse black hair. The girl is lying naked, huddled like a foetus at his feet, whimpering. His right arm is raised above his head, a heavy-buckled belt hanging down from it like a snake. Hanna has seen the posture before. In the orphanage. On the train.

The snake strikes down. The girl screams and rears up, her face streaked with tears through her long tousled hair. On the half-formed mounds of her breasts the tiny nipples seem to stare like horrified dark eyes.

The man is bellowing with rage, 'You're not bleeding! Why did you tell me you were? You're not bleeding! You're not bleeding, you lying little slut!'

Clearly beside himself, he brings the heavy belt down again with so much violence that he almost loses his balance. This time Katja sees it coming and half evades the blow. She also sees something behind him. For a moment she freezes in disbelief.

She exclaims, 'Hanna!'

The man, in the motion of raising his arm again, swings round to look. As a result the heavy candlestick comes down on his nose instead of the back of his head. He is momentarily stunned. As he goes down on his knees to cup his face in his hands the second blow breaks his knuckles. The third cracks his skull. He is blinded by blood. A bellowing sound turns into a gurgle in his throat. And still she goes on striking, beating, smashing, as if breaking the bars of a cage. From her throat come grunting, growling sounds. They may be smothered sobs, or not. She has never heard sounds like this coming from herself.

It is only when she gets too tired to raise the heavy brass thing any more that she is forced to pause, panting and gasping, her whole body heaving.

'You must stop now,' pleads Katja in a low moan. 'You have killed him.'

Hanna nods, dazed. She sits down heavily on the bed. The girl flops down beside her, reaches out to touch her, then withdraws her hand.

'What are you going to do now?' she asks.

Hanna shakes her head. She gestures towards the girl's skinny body and makes a movement with her elbows to say, *Put on something.*

Mortified, Katja briefly covers her chest with her hands, turns away, starts fumbling with the pile of day-clothes on the small table near the window (the shreds of her night-shift are spread across bed and floor). As she stretches her hands above her head to put on the pauper's dress donated by well-meaning ladies of the church, she unexpectedly breaks into a giggle. It turns into uncontrollable, hysterical laughter which goes on and on until she collapses on the bed. Only when Hanna reaches over to press the girl's body against her own does the laughter change into wailing.

'He looked so funny,' she sobs. 'In that smart uniform. And with his bare arse.'

Uttering low comforting sounds Hanna rocks the thin body; she can feel the girl's ribs.

Slowly the sobbing subsides. Katja begins to talk. It is confused and random, an uncontrollable flood interrupted only by deep convulsions which rack her body.

'This afternoon. There were so many of them. And then you hid me. But I could still hear them. Everywhere. And the women. It was like when we were on the farm where my father had his trading store. They killed him. With an axe they found in the shop. He was repairing the gate to the cattle kraal. My brothers were helping him. Gerhardt and Rolf. But those Ovambos didn't just kill them, first they . . . You know? And Mother and Gertrud and me just stood there. But they never touched us. They even left some food for us when they went away. The next day we went to the mission station that's six hours away. We first dragged the bodies into the house. To keep the vultures and stuff away, you know. Mother didn't want to go, but we made her. And then on the way she fell and broke her leg. Oh Jesus. We went to the station and brought the people back with us but the hyenas had got to her before we could. And there were vultures all over her. And flies, just everywhere. All over Father and Gerhardt and Rolf when we got back. The missionary tried to shield them from us, but we saw them. And smelt them. Later the soldiers came to take us away. The same ones as this afternoon. I don't mean the same men, but the same khaki uniforms. The German army. We were so happy when they came. Gertrud was smelling too, when she died in the desert. For a whole day I tried to scare the vultures off. And the jackals. But I was frightened of the hyenas. So I had to leave her there, you know. And anyway I couldn't stop the flies. All over the bodies. Over hers. I don't know where they came from. They were just there. But it was better when the soldiers came. No one came when Gertrud died. Only when my parents were killed. After two days, I think. Perhaps three. And the solders were really so good to us. They gave us food and water and everything. Only when they found black people in the veld they were not so good. On the way to Windhoek.' She shudders. 'You know what they did?'

Hanna presses the girl's face against her chest to smother the talk. But Katja struggles free from her fierce embrace.

'So when they came this afternoon I wasn't scared. Not in the beginning. Only when they. When he.' She tries to turn so that she can look again at the heavy half-naked body crumpled on the floor, but Hanna forces her head back.

That is enough now, her face says.

'What are we going to do with him?' the girl asks again.

Hanna looks at her, staring hard into her eyes. *Will you help me?*

They kneel down and begin to put the uniform trousers back on the dead man, turning their heads away, which makes the task more difficult. The girl starts giggling again.

Hanna utters an angry sound of reprimand.

'When they found black people in the veld they caught them and beat them and gouged their eyes out and tied them to anthills and left them there and some they hanged from thorn trees, you know, those big ones, the camel-thorns, and some they took and cut off everything, their ears and noses, their hands, their feet, their things, everything. And they put their things in their mouths and stood round them and laughed and smoked and drank schnapps. But they really were so good to us, as if they were our fathers or our big brothers, only some were quite young.'

Hanna grabs her by the shoulders and shakes her. *Now stop this! For God's sake, shut up!*

'You don't believe me? I tell you, I saw everything.'

You think I don't believe you? You think I haven't seen or lived it?

'And when they came this afternoon, I was happy to see the uniforms. This one too, he looked like the leader. When he put his arms round me and kissed me it was like my father, and I felt like crying, I was so happy, I remembered so many things, you know, from long ago, when we all, when Gerhardt and Rolf and Gertrud and I, but of course Gertrud died. And then all of a sudden he wasn't like my father any more.'

7

THIS, AS HANNA recalls it, is what happened in the afternoon. The detachment arrives just after noon, from the south. A group of officers on horseback, followed by a crowd of haggard soldiers on foot, fifty or sixty or eighty, then a wretched line of naked prisoners, hands tied behind their backs, strung like dusty beads on a rosary with thongs running from one neck to the next. Namas, by the look of them: short, slight people, yellowish in colour, their faces pinched and furrowed. Most of them are men, but there are women as well, and even a number of children. The rear is brought up by another band of soldiers with guns and whips and sjamboks.

They must be followers of Hendrik Witbooi, fighting on out of sheer habit or stubbornness even after their captain's death five months ago. In the early days of this war that has been ebbing and flowing through the vast land for years now there used to be a kind of gentlemanly code of conduct determining relations between the German army of occupation and the indigenous pepople; it is known that on one occasion, after Witbooi had been beleaguered on a koppie for weeks, he sent a letter to the German commander on the plain below ('My dear German imperial Herr Franz') detailing his needs: food, water, two boxes of Martini Henry ammunition, 'as is only fit and proper between large, decent and civilised nations'. But soon there was little evidence of honour remaining; and as time dragged on, particularly after Generalleutnant von Trotha took command, the war became as beastly as any other, engulfing large tracts of the colony as the general implemented his Tabula Rasa strategy. Sometimes it was reduced to a mere dribble of incidents, isolated guerrilla attacks on farms and outposts and military camps, but two years ago, in 1904, there was a sudden and total conflagration. The Hereros, finally uprooted from their ancestral lands by German expropriation and by the cattle disease that ravaged their herds and having nothing more to lose, unfurled wave upon wave of desperate attacks to drive the Germans – *Schutztruppe*, settlers, merchants, all – into the white-crested waters of the Atlantic. This time they were joined by most of the other native peoples, from the Kunene all the way down to the Orange. And after the violence had burnt itself out in the north it raged on in the south. Now, even after von Trotha has been recalled, his military successor, Oberbefehlshaber Dame, is continuing the campaign against the Namas. Which is where this detachment comes from.

Someone looking from a high rear window in Frauenstein gives the alarm. Within moments there are women clustered in every window like bats in a cave while the staff, with the diminutive but formidable Frau Knesebeck in front, form a protective phalanx in the backyard, between the kitchen and the barns and stables. The whole edifice is trembling with excitement. Strangers: visitors! And such a multitude of them. There is a sense of real occasion, something almost unheard of. And at the same time there is apprehension, fear, terror. All these military men – they cannot be up to any good. Such visits in the past have been restricted to small patrols of two or three or half a dozen soldiers at a time; and God knows what havoc they left behind. What lies ahead today cannot be imagined. Such an incursion from beyond the desert has all the impact of an event greater than history, it is the stuff of legends and of myth. This is the closest the war has yet come to Frauenstein; suddenly it is no longer a murmur of rumour and conjecture and possibility but something overwhelmingly real. It is here, it is now. They are aquiver with anticipation.

The commander is the first to alight from his horse. Clicking his heels, he bows stiffly to Frau Knesebeck.

'Gnädige Frau!'

'Whom do I have the honour to meet?' she enquires, tentatively extending a stiffly formal hand.

On a level with him, she finds his figure less impressive than when he was on horseback. Stockier, more fleshy, his legs somewhat too short for the heavy torso; and sweating copiously. Even so the khaki uniform with its many braids and brass accessories makes him seem a splendid specimen of imperial manhood.

'Colonel von Blixen,' he says, pressing sun-blistered lips to her knuckles.

His company is on its way back from Namaland, he informs her. He is happy to say that behind them lies an appeased land. There should be nothing more to fear from that direction. But his men are exhausted. Some refreshment would be in order. He glances up at the windows thronged with female bodies. Some entertainment too. If what they have heard about this admirable establishment is true.

'We keep a decent German house,' says Frau Knesebeck, pursing her lips. But it may well be accompanied, to the keen and possibly wishful observer, by the hint of a wink.

'We shall abide by all the rules of gentlemanly behaviour,' he assures her. His wink is less ambiguous.

'We lead frugal lives here,' she informs him. 'We do not have an abundance of victuals at the ready.' Noticing a narrowing of his eyes she hastens to add, 'But what we have is at Your Excellency's disposal.'

'Once back in Windhoek,' he says with a gesture of magnanimity, 'we shall arrange to make good to you whatever my men consume today. Tenfold.'

Frau Knesebeck makes a few quick calculations before she turns to her staff to give her own instructions. Six goats will be slaughtered, and any number of chickens. From the garden an abundance of vegetables will be brought in.

A foreign fever spreads through the corridors and recesses of the building as the women begin to make preparations for the feast while the men take charge of roasting the meat over large bonfires from the woodpiles outside the kitchen. From a distance, covered in ochre dust which leaves only eyes and mouths exposed, the prisoners stare in abject apathy. Two guards with sjamboks keep moving slowly along the rows to deal with anyone tempted to topple over from fatigue, hunger or pain. Before the afternoon is out, two bodies will be dragged off some distance from the house and left exposed to the predators that have been following them at a judicious distance over the last few days.

The soldiers eat outside. The officers are served at the long refectory table set in the middle of one of the seldom-used reception rooms on the first floor of the residence. Because very little light intrudes through the tall narrow windows – the whole place appears to have been designed from the need to shut out as much as possible of the outside world – there are chandeliers on the table and erratically flaming torches in brackets on the bare walls, lending a medieval, unreal aspect to the place. Frau Knesebeck is seated at one narrow end of the table, Colonel von Blixen at the other. Huddled against the surrounding walls, visibly torn between fascination and terror, are the thirty or forty female inmates, peremptorily summoned by the mistress of the house, ogling the excesses of the meal and the men partaking of it. They range from what seems like toothless crones (although it is doubtful that there is anyone above fifty) down to the barely nubile Katja. The girl is squeezed in between Hanna X and a squint-eyed youngish woman, Gerda Kayser, a comparatively recent arrival, whose face has been ravaged by smallpox. There is a constant flow of movement up and down along the broad stone staircase (where much later, in the night, Hanna X will drag her victim downstairs, thud thud thud) as the women on the staff carry off used plates to the kitchen and return with new laden dishes. Frau Knesebeck has had brandy brought up from the cellar. Very few of the inhabitants of Frauenstein have even been aware that such a supply is hoarded there. It must date back to the early, half-forgotten years of the place, presumably transported from Windhoek or perhaps Lüderitz on one of the wagons which still, a few times a year, traverse the desert with provisions Frauenstein cannot produce on its own – salt and sugar, oil and vinegar, coffee, paraffin and lanterns, small quantities of chewing tobacco, medicaments, shoes and clothing, needles and wool and reels of cotton, cutlery and crockery, occasionally paper and ink and pens for records and registers which are supposed to be kept although it is hardly ever done, bales and bolts of chintz or cheesecloth or sheeting, some basic farming implements. (From time to time there is some official error which results in large quantities of unexpected and unnecessary items being dumped in the yard: once a whole wagon-load of porcelain pisspots, once a pile of army uniforms, once a mountain of left shoes, a consignment of sheep-shears, a supply of pickaxe handles intended for a mine in Otavi or Otjiwarongo. So, too, presumably, once, the superfluity of brandy.)

As the meal progresses and the spirits flow more and more copiously, the officers grow steadily more rowdy. Some resort to eating with their hands, tearing meat from bones with their teeth; glasses and plates are broken; brandy is gulped directly from the bottles which continue to be brought up from the dark bowels of the building. And judging by their ever more irresponsible comportment several of the serving women must also be partaking of the liquid fire as they shuttle along an increasingly unpredictable route between cellar and dining hall. Frau Knesebeck's mouth resembles more and more the rear end of a fowl as Colonel von Blixen's gestures, accompanying his account of exploits on and off the field of battle, become more recklessly expansive and more precarious.

Here and there on the long sides of the table the general carousing erupts in raucous song; among members of conflicting groups of singers scuffles break out. More crockery is smashed, no longer in exuberance but in anger. Colonel von Blixen rises to his feet, steadies himself on his long arms, and thunders a long command ending in a string of verbs. Escorted by four more senior officers, the gang leaders in the brawl are ordered out. Stripped of the insignia of their ranks, they will accompany the footsoldiers outside on the resumption of their march. For a short while, under the scorching stare of their commander, the men remaining at the long table fall silent as they attempt, with varying degrees of success, to pour the next round of brandy in the abandoned glasses. The escorting officers return up the broad staircase, two of them on all fours.

'It is time to drink our toasts,' announces the colonel, who appears to have forgotten that they have already done so.

The officers rise with studied dignity. Three toasts are proposed and drunk. To their gracious hostesses. To the high command in Windhoek. To His Imperial Majesty, Kaiser Wilhelm II in Berlin.

'We shall now proceed with the enjoyment of the other delicacies so graciously put at our disposal,' announces Colonel von Blixen.

He pushes out his chair, takes a moment to steady himself with his hands on the high back, and begins to move in slow measured strides towards the nearest cluster of women against the wall. He stops to wipe his perspiring forehead with a large kerchief drawn, not without effort, from his pocket. Beaming the goodwill of the conqueror, he raises the chin of the first woman, briefly studies her face, moves on to the next.

'Herr Oberst,' says Frau Knesebeck, rising hesitantly at the far end of the table.

He pays no attention. By the time he reaches the fifth or sixth woman his comportment has become more brazen. He no longer merely lifts a head or a hand or pinches an earlobe but palpates a breast, tweaks a nipple, forces a knuckle between the lips of the woman in front of him. The tweaks become fiercer as he moves on. One woman moans lightly in pain. He raises his other hand to pinch both nipples. This time she makes no sound, but her face grows very white. When he comes to the twelfth woman he orders her to turn round and fondles her buttocks, grunts, moves on. At the next he grips with both hands the high collar of her dark dress and rips it open, exposing her breasts. In a reflex movement the woman tries to cover them with her hands. Von Blixen slaps her very hard across the face.

'Herr Oberst,' says Frau Knesebeck.

The woman drops her hands, looking down at the floor.

The commander moves on and on. Soon he no longer bothers to tear open the shirts or dresses in front of him, but barks brief commands at the women to do it themselves. It becomes boring. He returns to the table, refills the empty glass at his place, drains it in a single gulp, wipes his mouth with the back of his hand, resumes his inspection. They are now ordered to raise their skirts and remove their underwear, some with their backs turned to him, others facing him. He glances at their lower bellies, tugs at pubic hair, inserts a finger in a vulva, withdraws it in disgust when he discovers that the woman is menstruating. As is the next, and the next.

'Herr Oberst,' pleads Frau Knesebeck.

'Gottverdammt!' snarls von Blixen. He turns back to the table, instructs his officers to complete the inspection on his behalf. They draw blood every time. The colonel contents himself by finishing his round at some distance from the inmates lining the walls, merely glancing in passing at the odd face that appears briefly to interest him and gesturing to the nearest officer to sample her more intimately. More blood.

It is only when he reaches the girl Katja that the colonel comes to a standstill.

'You,' he says. 'Come here.'

Katja tries to slide behind Hanna X.

'Come here!' he shouts, so loudly that some of the women exclaim in fright.

The trembling girl approaches a pace or two. He beckons her with a finger. She stands in front of him.

'Now, girl,' he says. 'No need to be afraid.' With surprising gentleness, almost fatherly, he takes her face between his hands and leans over to kiss her on the forehead. 'Was this so bad?' he asks.

'No.' She manages to force a little smile.

'And this?' Von Blixen takes her by the shoulders – such thin shoulders, the blades behind protruding like incipient wings. He presses her slight body against him, still with a show of tender care.

She seems briefly to overcome her fear, even leans her head against his shoulder.

'Show me your tits,' he says.

'I don't have any,' she whispers. Coyly, archly, ashamed, terrified? It is hard to tell.

'Herr Oberst,' says Frau Knesebeck.

'I'll take this one,' he says, grasping the girl by the hand.

Hanna X makes a deep sound of protest in her throat.

There is a general low-key commotion among the women, inmates and staff alike.

'Silence!' shouts the colonel. His face is once again shiny with perspiration. It even glistens among the bristles between the joints on his fingers. He is still grasping Katja's narrow hand in his free hand. For another moment he glowers at the assembled women, then turns towards the nearest door, pulling the girl after him.

'I'm sorry, Herr Oberst,' says Frau Knesebeck. Suddenly resolute, she leaves the table and hurries past the colonel to block his way to the door. 'You cannot take this girl. She is in our special care.'

'Stand aside!' he bellows.

The small woman hesitates for a moment, then shakes her head. 'I'm afraid she is here under a special dispensation.'

'From whom?' he asks. 'What difference does it make?'

She stands her ground. 'We have instructions from the chief commanding officer of the German army in the colony, Oberbefehlshaber Dame himself,' she informs him without batting an eyelid.

He stares at her in silence, then looks down at the girl. 'Is that true?' In sudden rage he shakes her the way a dog tussles with a rag.

Katja merely whimpers.

Von Blixen faces his hostess again. 'I don't believe you,' he says, but his voice has lost some of its assurance.

'I have instructions to report directly to Governor von Lindequist,' says Frau Knesebeck calmly. 'If anything happens to this girl, who is Oberbefehlshaber Dame's niece, you will have to answer to him.'

8

FOR WHAT MUST be a full minute Colonel von Blixen stares piercingly into the eyes of his small hostess before he abruptly turns away from the girl, heads for the nearest woman, grabs her by the elbow and snarls, 'Come!' On his way out he snatches a full bottle of brandy from the long.

Katja blunders back to Hanna X, who puts her arms around the shaking girl and presses her against her own body. The other officers give them a wide berth, eddying past them like a stream past a boulder, each claiming a woman – prey or trophy – whom he drags off through the nearest doorway into the vast and various spaces beyond. Without deigning to cast another look at the girl, Frau Knesebeck turns to the members of her staff who are thronging in the doorway to the staircase. 'What are you waiting for?' she asks. 'There is all this mess to clear away.'

Throughout the interminable hours of the afternoon the place rings and shudders with the sounds of the men on their rampage as they go about their business. The walls reverberate with cursing and shouting, the screams of women, the crashing and thundering of furniture and utensils being smashed – beds and chairs, pitchers and ewers, pisspots, mirrors and window panes, doors, chests. In her own sparsely furnished room Hanna sits on her narrow bed, straight-backed and quiet, stroking the thin shoulders of the girl who is lying beside her, half asleep, whimpering occasionally like a dreaming puppy. From time to time the din appears to die down, then suddenly flares up again, moving from one part of the building to the next, up and down the stairs, spilling outside through doors or windows, then sweeping back. But at last the worst of the rage seems to have spent itself. From the yard come the first sounds of horses being saddled and readied to resume the journey.

That is when the door is violently thrown open and a man comes staggering across the threshold of Hanna's room. It is Colonel von Blixen.

'Ah!' he exclaims, steadying himself against the doorpost. 'I have been looking for you all over the place. You juicy little bitch!'

The girl struggles up through the confused remains of dreams. Hanna puts a hand on her hip. She appears calm, but her body is very tense.

'Come here,' says the colonel. In his red face the grin appears like a gash. There are smudges of blood on his uniform, and on his hands.

Katja shakes her head.

'Come here!' he thunders.

Hanna X draws the girl closer to her side.

The officer is clearly blind drunk, and now apoplectic with fury. He stumbles as he tries to approach, manages to get hold of one of the bedposts, stands swaying for a moment, then lunges towards the women.

Hanna X tries to move in between him and the girl but in the power of his rage he simply sweeps her out of the way, sending her sprawling on the floor.

'You heard what Frau Knesebeck said,' whispers Katja.

'To hell with her. To hell with Oberbefehlshaber Dame.'

Hanna comes to her feet, stroking into place the kappie with which she habitually covers her face. She makes a sound, but he doesn't even turn his head.

'Come here,' he tells the girl again. They can both smell him now. The drunk, the soldier who has marched through the desert for days, maybe weeks, and who has been fucking and vomiting his way through the labyrinthine afternoon.

This time, as if mesmerised, Katja does obey.

'That's a good girl,' approves von Blixen. He stretches both arms out, stiffly, with fierce concentration, and places them on her breasts. The girl goes red in the face, but she appears too scared to move.

'Blood,' he says, and spits on the floor. 'All these miserable women, bleeding, it's like a bloody slaughterhouse. But you are too young for that, I'm sure. It's you I want.'

He slides one hand down the front of her body and cups it over her pubis, grunting with satisfaction.

Several things happen at the same time. The girl jerks away from his grasp, loses her balance against the edge of the bed and falls on her back, her legs kicking briefly. 'I am bleeding,' she screams at him. 'I'm bleeding like all the others.'

Hanna X removes the kappie from her head to expose her face.

And right then Frau Knesebeck speaks from the doorway, 'Herr Oberst.'

Colonel von Blixen reacts as if he has been struck by a snake. What ultimately shatters him – the girl's taunt, Hanna X's face, or Frau Knesebeck's appearance – they will never know. But without a word the military man draws himself up, squares his shoulders, and marches out. They hear him all the way down the great staircase. The front door slams. Outside there are sounds of men and horses. Hooves trotting off, growing ever fainter in the distance. The interminable silence of the desert reimposes itself.

'Make yourself proper,' Frau Knesebeck curtly tells the girl.

Katja gets up and straightens the dress which has rucked up in her fall. Hanna X puts on her kappie again. The mistress of Frauenstein leaves, closing the door behind her with a firm, quiet click.

It is only several hours later, after night has fallen and the girl has gone back to her own room, that the colonel returns, unaccompanied, shaking in a silent inner rage that will not subside before he has vented everything that has been building up for so long.

Frauenstein is quiet. The dark has restored a curious bitter innocence to the place. The sad innocence of an orphanage when all the ordinary diurnal sounds have drained from it.

9

Sounds do not disappear, not ever, not really. Hanna knows this even when she is very small. What happens when they appear to fade away, like the sounds of the bell from the square, particularly at night, is that they grow very small in order to fit into a hiding place where they cannot readily be found by those who do not know how to listen. A small round place like a shell. This is what she discovers on the narrow grey beach of the Weser opposite the Europahafen one day when the girls of the Little Children of Jesus are taken on an outing by Frau Agathe. The day is gloomy and cold, but the river entrances her. Not for itself but because she knows it runs to the sea, which she has never seen, except in her dreams. And perhaps in her lost life before she was left at the orphanage, a life of which she remembers only brief unconnected flashes – one of which is of the sea, its sounds and smells, its white waves breaking. The sea is a place of miracles and magic. It goes all the way from Bremerhaven to the other side of the world, where the wind comes from, and where the palm trees of the Children's Bible grow and camels come by and the sun always shines. It is not cold and grey like here beside the Weser in Bremen, but an endless warmth. One can be naked in it and feel the sun on one's body, it turns you golden brown all over. Here in the orphanage, to be naked is very bad. There is the little girl, Helga, who is new and stays in bed all day crying, so Hanna crawls in beside her and they take off their shifts to be closer together, and Helga's sadness disappears and her own as well, but then Frau Agathe finds them together and it turns out that their badness is so bad that it is not enough for Frau Agathe to punish them, they have to be taken all the way up the street, both still bare as small skinned fruit, to the parsonage to be dealt with. That is where Pastor Ulrich awaits them, enormously round and fat, his moon-shaped red face beaded with sweat, the front of his black waistcoat stained by the past week's meals – egg yolk and cabbage and beetroot and meat and gravy – his large soft hands resting on his stomach. In his high-pitched voice he tells them that their nakedness is evil, a sin never-ever to be forgiven. In future he will summon Hanna every Sunday after church for an account of her sins during the week, and every week he will insist on finding out for himself – he can feel with his fat hand – if she has sinned again. And he will pinch her there, viciously squeezing the little lips together until they're bruised and sometimes blood-blistered. The sound of his voice, like the sounds of the great bell and of the oxen bellowing at the abattoir to which they're driven right past the orphanage in the Hutfilterstrasse, all those sounds shrink and grow very small in order to hide away. The same happens with good sounds. Like the sounds on midwinter day when everyone goes out in their brightest clothes, except for the orphan girls who wear grey, to skate on the frozen Weser. Everyone, even the very old who can no longer walk by themselves, but who can somehow still skate if they're put down on the ice upright, every single person in the town is there; there is such a crowd, Hanna is convinced that even those who have been dead for years must have come out to join them; and the noise they make mingles into one huge sound like the blast of the trombone in the brass band that plays on the Rathausplatz on holidays, and then it grows smaller and smaller until it can fit into that secret space of the shell she brings home from the grey pebbly beach of the Weser that day.

It is given to her by a small stranger she meets in the bright shallow water. Her name, she says without being asked, is Susan. She comes all the way from an island called Ireland and does not speak German very well (she has come here with her father, she explains, who is employed at the harbour with a lot of other foreign Catholic people from Thuringia and Bohemia and other places where there is no work for the men). Hanna asks to see the shell, and the little girl hands it to her with an endearing mixture of shyness and eagerness. It is beautiful, whispers Hanna, almost too beautiful to believe. Hold it to your ear, Susan tells her, you will hear the sea. Hanna has never heard of a thing like that, but the little girl nods solemnly and insists, Just listen. And she does and indeed, she hears the distant sea which hisses very softly in her ear, and brings to her all the lost sounds of the world, even from the far side of the earth where the palm trees are and the wind is born, and the singing of the sun, for oh the sun does sing. They play together for the rest of the day, Hanna and the little girl Susan with her very blue eyes and her very black hair, and it is as if the day itself, all of it, can now fit into a shell which will never stop its faint, small, perfect sound.

When she needs to pee and wants to run off, Susan says, Don't be silly, just squat down here, I'll keep watch so no one comes, and afterwards I shall too. So they first make a small round dam in the sand and she squats carefully over it, her feet wide apart and her dress hitched up high so that it won't get wet, and when she stands up again to correct her clothes, Susan peers at her stomach with large surprised eyes, and asks, What is this? And puts a cautious finger on Hanna's protruding navel. It's my belly-button of course, says Hanna, don't you have one then? And Susan pulls up her little red dress to take her turn to pee, displaying a sweet and perfectly indented navel. (There is a small mole a little way below it, and somewhat to the right.) You see? says Susan, yours is quite different. I suppose it's because you're not Catholic. Just then, from far away, where the other children are, Hanna hears Frau Agathe calling her name. Oh dear Jesus, I'll be in trouble, she says, breathless with fear. And they run back together, the small shell-gift still clutched tightly in her sweaty hand. You are not, says Frau Agathe, do you hear me? you are not, not ever again, to talk to strange children on the beach. They are Catholics, and that is worse than heathens. And on Sunday she has to report it to Pastor Ulrich who as always tells her to approach so he can feel with his fat finger if she has sinned, only it is not her non-Catholic navel he insists on probing. She is instructed again to pray, to be vigilant, and to repent of her evil nine-year-old ways, and he reads to her from the Bible, terrible things about hell and sulphur and damnation, but the sounds of the words are beautiful, whatever they may mean, words

stored in her small magic shell with all the other sounds. This side
of the shell there is only silence; if you look at it at arm's length,
you will never guess what is enclosed in it, a sea, a whole world of
sound, past and present and who knows future, and if you listen very
carefully, holding it close to your ear, you can hear it all. Not just
from the other side of the world, but the other side of everything,
the other side of silence itself.

It is a silence which she carries deep within her, from the lost
time before she ever arrived at the orphanage, a time before the
real time of hours and bells and loud voices began, the time of the
invisible sea, a time when the silence surrounded her and her three
friends, the friends no one but she could see but who were as real
as her feet or her belly-button or her narrow face in a mirror, their
names were Trixie, Spixie and Finny, but when she was brought to
the Little Children of Jesus they got lost along the way and she has
never found them again. She cried for days, until Frau Agathe put
an end to it with her strap, maintaining that such creatures could
only be manifestations of the Devil. Even so Hanna continued to run
away, albeit at increasingly long intervals, in search of them, only to
be found and brought back and beaten every time by Frau Agathe
and probed by Pastor Ulrich.

Beatings happen all the time in the Little Children of Jesus because
it is a Christian place where evil will not be tolerated. You get beaten
if you're late at prayers or for school, or for not being able to recite
the names of the books from the Old Testament in the proper order,
or for forgetting to bring in the washing, or for soiling your clothes
or scuffing your shoes, or for talking in the dark after the candles
have been put out, or for wetting your bed, or for having lice in your
hair, and most certainly if you run away to the big cathedral on the
Domplatz and hide behind a pillar to listen to the organist practising
Bach. Sometimes a beating is not enough and has to be accompanied
by other forms of punishment like being sent to bed without supper,
or locked up in the linen cupboard for an afternoon or overnight or
for a night and a day, or being forced to sit for a given time in a
cold bath, or to stand on two bricks in the corner until you faint,
or to learn long passages from the Bible by heart (never the easy or

interesting ones, but the genealogies) and if you don't get it right you get a stroke for every mistake, on your hands or your legs or the soles of your feet or on your bare buttocks with everybody assembled to watch. But this hasn't happened for quite some time now, for she no longer needs to run off in search of her lost friends, she now has this new friend Susan from her distant Ireland, and one day they will run away together and live happily ever after, the way it happens in stories.

Her favourite story is about the musicians who run away, the donkey and the dog and the cat and the rooster, all of them old and poor and no longer wanted by their cruel masters, and who then take over the robbers' house in the dark wood where they, too, at last, can live happily ever after. This is why she covets the small porcelain figurine which a girl called Ute brings to school one day. It is a sin to covet, God knows how severely she will be punished for it if they find out; but there is a worse sin, and that is to steal. Thou shalt not – thou shalt not – thou shalt not. Everywhere she goes she is surrounded by the dense hedge of Thou-shalt-nots. This small exquisite porcelain ornament showing the minute donkey and dog and cat and rooster is the one thing in the world she covets and which she decides to steal. There is no other way for her to hold it in her hands, to cherish it, to caress its delicate outline. During the interval she slips into the classroom and takes it from Ute's satchel, then hurries outside to hide it behind the girls' lavatory. After the break, when the disappearance of the figurine is discovered, they all have to open their satchels and sit with folded arms while the teacher moves along the rows to ransack their belongings. The little ornament is, of course, not found. Hanna leaves it in its hiding place for a week – furtively checking every day – before she carries it back to her bed in the Little Children of Jesus. It lives in her drawer inside her single spare pair of drab knickers; at night it sleeps under her pillow. But one of the smaller girls finds her with it and when Hanna tries to conceal it she drops it and now it is chipped. This is how she discovers that nothing one loves one is allowed to keep. Because now she has to get rid of it, but how?

God himself provides a solution. It is time for the Easter *Messe*, after the weeks of starvation when the meagre rations of the orphans are cut down to just under subsistence level (one has to suffer for the Lord). The girls are expected to produce small objects to be sold at the *Messe*, contributing a few pfennig to the church coffers and the greater glory of God. Most of them knit shapeless socks or crochet doilies. Hanna fabricates a small, rather wobbly chest of drawers from matchboxes smudgily glued together and a skewed cardboard mirror covered with silver paper. And on it, neatly centred, she places the Musicians of Bremen in all their fragile glory. This, she calculates, should appease God and perhaps cancel out the sins of coveting and stealing. She has already taken her leave of it. Now God may have it. He has so many useless things already. She has lately begun to have serious doubts about God. He'd better be careful, or she will stop believing in him altogether.

When Frau Agathe calls her in after the *Messe* to question her about the figurine, she can say with a very straight face that she 'found' it and thought God might like it. Even Pastor Ulrich's probing hand cannot elicit any further confession, and she is let off with a mere warning. With a profound feeling of relief she lies in her small bed that night, listening to the rain pouring down outside, her sole possession of any importance, her shell, pressed against her ear as she listens to the distant hiss of the sea and imagines going off very far away, hand in hand with a small girl from a strange land, a girl with very black hair and very blue eyes, across all the seas of the world to the palm trees of an oasis beloved of the breezes and the sun.

10

IN THE DESERT through which they are travelling now there are no palm trees. Nor any breezes, just a terrible February heat beating down day after day, gathering inside the canvas hood of the ox-wagon, suffocating, sweltering. But Hanna X is only distantly aware of it. She has no interest in finding out how, or why, or when she landed on the wagon which is taking her towards a place which is only a name as yet. Frauenstein. Below her aching back – there is no part of her body that is not aching; this must be the undying fire of hell itself – the motion of the wagon, jolting and rolling and swaying, is so much like that of the sea that on the verge of consciousness she believes that she is indeed, still, or again, on the ship on its indolent but relentless voyage from midwinter to midsummer.

The train journey is over; somehow, through a perverse and unwanted miracle, she must have survived that too. But she will not think about it. It is a black hole in her mind which she doesn't care to visit. In her thoughts it has not happened, it will never happen. (Even now, standing in front of the ancient mirror on the landing outside her room in Frauenstein, studying her reflection, she will not think of that journey. Not now. Soon it will *have* to be faced; before she eventually turns away she will have to face everything; but for now, please God, not yet.)

Adversity, Pastor Ulrich would say, is an ordeal of the Almighty. Catastrophe even more so. What would this journey on the wagon qualify as? But the question makes no sense. She and the Almighty parted company long ago. Who abandoned whom is a moot point. But surely it cannot just go on: there must be an end to suffering. At the moment just going on is all that happens, and all she can endure. She doesn't even know where they are taking her. She doesn't know who 'they' are.

The driver of the wagon and his two companions make no attempt to talk to their passengers, their load. They are black, and she is scared of them. She has never seen black people before; terrifying tales were told about them in Hamburg, before she left, when people found out where she was going. If one were a missionary, there might be some redeeming grace in the enterprise; but simply to go, like that, into a wilderness inhabited by godforsaken naked savages . . . ? It is a German colony, she would reply. There are good, ordinary German people living there. They need housekeepers and helpers. And wives, her interlocutors would insist, knowingly. That remains to be seen, she said. It still remains to be seen.

A military escort accompanies the wagon, four surly outriders. Good, ordinary German people. After what has happened on the train she is more scared of them than of the blacks; but at least, like the driver and his companions, they make no attempt at conversation. Sometimes two of them will ride off and return after some hours with an antelope draped over one of the horses. Kudu, gemsbok. The names are strange to her.

There are four other women on the transport wagon, rejects like her. They, too, will not talk, or only rarely. From time to time one of them may come over to the thin palliasse where she lies, to wipe her face or chase away flies or moisten her lips (or what remains of them) with a dirty rag. One of them, the youngest by the looks of her, tries initially to talk to her. 'What have they done to you?' she asks. Hanna shakes her head; they do not know about the painful throbbing stub in her mouth. 'Why did they do it?' the girl asks again. 'What on earth did you do to provoke them so? Why didn't you just let them be? We are not meant to resist the men. They always have their way. A woman must know her place.' Presumably she knew her place: yet what good has it done her? Here she is with them on the same wagon, going towards the same end, whether destiny or destination. The girl is silent for a while. But in the end she starts again, now with a whining tone of voice: 'One never knows, of course. I tried so hard to please them, but they just didn't want me. What do you think I did wrong?' Hanna makes no reply. 'You despise me,' says the girl, 'I know you do. But what right do you have? Just look at you. I mean, what kind of man would want you anyway?' Hanna turns away her head. Then she is left alone again. When her dizziness, or the pain, permits, she lies looking at them. They do not bear the kind of wounds and scars that disfigure her; but they have been marked too. Their bodies carry the imprint of their histories as hers does. It shows in the way they sit or stand or lie, the hunched shoulders, the knees drawn up, the faces turned away, the silent crying which they make no attempt to suppress, the snot they allow to congeal on their faces, the odour of armpits and groins they no longer try to hide. Rejects all. Yet these things hardly matter, they are no more than signs. There are other scars, invisible, which are incomparably worse and will not heal.

Not for a moment does the pain abate. It is like a body of liquid in which she has been immersed. Pain, God, pain. Why didn't she die? Surely no sin can be so terrible as to deserve this. Can they not simply leave her behind here to die? It should be so easy. But no death so far has been strong enough to take her. On and on, the pain goes on. On and on, they go on.

With every jolt of the wagon she feels diminished, eroded, dismantled, bone by bone. She is no longer who she is, nor who she ever was, only what she may be, a mere possibility of herself, circumscribed by pain.

There might have been some comfort to be drawn from her shell; but that has been lost somewhere along the way, possibly during the ordeal on the train. Such a small thing, but not having it marks the difference between memory and blankness, a possibility of hope and the certainty of despair.

Almost imperceptibly the wagon creeps through the vast landscape under the malignant sun. Occasionally they espy a tortoise, a blue-headed lizard on a flat brown rock, a gemsbok in the distance with heraldic horns; or birds. Quail fluttering up, screeching, when the oxen come too close; small freckled partridges; sometimes the specks of vultures drifting with wide wings on invisible currents of air. Once, miraculously, a flight of storks with black-tipped wings and beaks dipped in blood. She recognises them. At the end of summer she used to see them gathering on trees and rooftops in Bremen before they took off. 'To the south'. That was what people said. No one could be more specific. To the south. And now here they are. This must be the summer south. For a moment a strange elation fills her. She, too, has migrated like a bird. Perhaps she too will learn to fly. But the mere thought makes her dizzy. The white sun blinds her. Perhaps she has imagined it. This is a country of the imagination. There are mirages on the horizon, great lakes which shimmer in the heat and disappear as suddenly as they have appeared. A beach with palm trees waving in the breeze, upside down. Children playing on the sand, she can see the colourful patches of their clothes against the glare. She has another blackout. But the visions persist. A small black-haired blue-eyed elfin girl. A sudden donkey, a dog, a cat, a rooster with outrageous plumage. She can hear them bray and bark and meow and crow. And then she blacks out again.

When she wakes up there is no change in the landscape. It is as empty as before – emptier, because the brief creatures have disappeared – as empty as the world must have been just after God had said, *Let there be light*, and before there was anything else. Or perhaps this is the ultimate fulfilment of creation, this desert. The solid earth liquefying at the edges, melting into the sky. Its nothingness is complete. It requires nothing else, it is what it is, no more, no less, this sky, this earth, this glorious emptiness full of itself. God has withdrawn from it before his supreme failure, man, could leave an imprint here. The only redundancy is this wagon with its labouring trundling beasts, its accompaniment of men, its huddling women, she, Hanna X. Without them, without her, the landscape would be perfect.

To all sides it stretches out to meet the smouldering hollow of the sky. It undulates very gently. Like the sea on the equator. It is endless as the sea. Again she abandons herself to the motion. She is on the open deck. There is no one else. And suddenly she knows what she has to do. At last she will have peace, world without end. So easy. Why hasn't she thought of it before? Just move to the railing, lean over, one small heave, and over she goes, a falling, and a falling, a falling into nothingness, she will not even try to swim or come up for air, sinking, sinking, through all the layers of pain, into a deep oblivion, a susurration, fading, fading, as she dies at last.

11

THERE IS A kind of punishment in the orphanage which Hanna actually comes to enjoy, although she takes great care never to let on, otherwise they will devise something else. It consists of being ordered to spend hours, sometimes a whole afternoon, sitting on a hard bench at one of the long bare dining tables, reading the Bible. Afterwards she has to give an account of what she has read to Frau Agathe. For a long time she hates it, because the Bible is the book of the people who most terrorise her, stalking her even in her dreams. But then she discovers the good stories. And gradually she finds ones she likes more than the others. Mostly, they concern women who in one way or another cheat or charm or fight or wangle their way out of adversity. There is Ruth, poor and miserable, gleaning the field – whatever that might mean – of the rich man Boaz; until one night she crawls under his blanket with him and makes him notice her, so that he decides to marry her. (A rather silly story, she finds, as a matter of fact, but at least it got Ruth out of her misery.) And the shrewd Esther who marries King Ahasuerus after he has callously rejected his wife Vasthi, and then uses her power to promote her friends and punish her enemies. And of course the fabulous Salomé who dances her way into the heart of King Herod and persuades him to give her the head of John the Baptist on a plate; a rather nasty one that, but how else could the girl have had her way?

There are others that bring a glow of deep and dark satisfaction. The sister of Moses who deceives the daughter of Pharaoh to save the life of her little brother. Tamar, who tricks her father-in-law into sleeping with her so that she can unmask him as the hypocritical lord-and-master he really is. Hagar, rejected by the man who used her upon the wicked advice of his old wife Sarah, and then saved by an angel in the desert. The daughters of Lot who make their father drunk and lie with him so that their tribe won't die out. (Hanna is not quite sure about how lying with a man can lead to the survival of a tribe, but somehow it seems a shrewd way of getting what they want.) Deborah who becomes a judge over the whole of her nation and leads the armies of Barak against the enemy Sisera. And Jael who cajoles that same fearsome man, Sisera, into accepting some milk to quench his thirst, after which she covers him with a blanket and puts him to sleep in her tent, and hammers a long nail through his temples, pinning him to the ground. Good for her. And Delilah who betrays the savage, swaggering Samson to her people and makes him pay for the many men he has shorn of their foreskins (which Hanna believes to be the skin on their foreheads) or battered to death with the jawbone of an ass. And on and on, through all those gold-rimmed pages, to the triumphant vision of the woman arrayed in purple and scarlet colour and sitting on a scarlet coloured beast, with seven heads and ten horns: now that, Hanna thinks, is how she would like to ride through the streets of Bremen one day, accompanied by all the great bells of the cathedral.

12

I HAVE NEVER been able to understand why the wagon did not stop, or turn back. Even if Hanna X's absence was discovered only later, surely the most obvious reaction would have been to retrace the route as far as was necessary. Or can it be that they did indeed turn around but finding her motionless gave her up for dead and moved on again? But wouldn't they at least have made an attempt to bury her, even if it consisted merely of covering the body with stones or dry branches? Then again, there may have been so little communication between the women on the wagon and their drivers and escorts that the loss wasn't discovered before they arrived at Frauenstein – and by the time they returned the body would have disappeared; nothing unusual about that, given the prevalence of scavengers. But what about her female companions then? Or were they so deeply sunk in their own abjection that they didn't notice, or didn't care? Even so, we know that at least one of them, the young one, used to be concerned enough to look after Hanna from time to time – unless she preferred not to attract undue attention after the fact. A most irritating mystery, and not the only one in this story. Hanna X, forever hiding behind the trite symbol of the unknown.

She doesn't die, of course, even if to her it seems so at the time. When she comes to – hours later? days? she doesn't know, it doesn't matter – she is with a group of Nama people at their place in the desert. Her first thought as she struggles from darkness back to light, through many tiers of pain and dizziness, is that it must be an orphanage concert and that everyone is in fancy dress. Though 'fancy' makes a mockery of the weird blend of clothing and ornaments they are wearing: roughly sewn caps of lynx or musk-cat skin, but also wide hats with ostrich or pheasant feathers stuck to the brim; some shirts and skirts, but also strings of shell-beads or the bunched tails of jackals or zebras; a few jackets, but also ample karosses made of the pelts of dassies or gazelles; moleskin trousers, but also skimpy skin aprons to cover their shameful parts. A few of the men have guns, others bows and arrows. The women are naked to the waist, exhibiting breasts ranging from pubescent buds to the dugs of old crones, empty folds of skin sagging down to their wrinkled bellies, nipples like the scaly heads of lizards.

They are all chattering in what sounds like the twittering of birds, with strange clicks and sibilants and gutturals; but when they discover that she has opened her eyes some of them approach excitedly and start addressing her in broken German, which they must have learned from the occupiers of their land. Hanna can only shake her head. When they persist, she reluctantly opens her mouth and points inside at the absence of a tongue. Exclamations of shock and surprise and what may be sympathy. But even this small effort has so exhausted her that she sinks back into oblivion, though she is aware of hands lifting her head and a calabash pressed against her aching mouth and some sour, smelly, curdled liquid forced down her throat. Pain, pain.

Still, she must be getting better. The dark intervals become shorter. The returns to painful lucidity last longer, her thoughts grow more coherent, memory filters back. She would still prefer to be dead, and helplessly resents these people for not allowing her to die in peace. But the pain, she notices almost against her will, the pain is slowly dulling, ebbing, fading, no longer – or not always – as overwhelming as it was.

When she feels a warm wetness between her thighs and tests it with a finger she discovers that her bleeding has begun – the old bleeding from inside, not the bleeding of the wounds. Some of the women, the oldest ones, draw her legs apart to stanch it with tufts of grass; she can hear them clicking their tongues, tsk-tsk, as they stare at the mutilation of her sex. Only now does the nightmare on the train come back to her, and she retches at the memory. First there was her face. Then her mouth forced open, a piece of wood wedged between her teeth to give access to her tongue. Choking in blood. And then her nipples cut off. The viscous chicken-livers of her labia excised. Oh God, oh God. Give me a knife, she thinks, let me kill myself, how can you let me live like this? I am no longer a woman, a human being, I am a thing.

What would Pastor Ulrich say if he could see her now? She groans and grimaces. The Devil's hiding place, he used to call it. After what has happened to her on the train, how innocent his probings and pinchings and furtive fondlings seem now. But then the bitter bile rises up in her. The women have to keep her down with force. She tries to shout, *No!* but no recognisable sound gurgles from her throat. There was nothing innocent about that, she thinks in rage as the futile tears of her anger run down her burning cheeks. There may be a difference in degree, but not in kind. What happened to the woman on the train was just a variation and an extension of what had been done to the girl. It is all the same, there has been no let-up, not ever.

She sobs and groans in helplessness, which brings the pain back, and it goes on and on, until at last there is the respite of a blackout again. And this time, when she comes round, she has no energy for anger left. She can only moan and lie with drawn-up knees. There is no hope, no hope, there is no resistance left; this is her life, it has to be lived, that is all.

Through days and nights the old Nama women attend to her, bringing foul-smelling herbs and ground powders to apply to the wounds, feeding her unspeakably vile potions, forcing her to suck on a long-stemmed pipe and inhale the sickeningly rancid-sweet smoke which eases the tension and the pain, and brings oblivion in the end. They coax her into drinking curdled milk, sucking on strange-tasting roots and bulbs and tubers from the veld, slurping the yolk of an ostrich egg ladled from a shell positioned in the remains of a fire, until she can cautiously, painfully chew very small chunks of meat. Birds, probably. Later the strips cut from small buck, sometimes raw and succulent, sometimes boiled or roasted, sometimes dried.

More vividly than food or medicine or the comforting clicks with which both are administered, Hanna will remember the way they feed her with stories, of which the oldest of the women seems to have an inexhaustible store. It begins soon after she wakes up for the first time and lies staring dully, in a kind of uncomprehending stupor, at the landscape throbbing with sunlight and timelessness, under a sky from which all colour has been scorched. After watching her for a while, the oldest of the women – her name is Taras, which she says means 'Woman' – makes a sweeping gesture towards the surrounding desert. 'You wonder how it can be so dry?' she asks in her rudimentary German. 'It comes from a woman. The woman Xurisib, who was very beautiful, but very vain, the vainest woman in Namaland. And all the young men lusted after her, their purple wattles drawing lines in the dust. Even the old men would wake in the night with a branch planted in their loins, the way they dreamed of her.' Hanna lies with closed eyes and lets the words of the old woman wash over her like bright cool water. Xurisib, says Taras, was so vain that she even scorned the flowers that covered the earth after the good god Tsui-Goab had sent his rains. 'They don't last,' she said. 'Tomorrow they shrivel up and die, but my beauty will never wither.' All the people warned her, warned her, but Xurisib wouldn't listen. Then Tsui-Goab himself came to her in the shape of a mantis in a small bush that burned and burned and burned without burning itself out. 'You give me great pain, Xurisib,' he said to the girl. 'It is I who make those flowers come out after the rains, I am the giver of all good things.' But Xurisib laughed proudly and shook her head and her breasts quivered and her bangles sang. 'I don't need your flowers,' she said, 'and I don't need you. My beauty is all I'll ever want.' Then Tsui-Goab grew very sad and he went away, and Namaland became the dry place it is now. The rivers dried up and the trees died and the reeds withered and the voice of the birds grew silent, and all that was left was white sand and red sand and long thorns that scraped her legs. When Xurisib went back to her village, she found her people packing up their possessions to trek away, taking all the young men with them too. The girl wanted to go with them, but the headman wouldn't let her because he said there was a curse on her head. From that day on the Nama people have never stayed in one place. Always, always, always they are on the move. Xurisib stayed behind, and her skin became as dry as the husk shaken off by a snake, and her black hair turned grey, and in no time at all she was an old hag of a woman. She lay down on the ground to die. That was when the mantis came back to her and said from the burning bush, 'Xurisib, your life is over. But if you say my name I shall take away my curse.' And softly, softly, softly, Xurisib whispered the name of the god. And where the sounds of her voice fell, flowers sprouted from the parched earth. Again and again she said his name, 'Tsui-Goab, Tsui-Goab, Tsui-Goab,' until with her last breath she was shouting so loudly that the koppies in the distance reverberated with the sound. And the rains came, and the veld was covered in flowers from horizon to horizon, and Xurisib became a young girl again, with a shining face and firm breasts and strong legs and beautiful hands, and she danced the dance of the rain.

The voice of the wizened old woman turns into a chant, and some of the other women join in:

'Oh the dance of our Sister!
First she peeps over the hilltop, slyly,
   and her eyes are shy;
   and she laughs softly.
Then, from afar, she beckons with one hand;
her bangles glitter and her beads shimmer;
   softly she calls.
She tells the winds about the dance
and invites them too, for the yard is wide and the wedding
   great.

The big game come surging from the plains,
   they gather on the hilltop,
their nostrils are spread wide
   and they swallow the wind;
and they bend down to see her delicate tracks in the sand.
The small creatures deep below can hear the rustle of her
   feet,
   and they draw closer, singing softly:
   "Our Sister, our Sister! You have come! You have come!"

And her beads dangle,
and her copper rings glimmer in the dying of the sun.
Her forehead bears the fire-plume of the mountain eagle;
 she steps down from up high;
she spreads the grey kaross in both her arms;
 the breath of the wind dies down.
 Oh the dance of our Sister!'

There is a long pause. Then the old woman resumes, 'A few days later the flowers began to fade and shrivel up and die, and Xurisib quietly died with them. And from that day,' she says, 'if the rains come in Namaland and you listen very carefully, you will hear in the far-off thunder the voice of Xurisib calling out, "Tsui-Goab! Tsui-Goab! Tsui-Goab!" And then we know the land will live again.'

Story upon story, through days and nights, to while away the time, to make Hanna forget, to ease memory. For everything she sees or hears, everything silent or moving around the tentative settlement – casually shaped huts of rush and straw mats or skins laid on a latticework of bent branches – there is a story; sometimes various stories about the same object or event, stone or thorn tree, birth or death. No koppie or rock or aloe or quiver-tree or dried-up river bed or dust devil or erosion ditch or limestone ridge is without its divinity, benevolent or evil; all of it gathered in an eternal battle between the good god Tsui-Goab who lives in the red sky, and the devilish Gaunab who lives in the black sky.

When Hanna raises her hands to question what it all means, old Taras smiles and answers with a question of her own, 'How is your pain?' And Hanna nods, to indicate that she is feeling better. And Taras says, 'That is what stories are for.'

Sometimes she forgets to listen to the words and submits herself only to the flow of the language, the rhythms and repetitions and cadences, even in the old woman's halting and garbled German – *Dann liefen sie, dann liefen sie. Sie treckten, treckten, treckten: Then they walked and they walked, then they trekked, trekked, trekked . . .* – the pure and intricate music of the stories.

Or she listens to the Namas talking among themselves in their own tongue. All those complicated clicks. Sometimes she opens her silent mouth to imitate the movements of theirs, but gives it up. How can she ever converse with them? It is not just the loss of her tongue which forces her into silence, but knowing that there is nothing in the language she has brought with her which could conceivably say what she would so urgently wish to articulate. The things of this place, this space, in words not yet contaminated by others, or by other places. But that is impossible. Words bring their own past and their own dark geography with them, she thinks. Theirs are different. She listens intently when Taras patiently repeats them, as to a dull-witted child. *Khanous*, the evening star; *sobo khoin*, people of the shadows, ghosts; *sam-sam*, peace; *torob*, war. The names of animals: *t'kanna*, *khurob*, *t'kaoop*, *nawas*, *t'kwu*. Words that shut her out and turn their backs on her.

When at last Hanna is persuaded to take a few hesitant steps outside – first supported on the arms of women, later by herself – she is almost scared to set down her feet, for fear that it will not be the earth she feels under her soles but stories, live and hidden beings, natural and supernatural in turn, or at the same time.

13

THE WHOLE NAMA tribe – fifty or sixty of them, men, women and children – accompany Hanna X when at last she is ready to be taken to Frauenstein. And they walk, walk, walk, they trek and trek through a landscape of stories, until the strange unworldly edifice rises up from the horizon.

On their approach they pass sprawling vegetable gardens, surprising in this desert; and what appears like a desiccated patch of the garden, some distance apart, but which must be a graveyard. It is surrounded by a low wall, irregularly stacked. However, there are no headstones. Each of the graves, of which there may be a good fifty or so, in straight rows, has a crude wooden cross at one end, but these bear no inscription. There are no flowers either, no sign that anyone has bothered to tend the place and keep it in some order. The last row is not completed, but the remaining three or four graves in it have already been dug and are loosely covered with old weathered planks, with mounds of earth heaped up beside them, patiently waiting to receive whoever may be coming their way.

The small band of Namas hesitate for a while to inspect the site which seems so much less permanent than the burial cairns their people have raised across the barren land to commemorate their own dead and the many deaths of their hunter-god Heiseb – on the way here they have passed no fewer than three. After some time they press on towards the towering structure of stone.

A woman in a drab dress opens the huge front door to their knocking. She takes a step back when she sees the black people massed outside, but as she prepares to shut it in their faces she notices the white woman among them – blistered from the sun, haggard, her face mutilated – and hesitates.

'What do you want?' she asks.

'We brought a woman we found in the desert,' says the leader of the tribe, whose name is Xareb.

'Why did you come here? Why didn't you take her to Windhoek?' asks the woman.

'They tell us this is a place for women,' says the man.

The woman turns to Hanna X in horror. 'What have they done to you?'

Hanna merely shrugs, a hopeless gesture.

It is Xareb who turns to her and motions her to open her mouth. When she hesitates he does it for her, his sharp fingers pressing into her hollow cheeks. She moans with pain; the wound through which her teeth are visible has not quite healed yet. An angry altercation between Xareb and old Taras erupts in their Nama tongue.

'Wait,' says the woman at the door quickly and hurries into the dark interior, then comes back to close the door.

It takes a long time before Frau Knesebeck makes her appearance, flanked by several members of her staff. Two of them have guns, although from the way they are holding them it seems doubtful whether they know how to use them. There follows a near-endless discussion between Xareb and Frau Knesebeck, during which Hanna is once again required to open her mouth.

Then another wait in front of the closed front door. Some of the children are getting restless. There are many flies about them. Cicadas are shrilling ear-splittingly. The sun is right overhead.

When Frau Knesebeck returns she is accompanied by the four women who were on the wagon with Hanna X.

'My God!' exclaims one of them. It is Dora, the young one who tended her in her delirium. 'We thought you were dead.'

'So you know her?' Frau Knesebeck asks unnecessarily.

All four vociferously confirm it; then appear to be ashamed by the admission and try to retreat out of reach.

'You never said anything about another woman,' Frau Knesebeck challenges them.

'We lost her in the desert,' says Dora. 'She was already more dead than alive. There was nothing we could do for her. And the soldiers who came with us . . .'

'What about them?'

A pause. 'They said they didn't want trouble.'

Frau Knesebeck snorts with contempt. She comes a step towards Hanna. 'Come inside. You are in need of care. God knows what happened to you among these savages.'

Hanna makes a sound, raises an arm in futile protest, then meekly comes forward.

'We looked after her,' Xareb argues in anger.

'You?!' Frau Knesebeck waves dismissively at them. 'A white woman, a German woman, in *your* hands!' Annoyed, businesslike, she takes Hanna by the shoulder and pulls her across the threshold. 'Now get away from here, or there will be big trouble. All of you.'

Xareb stands his ground. 'We need food.'

'You are a no-good filthy lot!' says Frau Knesebeck in an icy rage.

The heavy door is flung shut. The sound reverberates through the dark building which feels dank even in midsummer. Outside there are voices raised in anger, the crying of children. Then silence.

'We shall have to bath you first,' says Frau Knesebeck. 'God knows what vermin you are infected with.' Orders are given; women hurry off to draw and boil water. They wait for a long time, to make sure that the Namas have vanished into the dull drabness of the desert, a mirage among mirages, the trickery of memory. Then Hanna is taken out through the front door again and round the house to the back: they cannot risk having the whole place infected and infested before she has been thoroughly scrubbed and washed and cleaned.

It must be at least an hour before Hanna has been painfully ridden of all possible contamination, given a shift to cover the shame of her broken, scarred body, and taken upstairs to a room. It must have been standing closed for a long time, because it smells overpoweringly of dry rot and decay.

'We shall pray for your soul,' announces Frau Knesebeck. 'Only God could have brought you alive through the ordeal with those savage scavengers.' Hanna raises, again, a hand in protest, but is stopped by the formidable small woman in front of her. She takes a deep breath. 'Unless it was the Devil.' But grimly she resolves, 'When we are through with you, Fräulein, you will be cleansed like a newborn babe. In the meantime we shall communicate with Windhoek.'

How the communication is effected, Hanna will never learn. Possibly through a *smous* who happens to turn up at Frauenstein three days later.

What she does get to know, about a month later, is the outcome of the enterprise. A small detachment of soldiers arrives at Frauenstein (Hanna, scared out of her wits, hides in an attic when she first sees them) to report that they have undertaken a punitive expedition to track down the malefactors. Deep in the desert they surrounded the tribe who had abducted and terrorised the woman taken from the transport wagon, and killed the lot of them – men, women and children all. 'We cannot allow this to be done to our women,' concludes the victorious commander; and his words are faithfully transmitted by Frau Knesebeck herself, to Hanna; who reacts by vomiting.

For ever after this news will be impregnated with the smell of the kitchen where she learns about it after she has been dislodged from the attic. The smell of cabbage soup. The smell of the orphanage.

14

THE ORPHANAGE IS pervaded with smells. Urine, carbolic acid, old leather, mould, despair. And food: sauerkraut, leeks, potatoes, fish heads steaming in a pot. But good smells too. Newly baked bread, milk straight from the udder frothing in the pail, freshly ironed laundry, shoe polish, a candle that has just been blown out. The parsonage smells of rat droppings and mould. But for her religion will always smell of Pastor Ulrich. A staleness, the smell of an old sofa on which dogs have slept. 'Closer, my girl, come closer. What sins have you brought us today?' He is so eager to hear. She will recite her little litany, knowing beforehand that he will answer, 'I'm not sure that is everything. But we'll soon find out, won't we?' First there will be his sermonising, the words spilling from his mouth and staining her: that must be, she sometimes thinks, why he wears his silly little bib, to catch the flow of words he spills as messily as the bits and pieces of the meals that smudge his waistcoat. And after the talking it is time to bruise what to him has always been the site of evil. She knows he is expecting her to wince, to mewl, to cry out, but she never does. That makes it worse, but she will not give him that satisfaction.

When she first notices the blood, one evening, she believes it is from the pinching. Only when it persists the next day does she realise that something is seriously wrong. Perhaps she will die. Which will be a pity because in a month they will be having their Christmas concert, to which she has been looking forward. They will all be getting starched white dresses. Not new ones, but newer than they have ever had before. She wouldn't like to have it marked with blood.

This she confides to the one teacher she cares for, Fräulein Braunschweig, who teaches geography and who encourages her to read when she discovers how famished the girl is for books. Sometimes Hanna spends several hours after school in Fräulein Braunschweig's classroom reading, reading, oblivious to the passing time. And there is no risk attached. For once, if she returns to the orphanage late, she can explain that she was kept in detention; Frau Agathe approves of such strictness. When she isn't reading, they talk endlessly. Fräulein Braunschweig has travelled much – all over Germany, from Hamburg in the north down to the Bavarian Alps, from Dresden in the east to Saarbrücken. Even to Vienna and Prague and Budapest; and once to Paris.

'When I grow up I want to travel too,' says Hanna. 'I'll go right round the world. I want to see everything.' There is a fever glowing in her chest. She puts her hand on the smooth surface of the globe in Fräulein Braunschweig's classroom. It spins slowly under her touch. 'All these places with the singing names.' She moves her finger randomly. 'Cordoba. Carcassonne. Tromsö. Novgorod. The Great Wall of China. The Bosporus. Tasmania. Saskatchewan. Arequipa. Tierra del Fuego. Sierra Leone. Yaoundé. Okahandja. Omaruru. I want to go where the birds go in winter. To the warm places of the earth. The far side of the wind. Where there is sun, and strange animals, and cannibals, and dragons, and palm trees.'

Fräulein Braunschweig encourages these imagined excursions. 'One day,' she says, 'perhaps I'll go with you.'

'You?!'

To her surprise Fräulein Braunschweig blushes. 'I've always dreamed of travelling too,' she confesses, like a schoolgirl. 'Years ago I had it all planned. I would be going with . . . a friend.' She pauses, then ends abruptly, 'Then he died.'

'I am so very sorry.'

The teacher never ceases to surprise the girl. To everyone else Hanna is the clumsy one, the one who always spills things, bumps into things, knocks things off tables and chests, loses her shoes, or her hat, or her pinafore, forgets to close doors or windows, mislays socks in the wash, stumbles over whatever finds itself in her way, the one who cannot tie her long hair up properly or fold a sheet straight, and who catches her thumbs in doors or drawers, and whose arms and legs are always mottled with bruises old and new; but to Fräulein Braunschweig she is more like a companion than a child.

Above all, Fräulein Braunschweig cares. It is she who sends for medicine when Hanna is not feeling well; or lets her lie down on a sofa, covered with a rug, when she faints in a class because she has been deprived of breakfast for some infringement or other. So it is she who notices that something is amiss that Thursday at the beginning of November and asks, 'What is the matter, child? You're looking pale.'

At first she is too shy to tell. But when Fräulein Braunschweig insists, she confesses with hanging head and burning face, 'I've been bleeding for two days now, Fräulein.'

'Where?'

Shamefaced, Hanna makes a vague gesture towards her lower belly.

'How old are you, Hanna?'

'Twelve. I'll be thirteen later this month, on the twenty-fifth.'

There is the shadow of a smile on the teacher's face. 'I think you're growing into a woman, Hanna.'

She is too bewildered to respond. And she is scared to admit what she still suspects to be the real reason, that Pastor Ulrich has fatally injured her. Because then too much will have to be explained.

'From now on you will be bleeding every month, my child.'

'How can that be?'

'We all do. Now sit down and listen carefully.'

At the end of it Fräulein Braunschweig provides her with a few strips of linen from the drawer where she keeps an endless supply of the most unexpected things for all possible emergencies; and she gives Hanna a letter for Frau Agathe, and an extra book to take with her to the Little Children of Jesus.

15

It is a book that will mark Hanna for the rest of her life. Not a book of stories or of travels, like most of the others Fräulein Braunschweig encourages her to read, but history. An account of the life and death of Jeanne d'Arc. In due course it will fill the emptiness left by the loss of her imaginary friends Trixie, Spixie and Finny; Jeanne will become more real to her than any of the other girls in the orphanage, including little Helga. In the fragrant darkness after the candles have been snuffed at night, she will exorcise her fear of the dark by imagining Jeanne in the narrow bed beside her; they will conduct long conversations that sometimes continue until the early dawn. Over and over the *Pucelle* will recount the simple facts of her short life: going about her domestic duties in the small dark family home in the hamlet of Domrémy in the valley of the Meuse, and playing truant, whenever she can, by visiting the tiny whitewashed chapel of Bermont lost in the woods, to which she is lured by the sound of bells. All her life she will be enchanted by bells. At the age of twelve, on a summer's day in her father's garden, she first hears the Voices which tell her that she has been chosen by God to put on man's clothing and lead an army to save King Charles VII from the English forces which have occupied her country. But for God's sake, what can *she* do? She is a slip of a girl, she is scared of the big world of violent men and political intrigue and battling armies beyond the humble hovels of Domrémy. Who will even listen to her? Her father would rather drown her with his own hands than see her in the company of soldiers. But through the years the Voices persist. At times she wonders whether she has gone mad. But this Hanna will not accept. Has she not, herself, spent hours with Trixie, Spixie and Finny? Such voices are only too real.

At last Jeanne breaks down the resistance of a credulous cousin who consents to take her to Vaucouleurs, the small garrison town twenty kilometres up the valley to meet Robert de Baudricourt, the first of her powerful patrons. After protracted negotiations, when Jeanne has just turned seventeen, he agrees to send her to Chinon where she will meet the knock-kneed, shifty-eyed, big-nosed Dauphin already hailed as Charles VII by some, although uncrowned as yet. Charles sees an opportunity to further his own interests without running any risk himself. After thorough examinations at Poitiers, Tours and Blois, including an intimate probing by no less a person than the Queen of Sicily, the Dauphin's mother-in-law, to establish her virginity, Jeanne is given permission to lead an army of several thousand men to the besieged town of Orléans. Officially there are several men in command (how Hanna, with her love of exotic names, relishes the taste of those syllables on her tongue: le Maréchal de Sainte-Sévère, le Maréchal de Rais, Louis de Culen, Ambroise de Losé, the rough and rude La Hire), but from the first day no one is allowed to doubt who is in charge. And on 8 May 1429, the six-month siege is lifted. The English begin to beat a retreat; throughout France the name of Jeanne d'Arc, a girl who cannot even read or write and signs her name with a cross, acquires the force of legend. Clouds of butterflies accompany her standard of buckram and silk, in blue and silver and gold; flocks of small birds descend on trees and bushes to watch her do battle. Barely a year later she will be betrayed and taken prisoner, in another year she will be condemned to death by the inquisitorial tribunal presided over by a bag of blubber, Pierre Cauchon, bishop of Beauvais, and – accompanied by the booming cathedral bells – burned alive on the Old Market Place of Rouen as a witch. How small the interval between virginity and sorcery. She is forced to suffer even the ultimate disgrace of having the last tatters of her burning clothes stripped from her to expose her blackened genitals to the jeering crowd. But from the pyre an English soldier sees a white dove flying out of the flames towards the heartland of France. Soon the English will be driven from the continent. And in 1456 a new tribunal will clear her name and annul her condemnation.

Which goes to show, Fräulein Braunschweig insists time and time again, that there are more important things than life or death. What matters is that Jeanne d'Arc prevailed because she remained true to herself all the way. She did what no one had thought possible. Her country was liberated. 'It is impossible truly to understand her, even after four centuries,' she argues with great conviction. 'All we can say is that she makes us think and she makes us question. She uncovers the dark places into which we may fear to look.'

Burning with pride and resolution, night after night, Hanna will drift off to sleep with Jeanne held so close to her in the small bed that she feels like flesh of her own flesh, dreams of her dreams. And when the day dawns, the book will be waiting under her pillow.

16

BOOKS WILL BE her undoing. Barely a week before the Christmas concert Frau Agathe summons Hanna one afternoon as she comes back from school. Though it is the middle of winter, it is an exceptionally bright day, so Hanna knows Frau Agathe will be worse than usual. She is always like that: when the sun is shining she will talk about the cold which is sure to come and kill all the flowers; and when she sees fruit she thinks of the vile worms inside; and when she hears someone laughing she will predict the tears that are bound to follow; and when everybody is celebrating Frau Agathe knows it will not last and then they will be sorry afterwards. Nothing is as liable to be punished as happiness. And on this bright day, when the solemn woman swathed in black awaits Hanna, clutching the girl's latest book in one ominous talon, she knows there is heavy weather ahead.

'What is this I found in your chest?' asks Frau Agathe.

'A book,' says Hanna.

'Do you care to tell me what book it is?'

'A book I'm reading. It is very beautiful.'

'*Die Leiden des Jungen Werther,*' snarls Frau Agathe.

'Yes,' admits Hanna, unable to fathom what the fuss is about. 'By Herr Goethe,' she adds, in an attempt to clarify the matter.

'It is not fit reading for a young girl,' says Frau Agathe, quaking with anger. 'In fact, it is not fit reading for any decent person.'

'I don't understand, Frau Agathe.'

'Don't play dumb with me.' The angular face of the pale, thin woman is contorted with fury. 'This is unadulterated filth. It is designed to lead the young astray, to deprave the mind. I will not tolerate such smut under my roof. This is a Christian institution.'

'Fräulein Braunschweig will not let me read filth,' says Hanna vehemently.

'Are you talking back to me?' exclaims the woman. 'A mouth like that deserves to be rinsed out with soap.'

Hanna turns to go.

'Where are you going?' demands Frau Agathe.

'Fetching the black soap for you,' says Hanna.

'You are indeed a child of the Devil,' the woman rages. 'God knows, we have done our best with you. But you are incorrigible. Now you will burn the book in the stove. I shall go with you.'

'I cannot do that,' says Hanna. 'It is not mine.'

'You're right. It is the Devil's book. Go to the kitchen.'

'I will not burn it,' says Hanna. There is no open defiance in her attitude, only a quiet resolution. And that makes Frau Agathe lose all control. She smacks the girl in the face with the book.

'Now come with me.'

Hanna touches her smarting cheek, and follows the woman to the kitchen. Frau Agathe flings open the small black hatch in the front of the stove. A deep red glow flares briefly into flames.

'Take the book.' Frau Agathe thrusts it into her hand.

Hanna clutches it to her chest.

'Burn it.'

Hanna shakes her head. Frau Agathe grabs a stove-iron from a hook on the wall. For a moment it seems as if she is going to attack the girl with it. But then, breathing heavily, she slowly replaces the iron. 'You will go to Pastor Ulrich,' she says with a strange kind of elation in her rasping voice. 'I shall give you a letter. Then we shall see.'

Half an hour later she is in the parsonage with the large fat man.

'Ah Hanna,' he says. 'What brings you here on such a pleasant day?'

'I have brought a letter from Frau Agathe,' she says stiffly. She hands it over, then stands back.

In silence he peruses it. His face turns as purple as a turkey's wattles, which signals unfailingly what is to come.

'Where is the book?' he asks.

'I have put it away, Your Reverend.'

'You were instructed to bring it here, were you not?'

'Yes, Your Reverend. But it belongs to Fräulein Braunschweig. It is not for burning.'

He gets up from the deep easy-chair, comes past her, closes the heavy door, and bolts it. She doesn't move.

He comes back, paddling like a large black waterfowl. Turns round to face her.

'Come over here,' he says, his face shiny with sweat.

Hanna doesn't move.

'I won't be touched today,' she says. It is like another's voice speaking through her, surprising her. It feels as if she isn't really down here with him, but somewhere high up on the rafters, looking down on the two of them, the large shapeless man, like a bundle of washing wrapped in black, the girl with the gawky body.

Pastor Ulrich gives a benign smile. 'And why won't you be touched today?' he asks in an unctuous voice. He seems almost to welcome the signs of defiance.

'Because Fräulein Braunschweig told me a month ago that I have now become a woman.'

'Indeed?' He raises his heavy eyebrows. He is sweating more profusely now; she can smell it. 'And how would we know that?'

For a moment she panics. Then a strange calm spreads through her. She raises her head and says, 'I am bleeding.'

His reaction briefly surprises her: 'Then it is time you start taking great care of yourself.'

'Thank you, Your Reverend. I shall take care. Fräulein Braunschweig has already told me all about it.'

He narrows his eyes as if he suspects she may be sarcastic. 'Your body is the temple of God,' he says. 'Men may feel tempted to defile it.' He takes out a large kerchief to wipe his face, then blows his nose in it.

'What do you mean, Your Reverend?'

'They may . . .' He cleans his throat. 'They may attempt to touch you in lewd ways.'

'The way you touch me, Your Reverend?'

He seems ready to explode with indignation. 'How dare you say that?' he asks in a near-whisper.

'The way you touch me: is that not a sin then, Your Reverend?' she asks.

'What I have done to you, my daughter,' he says, 'has been done in purity of mind and generosity of spirit, in the name of God. To exorcise the devils which reside within you. In that place.' He makes a gesture towards her, but drops his hand. There is a long silence. Then he approaches slowly. 'What you need right now,' he says, 'is a proper cleansing. Before you are consumed by the fires of hell that burn in that secret place of your body.'

'If there are devils in me, then they're mine. And you have no right to drive them out,' she says. There is a recklessness and a passion in her now, which seem to excite him unbearably.

He comes still closer. She backs away. He follows. It is a scene an onlooker might find comical; to them, trapped in it, it is deadly serious. She backs. He follows. Until she feels the wall against her shoulderblades and knows that no further retreat is possible. He comes still closer.

'Don't do this, Your Reverend,' she says. Her voice falters briefly.

'It is for your own good,' he says. She can smell his lunch on his breath. Leeks, onion, chicken. 'It is my duty to take you in charge.'

'Can you not leave it to God?' she asks. 'Or do you think he may also take advantage of me?' For the first time ever her defiance is open; but it is her life she is fighting for.

'This is blasphemy!' he gasps. 'Are you not scared unto death? *It is a fearful thing to fall into the hands of the living God.*'

She mustn't say this, she mustn't; but she does: 'If God is like you, Your Reverend, I won't have anything more to do with him. Not ever.'

17

.

It has dire consequences. In later years – and also this night when she stares, darkly, at her reflection in the mirror on the landing – she will think of it as her first death. (The very early one, before she came to the Little Children of Jesus, doesn't count, because she has no recollection of it.) Pastor Ulrich personally accompanies her back to the orphanage. On the way he tries several times to clutch her hand, but she evades his grasp.

She has to spend a week locked up in the cellar where the peat is kept. A dark so absolute she cannot see her fingers when she holds them up to her face. She has always been terrified of the dark, but this is so far beyond terror that she can no longer consciously feel it. It is just something that is lodged inside her, a blackness into which she retreats and which paralyses her. They have taken away all her clothes. She is given no food. Only water, twice a day. Once a day someone comes with a cane to administer a beating. When at last she is allowed out she can barely walk. The light hurts her eyes, piercing them like shards of broken glass. She is taken to Frau Agathe's cramped study cluttered with heavy dark furniture. Pastor Ulrich is there too. She can smell him before she sees him.

'My child,' he says, his voice marinaded in loving concern. 'I hope you have used your time to think on God and his mercy.'

Hanna shows no reaction.

'It is the Devil,' whispers Frau Agathe.

'What do you have to say?' Pastor Ulrich prods her gently.

'Why do you hate me so?' she asks with stiff lips.

'You are wrong, my daughter,' he says. 'We love you. God loves you. What we hate is the Devil that has taken hold of you. We shall get rid of him whatever it takes.'

She shrugs wearily.

'This weekend you have your Christmas concert,' he reminds her. 'Are you ready to take part in a spirit of celebration, with a mind and a body cleansed of sin, to the greater glory of God?'

'I do not want to have anything to do with your concert,' she says. 'I do not want your God.'

Frau Agathe sits down on a chair, gasping for air like a fish on land, too horrified to speak.

He, too, is breathing deeply. He asks, 'What is it you want?'

'I want my books,' says Hanna. 'I want to go back to Fräulein Braunschweig.'

'Unless you repent you will never set foot in that school again,' says Frau Agathe in a piercing voice. 'All you bring back from there is bad habits and an evil heart.'

She cannot believe it. She stares at the grownups in dismay. All her thoughts go tumbling in disorder through her mind. But she does not speak.

Frau Agathe stands up. 'I shall leave you to Pastor Ulrich,' she says. As she prepares to close the door behind her, she adds, 'I shall pray God for your immortal soul. But I have very little hope.'

'Please don't go,' says Hanna.

Frau Agathe looks at her with a frown between her pale grey eyes. 'What do you mean?'

'Pastor Ulrich does sinful things to me when we are alone.'

The tall thin woman stares at her as if she has seen a ghost. Then she thrusts her bony face into her hands and starts shaking. 'How dare you, how dare you, how dare you?' she stutters. But Hanna cannot make out whether it is addressed to her or the pastor.

He is livid. But is it with rage, or fear?

'Do you think,' he asks in a voice so low she can hardly hear it, 'do you think any man – do you think that I, a man of God – will even consider laying a finger on one as despicable and as wretched and as evil and as ugly as you?' He is breathing deeply, unevenly, as he does when he is alone with her.

I may be despicable, she thinks. And I know I'm wretched. I may be evil. But don't tell me I am ugly. For God's sake, don't.

She is taken back to the cellar for another week. She no longer feels the hunger. She is barely conscious of the pain when they come for the daily beating. But she is aware of the cold. It creeps into the marrow of her bones. She is shivering, day and night. Her head throbs with pain, she is racked with fever. Sometimes she hears voices. Fräulein Braunschweig saying, 'You must read this. *Die Leiden des Jungen Werther*. It is a very beautiful book.' The small piping voices of invisible children, Trixie and Spixie and Finny. And unknown voices too, chanting the music of far-off names – Guadalquivir and Macchu Pichu and Smolensk and Ondangua and Barbezieux and Parramatta. They may be the voices of angels. Sometimes they change into animal sounds, the braying and barking and mewing and crowing of the Musicians of Bremen, drowned out by the glorious booming of the cathedral bell, and then silence, nothing but silence.

'This child is dying,' says an unfamiliar voice one day.

Frau Agathe's voice replies, 'She is acting up.'

Then back into the dark. There are rats scuttling about. They gnaw at her hair, her fingers, her frozen toes. They are speaking to her in eerie squeaking voices. Come with us, they tell her. Let us get out of here and drive out the grownups from the Little Children of Jesus and take possession of it. But how will we get out of this black hole? she asks. No problem, they say, we'll gnaw through the door.

It happens so quickly that she can hardly believe it. A shimmering of daylight filters into the cellar.

Come, they shriek at her. We can't wait, we must surprise them! Her weakness, the fever, the shaking of her body, all miraculously flow out of her as she gets up and, grabbing a coal shovel from the wall next to the broken door, follows them up the broken stone staircase. The rats must have communicated with others of their tribe beforehand, because when they reach the ground floor above they are joined by thousands of other rodents that come swarming from all sides, through doors and windows, down chimneys, pouring from the ceilings.

They part to all sides like a dark sea to let her pass. 'You must lead us,' they say. 'You know the place. Take us straight to them.'

With Hanna at the head, they converge on Frau Agathe's room. The door is locked, Hanna discovers when she tries to force it from outside. From inside they can hear a humming of low, anxious voices. Frau Agathe and some other women. Pastor Ulrich. This is perfect. Hanna motions at her cohorts to storm the place. Once again the rats swoop to the door. Within minutes there is nothing left but a heap of white splinters and a gaping hole. The grownups are cowering against the far wall.

'Please understand,' squeaks Pastor Ulrich in a falsetto voice. 'Everything we have done has been in the name of God. We really mean well. We bear you no malice.'

They are not permitted any further argument. The rats come swarming forward and overrun the five or six figures in black. There is one large general sound of gnawing, within which smaller eddies can be distinguished – the wet slithering of mastication, squeaking tussles and fights over fingerbones and toes. And in no time at all only bones are left, smooth and very white.

From there the rats spread out in all directions. Children are set free from dormitories and study halls in which they have been locked up. In a frenzy of jubilation they ripple through the corridors and spill out into the streets. They are heading for the river, and from there to the sea, Hanna knows. And as soon as the work is done – the great stone building crashing to the ground behind them, sending up a huge cloud of dust – she runs to join them. The sea, the sea. And playing on the beach, blissfully unaware of catastrophe as she builds a sandcastle at the lacy edge of the water, a small girl with black hair and the bluest of eyes is caught in the dazzle of the sun. Behind her are palm trees waving like tall hands beckoning. This way, this way.

She comes to, hazily, when her body is picked up by many hands, and a blanket is thrown over her, and she is carried out, and upstairs.

'I'm afraid it is too late,' a voice says. 'The girl is dead.'

'She had to sit out her punishment,' says Frau Agathe. 'What will become of discipline if we give in to every little prank? At least we've driven the devils out, praise God.'

When she wakes up again she is in a strange white room. So she must be dead, she thinks, and this is heaven. God may turn up at any moment. Which may be problematic, as she no longer believes in him. Perhaps she should tell him, Can we agree on this? I will not believe in you, if you will not hold it against me.

But the man who comes in is not God. It is Pastor Ulrich. (He had eggs for breakfast, and pork sausages, the stains on his waistcoat disclose.)

She shuts her eyes, but he doesn't go away. Through trembling lashes she peers at him. He stands looking down at her for a long time, before he goes to find a chair from a corner and pulls it up right next to her bed.

'My daughter,' he says.

Hanna pretends to be asleep.

'Hanna.'

She still says nothing. Will he not get tired and go away?

He will not. She feels a movement on the bedclothes. He has inserted his hand under the top blanket. For a while he keeps very still, then the hand begins to move closer as if it has a life of its own, like a fat crab. It touches her hip and goes still again. She lies very rigid.

He whispers, 'Hanna.'

She does not answer.

'Surely it cannot be worth it,' he says, as if he is talking to himself. 'We can come to an understanding. You can go back to school. You can even go on reading your books, provided they are not too lewd or ungodly.'

She does not answer.

'My only concern is for your well-being,' he says. 'You had us all very worried indeed. Double pneumonia. But you will soon be well, the doctor says. Are you not glad?'

She remains wrapped in silence as in a cocoon. No butterfly will hatch here.

'You are really a good girl, Hanna. I am prepared to talk to Frau Agathe.'

Hanna says nothing, but her whole body keeps rigid. He must know she is not asleep. The hand begins to move across from her hip. It reaches what it has been trying to find, and comes to rest, the thick fingers cupped over it.

'Hanna?'

'I shall tell God,' she says through clenched teeth, her eyes still tightly shut.

He utters a small harsh laugh. 'If God has to choose between you and me, who do you think he will believe?'

'Then I shall tell Fräulein Braunschweig. She will believe me.'

The hand freezes, opens limply, moves away. She can breathe again.

'Whatever happens,' he says, 'you will have brought upon yourself. You understand that, don't you?'

'I'm going to die,' she says quietly.

Suddenly he erupts. 'Then die!' he shouts at her. 'For God's sake, die! But don't come crawling back to me afterwards asking for forgiveness.'

She doesn't bother to respond. Her eyes are still closed when he leaves. The bed is swaying, rocking, drawn along by a gentle invisible current, like a small boat on the sea.

18

THERE ARE A hundred and ten women on the *Hans Woermann* which leaves Hamburg harbour on a miserable dark day in mid-January. The ship carries twenty first-class passengers, so the women transported to the colony of German South-West Africa are housed in rather unprepossessing quarters. Thirty of them, entered on the register as the more educated or cultured of the crop, the 'gebildeten Mädchen', because they can afford to contribute the sum of 150 marks to their passage, are lodged in second-class cabins, each with a bunk to herself. But the majority, the sixty 'einfachen Mädchen', transported at the government's expense in third class, are herded into dingy cabins below sea level, two to a bunk designed for one, four bunks to a cabin. It is the only way to create space for the five thousand tons of freight which make the journey affordable; the Company turns a blind eye, and the passenger lists are amended accordingly.

It is on the list supplied by Frau Charlotte Sprandel of the Kolonialgesellschaft in Berlin, on behalf of Johann Albrecht, Herzog zu Mecklenburg, that an unfortunate spattering of black ink first designates one of the passengers as Hanna X.

The woman assigned to share a bunk with her is Lotte Mehring. The name immediately calls up the most intimate memories from Hanna's past, *Die Leiden des Jungen Werther*. But it is so much more than a name. It is a new reality. Lotte is a small slender girl with wispy blonde hair, mousy but not unattractive. A few years younger than Hanna, widowed at twenty-two, she has been shipped off by her late husband's family before she could claim any of the meagre inheritance his seven brothers preferred to keep to themselves. Not that she would have wished to hold any reminder of the brief marriage which brought her little more than sweat and tears, black eyes and broken arms and a miscarriage, which she will relate in a low whisper to Hanna during the long nights they lie together on the narrow bunk which reeks of despair and stale urine.

'Why did you marry him then?' Hanna will ask one night.

'He wanted me,' Lotte says simply.

'Did you not know he would use you so?'

'No. But even if I had . . .' Lotte presses her small forehead against Hanna's hard shoulder. 'I'm sure I would have married any man who came along to take me away from our family.'

Hanna shakes her head uncomprehendingly. 'At least you *had* a family,' she points out. 'I had only the orphanage, until they placed me out in service.'

'You don't know how lucky you were.'

'You don't know what you're talking about, Lotte. You should have seen that place. If I told you about Frau Agathe.' A quiet shudder. 'And Pastor Ulrich . . .'

'He could not have been as bad as my father. And my two brothers.'

'But surely . . .' She cannot speak the rest.

'The first time he came to me in the night,' says Lotte, 'I was not quite ten. My brothers began soon after.'

'But where was your mother then?'

'She pretended not to know. She was too scared, you see. If I went to her she would get very cross and say it was all lies. And then she'd tell him what I said and he would beat me. And her too.'

Lotte will begin to moan softly, as if in pain, and Hanna will hold her against her body, rocking her very gently until the crying has subsided.

'Please keep holding me,' says Lotte after a long silence. She moves her fingers across Hanna's face in the dark, and then stops in surprise. 'Why is your face wet? Have you been crying too?'

She cannot speak. She only nods. The dark makes confidences possible which would otherwise be unthinkable.

'But you . . .'

'Don't talk now,' says Hanna.

In the dark, in the slow dance of the ship on the sea-swell, they hold one another, the small slight body and the stronger more unwieldy one. Holding, holding. Lotte is almost as real to her as Jeanne d'Arc, years ago, in her small bed in the orphanage. And almost imperceptibly their hands move across each other's face, more lightly than the quivering of a butterfly wing.

'You know,' says Hanna once, 'no one has ever held me. Not even when I was very small. No one came at night to tuck us in. We were taught to be strong, to devote ourselves to God and good things, touching was bad, it made one weak. Except once, when a new little girl came to us, Helga, and she was crying so much, she would keep us awake at night, I went to put my arms around her and hold her. Just hold her. But then Frau Agathe found out about it.'

'Tell me,' says Lotte.

And so it becomes Hanna's turn. And then Lotte's again. And in the dark they hold each other very close, body to body, feeling the new warmth they generate between them. Conscious, always, of the night outside, and the cold of the sea, the endless near-black depths below them, this warmth becomes infinitely precious, a wholeness, a small but brave affirmation that yes, they are here, Hanna and Lotte, two lonelinesses merging, two histories, a single breathing living being, beautiful in the dark, vulnerable yet strong while it lasts. What is this I, this you? From what immeasurable distances do we come, what light or darkness are we heading for – nights swarming with stars, palm trees waving in the wind, glimmering in the sun – how much of eternity can be stored up in an hour, a single moment? I love you.

She invents not only the geography of Lotte's body but her own, a new and breathtaking discovery: that this body she has learned to despise, to loathe, can be capable of so much pleasure, can give so much joy. That what used to be a source of pain and revulsion can now be an affirmation, a place of celebration. This you have given me, this I can give back to you. This is me, at last, now and for ever. Me, Hanna X.

Their bodies are slowly turning and moving, their hands are moving, fingers clasp and unclasp, what journeys of discovery they undertake through the nightscapes of bodies folding together, intertwining, turning the everyday into miracle – you, me, us, always – naming and unnaming, ears, eyes, throat, shoulders, elbows, breasts, belly, knees, feet, hills and valleys, palm trees, hidden springs, the ever-secret depths and folds of your body, mine and not mine, yours and not yours, tongue to tongue, breathing in of my breathing out, whisper of my whispering, you, me, us.

If anyone ever finds out, something terrible is bound to happen, so they take great care never to be seen together during the daytime. They go about their business with the other women. The *einfachen Mädchen* in third class are required to help the sailors with domestic duties: cleaning their own cabins, scrubbing the deck, serving in the kitchen. But the night belongs to them. They lie talking for hours, sometimes until daybreak (even though one cannot see the day dawn in the perpetual darkness of the lower decks). In between they make love, or simply lie together in a long embrace.

'What will happen when we get there?' asks Lotte.

'We will find somewhere to live together,' says Hanna.

'The government paid for us, they will claim us. We owe them.'

Does Hanna not know all about this kind of owing? It is what she learned to hate more than anything else about her indenture. 'I will not let it happen again,' she assures Lotte.

'But *how*? We are in their hands, we are not allowed to make decisions, we are women.'

'We shall find a way.'

'It won't happen by itself,' Lotte persists. 'We'll have to plan before we get there.'

'Something always happens. You didn't plan your husband's death, it just happened.'

'One of his brothers killed him.'

'But you were saved. And you were not involved in the killing.'

There is a long silence, before Lotte says, 'I was. I planned it. I bribed his brother to do it.'

'How did you do it?'

'I promised him – it doesn't matter. It worked. That is all.'

'It will work again.'

'They will find a way to stop us.'

With all the heedlessness of her newly discovered state Hanna says, 'Nothing can stop us.'

'My Hanna, my Hanna.' And in love and anguish she begins the stroking movement which she knows will drive Hanna to hopeless pleasure.

But she is, of course, right. It cannot last. The irruption into their joined privacy comes unexpectedly. As the journey continues the sailors take to visiting the women at night, particularly the most vulnerable among them, in third class. And the fact that they are welcomed by some of the women – for all kinds of reasons that proliferate in the dark – makes them bolder in imposing on others. There are small profits to be made from such encounters: favours in various forms, food, inconsequential gifts, promises of one kind or another. And these alleviate the tedium of the weeks at sea, instilling flickerings of hope in some who have already given up or resigned themselves to deception and disappointment.

For some time this does not affect Hanna and Lotte. They inhabit a small island which seems inviolable. Until one night a few very drunk men blunder their way into the cabin at the end of the passage. They do not bother to pick or choose, but grope at random at the female flesh barely concealed under shapeless cotton or linen shifts. One of them drags Lotte away. She fights with all the viciousness of a trapped rodent, but it only makes him randier. When Hanna joins in and attacks him from behind he is nearly overpowered. But then she is set upon by one of the other sailors and sent sprawling in a corner by a blow to the head. By the time she is on her feet again they are gone.

One of the other women takes her by the hand. 'Just leave them, dearie. They're in such a state they'll kill you if you try to interfere.'

'But you don't understand,' sobs Hanna. 'They can't take Lotte. They have no right.'

'They have every right, my girl,' says the other woman. 'We should just be thankful that we've been spared. For tonight. There are still six nights to go.'

There is a sickness in her which is not of the body. She remains hunched up in a corner of the bunk, waiting for Lotte to come back, praying open-eyed, praying to the God she doesn't believe in, to make sure Lotte isn't hurt too much. What this may do to them, she is too scared, too numb, to figure out.

But Lotte doesn't return. Has the man killed her?

No, she discovers later the next day, it is much worse. The man has claimed her. Lotte will spend the rest of the voyage on his bunk with him. Even during the daytime he keeps a hawk's eye on her as he goes about his tasks, never far away. The two of them are not allowed a minute together to talk.

It is soon over though. Two days later, in the afternoon, the news spreads from deck to deck: a young woman has committed suicide. She has slit her wrists in the bathroom. Hanna does not need anyone to tell her who it is.

It is only the next day when, after a cursory service presided over by the captain, Lotte is buried at sea – her body, that small beloved body, sewn into a canvas bag, laid out on a wooden stretcher and summarily tipped overboard, followed by some makeshift wreaths – that Hanna discovers the horrible mistake. The name of the dead woman is announced to have been hers, Hanna X's.

She hurries to the captain afterwards to have the mistake corrected, but the officers surrounding him deny her access. When she finally grabs one of them by the lapels to shout, half dementedly, that she, Hanna X, is still alive, that the dead woman is Lotte Mehring, he disengages himself with visible irritation and promises to look into it. But when she corners him again a day later, he tells her she is mistaken. Enquiries have been made, they have checked the cabin number and the bunk, and the deceased woman is indeed Hanna X.

'But I am Hanna X!' she exclaims. 'Here I'm standing before you. Do you think I don't know who I am?'

'Listen, woman,' he brushes her off gruffly, 'I don't know what is up with you. We have gone through all the records, you have given us a lot of trouble, so why don't you just accept the facts?'

'The facts are wrong,' she says. 'Look at me.'

He gives an indulgent, superior smile. 'Suppose,' he says, 'just suppose you are right, which you are not. Even then, do you really think we can change the documents now? Do you realise how many forms we have had to fill in?'

'Then who am I?' she asks him. 'If you are so sure, tell me.'

'I really could not care less,' the officer says brusquely. 'Now please just leave me in peace and accept that Hanna X is dead and buried.'

19

THE WIND. THE wind always comes from *somewhere else*. At night in the orphanage, slowly retreating from the edge of death, she lies listening to the comforting sound of her friend, the wind. She must have been very small when she first became aware of it. She was suffering from a bad cold and couldn't sleep; and all the time the wind was there to keep her company. In the morning she told Frau Agathe, 'The wind has a cold too, I could hear her sniffing all night.'

And Frau Agathe replied, 'If you can think up such nonsense you're not sick any more. So get up, make your bed and go and weed the garden.'

Ever since then she has been thinking about going on a journey to find out where the wind comes from. The far side of the wind would also be the other side of silence.

20

In the early days after her arrival at Frauenstein with the band of Namas Hanna keeps mostly to the small grey room assigned to her, exposed to all her memories. The in-between time with the Nama tribe – between an old life and the beginning of a new, between the sea and the desert, between the train and Frauenstein, between life and death, consciousness and oblivion – remains a fluid and confused assortment of images, watercolours running together on a sheet of paper, a space of stories and possibilities and impossibilities. Her thoughts keep wandering. The train journey – no, not that; that must be excluded from memory. The voyage on the *Hans Woermann*, then. Lotte. For the first time she is free to mourn, and she does. A mourning as much for herself as for the young woman who briefly shared her bunk, her life. A woman undone by the vagaries of officialdom when the name of Hanna X was entered on the records. She is dead, she will think. And that is true, for nothing remains of the person she once was or may have been. So she must be dead. And in a way this links them even more fatally and more wonderfully together.

She need not fear the outside world any more. The worst that could ever have happened to her has happened. Lotte's death, the train, her own death in the desert. There is nothing more they can take from her. She has arrived at an inviolate stillness. That careless action by the scribe on the *Hans Woermann*, sealed by what then happened on the train, has put her at a remove from the ordinary lives of ordinary people.

It is confirmed, if confirmation is needed, by what occurs when the commando bring the news about their triumphant expedition against the Namas to avenge the wrong they believe has been done to her.

To celebrate the victory they are invited in, and as is the wont of Frauenstein, they are treated to dinner and granted the freedom of the house. As has happened in the past and will be repeated in the future. Hanna, who at first hid in the attic, is now cowering in her room, still petrified by the news, and even more so by the memories of the train they rekindle. But there is no need to fear. When three, four, five of the soldiers burst into her room she looks up at them from the small rough table where she is seated; and when they see her face they gape, and stop in their tracks, and retreat, and close the door very solemnly after them. Which brings the reassurance that, indeed, she has nothing more to fear. But also the painful confirmation of final and utter rejection. Even these scavengers have turned her down. She has sunk lower than any woman, lower even than the animals or wild melons with which these men will copulate if there is nothing else at hand.

From that day on she will never go about with her features exposed. The large pointed kappie will cover her head and obscure her face, day and night. Not even the remonstrations of Frau Knesebeck will make her reconsider. But why does she really wear it? To spare others, or herself? To confirm, finally, her indignity, or to safeguard an ultimate shred of pathetic dignity?

Not that anyone would bother to ask. They know, now, that she is incapable of answering. But it goes beyond that. Because she cannot speak they seem to assume that she is mentally deficient. When they address her, they choose simple words, which they articulate very slowly, and very emphatically. For God's sake, she would like to tell them, I am not deaf; I am not an idiot; I understand perfectly. In the first days, even weeks, it will make her cry in helpless rage when she is alone; she will tear curtains from the windows, or break things, or beat her hands or her head against the walls until her knuckles bleed or her forehead is swollen with unsightly bruises. (Their only reaction is to shake their heads and commiserate: the poor thing, the mad woman whose mind is quite unhinged; one has to be very patient with her, treat her even more circumspectly, she is like a small child.) But very slowly she comes to resign herself. There is no sense in trying to resist. This is her life, now. It has to be lived somehow. And perhaps it is not without consolation that she is allowed to retreat ever more deeply into herself.

In the Little Children of Jesus she used to go to the most extreme lengths to please Frau Agathe and the others, to invite their approval if not their love. True, in their eyes she never went quite far enough: she could not prostrate herself utterly, or ingratiate herself, or be obsequious – which is why they continued to think of her as stubborn and intractable, and punish her the more for it. And of course she had her long, flowing cascade of hair, which convinced them that she must be suffering from the sin of pride. But what she craved, *because* she was so clumsy and always spilled things, or broke things, or did the wrong things, was to make them realise – please, God! – that she was *trying*; that she, too, needed to be acknowledged, however grudgingly. But now not even that effort is necessary. She can withdraw entirely and they will shrug it off: that is the way she is; after what those savage Nama people have done to her, how can one not grant her the right to be 'otherwise'? Poor thing, poor ugly wretch.

In the beginning, particularly after the visit from the avenging commando, Hanna has an unbearable urge to speak. She has to tell Frau Knesebeck about her stay with the Namas. The ghastly mistake made by the soldiers cannot go unchallenged. But there is no way she can communicate in grunts and moans and wails: when she reacts in this way to the soldiers' tale, the staff believe that she has lost her wits by the reminder of her ordeal among the savages, and she is forcibly if sympathetically taken to her room. That is when she decides to write down her story. Communicating in frantic signs to Frau Knesebeck – who somehow has assumed that she is illiterate – she is finally pacified with a stack of paper, a pen, spare nibs, an inkwell. It has become the only way open to her to grope through the wall of silence surrounding her, reaching out to someone out there who may respond. There *must* be someone, something, at the other side.

Throughout the night, by the dull light of her single candle, she writes, in the large looped childish calligraphy they taught her in the orphanage. It is irregular and spoiled by blots and splashes and smudges, because the emotions are still not under control. Two nibs are broken. Her hands are stained black, and some of it has come off on her face.

From time to time she has to stop altogether to calm down, walking around the room, or wandering up and down the stairs through the huge gloomy building. But always she returns to the task, driven by the need to tell her story. It may be too late to do something about the fate of her Namas – 'her' Namas is how she always thinks of them – but at least someone must know; it may change the future for others.

Laboriously, painstakingly, she writes down everything she can remember about her stay with the tribe – her confused memories of the early days, faces, words; the way the women cared for her, the herbs and concoctions they made her swallow, the ointments and unguents they applied to her wounds. The singing she listened to, the dancing when the moon was full, the curious instruments they used to make their music, the monotonous but mesmerising rhythms of the *t'koi-t'koi* and the *ghura*. And then the stories in their pidgin German, the endless inventions of the old women. The care they took of her, the generous attention to ensure she wouldn't get too tired on the long trek to Frauenstein.

In the early dawn she takes the wad of papers covered in her messy scribbling down to Frau Knesebeck's office.

'You're up early,' the spruce woman says.

Hanna merely shrugs impatiently, thrusting the papers into her hands.

'Very nice,' says Frau Knesebeck in the tone one adopts for a small child. 'Not very tidy, but I'm sure you have done your best.' She opens a drawer and puts the papers into it.

Agitated, Hanna comes round the desk, opens the drawer again, points excitedly at the papers.

'Don't worry,' Frau Knesebeck assures her. 'I promise you I shall read it with great attention.'

But Hanna tugs at the woman's elbow, points at her eyes, pats on the papers, pulls them out of the drawer again. *Read, read now!* she tries to say.

'Now calm down,' Frau Knesebeck reprimands her firmly, with a hint of annoyance in her voice. 'I'm very impressed with the effort you have made. Now you must give me some time to peruse it.'

Breathing heavily, Hanna remains standing for some time. Only when

Frau Knesebeck makes it very clear that she has other business to attend to does she turn to go out, her shoulders sagging. In the late afternoon, hearing Frau Knesebeck in the laundry, Hanna returns to the office, removes the papers from the drawer and replaces them on the middle of the desk.

Exhausted as she is, she finds it impossible to sleep that night. Once again she spends hours at her table writing, writing. This time she doesn't dwell on the Nama tribe but writes randomly whatever comes to her mind about the more distant past – her life in the orphanage, Frau Agathe, the long-ago day beside the river when she met the little Irish girl (the shell is gone now, she writes, lost in the course of that nightmare on the train, lost for ever, and the sound of the sea with it), about Trixie and Spixie and Finny. In the morning she takes the new clutch of papers down to the office.

Frau Knesebeck motions to a corner of the desk where Hanna can put down her latest offering.

But Hanna remains standing.

'What are you waiting for?' After a moment, Frau Knesebeck forces one of her thin-lipped smiles that look like wincing. 'Oh I see.' She pulls open the drawer and removes the previous stack of papers, pushes them across the desk towards Hanna. 'Yes. Well.' She presses her fingertips together. 'I have read your outpouring with great attention. It must have been unbearable, subjected to the whims and the cruelties those natives inflicted on you. Even worse than I'd imagined before. You are a very brave person indeed. I commend you for it. Now' – she rises briskly – 'hopefully you have written it all out of your system. You will soon feel a new woman.' She looks at the new pile on her desk. 'I shall look at this as soon as possible. But I do think you should now put this behind you. We do not want to perpetuate such a bad memory, do we? The crime has been punished, your suffering has been avenged. We can now move on.'

The third night Hanna does not even try to make sense in what she writes on the many pages she covers with her rambling notes – increasingly tired, disconnected, leaden. Quotations she recalls from old books, snatches from the lives of Werther or Jeanne d'Arc, random rhymes, nursery songs, slogans from the streets of Bremen, long words from school dictations, deliberately misspelt; and then, driven by a rage she cannot explain herself, all the curses and swear words she has ever heard, the ones for which her mouth used to be rinsed out with the foul-smelling black soap. Even the unforgettable sentence the man on the train spoke that night.

Almost gleefully she takes the new stack down to Frau Knesebeck in the morning and exchanges it for the previous instalment.

'Another effort?' the woman asks, irritation now on the surface of her voice. 'I've looked at yesterday's of course. Well done, indeed. But I really believe we have now exhausted the experience.' She places the latest pile of papers in her drawer. 'I shall of course look at this too. But you realise I have other work to attend to as well. I shall let you know when I am ready.'

Three days later Hanna returns to Frau Knesebeck's office and patiently waits at the door until the woman sharply raises her head to ask, 'Well, what is it this time?'

Hanna points towards the drawer.

'Yes, yes, of course.' She opens the drawer and takes out the manuscript. 'It is quite remarkable that you should have made the effort. You can be proud of yourself. We certainly are.'

Shaking with barely controllable rage Hanna rushes to the desk. In a long raking movement she sweeps up her papers and goes to the door. Tears are streaming down her face, but she makes no sound.

'I do think you should take more care with your writing, though,' says Frau Knesebeck behind her. 'It gives the impression of being rather hastily written. The letters are not always shaped properly, the lines are uneven, and there are far too many blots.'

In the oven at the back door, where a fire is flaring in preparation for the day's baking, Hanna spends half an hour burning everything she has written, each sheet separately. At first she is shaking with rage. Burn, burn! As if it is her own pyre. But as she grows more weary and her movements slow down, a deeper, inexplicable satisfaction spreads through her. Yes, this is a necessary act. How could it be otherwise? What she has written did not deserve to be told. It was not the truth, couldn't ever have been the truth, the whole, and nothing but. How could she have presumed so much? The truth cannot be told, that is why it is the truth.

Later in the day she leaves Frauenstein to die.

21

A LITTLE WAY down from Lotte's navel, and slightly to the right, is a small mole. Hanna will often linger there before she resumes with the tip of her tongue the journey of love.

22

THERE IS NOTHING furtive about her going off into the desert. In her childhood when she ran away from the orphanage, she always made sure that her absence would not be detected too soon. Also, in those days, on every occasion she had a clear idea of where she was going. Once, when she was very small, she hoped to reach the moon. On another occasion she tried to reach the place where the wind comes from. Sometimes she tried to find the way back to Trixie, Spixie and Finny. At least twice, in a more practical frame of mind, she left the dank building in the Hutfilterstrasse, followed the intricate warren of streets to the Rathausplatz and the St Petri Cathedral, cut through the Schnoor quarter and crossed the darkly flowing river on the free ferry to the Weserstrand on the far side, opposite the large basin of the Europahafen. But on neither occasion was there any sign of the girl who had once played there. And so both *Ausflügen* ended in a sad return.

This time, however, it is different. She is not going towards anything at all: it is purely a movement *away from*. And she neither hides nor advertises her going. It is immaterial to her whether she is observed or not. In the early days of her stay at Frauenstein she was never left alone; there were always women appointed to keep an eye on her. But their vigilance soon wilted in the heat. Why should it matter to them whether she is here or somewhere else? No one particularly likes or dislikes her. She is tolerated, as everybody else is; no more, no less.

She has taken nothing with her, no food, no clothes, not even a bottle of water. If she still had her shell, she might well have brought that along; but now it is gone, with all its irretrievable memories. Her wide bonnet, too, is left behind; someone else may find it useful, it is still quite new. One needs so little on this last trek. There is no sadness in her, not even reluctance. It is simply something for which the time has come. If anything, she feels anticipation at joining Lotte in death. It is not a religious expectation of an afterlife – in her early rejection of God she has also turned her back on both salvation and damnation – but a quiet contentment in accepting that what has happened to Lotte will now happen to her. In a way the Namas are also drawn into it. But they didn't choose their death, they were overcome by it; with Lotte and with her it is different, an act of choice.

It is Lotte she feels closest to in this infinite space. All boundaries, even of time, are quietly effaced. In this extremity, as in the extremities of love, they are together again. How would Lotte react to her scarred face and body, if she were here now? The question is irrelevant. They are together, there is no difference between them, they are the same, body and body, mind and mind, dream and dream, more intimate than marriage. It is such a necessary journey, into the self.

At the same time, she may think, this is perhaps the closest one can get to that *beyond* which she has always sensed at the far side of everything she knew. When she was a child it was associated with the other side of the sea, which to her was Ireland, where the little girl Susan came from. Much later, when she applied to go to German South-West Africa, that distant land nudging the turbulent Atlantic came to represent *beyond*. But now that *there* has become *here* she knows it is much more complicated than she has ever thought. What defines *beyond* is, after all, the acknowledgement that it cannot, ever, be attained. Except possibly on this final journey.

Desolate as the landscape around her may appear to be – red earth, rocks scorched brown and black, outcrops and ridges and banks of stone, stunted trees and *bossies*, sparse dry tufts of grass – to her it is not empty but dense with the life of the stories the Namas so endlessly told her. The thin dust devil twirling in the distance is the devil, *sarês*, in search of a victim. The shrilling cicadas are praise-singers of the god Tsui-Goab. The dry bed of a long-disappeared river is the trace of a magical snake. And when night falls and she lies down to rest, prostrate on her back, her head on her folded arms so that she can gaze up at the slow cartwheeling of the stars above, she recognises in the Milky Way the white ashes scattered by Tsui-Goab after he had defeated the evil god Gaunab so that all the world could be warned of the route he took to his home in the Black Sky. And the brightest light of all, that of the evening star *Khanous*, was once a brilliant girl among the Namas who warded off an attack by treacherous San warriors by sacrificing her virginity to the enemy in order to save her father's tribe.

Hanna is amazed to discover how much she can recall of what she was told by Xareb's people. Even during the days and nights when she was dazed and only half awake the stories must have insinuated themselves into her torn and bruised body like draughts and ointments with healing powers beyond all explanation. ('There is no pain and no badness,' she still hears the dry voice of old Taras in her ear, 'that a story cannot cure.')

The journey becomes, not a return to, but a kind of consecration of her stay with the tribe. They are the only people who have never, not once, recoiled or gaped in horror or disgust at her disfigurement; she was simply a person in need. Even among the outcasts in Frauenstein she remains an aberration and a curiosity. And how can she blame them? To herself she is a freak. When she wanders through the hollow space by day or night and catches in passing the merest glimpse of her reflection in a mirror, she averts her eyes; she will not face the ghoul she has become. But here in the desert, restored to the memory of the small people who saved her life and tended her – and paid the price for it – there is no danger of reflections; she can be whole again. She no longer feels the need, as in her bed in Frauenstein at night, too scared to face a mirror, to palpate the surface and contours of her face, her breasts, her cunt as if, like one newly blinded, she has to learn to read with her fingers the half-obscured and horrifying text of herself. Here, back with the Namas of her mind, she can simply *be*, there is no need of confirmation from the outside. It is a kind of purification of body and mind, stripping herself down to the elements, the perfect preparation for death.

It is not only the stories that come back to her. On the second day, when the thirst grows really bad, she finds herself kneeling beside a shrivelled plant that looks like nothing on earth; and as she instinctively begins to burrow into the gritty earth she realises suddenly that she is doing what Xareb himself has shown her digging for a *norra* root. The satisfaction the cool acrid juice brings her is better than anything she can remember from Bremen. It is an experience repeated with other forms of nourishment from the veld: the prickly leaves of *aruma*, the small green melons of the *tsamma*, the orange pods of *kukemakranka*. Many of the names she has forgotten, but she remembers what the plants look like, where to look for them, what they taste like. A couple of times she does make a mistake and pays for it with excruciating cramps or bouts of vomiting or diarrhoea; once it is so bad that she is convinced she will die.

But she recovers, and feels inordinately proud of herself. That is when, with a wan smile, she realises how mixed up everything has become in her mind: for why should she be relieved to have recovered if death is in fact what she has been looking for? She knows now that this is not the way she will meet her end, just as a good swimmer would be foolish to attempt suicide by drowning.

Xareb's people have saved her again, she thinks. And having revived herself with the juices of another tuber and some fiercely bitter aloe leaves, she calmly turns back to the east where she has set out from and begins to retrace her steps – quite invisible, her feet having left no imprint on the hard earth to start with – all the way through the desert which has now become a home to her, back to Frauenstein.

From very far away she sees the fantastic fortress rearing up against the lurid blaze of the sky. And a little distance beyond, the rocky outcrop which marks the head of the magic fountain. From this direction the formation in the shape of a woman is clearly recognisable, her torso half contorted as if struggling against her own petrifaction to turn back, back, to whatever lies behind her. This, she thinks, perhaps wryly, is what happens to women who try to look back.

A story told by the old woman, Taras: of the trickster-god Heiseb who left his tribe as a young man to see the world, and stayed away for a time without time; and when one day he came back, covered in dust and dirt, his skin wrinkled with memories and distances, a prodigal son stumbling at last into the almost-not-remembered village, there is no one left to welcome him, only an assortment of rocks and stones. Which is why dotted all over the landscape the innumerable graves of Heiseb are still marked with cairns to which every passer-by, woman or man, is required to add another stone. And Hanna, too, carries home a stone from her wandering and deposits it below the outcrop before she turns to enter the forbidding house of the women. It is difficult to say what she feels. Sadness? Regret? Fear? Relief? Satisfaction? Probably only something like resignation: she has gone away, she has come back, she is here now. And will be for the rest of her life.

She is tired, yes, to the point of exhaustion. Emaciated. Her shoes have been worn through and her feet are bleeding. Her face is blistered from the sun, a fiery purple red as if the skin has been stripped off. Now there will be shade and water and rest. Not necessarily sleep: it is not oblivion she wants, but an even, continuous consciousness.

Frau Knesebeck is in her office when she comes in. Hanna hesitates in the doorway. The woman at the desk looks up. Her expression registers no surprise. 'You are back,' she says.

Hanna nods.

Frau Knesebeck looks at the clock on the wall, its formal face flanked by eagles with spread wings, carved from dark wood, highly polished. 'It is time to milk the cows.'

Hanna goes out. She is not even upset that there will not be time to wash or change her clothes before she goes to the cowshed. It can wait. The routine is more important: it has been running its course since long before she arrived and will continue after her death. Rising early – no bells are rung at Frauenstein, the women are expected to follow the daily timetable by rote – to milk the cows and turn the animals to graze, then to separate the milk and keep the cream in the cool-room to make butter. Taking out the slops to the garden and the long outhouse with its row of holes in the wooden bench. Preparing breakfast, then washing the dishes. After which it will be time to do the laundry, or the ironing, or the darning and mending, or washing the windows, or polishing the floors, or cleaning the sheds, or chopping firewood, depending on the day of the week. Something for every hour of the day. Making oneself useful, keeping oneself occupied.

And there is reassurance to be drawn from the unvarying course of the daily programme, leaving little time for private emotions, for dwelling on an irrecoverable past or an impossible future. Everything is here, now, and for ever. She must cut herself off from feeling, even from the acknowledgement of feeling. It is too dark, too dangerous, too unpredictable, a wilderness into which she dare not venture. Only at night, sometimes, there is the treachery of dreams. Most of them are terrifying. Pastor Ulrich, Frau Agathe, the peat-shed, the closing of the heavy door in the parsonage study. Or the train, always the train – nightmares so horrendous that she is awakened by her own screams. The comforting dreams are more rare. Hearing the voice of old Taras in her ear, spinning her stories; or watching the children at play; or joining the tribe as they gather food or repair their huts or bring in bundles of firewood or slaughter a goat. Even more rare are the nights when Lotte takes shape from the dark to share her bed; within the dream she will awake to feel the caress of a hand, light as the whisper of the wind or a butterfly alighting on her breast (she still has nipples) or between her thighs (she still has a cunt). And with her own hands and lips she will return the caress and feel a body assume its substance from her touch. And she will discover that desire is still possible, even if it is unbearable. Then she will lie awake for the rest of the night, her body rigid with yearning; waiting for the bleak dawn to spill into her room and bring with it the first sounds of a new day, an old routine resumed.

23

ROUTINE IS ALSO what marks her years in service. Soon after she has recovered from the pneumonia, even before she has completely regained her strength, she is placed out for the first time. Frau Agathe has found 'just the right people' for her – a couple with four small children, a fifth on the way. Hanna is still devastated by the knowledge that she will never go to school again; but there is some consolation in the prospect of leaving the Little Children of Jesus for good. And she persuades herself that the couple who will be employing her, the Klatts, seem all right. Frau Hildegard, straight-backed, with steely eyes, her blonde hair drawn into a tight bun behind her head, is emphatic about her belief in strict discipline; one would have to step carefully with her – but then, Hanna is used to that. And Herr Dieter appears friendly enough, a jovial, prosperous-looking banker with a large smooth pink face.

There is one problem at the beginning, but it does not, at least not at first, seem insurmountable. The orphanage does not allow her to take anything away with her when she leaves – with the sole exception of the shell from the little foreigner on the Weserstrand, which Frau Agathe scornfully dismisses as childish nonsense. Even her worn and frayed clothes must be left behind for some sad successor. Which means that Herr and Frau Klatt will have to provide a new outfit and at least one change; this is readily resolved when Frau Hildegard and Frau Agathe come to an agreement that whatever is supplied by the Klatts will be deducted from Hanna's wages at a fixed rate. As it is standard practice for half of the wage of 40 marks per month to be paid directly to the convent, it leaves a mere pittance for Hanna's own use. This doesn't bother her much, as she has never had money anyway. But it does become problematic when she discovers that there are all kinds of hidden expenses she has to meet: small items like soap and candles and even sugar, and her meals over weekends, when she is theoretically off duty (although with nowhere to go she has little choice but to stay on in her cubbyhole of a maid's room in the cold, dark attic of the Klatts' home; which also means that she remains at their beck and call). And of course she is expected to bear the cost of all breakages. Given her habit of dropping plates and dishes and cups, and even more expensive objects like the vases or ornaments she is required to dust every other day, the deductions very soon exceed her wages. In addition, Frau Hildegard has devised a system of fines for everything she regards as a transgression or a dereliction of duty: oversleeping in the morning, arriving late for meals, forgetting to bring in the washing, neglecting to clean up after the children, reading during working hours, or simply 'causing a nuisance'.

These costs mount up so rapidly that after the second month Hanna realises she will not be able to work off the debt in a whole year. When she raises it with Frau Hildegard, the woman dismisses it laconically:

'No need to worry about it. If you behave yourself you'll be with us for many years.'

'But with no money at all?'

Frau Hildegard shrugs. 'That's entirely up to you, isn't it?'

By this time Hanna has established that Frau Hildegard is not a happy person. More precisely, that her only happiness derives from being unhappy. She bears the world a permanent grudge. The reason is not quite clear, as Herr Dieter has assured her a comfortable enough life – though not, as she is always quick to point out, as comfortable as the life she was used to in her father's home. She has a grudge against her children, she has a grudge against most of her friends, she has a huge grudge against her in-laws, she has a grudge against her dark house and, above all, she has a grudge against her husband because he always grins as if life need not be taken seriously. Very soon, inevitably, she also develops a grudge against Hanna.

At the end of the third month, when Frau Hildegard mentions in passing what her accumulated debt now amounts to, Hanna asks to see her account.

'Account?' asks Frau Hildegard. 'What do you mean, your account? Isn't it enough if I tell you what you owe?'

'Please, I want to see a paper,' says Hanna.

'I don't have time for it now.'

'Then can I have it tomorrow?'

After four days of gentle enquiries Frau Hildegard brusquely deposits a handwritten statement next to Hanna while she is doing the washing. 'I trust you will find it in order,' she snarls.

That evening after work Hanna carefully studies each item and marks with a cross what she finds unclear. When she serves breakfast the next morning she places the amended statement next to Frau Hildegard's plate.

'I marked the things I don't understand,' she says quietly.

'I didn't think you could read,' snaps the woman.

'This little one is cleverer than you think,' remarks Herr Dieter, laughing.

'I don't see anything funny in it,' his wife hisses at him. She turns to Hanna: 'I'll attend to it when I have time.'

When after another two days she appears to have dismissed the matter Hanna gently reminds her just as she prepares to go out shopping.

'I made out the statement myself. I'm sure it is correct,' says Frau Hildegard, turning away to put on her hat.

'Then if you don't mind, I'd like to go through it with you,' says Hanna.

The paper, it turns out, has been misplaced.

'I remember what was wrong,' says Hanna, unperturbed. 'First, you said I broke three cups. It was only two. And that I lost one of Herr Dieter's shirts in the wash. But it was only a sock, which little Gretchen took to make a puppet. And . . .'

Frau Hildegard explodes: 'Are you telling me I'm a liar?'

'No, Frau Hildegard. I'm only saying there were some mistakes. And when one has as little money as I have a single pfennig can make a difference.'

'Are you complaining about your wages now?'

This is when Herr Dieter comes in from the garden to go to the bank, leaving mud-tracks all over the floor, which Hanna will have to mop up later. 'What's all this squabbling about?' he asks benignly, winking at Hanna.

'This – this *wench* is accusing me of cheating her!' (The word she uses is *Dirne*.)

'It was only a few mistakes, if you please, Herr Dieter,' Hanna points out in a faltering voice. 'She says I lost one of your shirts in the wash . . .'

'I can't remember missing a shirt,' he says. 'A sock, yes. But I think I saw Gretchen making off with it.'

'Are you siding with a young guttersnipe against your own wife?' asks Frau Hildegard, nostrils flaring. 'And in my condition . . .'

'I'm just trying to be fair,' he says jovially. 'Anyone can make a mistake.'

'I do not make mistakes,' Frau Hildegard hits back, tearing the hat from her head and marching off to her bedroom where, they both know, she will now spend the rest of the day with compresses on her forehead.

'I'm so very sorry, Herr Dieter,' stutters Hanna. 'But I need my money, and in this way I shall never earn anything.'

'I'll sort it out with her,' he promises. And he gently pinches her cheek. 'Leave it to me.' Just before he turns away he appears to change his mind and comes back. 'Would you be interested in earning a few pfennig on the side?'

She looks hard at him, but there seems to be no guile or threat in his smiling pink face. 'I'll do anything, Herr Dieter.'

'At what time do you finish your work?' he asks.

'At eight o' clock, Herr Dieter. But sometimes Frau Hildegard wants me to do the darning after that.'

'Not tonight,' he says firmly. 'Come to my study just after eight.'

She doesn't move. 'Herr Dieter . . . ?'

'Now off you go,' he orders with a bright smile.

All kinds of uneasy thoughts keep tumbling through her mind as she picks her way through the day's tasks: making the beds and sweeping the floors, taking the children to the park, going to the market, cooking lunch, doing the washing, polishing the silver, preparing dinner, putting the children to bed. And then it is eight o' clock.

He looks up when she appears in the doorway to the Herrenzimmer.

'Close the door, Hanna,' he says, pushing away his ledgers, leaning back, folding his arms on his broad chest. 'Come closer. You're not scared of me, are you?'

She shakes her head, swallowing hard. The scene suddenly reminds her so much of Pastor Ulrich's parsonage that she breaks out in a sweat.

'How old are you, Hanna?'

She tells him. Then adds in a hurry, 'I don't do bad things, Herr Dieter.'

'I wouldn't dream of expecting bad things from you,' he says, so kindly that her misgivings begin to seep away. 'Come, sit down.' He points to an easy-chair at the other side of the desk.

She approaches, but chooses not to sit down.

'I'll be frank with you, Hanna,' he says. 'You're not what one would call a particularly pretty girl.'

She looks at him without expression.

'But you do have lovely hair.'

Still no reaction from her.

'Show me your titties,' he says in a matter-of-fact tone as if he is asking to check her fingernails.

Hanna takes a few steps back, turning her head fleetingly to calculate the distance to the door.

'I promise you I'm not going to lay a finger on you,' he says. He thrusts a hand in the pocket of his house jacket and takes out a small assortment of coins and puts them on the corner of the desk. She does not count them openly but even a quick glance tells her that this may amount to several days' wages.

She makes no movement.

'Take off your shirt,' he says again, tapping one finger very lightly on the small pile of coins.

'Please, Herr Dieter,' she says, her voice catching in her throat.

'I'm sure you have very charming little tits,' he says.

'You really are not going to touch me?' she asks.

'I give you my word.' He remains sitting in his big chair behind the desk.

She stares at him for several seconds, then at the money, before with a little shrug – what strange creatures men are – she raises her hands and starts unbuttoning, with dumb fingers, her plain white shirt. Again she looks at him, then draws apart the two flaps.

'Take it off.'

She takes a deep breath and shakes the garment from her shoulders, still briefly, instinctively, covering her breasts with her hands, then resigns herself, her eyes fixed on a spot on the floor. Embarrassed, vexed with herself, she feels her nipples stiffen.

He is silent for such a long time that she finally has to look up. There is a curiously intense expression on his fleshy face. But he says nothing. At last he gives a small, stifled moan, moves one hand across his face, and says, 'You can go now. Thank you.'

She is in such a hurry that she only does up half the buttons; and she is already at the door when he says, 'Your money.'

Flustered, she turns back, glances cautiously at him – but he seems to have lost interest in her and has returned to his ledgers – and shuffles hurriedly to the desk, scoops up the money, dropping a few coins, bends over to retrieve them, bangs her head against the desk as she straightens up too quickly, and scurries out.

Nine days later (Hanna keeps count), when she is summoned to the study again after the day's work is done, she once more, perfunctorily, as if she is taking off a sock, bares herself to the man's command; but this time he gets up behind the desk and says, 'Would you mind if I touched them?'

'Just touch?' she asks.

'Just touch.'

'All right. But that will cost more.'

In the weeks that follow, his touching, which at first is a mere brushing with the fingertips, becomes bolder; some times, when he has been carried away somewhat by the squeezing and kneading, her breasts feel tender and painful and keep her awake during the night.

She never lets on though, but she does insist, very apologetically, on a few extra pfennig.

The time comes, soon after Frau Hildegard has been confined with her fifth child, when Herr Dieter asks, as a special favour, if she would mind taking off all her clothes. Only if he promises not to touch her below her navel, she says. He accepts. Later he will offer her double the past rate for the privilege to touch, but Hanna refuses. It is a difficult decision, because it may mean two whole marks more, and Frau Hildegard has really gone crazy with her fines in recent weeks; but in the end she remains resolute. She will not have another Pastor Ulrich, not even if he pays.

24

In the meantime the daily routine becomes ever more charged with chores and duties. Since the birth of the new baby the other children have grown more demanding; it is seldom before ten o' clock that Hanna is allowed to creep upstairs with her meagre light. (She has considered giving up the candle to save money, but she is too scared of the dark where terrible things lurk.) Many nights she is required to carry the baby upstairs with her, if Frau Hildegard, who bears the child a most unconscionable grudge, needs an undisturbed sleep. And he seems to have permanent diarrhoea, which means so much more washing. In addition there are all the errands to be run, what with Frau Hildegard incapacitated most of the time.

The only escape, on some of her rare days off, is the visits Hanna pays to Fräulein Braunschweig at her old school. It means spending a few of her hard-earned pfennig on the tram, but there is no other way as the Klatts live far from the centre and if she goes on foot it will take the whole afternoon. They talk non-stop. There is always so much to tell, not about the work because it is not worth wasting time on that, and not about Herr Dieter, because she finds that too embarrassing; but about the children whom she likes even in spite of the trouble they cause and the pranks they play on her; and about her thoughts, and the books the teacher has lent her, and her dreams of a distant future when she will be out of service and working in a library or a bookshop, earning money for her travels around the world.

The visits are soon switched from the old classroom to Fräulein Braunschweig's small apartment two blocks away, in a small alley near the Marktplatz. In the beginning Fräulein Braunschweig always has coffee ready for Hanna when she arrives; but when she discovers how voraciously the girl sets upon the sweetmeats she has prepared a few casual questions bring to light how little Hanna gets to eat in the Klatt household (a diet mostly of black coffee and stale bread, and leftovers if she's lucky); from then on she makes sure that there is a full meal waiting on visiting days.

As the friendship develops, Fräulein Braunschweig also begins to tell Hanna more about herself. About the young soldier, Otto, she once was engaged to and with whom she'd planned to see the world. But then the war with France broke out and he had to go.

'On the last night before he left,' she says, 'I couldn't stop crying. I just knew he was going to die. But he was so full of life, so happy, he believed so much that great things would be happening to him in the war. And then – I suppose it was inevitable – then he . . . then we . . . well, we were engaged and everything, so we thought . . .' A long pause. 'And the next day he went away. And he was killed. And only after that I found I was pregnant.'

Hanna presses the teacher's hand between both of hers. She is crying. It is, ironically, Fräulein Braunschweig who has to console her.

'I was too confused to think straight,' says the teacher. 'And of course I was still so young. All I could think of was what my parents would say. So I got rid of the child.'

Hanna feels the skin on her jaws contract.

'Oh poor you,' she says, 'poor, poor you.'

'That's enough,' says Fräulein Braunschweig firmly. 'It all happened very long ago.' She gets up, reaches out and briefly presses Hanna's face against her. 'In a way, you know, I've come to think of you as the child I haven't had. So it's not so sad after all. Come, I think it's time for the books.'

Fräulein Braunschweig allows Hanna to browse at will through her bookshelves. Over the months her small collection of travel books is unobtrusively extended to make sure that there will always be something new. Turkey, India, the Greek Islands, Ireland, South America, Africa.

They do not speak about Fräulein Braunschweig's past again; but it is not necessary. She has said as much as she is prepared to say. And there is so much else to talk about.

Many times their conversation returns to Jeanne d'Arc with whom Hanna continues to have an intensely personal relationship. There are episodes from Jeanne's life which never fail to intrigue and delight her. The journey from Vaucouleurs to Chinon, when she innocently sleeps every night between her escorts Poulengy and Jean de Metz, impressing them so deeply with the innocence of her simple and forceful presence that they never think of touching her. Her disarming, girlish fondness for pretty clothes: a kidskin girdle, padded hose, leather shoes, finely wrought chain armour of polished steel – and of course her extravagant standard with its triumphant legend *Jhesu Maria*. The story of how, during the siege of Orléans, Jeanne is wounded by an arrow which penetrates fifteen centimetres into her flesh just above her left breast; she dissolves in tears, yet has courage enough to pluck it out with her own hands before she allows her soldiers to stanch the blood and dress the wound with olive oil and lard. And also the story of how, imprisoned in the castle of Beaurevoir *en route* to her trial and death in Rouen, she lapses into despair and, disregarding, for once, even the admonitions of her Voices, hurls herself from a tower twenty metres high, without even spraining an ankle. On and on the stories flow, and Hanna absorbs them all as if to quench a real and parching thirst.

On summer afternoons Fräulein Braunschweig sometimes takes a walk with her through the old town and tells her stories from the past, snatches of history interspersed with fantasy; apart from the story of Jeanne, Hanna is especially fond of the fairytales collected by the Grimms. It is as if the darkness in them illuminates obscure corners of her own life. The scarier they are – the opening of Bluebeard's secret chamber, the killing of the little Gooseherd's horse, the deaths of Snow White, the unfairness of the princess towards Rumpelstiltskin, the stepmothers and witches and wicked queens – the more enthralled she seems. If Fräulein Braunschweig is perturbed by this morbid fascination she never tries, at least not openly, to discourage Hanna. The poor child, she may think, has little enough to hold on to in the monotony of her dreary days; she may as well be indulged a bit. If there is time, the teacher will offer her informal lessons in the subjects she liked most when she was still at school: history, geography, literature. It remains rather rudimentary, but Hanna soaks up everything. When it is time to leave, it is like returning from one kind of world to another.

Invariably, Hanna is invigorated when she arrives back at the Klatts'. This, after all, is only temporary. There will be an end to it. One day it will be over and she and Fräulein Braunschweig will set out to explore the far and improbable places of the world. But soon this vigorous optimism abates. Every month, when the new statement comes, she falls further into arrears with her debt. It is slowly dawning on her that it will never ease, and can only get worse. This is the whole logic behind her indenture. For better or for worse, in sickness and in health, this will last till death.

This makes Herr Dieter's tempting offers of increased payment for more exquisite favours that much more difficult to resist. Even so it takes many months before she agrees to go beyond exposing herself and administer more blatantly to his needs. It is only because he is so understanding and kind about it that she concedes at all. Initially he is satisfied to undo his trousers and sit back to be fondled with her well-meaning if clumsy hands. As with everything else, her gaucheness is painfully evident; yet in this kind of fondling it appears to add to his appreciation, and hopefully his enjoyment. Beyond this manual manipulation she will not proceed, although he begs for her mouth; that she finds dirty, a sinful act. Not against God, who does not exist anyway, but against the body itself. (There are still many years to go before Lotte will come into her life.) She is bemused to see a grownup, important man grovel so, to hear him plead so urgently – and offer so much money – for a favour as derisory as that. And perhaps, she sometimes thinks, it may not even be so bad, really; if in the beginning she was revolted by the sight and feel of his spurting seed, she gradually relaxes into vague amusement. In a detached way she feels almost proud to discover how much pleasure she can dispense. But she will not cross the boundaries she has imposed, whether through instinct or contrariness.

Still the daily burden of work continues, and stealthily increases.

As do the costs incurred: because the children have found out about the fines their mother imposes and now know how to blackmail Hanna into doing whatever they wish. If that fails, they will break something precious and blame her for it. Worse than any fine or punishment (because sometimes Frau Hildegard, more and more unhappy with the world as time goes on, will also deprive her of food; or take the strap to her, beatings which seem to work her up into a frenzy where she can no longer control herself at all) is the fatal knowledge of that debt piling up, piling up, measuring the lengthening distance between the present and the possibility of release.

The only brief moments of escape are those late-night visits to the study with its pool of light among the textured shadows, the shiny surface of the big desk, the deep red of the leather upholstery on easy-chairs and couch, the eyes of her benefactor as he watches her strip off her clothes with gawky, graceless movements, discarding a shirt, shifting a skirt down her legs, stepping out of dropped knickers (and more often than not catching her foot in them and briefly losing her balance); or as he leans back to abandon himself, with eyes tightly closed, to the fumbling of her chafed hands in his lap.

Whether she ever derives some fleeting pleasure or excitement from it herself is difficult to tell. She is aware, almost every time, of her nipples hardening. And occasionally, truth be told, she becomes wet, which flusters and unnerves her so much that she promptly and awkwardly puts on her clothes again. For this is the most intimate betrayal of all: by her own body. But pleasure? Unlikely. And yet it is not a purely mechanical or mercenary encounter either. The few coins, the four or five or sometimes even ten marks, do matter, and she does not hesitate to raise the price if she has worked unusually hard or he shows particular enjoyment. But that is not all. There is an intricate exchange in it as well, a subtle sharing perhaps; or possibly the mere knowledge that, even if it is only for a few minutes, half an hour, exceptionally an hour, she has been of service to someone, she has done something that is appreciated, in a dark and subterranean way she has been acknowledged.

For she will always carry with her the early words he spoke to her: *You're not what one would call a particularly pretty girl.* (But then, oh don't forget, don't ever forget!, he added, *But you do have lovely hair*.) And even more so the conversation she overheard very soon after she first arrived in the Klatt household. Frau Hildegard and one of her neighbours, a bosomy, cheerful woman named Käthe, were talking in the lounge; Hanna brought them coffee and Torte, and left. But as she closed the door behind her again she heard her name, and stopped to listen.

Frau Käthe is speaking: 'Poor thing. So very plain. Not very appetising to look at, is she?'

'We did not hire her for her looks, Käthe,' Frau Hildegard says pointedly.

'No, quite. That much is clear. But I always say looks are important for a girl. That's all a man will notice.'

'Just as well then,' comments Frau Hildegard with a harsh little laugh. 'Then we know our menfolk will be safe. A pretty woman is an invention of Satan.'

'How can you say that when you have such striking looks yourself, Hildegard.'

'I was talking about servant girls,' Frau Hildegard puts the matter beyond dispute.

'Well, of course, I've heard it said that for some men a plain woman is a better proposition, because the plain ones are more grateful for some attention.'

'There is plain and plain,' Frau Hildegard trumps her. 'This one, as you have no doubt noticed, is *severely* plain. So we can both rest easy.'

Their laughter drowns out the tinkling of the coffee cups.

And so there is of course more than a touch of irony in the fact that it should be Herr Dieter's dalliance which leads to the abrupt termination of Hanna's service.

Not that they are ever discovered together, nothing as melodramatic as that. (If only it *was*, Hanna may, perversely, think after it is all over and the dust has settled and she is back in the orphanage.) What happens is that Frau Hildegard, driven by her concern for propriety and diligence, ventures up to Hanna's little box of a room in the attic on a tour of inspection, one day while the girl is off to market. There is nothing untoward to be discovered among Hanna's pitiful possessions. Except, perhaps, the shell from the girl on the beach; but it holds no interest for the lady of the house. What does attract her attention, however, is a tear in the old stained mattress in the corner. Is it suspicion, or sheer nastiness, that makes the woman stoop to put a hand through the tear and pull out a soiled linen bag half filled with coins? She has no wish to count the money, it is dirty; but at a guess she would say that it may well be a few hundred marks. The equivalent of a whole year's wages. *Before* the share of the Little Children of Jesus has been deducted. Stolen. All stolen from the household over these many months. That is the only logical conclusion.

Frau Hildegard chooses the hour of dinner, that evening, when the whole family is assembled at table – Hanna hovering in the background serving, almost too tired to stand on her feet – to produce, with a show of disgust, the dirty bag which she places on the corner of the long table next to Herr Dieter's plate.

Everybody stares. Hanna takes a step back. Her only comfort is that she is in the half-dark; hopefully no one can see her face.

'And what might this be?' asks Herr Dieter, fingering the bag with mild distaste.

'You ask that person,' says Frau Hildegard, half turning to point at Hanna. 'I found it in her mattress. Perhaps she will care to explain.'

Everybody waits, Herr Dieter too.

'It is my money,' says Hanna. She reaches for the bag, but Frau Hildegard sweeps it out of her reach.

'As far as I know you have nothing but debt. And this is a substantial sum.'

'I'm saving it to pay off my debt.'

'I couldn't care less what you want to do with it, my girl. What I wish to know is where you got it.'

'I earned it,' says Hanna, barely moving her lips.

'*Earned* it?'

Another long silence. Hanna looks at Herr Dieter, but he is more interested in reaching for the beer bottle to fill his mug, his head turned right away from her.

'At the market,' says Hanna. 'Doing things for people when I go there. Carrying and stuff.'

'I keep a close watch on your coming and going,' says Frau Hildegard. 'You have never been away for long enough to do such things. Anyway, this is not the kind of money people pay for small errands.'

'It took months. Ever since I came here.'

'You are lying to me, Hanna.' A pause. 'Is that so?'

This time the pause becomes almost unbearable.

'Yes, it is,' Hanna admits at last.

'Then what is the truth?'

'I earned the money with my body.'

Herr Dieter chokes on his beer.

'You did *what*?'

Hanna retreats until her back is against the wall.

'Hanna, talk to me.'

Hanna looks imploringly at Herr Dieter, but he avoids her eyes.

After another silence Hanna says, so softly it is barely audible, 'You pay me so little, I have no choice.'

Frau Hildegard gets up. Her chair scrapes the polished wooden floor.

'A thief *and* a whore,' she says, spitting each word out separately. 'I shall not have that in my house. We are decent people. Tomorrow Herr Dieter will take you back to the orphanage. With some luck you will end up in prison. It is a pity they no longer send criminals to the pillory.'

25

THE DAY AFTER Hanna returns to Frauenstein from the desert she calmly and deliberately hacks off her long hair. When she enters the dining room for lunch, Frau Knesebeck looks at her with stern disapproval, but soon composes herself. All she says is, 'Did you have to do that? Were you not ugly enough as it is?'

26

LIFE IN THE orphanage runs on as if she has never been absent. Hanna receives the routine punishment for working girls who have been dismissed – rations reduced to bread and water for a week, concluded with the public exposure of the culprit to the collective, rehearsed jeering of the assembled children and their overseers. Afterwards, through the considerable skills of Frau Agathe who has a reputation for inventing impressive references (signed by herself, by Pastor Ulrich, and imaginary employers), she is dispatched to a new placement. It is somewhat more distant than the first, but it is still possible, with half an hour of additional travelling each way, to continue seeing Fräulein Braunschweig; so Hanna can resign herself to it.

The problem, as she soon finds out, is that her debts from the Klatt household have not been written off but are carried over to her new employment. Frau Agathe having paid the full account produced by Frau Hildegard, without soliciting any comment or verification from Hanna, the new employers, the Hartmanns, are now required to reimburse the Little Children of Jesus.

They are a tight little family, but not a very happy one, as if they occupy the same space without really touching each other. The only child, Peter, who is twelve, has such a frail constitution that he cannot go to school and has to be taught at home by his mother, Frau Liesel, who was a teacher before her marriage. Herr Ludwig works for a firm handling imports and exports in a large brick building at the Europahafen. Hanna has been hired to do the housekeeping so that Frau Liesel can devote all her time to Peter.

Which does not prevent her from going out almost immediately after her husband has left for work in the mornings and seldom returning home before mid-afternoon, leaving Hanna to take care of Peter's lessons, an arrangement that suits everyone. It is likely that were he to know, Herr Ludwig would not approve, but he is studiously kept in the dark by his energetic wife, who draws Hanna into the conspiracy with a wink, some dark threats, and sporadic small rewards.

What Peter suffers from appears to be asthma, but Hanna is tempted to believe that the parents are really over-protective, following the loss of no fewer than three other babies before his birth — two of them stillborn, one dead just before his first birthday, as Frau Liesel never fails to remind her young housekeeper in tones of hushed and dire drama. To Herr Ludwig the survival of a son and heir is of primary importance, he himself being the last in a long line of almost-notable men, most of them in military service. (The only reason why he turned to commerce was that his own health had never been robust; also, he already had two older brothers in the army. No one could foresee that both would die within months of each other, one on duty in East Africa, the other in a duel not much spoken about in the family.)

Supervising Peter's homework is for Hanna a way of resuming her own lessons and her own reading. Her eagerness also brings a faint glow to the boy's pale face, though he remains weighed down by the suspicion that he will never really be as brilliant as his parents expect him to become. At least she can share with him her enthusiasm for the sufferings of the young Werther, the exploits of Jeanne, the far places of the earth.

When Frau Liesel comes home in the afternoon — often flushed and with shiny green eyes — Hanna is called to run her a bath, where she reclines for an hour or so, stepping out just in time to hear the boy's lessons. Sometimes, when Herr Ludwig comes home a bit early, he joins the little gathering, invariably lavish in his praise for the merest flickering of brightness demonstrated by his son. Sometimes, when the boy falters, Hanna cannot restrain herself from eagerly prompting him — the dates of the Seven Years War, the capital of Peru, the river that forms the northern border of the new German colony of South-West

Africa – and this attracts Herr Ludwig's interest. One late afternoon, the revision done, when mother and son retire to Peter's bedroom to pack away his books and have their customary cuddle, he turns to Hanna and looks at her so intently that she begins to fidget and drops the coffee cup she is about to place on the tray.

'You are a bright girl, Hanna,' he says as she squats to pick up the pieces. 'Why didn't you finish school?'

She puts the shards on the tray, causing a teaspoon to fall.

'I had to go into service, Herr Ludwig,' she says, feeling her cheeks burn as she kneels down again.

'You must try to keep it up.'

How? she wonders with a brief rush of anger. But she just nods and mumbles, and gets up. In the process she nearly knocks the tray off the sideboard, but fortunately manages to salvage it at the last moment.

'Why don't you come to my study tonight when your work is done?' he says. 'There's something I'd like to show you.'

Please, she thinks, not again.

'Hanna?'

'Herr Ludwig?' she croaks, not daring to look at him.

'I asked you a question.'

'I – I can't, Herr Ludwig. Please. If you don't mind.'

This time she drops the tray.

When she has finished collecting all the pieces and cleaning up, he says quietly, 'I'll be waiting for you.'

After supper, having taken twice as long as usual over the dishes, she sits down at the kitchen table and stares at her hands, red from the hot water. In her mind she repeats all the questions and answers she can remember from the afternoon's lessons. Then she looks up at the clock on the wall. It is almost nine. Now, surely, he will have gone to bed.

Dragging her feet, she goes to the study. There is a sliver of light under the door. Perhaps he has left the lamp burning.

But he is still working, comfortably seated in a large armchair, a clutch of papers on his lap.

He looks up and smiles indulgently. 'It took you a long time,' he says.

'I'm sorry, I . . .' Her voice trails off.

'I must have a word with Liesel,' he says. 'We cannot burden you with too much.'

'No, no, please, it's all right, really.'

Without any warning he asks, 'How did you know about the Kunene River?'

She stares at him blankly.

'The northern border of the colony of South-West Africa,' he prompts her.

'I try to listen when Peter does his lessons,' she mumbles, dreading that she will give anything away that might reflect on Frau Liesel. She adds precipitately, 'I like the names of faraway places, Herr Ludwig.'

'My company's ships go to harbours all over the world. China, Africa, America, everywhere.' He takes off his reading glasses and looks at her. 'Perhaps, if you continue with your studies, you can come and work for me one day and travel to some of those places.'

'Please don't mock me, Herr Ludwig!' she suddenly explodes. 'How can I continue with my studies?'

'To begin with, you can tell me if there are books I can get for you.'

'I have no money apart from what I earn here, and most of that goes to pay my debt.'

'We will have to see about that,' he says. Then he puts his papers on a low table beside the chair and gets up. 'But that is not why I asked you to come to the study.'

This is it, she thinks. He comes towards her. She edges away, trying to shrink out of reach. But he moves past her to a small table with immaculately inlaid squares in pale and dark wood. Two rows of intricately carved pieces, ivory and ebony, have been set up at either end.

'Do you know what this is?' Herr Ludwig asks.

'Some kind of game?' she guesses. At the church *Messe* the children were sometimes allowed to play draughts, but these pieces are different, more various and more exquisitely turned.

'It is a chess set,' he explains. 'If you wish, I can teach you to play.'

'What for?' she asks suspiciously.

He smiles. She looks at his face in the amber light of the lamp: its finely chiselled features as if it, too, has been carved from wood – keen eyebrows, high cheekbones, a firmly set chin, a nose like the beak of the eagle preferred by Chancellor von Bismarck who recently resigned in sullen deference to the new young emperor, Wilhelm II. His hair is wavy, combed up high in front, then stroked severely back.

'Just to see how good you are,' he says. 'I've tried to play with Frau Liesel, but she gets bored too easily. And Peter, I'm afraid, has shown no aptitude yet.'

'And if I don't play well I get punished.' It is a statement, not a question.

'If you don't play well, you lose. That is all. And then you try again, until you get better.' He gives an almost boyish smile. 'We can make a deal: every time you beat me, you can ask for any book you wish to have.'

'And I don't pay for it? Not even afterwards?'

'Of course not. You earn it by winning.'

'And what will you ask of me if you win?'

'I want no more than the pleasure of playing. My evenings are very boring.'

'Is your wife not waiting for you?'

He hesitates for a moment. 'She reads, and then she goes to sleep,' he says with just the slightest tightening of his jaws.

'What can be the pleasure of playing with someone like me?' she insists.

'There is no one else. Liesel doesn't like my friends to come over.'

'You can go out.'

'I cannot leave her here alone.' Almost apologetically he adds, 'You see, after the children we lost . . . and with Peter so sickly . . .'

'Now I understand.' There is a slow, bitter twitching of her mouth. 'You want someone you can beat. You will only teach me because you know I can never beat you.'

'Why don't you give it a try? If at any time – tomorrow, a week from now, a month, no matter when – you decide you don't like the game, we can stop.'

There is a prolonged silence. Even the light seems to defer to it. Then Hanna says, 'Show me.'

It is midnight before he insists that she go to bed.

During the next day she finds time – makes time – between bouts of other work, even when she is supposed to be with Peter, to slip into the study and rehearse the moves of the pieces on the chessboard. 'Think of it as a military campaign,' Herr Ludwig has told her. 'Think of it as a battle plan. If your enemy makes certain moves, there are others you can make to counter him: stop him, waylay him, forestall him, lure him in a different direction, pounce on him from behind. And for every move you make, you can be sure he will think up something else in turn; so keep him guessing, don't let him see what you really have in mind before it is too late. Always try to stay one step ahead, try to read what is happening inside his head.'

Her first thoughts, last night, were, *I shall never learn this, I'm just not clever enough.* But all through the night new thoughts, possibilities, manoeuvres, strategies, moves, shifts have been careering through her mind. Now she is exhausted, but she cannot rest before she has tried them out. When Peter complains she tries to draw him into her game, but he soon loses interest and she has no choice but to give it up too.

That evening, after the dishes have been done, she cannot wait to go to the study. To her chagrin she turns out to be so tired that she plays worse than the night before, and Herr Ludwig insists that she retire early. Those are frustrating weeks. Hanna is not very good; but she will not give up, and she has endless patience. One evening there is an unexpected crisis, when Herr Ludwig, in an attempt to bolster her confidence, makes a silly move at a crucial point, loses his queen and finds his king mated.

But instead of seeing her jubilant as he expected, Hanna erupts in a rage that catches him completely by surprise. He never thought this compliant, placid girl could be so angry. She pushes her chair back and jumps up so furiously that it falls over; in a single sweep she rakes all the pieces from the board, scattering them across the floor.

'Why did you do that?' she shouts at him, her face red and

contorted. 'You have no right to humiliate me like that. Just because I'm a servant girl!'

'I'm sorry, Hanna,' he stammers, genuinely upset. 'I lost my concentration for a moment, I made the wrong move . . .'

'You did not!' she screams. 'You're not so stupid, you did it on purpose. You let me win. Because you despise me, because you think I can never win on my own. I won't play with you again, not ever!' And she runs to her room, sobbing.

In the night her rage makes way for shame. What on earth has possessed her? She never knew she had this in her. But at the end of it all there is only one simple and terrible fact to face: he is the master, he can do anything he wants, she has no right, no right at all, to question him, whatever he may wish to do. And to storm at him like that! Calling him du. It is the end. She will be sent away in disgrace again. And she deserves it. She has wrecked everything. Any chance of beating him, of winning books from him, of studying, of one day working for his company and travelling the world, everything, everything.

When she takes his breakfast in to him (Frau Liesel and little Peter are still in bed) she starts to apologise but breaks into tears and cannot go on. He gets up from the table, takes her by the shoulders and says gently, 'I am sorry, Hanna. I am very, very sorry. I never meant to hurt or insult you. Will you please forgive me?'

It makes her cry more hopelessly. But that evening, very quietly, and without talking about it again, they return to the small chess table against the wall.

And a month later, perhaps a bit more, the unimaginable happens. After an intense and drawn-out game spread over two long evenings, which Hanna tries to approach like the siege of Orléans, it dawns on her that she has him at her mercy. One move of a bishop and his king will be cornered. There is no way out. She has done it. Never in her life has she felt such a sense of power. That is when she sits back, the shadow of a smile on her lips, savouring it, only for a moment, before she leans forward again and moves her bishop out of the way, letting Herr Ludwig's smooth white ivory king off the hook. Which will make it possible for him to capture hers.

Herr Ludwig looks up in dismay. He studies her face as if it were a military map and cannot believe what he sees.

'What have you done?' he asks in a smothered voice. 'Hanna . . . ?'

'What do you mean?' she says, unperturbed. 'You win.' In the caress of the light her face looks timeless, much older than her tender years – how old is she? fifteen? sixteen? – but at the same time much younger, with all the intricate innocence of a child building castles on the sand.

After that they continue with their evening games; more often than not he wins, occasionally they play to a draw, but from time to time she beats him fairly, squarely, and wins a book. Especially when she imagines Jeanne hovering behind her to repeat her early triumphs – Jargeau, Beaugency, Patay – or to attempt new strategies which will convert previous defeats into victory, even below the walls of Paris and Compiègne.

Not that it has any hope of lasting. And afterwards, predictably, she will come to think of it as having been inevitable from the beginning: the very fact that happiness exists, means that it will end. As simple as that.

What happens can be directly blamed on the chess. Frau Liesel is not unaware of their games in the evenings, but this causes no more than a fleeting whiff of annoyance, certainly no serious suspicion; if anything, the discovery allows Frau Liesel more scope for her own diurnal fugues. It only turns problematic when Hanna begins to take more time off from her lessons with Peter in order to practise her chess strategies.

One afternoon while she is in the study working out a new move Peter, bored stiff with being alone, is tempted outside by some boys kicking a ball in the small park across the road. Hanna does not become aware of it until the front bell is rung and she finds Peter on the doorstep, writhing in agony and gasping for breath, his new-found friends having dissolved into the crisp wintry air.

By the time Frau Liesel returns from wherever she has spent her day the boy has been revived, thank God, but he is still shaking and deathly pale. Before the distraught mother has administered her own medicaments and concluded her hysterical inquisition of Hanna, the father arrives. Even much later, thinking back, the girl will remember it as a scene of total confusion, everybody speaking at the same time and the boy, finding himself the centre of attention, acting up in high melodrama. Inevitably, Hanna is designated the culprit for having abandoned her precious charge; but what Herr Ludwig demands to know is where his wife has been. There is a hailstorm of accusations and counter-accusations, but the more Hanna tries to cover for Frau Liesel the less the latter's absence can be explained. Only one outcome is possible, since it just wouldn't do for the mistress of the house to bear the brunt of all the accusations.

'I hate you, I hate you!' Frau Liesel shouts after them as Herr Ludwig and Hanna finally drive off in their cab, back to the Little Children of Jesus; but whether it is directed at her husband or the girl, or perhaps even at Peter or herself, is impossible to say for certain.

'I am so very sorry,' Herr Ludwig apologises along the way through the glistening cobbled streets. 'Please believe me, this is not what I wanted at all.'

Before they reach their destination in the Hutfilterstrasse he slips her some money, and he assures her that her box of books will be dispatched the following day. (Although these will be promptly confiscated by Frau Agathe.) A few days later a small chess set will also be deposited for her at the orphanage, but Hanna will refuse to accept it. All that matters, as far as she is concerned, is that she is, once again, back where she first came from.

27

THIS WILL HAPPEN so many times over the ensuing years that Hanna loses count. All she knows is that with every return and every new beginning there is a diminution of hope, like light draining from a winter's day.

There is only one advantage, if it can conceivably be called that, which is that in the process she is exposed to an amazing variety of skills – though it should be said that she remains as clumsy at all of them as ever she was. She brings the same anxiousness to please to each new placement, accompanied by the same inability to do anything quite right. She still breaks crockery and loses cutlery or shrinks or stains items in the wash, still forgets exactly what has to be done exactly when, still catches her fingers in drawers or cupboards or bumps against furniture or door jambs. But oh God, she tries so very hard.

Over the years Hanna will look after infants, poultry and even larger livestock; change the nappies of the very young or the incontinent old; milk cows and goats and once a sickly young mother; read to a woman with cataracts on her eyes, to somebody's illiterate uncle and any number of boisterous children; look after the irascible deaf man and his even more irascible daughter mentioned before (which involves the need for proficiency – at the cost of many a frenzied beating – in sign language); keep senile old women of both sexes occupied; prepare food and wash dishes, sheets, clothes of any description and feet of various sizes; make beds, butter and cheese; do hair and odd bits of carpentry; unblock drains, sewage pits and ears; cut down trees and the amorous attentions of sons, fathers, grandfathers, great-grandfathers, uncles or nephews in the household; kill chickens, lice, newborn kittens, rats and expectations; wax floors and moustaches; prepare poultices, plasters and concoctions to cure or calm headaches, inflammations, congested lungs, stomach cramps, gallstones, bladder infections, female complaints, male complaints, rheumatism, bunions or cancer.

Some of her placements are better – less appalling – than others. She may be allowed a full day off every week (the luxury of spending unhurried hours from dawn to dusk with Fräulein Braunschweig); she may be granted access to an employer's library; she may be given the same food as the rest of the family (though never sitting down at table with them); she may have light in her room, or a bed; she may be allowed to sleep until six in the morning, seven on Sundays; she may be fitted out in a new uniform for Christmas; she may be given permission to lie down when she is sick or has menstrual cramps; she may go to church of a Sunday morning to listen to the organ even if she pays scant attention to the preacher. Some placements, of course, are worse than whatever passes for the 'rule': there may be stiffer penalties for transgressions than even Frau Hildegard could dream up, or savage beatings administered by the master of the house (usually on Friday evenings when she has to line up with the children, and sometimes the wife, to review the week's infractions), or black bread infested with weevils, or rats running riot in her bedroom, or icy draughts cutting right through her in winter, or a criminal insufficiency of food or clothes.

Often there is some form of sexual harassment to contend with. In a few homes it does not progress beyond predictable gropings in passing. Others are more serious. Some nights, when the lord of the house slides into her narrow bed at hours when she least expects it, she has to make an escape – pleading sickness, or the curse, or an infectious disease; excusing herself to go to the outhouse and not coming back (on one occasion spending the whole night shivering outside after he has locked her out) . . . More often than not she is required to offer variations of her administrations to Herr Dieter; but she soon learns to absent herself: it is not she who performs these slightly silly obscenities, but someone else, while she migrates for the while to a different space where she may observe from a distance the man observing her. And she never agrees to go beyond the limits once imposed on Herr Dieter. On a few occasions her refusal provokes assault, but she perceives very soon that the masters cannot always let themselves go completely. Because at the other end there is always a wife to account to.

Even in the better positions she cannot always rely on payment, whether in money or in kind, for these unscheduled services. In fact, the first time she dares to request, in a very subdued manner, some kind of reward she gets her face severely and repeatedly smacked. But in the end there is a weird pliability in them: as if not she, but they, are in a position of supplication. A man remains a mystery to her – that someone so big, so strong, so imperious, so peremptory, can be at the mercy of such a very small squiggle of his anatomy. (Once the seed has been spilled, of course, his manner tends to change abruptly, as if there is now in him a need to avenge the humiliation he invited in the first place; and she rapidly learns when to make her getaway.) And so she can continue, like a squirrel or a crow, to hoard away her 'little gifts', in the hope, always in the hope against hope, that one day she will be able to buy herself out of her debts and be free to go where the wind or her wildest dreams take her.

28

THEN ALWAYS BACK to the Little Children of Jesus, in disgrace; humiliated, cast away, waiting for the punishment to come and the new confirmation of her utter worthlessness as she lies on the hard narrow bed temporarily assigned to her, or sits huddled in the branches of a tree laden with luminous fruit like dull red lights glowing in the dark, apples heavy as sin.

And always out again, after Frau Agathe has forged new references and testimonials in order to rid the orphanage of her. For better or for worse. No, after the Hartmanns it is always worse. Except once; and that will be the last of her placements, a good twelve years after the first. It is an old couple who come for her in a coughing, smoking, straight-backed car, black as a coffin, a Daimler-Benz. It is Hanna's first ride in a car and she is terrified, but under the collective envious gaze of the entire orphanage assembled in the Hutfilterstrasse, she tries to strike a regal pose and can barely refrain from waving her nail-bitten hand like a queen.

The Kreutzers live on a small farm some distance out of town, on the road to Hamburg. Herr Wolfgang, who insists on being called Opa, used to be a violinist with an orchestra in Bremen until his hands turned useless with arthritis; and Frau Renate – Oma – designed costumes for the opera. Now they are happy to spend their old age on the farm, driving into town for the occasional concert; when they learn about Fräulein Braunschweig, they even drive Hanna to her ageing teacher's apartment once a month, otherwise she would no longer be able to visit. They have several grown-up children but haven't seen them in years. The life they lead is very quiet. There are a few farmhands to take care of the animals and the fields, so Hanna has only the house to look after. The old people grow very fond of her; soon she is like a child of their own. Having generously taken charge of her debt to the Little Children of Jesus they will now pay her the full 50 marks she nowadays earns every month. And when they die, Opa says, she will inherit the farm.

Her main task is to read to Oma in the afternoons, as the old woman's eyes are very bad. Opa spends most of his time in his music room, reading old scores and chuckling from time to time, as he constantly finds secret jokes in them, particularly in Haydn and Mozart. For the rest he works on his 'instrument', which no one but Oma has ever been allowed to see as it is reputed to be something exceptional. He does like to talk to Hanna about it, mainly because she is such a good listener: she can sit for hours without moving, drinking in every word, never allowing her eyes or her attention to stray.

'It is the ultimate instrument,' he often tells her. 'The whole of the history of music has been a movement towards this. Not a piano, not a cello, not a violin, not a harp or a flute or a French horn, although each of these has its small share of the sublime. No, this is different. I think of it as the summum of music, the absolute, the ne plus ultra.' (Half of the words Hanna cannot understand; but she memorises them and will later look them up in Fräulein Braunschweig's dictionaries or encyclopaedias.) 'You know what happens when pure white light strikes a prism?'

'It becomes a rainbow,' says Hanna, faithfully recalling Fräulein Braunschweig's teachings.

'Just so.' He beams his satisfaction over the half-moons of his gold-rimmed reading spectacles. 'You're a clever girl. Now you can think of all the colours of the rainbow as different musical instruments. Do you see what I mean?'

She frowns and shakes her head. 'I'm not sure, Opa.'

'You wait.' He smiles. 'It will soon be finished. It has taken me years to think it through, but actually it is very, very simple. You shall see. You and Oma will be the first to hear it.' He raises a gnarled finger: 'And the beauty of it is of course that I shall be able to play it. Even with these old hands. *Anybody* will be able to play it.'

'I don't think so, Opa. I'll try, but I'm sure I'll be too clumsy. At the Little Children of Jesus they tried to teach us so many things, but I've never been good at anything. Running or the high jump or embroidering or making rag dolls for charity or playing the recorder. I'm just not good enough.'

'You will play my instrument like an angel,' Opa assures her. 'Just be patient.'

It takes two years of patience, but there is a special satisfaction in the waiting: the old man has so much confidence in her, he is so sure of the outcome, so truly delighted at the prospect, that Hanna gradually dares to believe that perhaps, who knows, this once . . . And while Opa is locked up in his soundless music room for afternoons on end, she hums or whistles out of tune while she cleans the house or washes the dishes or reads book after glorious book to Oma in the living room where they even have electricity.

When she isn't busy and the weather is good – not very often, but it happens – she goes up the stairs to the large balcony that juts out from the top floor. Sometimes she reads. Mostly she just lies on her back, staring up at the sky, watching the drifting clouds, the shapes they form, their endless changing, dissipating and reforming, their slow swirling, their near-motionless dreaming like white swans on water. She loses herself in their fantasies of ships and birds and dromedaries and waving palms and unicorns and magic castles on faraway beaches of Ireland and Africa. Shapes that come and go and are lost for ever and remain in the memory for ever. It is as if she herself becomes a cloud and drifts and sails and swims, it is like flying, it is bliss, the only true bliss she has ever known – except for that forever day with Susan on the beach.

Sometimes a fleeting, never-quite-catchable memory filters into her mind and she seems to remember lying just like this, in green grass, as a very small child, in a time before the Little Children of Jesus. And her three imaginary friends are with her. But the image is too vague, and too brief, to hold on to. Still there is reassurance in it, as her life before memory began is now strangely reconciled with the hereness of her lying on the balcony and the possible shapes of the future. Even God becomes slightly, if only slightly, more comprehensible –

not the dirty old man of wrath and vengeance who presides over the Little Children of Jesus, but someone altogether more smiling and musical, who resembles Opa in many ways.

Then at last, out of the blue, one day, Oma comes upstairs to the balcony to call her: 'Hanna, Opa has something to show you.'

She sits up quickly. 'Not the . . . ?'

'The instrument,' says the old woman, her fading eyes bright with light. 'It is finished.' She pauses and adds, 'I hope you won't be disappointed.'

'How can I be disappointed? We've all waited for so long.'

'Well,' says Oma soberly, 'it is perhaps not quite what one expected.'

'But it *is* special?' she asks breathlessly.

'Oh it is special enough. And if you think of it, exactly what he promised.'

She hurries down the stairs, misses the last step, falls, gets up again, dusts her torn dress and dashes to the music room where Opa sits at the window. Light falls through the small panes, making delicate brush strokes across his bald head and the shiny object he is holding on his lap. She stops and stares. For a moment she is disappointed. It looks so ordinary. Like a violin, somewhat rounder, the wood beautifully polished, and with a single string. It isn't taut at all, but hangs limply over the surface where the sound hole of an ordinary violin would be.

'Try it,' he says, handing her the instrument, and the bow to go with it.

'How does one hold it?' Hanna asks.

'Any way you like.'

She glances at him, holds the instrument some distance from her body, and lightly touches the single string with the bow.

'It makes no sound,' she whispers, embarrassed.

Opa laughs with deep contentment. 'That is it,' he says. 'Do you understand now? *That is it.*'

Two days later, without warning, Opa dies quietly in his sleep.

'I want you stay here with me,' Oma tells Hanna at the funeral.

But the couple's children, who have never put in an appearance in the two years Hanna has been there, arrive from all over Germany and insist that the farm be sold and their mother move in with them, one after the other. They annul the inheritance Opa has promised Hanna long ago.

Now she will have to fend for herself, or return to the Little Children of Jesus. But she is in too much shock to choose either. Instead, she takes a handful of Opa's pain pills, and dies.

29

FROM THE VERY beginning of her stay at Frauenstein Hanna becomes aware of the ghosts that haunt the place. At first they are visible only in mirrors in passing; and when she turns round there is nothing to be seen. But once she has become used to them, or they to her, the encounters are more direct, face to face. Sometimes she meets them singly, at night, when she cannot sleep for fear of dreaming about the train; otherwise in twos or threes. Sometimes there is a whole dark throng of them swarming up the broad stairs, with a whispering sound, and a movement of glacial air sweeping past. But for some reason they do not scare her. If anything, they stir up a feeling of great sadness. They look at her with their terrible and terrified eyes; and she understands as no one could who has only ever lived and who hasn't travelled through the landscapes of death as well, as she has. And looking into her own eyes in the mirror tonight, she recognises herself and realises why. With them, only with them, she shares the intimacies of life as well as death. She knows they are the women from the unmarked graves outside, the nameless ones, forgotten by everyone, relegated to obscurity as if they had never existed. Which is why they cannot come to rest but have to go on wandering, to be accosted, and in some obscure way acknowledged. *Someone* must know. She feels so close to them. Not only because she herself has died so many times, but because she will be forgotten like them, and take to wandering too, until perhaps someone, someone, somewhere, will one day be reminded of her story and speak her name in the silence, Hanna X.

30

No, THE PILLS do not kill her. She vomits copiously and is ill for three days, and then recovers and knows she has to leave the Kreutzers' farm. But this time she will under no circumstances return to the Little Children of Jesus. She is no longer a child, she has a life of her own. Behind the backs of the spiteful Kreutzer children Oma manages surreptitiously to slip her some money and an eloquent letter of reference, and arranges for a neighbour to take her to Bremen, with a suitcase of clothes and a box of books; and oh, her magic shell. For a few weeks she stays in Fräulein Braunschweig's small apartment where she sleeps on the couch until they can devise a way out.

It is the teacher who first brings news of the drive to recruit women – as domestic workers, possibly as consorts – for the German colony of South-West Africa. And in no time the decision is made. Is this not what she has been dreaming about all her life? Moreover, the news seems to revive some of the teacher's own deep memories – of the time she was engaged, and how she and her Otto used to talk about their travels around the world, and how enthusiastic he was about going to East Africa or South-West Africa with her. If Hanna goes it will be, in a way, a rounding off of some of her own dreams. Fräulein Braunschweig accompanies her on the train to Hamburg. With some of the money Oma has given her, they buy her a new outfit; and this gives Hanna new confidence, even after the train journey and two days in a ratty little boarding house in Hamburg. The interview with Frau Charlotte Sprandel of the Kolonialgesellschaft, who has travelled all the way from Berlin, is constantly postponed because of the stampede of women – some as young as fourteen or fifteen, others as old as fifty or sixty – clamouring for the opportunity of being chosen.

'There are too many,' Hanna says several times. 'They will never take me.'

'You are exactly what they are looking for, Hanna.'

'I am too severely plain, Fräulein.' The phrase has been branded into her mind where it hurts most and lingers longest. She tells Fräulein Braunschweig about the conversation between Frau Hildegard and her friend.

'They were jealous of you, that's all.'

She cannot suppress a bitter laugh. 'What on earth do I have that anyone could be jealous of?'

'You have a good mind, child. And you're a willing worker. You have genuine enthusiasm. Not many people have that.' She smiles, and suddenly looks years younger: 'And you do have beautiful hair.'

The interview, when at last it is Hanna's turn, takes place in a high bare room in a yellow office building near the harbour. Frau Sprandel, splendid in black and fur (for the day is cold and drizzly), sits behind a long table, flanked by several other people, all of them men, most of them elderly and officious. Nobody shows any interest in the new applicant; they must have interviewed so many already.

'Come, come, Fräulein,' says the furred lady with visible irritation as Hanna tarries on the doorstep, 'we don't have all day.' She reads Hanna's name from a document in front of her. 'This is your name?'

'Yes, Frau Sprandel.'

'You are aware of the kind of person we are looking for?'

'I have read the notices, Frau Sprandel.'

'All the applicants – and there are many of them – are evaluated on the basis of their merit and health.' She places great emphasis on the impressive-sounding words *Würdigkeit und Gesundheit*. 'What makes you think you qualify?'

'I don't think I qualify at all, Frau Sprandel.' There is a sudden rustle among the papers in front of the dignitaries at the table. Now they are all paying attention. Hanna presses on resolutely: 'I'm a clumsy person and I always break plates and things and often I don't finish my work on time. But I've never been scared of work and I try very hard and I have always had good health.'

'Hm.' Somewhat to Hanna's surprise she detects a hint of approval in the lady's attitude. Frau Sprandel returns to her documents. 'I have looked at your references. I notice that you were brought up in an orphanage. the Little Children of Jesus. A good Christian institution, I believe.'

Hanna feels her jaws contract. But as evenly as possible she says, 'That is what Frau Agathe and Pastor Ulrich used to say.'

'You don't agree with them?'

'No, I don't,' Hanna says quietly. 'But there is really no need for you to take my word. Few people do.'

Frau Sprandel changes her angle of approach: 'Would you say the orphanage was the kind of place you would rather not have been?'

'I often ran away when I was small,' Hanna replies with complete candour.

'Would you do it again now, if you could?'

'No.'

'Why not?'

'Because it doesn't work.'

'Yet you are interested in going to South-West Africa. Is that not running away?'

'It is not Germany I want to get away from, Frau Sprandel. It is Africa I want to go to.'

This prompts much whispering all the way down the long jury table, while Frau Sprandel sits studying Hanna with narrowed eyes. It takes quite a while before she returns to her notes. 'Would you describe yourself as a city girl?'

'No, Frau Sprandel. Bremen is not a big city. And for the last few years I have been working on a farm.'

'Hm.' She nods and looks sideways a her co-adjudicators. 'The one requirement we are very strict about is that our recruits must be *vom Lande und nicht von der Stadt*.' A murmur of approval ripples along the table. 'You must realise that Africa is not Germany. It is a wild place.'

'I have always wanted to go to wild places, Frau Sprandel.'

'It is not for the romantically inclined,' the woman says curtly. 'German South-West Africa is a country larger than the whole of Germany. It has half a million of inhabitants of which fewer than five thousand are colonists.' She pauses to let the information sink in. 'In addition there is a garrison of some eight thousand troops. But the vast majority are natives. Raw, uncivilised, savage tribes from which one can expect neither help nor mercy, only open hostility.'

Hanna nods, feeling her throat constrict.

'The only more or less civilised place is the capital town of Windhoek on the central plateau, and even that has fewer than one thousand inhabitants.'

Hanna, who has been trying to listen demurely, can no longer contain her enthusiasm. 'I have read,' she says, 'that there are three roads running from Windhoek. There is a rough road past places called Okahandja and Otjimbingwa to the coast, another south to Rehoboth and Mariental to Karasburg, and a third north to Omaruru, Otjiwarongo, Outjo and Tsumeb in Hereroland.' She stops to catch her breath. 'Have you ever heard such beautiful names, Frau Sprandwel?'

A small titter of giggles and coughs from behind the table.

'I'm afraid it's only the names that, to some people, may sound beautiful,' the regal lady says in reprimanding tone of voice, but it does not sound altogether humourless. 'My understanding is that it is mostly inhospitable desert.'

'I love the sun, Frau Sprandel.'

'I must warn you that it is a climate of extremes, Fräulein. It will not be an easy life.' Another calculating pause. 'Furthermore, it is dangerous. Six years ago there was a war between our people and the war-mongering Hereros in the north of the territory. Many of our colonists were murdered.' A brief clearing of her throat. 'Fortunately quite a few thousand of the Hereros were also exterminated, and soon after that a widespread cattle disease dislodged most of them from the land and forced them into constructive employment on the farms.' Her eyes appear to look right through Hanna. 'But from dispatches out there we learn that hostilities are once again building up. In due course there may well be another war. For the moment Germany entertains good relations with some of the wiser leaders, who realise that without us they are doomed. But there are some savages among them' – she briefly consults her notes and shakes her head – 'with names no Christian person can hope to pronounce, and who will not learn. Should they ever succeed in fomenting a general uprising among all the tribes of the land, our garrison will be stretched to the limit. So it is only fair I should give you due warning.' This time the pause seems almost interminable. 'Are you still serious about going to such a place?'

'Oh yes, I am, Frau Sprandel. I've read everything about it I could lay my hands on.'

'The work will be extremely exacting.'

'I shall do any honest work expected of me.'

'Are you by any chance engaged to be married?'

Hanna shakes her head.

'You realise some of the men offering work to immigrant women may also have an interest in . . . finding a companion, a spouse.'

Hanna swallows but keeps her face straight. 'If it is a good man I will not have any objection, Frau Sprandel.'

'And what, in your eyes, is a good man?'

'Someone, I hope, who will have some respect for me.'

Another ripple along the table, but there is little mirth in it.

'That is a good Christian sentiment,' comments Frau Sprandel, fingering the collar of her fur coat. 'But one cannot expect too much refinement or delicacy in a colony of that nature, you appreciate that?'

Hanna breathes in deeply. 'Some of my employers over the years have not been very delicate either, Frau Sprandel. I think I can handle that.'

There follows a long whispered consultation along the table. Then Frau Sprandel turns back to Hanna. 'Now that you have heard our questions, is there anything you would like to ask of *us*?'

Hanna pauses. Then she asks very calmly and seriously, 'Please, Frau Sprandel, will there be palm trees in South-West Africa?'

This time the laughter is more generous.

'I have told you that it is a desert land, Fräulein,' replies the regal lady in the middle of the table. 'I think we can safely assume that there will be the odd oasis with palm trees.'

'In that case I shall go,' says Hanna.

'We haven't offered you a place yet,' Frau Sprandel pointedly reminds her.

Hanna blushes scarlet. Now she has ruined everything. 'I'm sorry, Frau Sprandel, I didn't mean . . . It's just . . . When I listened to the sea in my shell – I got it from a little girl on the Weserstrand – and it wasn't just the sea, but palm trees too – and from that day I *knew* that if there was such a place I must go to it. So please take me, I'll do anything you want.'

'Can you make any contribution to your passage?' the woman asks.

'A contribution . . . ?'

'In cash.'

'No. No, I'm sorry. I didn't realise . . .'

'Third class,' says Frau Sprandel and turns first left, then right, to her colleagues. 'Agreed?'

'Agreed.'

'You may go,' announces Frau Sprandel. And as Hanna stumbles out in a daze, forgetting even to thank them, the furred lady adds a flippant rider: 'As long as you don't expect too much of your palm trees.'

31

THERE ARE VERY few palm trees, all of them tattered and frayed by
the wind, when the women disembark at Swakopmund from the sloop
which has brought them from the *Hans Woermann*, at anchor in the deep
sea. Hanna is hardly capable of observation, drenched to the bone by the
angry waves through which the small sloop has had to plough. Several of
the passengers' boxes and bundles have disappeared into the inky sea.
Hanna is too numb to care. It is a cold grey day, as if they have never
left Germany. There must be some mistake. But she refuses to give up
hope; this is only the point of arrival, it doesn't count, the oasis will be
inland, she must be patient.

After the long weeks at sea the land under her feet appears to heave
and sway. She has to catch hold of a railing to steady herself. Closing her
eyes against the fog she can see the palm trees of her Children's Bible
again, and the real ones of her dreams. From her pocket she extracts the
shell that has come all the way with her, from midwinter to this angry
midsummer. She presses it against her ear and smiles, because the sea
is still there, the sibilant sea.

She wanders away from the others, but is called back. They are
shuttled into groups of ten and taken to a large building in ornate
colonial style, where they are ushered, one by one, into a series of
offices. This is where they will meet their future employers, their
prospective husbands. For this, she knows, they all know, is what they
have come for. And she is resigned to it.

At first sight, as she comes into the small office that smells of
dust and tobacco and stale sweat, the prospect is not inspiring. The
man sits with his back to her. A middle-aged peasant, is her first

impression. His whole body, his ill-fitting jacket, the back of his narrow head, everything defines him as a loser — a mean-spirited, vicious, hard-drinking, abusive loser.

He gets up to face her. She goes past him to the empty chair opposite, and sits down. He clears his throat and turns his dirty hat in his hands, then he sits down again. The official behind the large desk reads out the man's name, but she isn't paying attention and only absently picks up something sounding like Grossvogel.

And then he reads, 'Lotte Mehring.'

'I am not Lotte Mehring,' she says, flaring up.

'That is what it says here.'

'Then it is a mistake.'

'What is your name?'

'Hanna.' She will add the surname now lost to us.

The official looks flustered. 'But here it says Lotte Mehring.'

'Then you must please change it.'

'I'm not allowed to. I can only go by the register.'

Unexpectedly, the matter is taken out of his hands. The man sitting opposite her grins in her direction. 'Hanna,' he says, leaning forward in a show of familiarity. 'Now that's a good name for a woman. Hanna.' He grins again. Several of his teeth are missing, the rest are tobacco-stained. He has a bristly moustache. His face is a dark reddish brown; but there is a white rim around his narrow forehead where the hat has kept out the sun. He puts one large paw on her thigh. He smells of beer and chicken shit. 'Well, Hanna. You are to be my wife then,' he announces.

The official tries to say something, but he has become quite irrelevant to them.

At first she feels like bolting, blindly, no matter where, the way she felt that day during her illness when Pastor Ulrich put his hand under the bedcovers. She cannot explain it to herself: only minutes ago she was prepared to resign herself to almost anything. Then why this onrush of panic? Perhaps it is brought on by Lotte's name, by remembering everything that might have happened, should have happened, and now is slipping for ever out of reach. She can barely contain the rage and resentment that seethe in her against this moment which will decide the rest of her life. In the debilitating knowledge that he is the very last she wants, but the only one she may ever be allowed to lay claim to.

But she knows she cannot resist them openly; she must stay calm whatever the cost. She dare not antagonise them too much. Not right now. She takes a deep breath and says, 'I am sorry. But I cannot be your wife.'

He stares in disbelief, his eyes bulging slightly. The yellow whites are streaked with red. 'What do you mean?' he asks. 'Why not?'

'Because you're ugly and old,' she says.

'Now,' says the official behind the desk. 'Fräulein Lotte, or Hanna, or whatever your name may be, you should be grateful that there is someone who wants you.' But her stare appears to unnerve him. He looks at the middle-aged suitor. 'You are of course free to change your mind, Herr Grossvogel.'

The man rises and possessively places his hand on her hard shoulder. 'I think *she* will change her mind,' he says. 'All it takes is a little firmness. There are ways and means.' Again his ingratiating grin. 'And four days on the train can make quite a difference. You did say four days, didn't you, Meinherr?"

'Four days,' the official confirms. He gets up behind the desk, now visibly in a hurry to put the formalities behind him before they are bedevilled by further complications. 'Well, my best wishes to you both.'

But a few hours later, as the train pulls out of the station under a sky bleeding like a slaughtered carcass, there is an early hitch. The man to whom she has been assigned pulls Hanna into their compartment and slides the door shut. Unceremoniously he begins to unbutton his corduroy trousers. On the bunk opposite another couple is already fucking.

Hanna remains standing with her back pressed against the door. 'Do you have palm trees?' she asks in a strained voice.

He gawks at her. 'What the hell's the matter with you? Where do the palm trees come in?'

'Do you have palm trees where you live?' she repeats.

'Woman,' he says, 'don't waste my time. Take off your bloody clothes.'

'I shall let you do this thing to me,' she says, 'but only if you can give me palm trees in the sun. Otherwise no.'

That is when he slaps her in the face.

And Hanna slaps him back.

This he has not expected. With his hand to his stinging cheek he retreats out of her way.

The naked man on the bunk opposite pushes himself up on his arms. 'Will you two shut up and get on with it?' he asks before he plunges down on his woman again.

'But did you hear that?' whines Herr Grossvogel. 'She doesn't want to let me.' In a sudden new surge of fury he lurches towards Hanna.

It is a very confused scene that follows. Hanna is fighting with everything she can muster, scratching and biting and kicking, butting him with her head, all of this in silence, except for the violent rasping of her breath. When she fiercely raises a knee into his groin he folds double, begins to retch. She turns round to escape. But then the man opposite joins the fray. Grabbing Hanna from behind he hurls her to the floor. And suddenly the other woman also jumps up and jerks at Hanna's long hair. Between the three of them they manage to force Hanna down. It is in fact the woman who tears off her clothes and grabs hold of her feet while Herr Grossvogel kicks off his trousers to take the plunge. As soon as he has her pinned down on the soiled floor the two naked lovers resume their own coupling.

But Hanna is not giving up. Once the other couple are again engrossed in their own actions and while the man on top of her is still fumbling to find his way, she manages to gain a grip on him where it hurts, and rolls from under him. Clutching her torn clothes to her breast she pulls the door open.

'Fuck off!' her would-be husband shouts after her. 'I don't want you anyway.'

She runs down the narrow corridor to the next coach. There she steps back into what is left of her clothes and remains standing at a window, her forehead pressed against the cool hard pane, seeing nothing of the darkening bare landscape streaming past.

How she aches to be back on the sea.

32

At MIDNIGHT, AS you cross the equator, the sea sighs and turns in its sleep; and then there is a stillness unmatched by any other silence you have ever known. It would not surprise you if, as in ancient legends, you suddenly found yourself going right over the edge of the world into a void too vast to understand; and what lies at the other side of it is entirely unknown, unknowable. The sea is a magical darkness, shot through with lines and flashes of phosphor. And there are flying fish. Nothing is improbable any more.

33

IN THE NARROW train corridor, as the night wears on, Hanna is joined by two or three other women, later by more; after some time there are ten or twelve of them standing close together, not talking, but seeking comfort in the closeness of other female bodies. At least they are out of it, she thinks. They have survived.

But it is still only the beginning. And the evening and the morning are the first day.

In the deep of the night, while the train is stationary at some unnamed siding and the sheer weight of a yellow bulbous moon seems to drag it down to the horizon, men make their appearance from elsewhere on the long train and converge on the string of women. Some are asked, even obsequiously; others are simply dragged off by the arms. It is the second round. What Hanna will remember, afterwards, is how one man after the other approaches her from behind, saying things like, 'Hello, beautiful' or combing fingers through her hair; and how they withdraw in disappointment or disdain when she turns round and they see her face. How many times in the past has it happened to her? Yet this must be the first time their derision comes as a relief, a bitter pleasure. But it does not last. The men are too drunk, and too desperate. Hanna will be unable to recall details later; she will not want to. And by the time the disgruntled lovers grow too unsteady on their feet, too inebriated, too frustrated to persevere in their hunt and are replaced by soldiers who initially kept to their own coach at the front, the macabre version of musical chairs becomes increasingly hectic, with ominous undertones no one can mistake any longer for pleasure or play.

It must be on the second day, or perhaps the third, that Hanna — the worse for wear and weariness, yet still in a manner of speaking unscathed — is forced into a compartment by what, from his braids and insignia, must be a particularly high-ranking officer. There are two others looking on, too drunk to join in but not too drunk to contribute crude interjections of encouragement or jest. When she tries once again, only more tired and dejected than before, to evade what seems at last to be inevitable — by turns arguing, pleading, shouting abuse, appealing to his sense of honour as a military man representing the Kaiser — he merely laughs.

'Why pretend to be what you're not?' he asks. 'You're a whore. That's why you're here.'

'I am not a whore,' she says in quiet rage. 'I came here to find work. I have never slept with a man.'

'You've never slept with a man?'

She raises her head, stares him defiantly in the eyes. 'No, I haven't. And I will not do it now.'

For a long time he studies her with the keenness of a botanist looking at a new species of plant, or perhaps a boy inspecting a beetle he has shorn of legs. 'Do you know who I am?' he asks at last.

'It makes no difference.'

'I am a captain in the imperial army.'

Hanna shrugs.

'I am Hauptmann Heinrich Böhlke.'

'It is a name,' she says.

'You can count it an honour that I have selected you. You do not look like a woman who has much choice.'

'My body is my own,' she says.

'Not on this train. You are here at our pleasure. More precisely, at *mine*.'

'I would have expected you to show some respect.'

'I am a man, you are a woman. That's all. And I think we have wasted enough time.'

She shakes her head. But she cannot control the trembling of her body.

'After this,' he says, 'you can return to whatever way of life you choose.' A brief but humourless smile. 'In fact, after this you will not want another man.'

She does not know – and afterwards will not understand – where she finds the temerity to say, 'That is not for you to decide.'

'Look, Lotte,' he says. There is now a low, more dangerous edge to his voice. 'That is your name, isn't it?'

'No, it isn't.'

'Then what is it?'

She shrugs.

He narrows his eyes. 'It makes no difference,' he says. 'There is only one thing you have to understand. Are you listening to me?'

She shakes her head.

There is a very small, very unpleasant grin on his face. 'When I fuck a woman,' says Hauptmann Böhlke of the imperial army in a voice as still and keen as a blade of very fine steel, 'she stays fucked.'

And then he fucks her.

34

It is still not the end. It is actually a long way from the end. She will refuse to remember what happens, but it will come back to her regardless. At some stage she is alone in the corridor again, her whole body aching, a feeling of blood and singeing fire between her legs. At another stage there are, as before, women with her. Some of them cannot stand and are crawling on hands and knees. And then the men return. Different ones, or the same ones. No one seems to care any more. Hanna doesn't.

But this, whether she wants to or not, this she will remember. That Hauptmann Böhlke comes back to find her. It is night. Some time in the night, one of the nights. Has he not had enough? Or is he furious that when he first took her, when she realised there was nothing more to be done about it, she neither resisted nor showed any sign of life at all? He might have had his way with a corpse. And now, who knows, his pride may be at stake. Otherwise the woman may not stay fucked.

Of this time she will remember that she is stripped naked. (There are not many tatters of clothing remaining anyway.) And that she is forced on her knees in front of him. And that something is pushed against her mouth. It is very hard, yet it has the softness of human flesh. And that he is shouting at her in a kind of frenzy, 'I'll make you remember this! Take it! Slut! Whore!'

She thinks of what so many others have tried to make her do; but they never succeeded. Only this time she cannot avoid it. She gags, but he will not let her go. His hands are clamped to her head, on either side, his fingers entangled in her long hair. She hates her hair. He goes on shouting obscenities.

And she will remember — but this will never be a clear, precise memory — that after a long time, when she cannot resist any longer, she breaks down and accepts in her mouth what is thrust into it. And that, then, blindly, when there is no other way out, she bites. And that she doesn't stop, not even when the blood comes streaming from her mouth, more blood than she would ever have believed possible, a red fountain pulsing into her mouth, choking her, gushing all over the place and the braying men. Screaming, his body collapses over her.

Whether the end comes soon after, or only much later, she does not know. All she knows, and this quite clearly, is that it is now indeed the end because it can go no further.

She is thrust into a compartment. It is crowded with men in khaki uniforms. In a far corner huddles the captain. He is wrapped in a blanket and looks very pale, but it seems he insists on being there.

'Now I'll show you what I meant,' he says through clenched teeth, but whether in rage or pain is hard to tell.

She wants to clutch her shell in the palm of her hand but there is only emptiness.

They are all around her. They are taking off their belts with the heavy pointed metal studs. Some of them have army knives. One of them produces a piece of wood which he wedges between her teeth.

That is how Hanna X dies, this time.

35

I MUST RETURN to the scene in front of the mirror, where the life of Hanna X first assumed, for me, the shape of a story to be patched together, piece by piece, from the threadbare facts of history. Here, in front of this mirror, it is time for her at last to look. Nothing can be avoided any longer. Her face. Her body. The whole of her physical truth, everything that has been inscribed on her to tell her where she has been, who she is. Obscurely in the background, barely visible in the light of the candle on the blemished surface of the mirror, looms the host of dull grey ghosts – not threatening, but as it were in solidarity, to show that they are here too.

Holding up the long candle close to her, she gazes at the image of herself she has eschewed for so long. With her free hand she lightly touches the surface of her face and of her body. Almost the touch of a lover – if she closes her eyes she may imagine Lotte's fingers, Lotte's lips; but this is not a time for closing the eyes. It is a time to see, to see, in order never to forget again.

This is what has been done to her. Not because of anything she has done, but purely because she is a woman. And because they *could*.

This is who she is now. Almost in wonder she moves her fingers along her skin. How curious, this urge they have, all of them, to leave their mark on a woman's body. As if despair lies behind it, and fear, a deep but very ordinary fear, a fear perhaps of death, their own. In each the need, the terrifying urge, to scar and leave his mark. And only her body available for their inscription. Ever since Pastor Ulrich first took her lips between his fingers to hurt them, to try and make her wince and cry (which she didn't). Until that last man on the train, Hauptmann Heinrich Böhlke.

She touches with a single fingertip the scars where her nipples used to be. Her belly, her protruding navel (for she is not Catholic). Then slightly parts her legs and leans forward, reluctant to look; but for once she knows it cannot be disowned or avoided. The site of the ultimate humiliation. The secret tenderness, the small extremity of pure and infernal joy, once offered to Lotte and assumed by her, now gaping and absent. *When I fuck a woman she stays fucked.*

Wax drips on her naked belly. The pain is almost pleasurable. *I am still alive*, she thinks. It comes like relief, like rain to this parched land. *I can still feel pain; I can still feel. It is not all gone. I have returned from the dead.*

She is ready to take her leave. This is not another escape. She will not be running away from something again, but *towards* something. What has happened in this place today, what they tried to do to little Katja, has awakened her from her sleep of death. Because it was to her that it was done. Like all the humiliations of her life, inflicted by all those involved in her slow dismemberment. Now she must begin to re-member herself. There is something in her which has never been there before and which gives shape to all that has happened to her, and inside her. It is hate. Tongueless, she tastes the word in her mouth. Hate. It has the bitterness of a medicine that restores life.

On the face of it, she has always borne whatever they chose to visit on her, but she has never yielded, she has always withheld consent. However meek she may have seemed, this deep stern resistance has always been there. When they went too far, sometimes the only way to express her protest was to run away; at other times it made her stand up to Frau Agathe and Pastor Ulrich and Frau Hildegard, or draw the line with Herr Dieter and his successors; always, deep down, she has lived a restrained and muted No to them and their world. Now she will no longer do it quietly. She has at last acknowledged hate. It gives a purpose to all the turmoil inside her. It has made her kill the man who tried to rape Katja. The knowledge brings with it a strange, almost exhilarating, freedom. They no longer have any power over her. Because now it is up to her to decide what she will do with her hate.

Breathing very calmly, holding the tall candle in her steady hands, she returns to her room. She puts on a long dress and her sturdy boots, then packs a few necessities on a sheet from her bed. On top of the clothing she puts the dead man's Mauser and its bandolier of cartridges, and the Luger pistol she removed from his belt before she dragged his body to the fountain, thud thud thud. Then she goes down to the kitchen to find a good strong knife and a few indispensable utensils. The journey may be long. Once she is satisfied that nothing important has been left behind, she returns to her room, ties the sheet into a bundle which she slings over her shoulder.

She blows out the candle. On the dark landing she stops in front of the mirror for a last look. She gazes past her own image to the rustling throng of grey shadows behind her. The sisterhood of silence. There is almost a smile on her disfigured face. She will not be fucked for life.

As she turns to descend into the deep stairwell that reaches down, in the faint light, towards the darkness below, a voice says behind her, 'Where are you going?'

Two

36

EVEN IN WELL-documented accounts of the men who dominated
the turn of the twentieth century in South-West Africa – the early
governors who took charge after nearly a century of pioneering by
missionaries and traders and miners: Curt von François (1891–1894),
Theodor Leutwein (1894–1904), the infamous Lothar von Trotha
(November 1904/November 1905), his less bloody-minded successor
Friedrich von Lindequist (1905–1907) – the individuals tend to remain
shadowy figures in the background of their own story, obscured by
historical facts. This is also true of indigenous leaders like Samuel
Maharero or the redoubtable Hendrik Witbooi (whose extensive
diary, for all its vividness, relies more on the consideration of external
facts than on the internal motions and impulses and calculations that
made him the man he was). Which means that in all these cases
documented history still has to be reconstructed, reimagined for
a grasp of the identities caught up in it. How much more so the
life of someone like Hanna X. And yet she was *there*, that much I
know. And having reached this turning point in her story I have no
choice but to continue. I believe more and more that as a man I owe
it to her at least to *try* to understand what makes her a person, an
individual, what defines her as a woman.

Like Hanna herself I must go on. And the first image I have of
her after she left Frauenstein is of her moving through the desert
landscape, one of two very small figures in a vast expanse, under a sky
speckled with distant vultures. It is the first sign of life she sees in two
weeks, as they spiral very slowly, effortlessly, wide wings motionless,
gliding on their high thermals. They are in no hurry to come down;

whatever they have noticed below cannot yet be dead. But there must be *something*, otherwise they would have moved on already.

Hanna motions in their direction with a brief movement of her head. The girl nods.

She is still not sure she should have brought the girl with her. But what else could she have done? When she heard that voice softly calling her name in the dark as she prepared to leave Frauenstein she froze in her tracks, one foot already poised on the top step. Katja. She'd counted on the girl being still trapped in her death-like sleep. Now something would have to be done, and quickly. It cannot be long to daybreak. Leaving her bundle at the top of the stairs she hurries back and takes the girl by the arm, motioning urgently that she must return to her room. But Katja stands her ground.

'Where are you going?' she asks again.

Hanna gestures impatiently: outside, away, *now*.

'You're not going without me. You can't leave me here.'

You don't understand, Hanna tries to convey to her in the sign language they've begun to devise. *I cannot stay in this place.*

'After what has happened . . .' says Katja, her voice choking. 'Please. I need you. I won't let you go.'

Without a tongue, how can she possibly persuade Katja to stay? And time is running out. Also, even if she has no wish to admit it, she has become, in a way, responsible for the girl. Ever since Katja began to cling to her, following the death of her sister in the desert; and much more so, now, after the events of the night. For a long time Hanna cannot make up her mind. What finally resolves the question is the strange feeling she has, looking at the terrified young girl, that she is again looking in a mirror and seeing, this time, a younger version of herself. Katja is prettier than she has ever been, yes; but there is the hair, the long blonde hair cascading over her shoulders, the hair that used to cause people seeing her from behind to assume that she was beautiful; the hair that once captivated Pastor Ulrich, the hair that men urged her to wind around their privates as she caressed them with closed eyes; the hair she cut off soon after she'd come to Frauenstein, to help rid her of the nightmare on the train. And here is Katja now, thin and vulnerable in the pauper's dress she put on after the murder, Katja with the selfsame wealth of hair. Taking the girl with her into the wilderness will be like giving *herself* a second chance, rescuing her not only from this forbidding fortress, but from everything that can restrict and immure and menace her, all the rules and regulations and prescriptions of the world – Katja the orphan, lonely, threatened from all sides.

So in the end she resigns herself to what has come to seem inevitable. She accompanies Katja back to her own room and helps her pack another bundle. The first feeble daylight comes leaking through the small windows as they pick their way downstairs and then outside, across the bare yard, past the outbuildings and the vegetable garden and the graveyard, past the rocky outcrop that marks the spring, past the rock formation in the shape of a woman turning back to whatever she has left behind, and out on to the open plain that stretches ahead of them to meet the sky where the first lurid streaks of dawn are beginning to show.

Below the rock she stops to glance back one more time, almost as if expecting to see something, someone, following. But who? The ghosts, perhaps. In a way it might have been reassuring to see them following in her wake, that grey, immaterial host. But they must have their own reasons for staying. They must remain behind as once, lost in the distance, she left behind her imaginary friends when she was transported from her first and unremembered life to the unforgiving walls of the orphanage. And now another life is beginning. What it may be, she does not know yet. But she has chosen it, and must go on.

No need to hurry. After her previous experience, and Katja's, they know there is little danger of being followed: Frauenstein will rely on the efficacy of the desert either to destroy them or to send them staggering back. Unless the corpse is found, and there is little chance of that, no one is likely to care about them any more. She takes her time to initiate the girl, as they go on, into the skills she can remember from the Namas: how to find *tsamma*, roots and tubers, thick-leaved succulents, and to distinguish between the edible and the lethal; how to recognise the markers of buried ostrich eggs filled with water by nomadic Namas and Bushmen; how to be alert to the flutterings and the brief twitterings of the small grey birds that can lead them to the nests of bees in hollow tree-trunks or anthills ripe with the sweetness of golden honeycombs.

They communicate as they have done in the past: Katja talking and asking, Hanna replying with spare but eloquent gestures or with a scribble of key words, no longer on paper as once in Frauenstein, but scratched on a patch of sand or hard bare earth. They should try to find a Nama settlement or a group of nomads, she has suggested. For the moment she is not yet ready to offer any further explanation. Apart from the time she spent with the Kreutzers, and with Lotte on the boat, her stay with the Namas has been the only interlude in her life in which she has approached a state of near-contentment, containment, perhaps of happiness. That tribe is now annihilated, but they may find others. And for what she has in mind she will need the strength of numbers. As many as she can find. An army. But she has no hurry. This clear, limpid hate that drives her is as patient as the desert sun; as inexorable too. A fire in the guts.

What strikes Hanna as almost uncanny is the way in which Katja seems to need fewer and fewer written words or phrases from her: their communication is becoming almost telepathic; as if the girl is turning indeed into a version of herself. She is tough too, much tougher than one would expect from her frail body. It was, perhaps, not a mistake after all to have brought her along. Even if two weeks is hardly enough thoroughly to put her to the test.

From time to time they come across the remains of some Nama settlement – burnt-out huts, kraals of branches torn apart, the carcasses of goats, a few cattle, dogs; bones of people scattered by scavengers. These must be signs of the war that has been ravaging the land and of which they have heard so much; but except for the single recent occasion when the army detachment and its prisoners arrived at Frauenstein it has never been more than rumours or reports. This is more real, more stark, yet there is a curious sense of absence about it, a denial of life. Ultimately the signs point nowhere.

But now there is something happening ahead, announced by the slowly cartwheeling vultures. It is unnecessary for Hanna to gesture or for Katja to say a word; they do not even exchange glances. Yet both have quickened their step. The discoveries of their desert trek, so far, have been unremarkable, although to the two women they are momentous in their way: a secretary bird caught in what seems like an extravagant and faintly ludicrous dance with a snake; a family of meerkats surveying the plains; tufts of dry grass swept up in an otherwise invisible whirlwind; small clouds sailing across the sky and disappearing again; a trail of ants crossing their path. Insignificant in themselves, yet each an unsettling portent of life and death pursuing its course without a moment's respite. But this — those vultures and their still unseen target — is more overtly dramatic in the total stillness of the desert.

'A sick animal perhaps?' Katja suggests as they draw nearer. 'Perhaps a buck wounded in a fight or mauled by a lion? Or a little one abandoned by its mother.'

Hanna shrugs.

They come still closer.

Hanna touches the girl's arm to hold her back. She clenches her fist to indicate a man.

Yes, it is a man. Or was once. Before he was tied down, on his back, over an anthill, outstretched arms and legs fastened to stakes driven into the ground. The front of his body, from neck to knees, is black with dried blood through which a criss-cross pattern of stripes can be discerned. His sex has been mutilated, the testicles cut off. A cloud of flies rises in an angry buzz as they approach. Hanna tries to turn Katja's head away, but the girl resists as she kneels beside the spreadeagled body, her eyes staring.

'Is he dead?' she asks after a while, her lips dry and barely moving.

As if in reply the man utters a low groan; his body twitches, the only movement of which he seems capable.

Hanna kneels beside him, unties her bundle, takes out her long knife, proceeds to hack and saw through the thongs that tie his wrists and ankles.

Water, she signals to Katja.

The girl approaches with an earthenware jar she has brought with her. There is little liquid left, but what there is she sprinkles on the man's dark, swollen, cracked and bleeding lips.

Careful, motions Hanna. *Take your time. Otherwise it will all be wasted.*

They try to move him into a more comfortable position, but he seems unable to of comply, even to understand. His back, they discover as they cautiously and clumsily drag him from the anthill, is inexplicably unscathed. It is a giant of a man, built like a bull, but now in such a sorry state that they may well have come too late. He appears delirious.

Who could have done this to him? Hanna tries to convey to the girl. *And why? Do you think he was punished for doing something terrible? Murder, or . . .* She drops her arms, unwilling to proceed.

'He is black,' says Katja. 'In this land, I have found out, that can be enough of a crime. I sometimes saw them when they came crawling on all fours to my father's trading post. He always tried to shoo us away; it was not for our eyes, he would say. But we would look anyway.'

But why beat a man like this . . . ? Hanna tries to ask. *On his chest and stomach and the front of his legs . . . and there –* she points – *and not on his back?*

Katja shrugs. 'This is how they do it here,' she says in a small, strained voice. 'The Hereros call it the German way.'

We must find some shade for him, gestures Hanna.

'There is no shade.'

He will die here. Involuntarily Hanna glances up. The vultures have descended much lower than before. At times they come so close that one can make out the obscenely naked necks, the fierce stare in the unblinking yellow eyes. She looks around, gestures. *We'll have to make shade to protect him.*

'How?'

Give me a hand.

From a stunted thorn tree they spread open the sheet that held Hanna's few possessions and into its inadequate shade they half carry, half drag the body of the man who moans weakly in agony. Hanna drapes a shirt over the blackened, bloody stump that remains of his genitals. Overhead, the vultures utter screeches of protest, flutter their wings in anger, then take off; after a while a few of them return again, dive down as if to hurl themselves into the ground, only to swoop up at the last moment and resume their spiralling, but now upward, higher and higher, dwindling into mere pinpricks.

There is little more the women can do. The man's wounds should be cleaned, he is racked with fever, but they have no water. And in this shimmering heat which blinds the eyes every motion is exhausting. They can only wait. When at last the sun begins to liquefy, Hanna leaves Katja in charge and goes off to look for medicine. It is so long ago that she was tended by the Namas; she has forgotten much. But she does find a few small dry shrubs which look vaguely familiar; if they are what she hopes they are, they might help for fever. And a *gli* root for a concoction to make him drunk and help him to forget the pain.

The dark comes very suddenly, but there is an abundance of firewood about and using one of the tinderboxes they have brought with them they can get a fire going. Just beyond the reach of the flames there are green eyes shining in the night, appearing now here, now there; and the eerie cackling of jackals, the calls of a hyena. Katja is terrified. Hanna holds her close, making soothing, humming sounds; and from exhaustion the girl drifts off into uneasy sleep. But Hanna stays awake to feed the fire, and from time to time to force some more of the bitter juice from her shrubs through the swollen lips of her delirious patient. He responds with low, rumbling groans like an ox in pain. If he makes it through the night, Hanna thinks, he may survive. If not, the vultures will be back in the morning.

37

IN THE MORNING the vultures have not returned. The dark giant will survive. They feed him small morsels from the hard stale bread they still have left, and moisture from a *tsamma*. Katja keeps at a safe distance: she has too many nightmare memories from the time the Hereros attacked her father's trading post and killed all the men. But she watches intently while Hanna feeds him from the *tsamma*. What an amazing melon it is, Hanna thinks as she cautiously makes a hole at the top as she once saw the Namas do, and inserts a sturdy twig which she twirls until the flesh inside is pulped into a liquid which she feeds to the debilitated man. Once it is all finished, she will shake and scratch out the seeds to roast, or to grind into flour. And the shell, carefully preserved, will be kept to serve as a container or even a cooking pot.

Slowly, as the days creep by, the man's condition improves. In the beginning, when he is awake, he just lies staring at them with suspicion in his eyes narrowed into slits. But after a day or two he utters something in a voice like a subterranean rumble. It is in a language they do not understand.

Hanna nudges Katja, who asks, 'Do you speak German?'

'They make me learn,' he replies, his mouth struggling to shape the words. 'Otherwise I get no work.' Then he adds with what seems to be a statement of superiority, 'I am a Herero.'

'The land of the Hereros is up north,' Katja quickly reminds him. 'The other side of Windhoek. Not down here.'

'They kill my cattle,' he says in a rush of anger. 'They kill all our cattle. They kill the fire of our ancestors. So what must I do?

I come here to find work. Otherwise my people will die. My wife, my family. That way, far away.' He motions to the north. He tries to push himself up on his arms. In what sounds like a tone of accusation he demands, 'Who are you?'

Katja first glances at Hanna, then says, 'I am Katja. She is Hanna.'

'Why are you in this place?'

'We found you here. We couldn't just leave you.'

'We cannot stay here. He will come back to see if I am dead.'

'Who will come back?'

'The one who put me here. The baas.'

'Where does he live?'

'His farm is that way.' He gestures. 'Not far. One day.'

For the first time Katja ventures a question on her own: 'Why did he do it to you?'

He mumbles something unintelligible.

He must tell us, Hanna conveys to Katja. *We must know if he is a thief or a murderer*. The girl puts it into words.

For a long time the stranger stares at them; his attitude is defiant, hostile, even menacing.

'Why you ask?'

'We must know who you are,' explains Katja, at Hanna's prompting.

'And I must know who you are.' His gruff voice sounds almost taunting.

'We come from the farm Frauenstein.'

'People go to that place. Nobody come from there. That is what I hear. If you go there you stay there.'

'We were not safe there.'

'Why does she not speak?' he asks, pointing his chin at Hanna.

'She has no tongue.'

'Who do that to her?' He moves his hand across his face.

'Soldiers,' says Katja. 'An officer in the German army.' Hanna communicates something to her in sign language, and she asks, 'Why did your baas do this to you?'

A long silence. Then a smothered growl. And he says, precipitously, and in a fury too urgent for his broken German, 'The baas want to take my wife. I stop him.'

'Who is your baas?'

'His name is Albert Gruber. He is a farmer.'

Doesn't he have a wife of his own then? Hanna wants to know, through Katja.

'He bring a wife from Germany, yes.'

'Then what happened?'

'She make music. He beat her. She drink poison stuff.' A pause. 'Now he want my wife, he take her.'

'What is your name?' asks Katja.

'Kahapa.'

For the moment that is the end of their conversation. But over the next few days, as he gradually grows stronger, he becomes less obdurately reticent. And once they have given in to his increasingly insistent demands to be moved away from that place, his suspicion about them seems to be allayed. Between the two of them they help him to hobble along, stopping to rest every fifty or hundred metres, until they can no longer see the spot where he was exposed. In the shelter provided by a small koppie they make a new halt, shifting around it as the sun moves the deep shadow.

On Hanna's firm instructions, Kahapa has torn a broad strip off the sheet from her bundle to wind it round his waist. His attitude makes it clear that he resents the outfit; perhaps it makes him feel like a woman. But he keeps his protests down. He owes them too much.

Hanna draws a peculiar satisfaction from the care she bestows on the still almost helpless giant. For perhaps the first time in her life someone depends utterly on her. Even the woman with the cataracts she once read to, the deaf man and his daughter to whom she spoke in signs, were not truly dependent on her: she was a hired help, she was paid to do her work (however paltry the wage), she could be – and was in the end – fired. Here is a life for which she alone is responsible. And it has been her choice. Katja is in it with her, yes. But it is no simple role the girl fulfils: Hanna has come to rely on her – as an interpreter, a helper, a support – but she also needs Hanna in the intricate processes of survival; and she has her own needs, fears, hopes, demands.

Sometimes, when the injured man dozes, they talk with their hands, a language that becomes more nuanced by the day. If they need to talk at all: for long periods they simply sit together, looking at each other or not, allowing their thoughts to come and go in a silent osmosis.

'What are we going to do with the man?'

We must wait until he is healed. Then we'll see.

'Is it for him to decide then?'

No, but he is with us now. We shall decide together.

'And after that?'

We'll go on into the desert. (She will not yet talk to the girl about the hate. The hate that burns like a sun and gives light like a sun.)

This is what it means to move into the interior, she thinks. Not arriving on a boat, meeting people, talking to strangers, bringing with one a language made beyond the seas, bestowing words on things – stone, bush, root, earth, sky – but walking into it, merging with it, body to body. The way, perhaps, it was with Lotte in the total darkness of their submarine cabin.

'But how far do we go on?' asks Katja. 'Until what happens?'

Until we know what is on the other side.

'Suppose it never ends?'

Then at least we'll know the desert.

'Are you not afraid, Hanna?'

Of what?

'If someone comes, some time . . . ?'

We are armed.

'Do you know how to use a gun?'

No. A smile. *You are right. We must learn. Perhaps this man, this Kahapa, can teach us.*

Kahapa does, once he can stand up on his own again and the smell of his festering wounds diminishes and his strength returns. With endless patience he shows them how to load, and take aim, and shoot. When Katja finds the Mauser too unwieldy she is given the Luger. Neither becomes really proficient, but at least they no longer pose a danger to themselves. Then Kahapa takes them on a hunt. He shoots a springbok, an old crippled animal presumably rejected by its herd. The meat is tough and stringy, but they feast on it for days.

It is while they are sitting beside the fire Kahapa has made to roast the meat that he begins to tell them about how his people first came from what he calls the Far Country, a place without a name, hundreds of years ago, bringing the sacred fire of their ancestors with them. And where they settled in the new Hereroland, from Aminuis to Epukiro, to Otjimbungue, to Otjituuo, to Otjihorongo, to Ovitoto, to Tses – all these places with the magic names that ring in Hanna's ears – they brought their fire with them, each new settlement or tribe lighting its own from the coals of the first fire, so that it would never die. At the great omumborumbonga tree in the region of Okahandja, he explains, the two brothers who arrived together first separated. The descendants from the one became the Ovambos, who remained in the north; from the other brother descended the Hereros who spread down across the whole countryside as far as the Nossob River and covered the grassy plains with their great herds of cattle.

But then came the Germans – and Kahapa's voice trembles with subdued rage – and started occupying their land and taking their cattle; and the Namas from the south began to make raids into Hereroland to lay waste great tracts of it; and the terrible cattle disease destroyed the herds; and the destitute people were forced to become labourers on the farms of the very whites who had scattered the ashes of their forefathers' fires.

'And now I am here,' he says. 'But I shall not stay here. First I shall go to the farm where he do this to me and take back my wife. And one day I shall go back to our Great Place in Okahandja where our chiefs lie buried.'

A few days later, when the last of the meat has been consumed, they finally set out in the direction Kahapa has pointed out.

Are you sure you're strong enough for this? Hanna makes Katja ask him.

The tall man growls deep in his throat. 'I am ready,' he says. 'Ndjambi Karunga, the god of my people, will help me.'

They are both in trepidation of what may come from a confrontation. Katja, especially, shudders at the prospect.

'We must try to keep him away from that farmer,' she pleads with Hanna. 'The violence will be terrible.'

What must happen must happen, Hanna replies. *Kahapa has to do his duty*.

Katja shakes her head in despair, but she is given no choice.

Proceeding very slowly and making many halts, they take a full day and a half to reach the farm. Kahapa leads the way. The landscape has become more turbulent, with high ridges and outcrops breaking the plains; and the farmhouse, little more than an unplastered hovel of stone and reeds, sits high and exposed against a rocky slope. The farmer must have spied them from a long way off because he comes down to meet them, gun in hand, clearly intrigued by the unusual visitors. He is a man with a wild beard discoloured by tobacco juice, on his head a filthy hat decorated with a strip of leopard skin around the brim. They are very near to him before he recognises Kahapa. His small eyes set close together register unspeakable shock.

'I left you for dead,' he stammers. 'How the hell did you survive? And what are you doing here?'

'I come for my wife.'

'The *meid* is not here.'

Kahapa takes a deep breath. 'You kill her too?' he asks.

The man retreats a step. 'She ran away.' He is clutching the gun very tightly, evidently not prepared to take any chances.

'You lie,' snarls Kahapa. 'If she run away she come to me where you put me.' He takes a menacing step closer.

'She didn't know her place,' the farmer retorts. But behind the anger in his voice one senses real apprehension.

'Where is she?'

'How must I know? I told you she ran away.' In the background, at the front door and around the corner of the house, other figures appear. Judged by their miserable appearance they must be labourers. Three barefoot women, a shirtless man with tattered trousers. Sensing their presence, the farmer glances round. He appears openly nervous now. 'Go ask them,' he says curtly.

Kahapa stares hard at him. 'I want my wife,' he says, coming slowly past the farmer.

The man edges out of his way. For a moment Hanna and Katja are afraid that he may shoot from behind, but their presence appears to make him hesitate. They prepare to follow after Kahapa, covering his rear.

'You two can stay here,' says the farmer quickly, stepping forward to block their way. He is looking at Katja with some interest. In a way Hanna finds this more ominous than his belligerence towards Kahapa.

'Where do you come from?' the farmer asks, an unpleasantly cajoling tone in his voice. 'Did this bastard try to do you any harm?' Only then does he notice Hanna's face under the hood of the kappie. He takes a step back. 'What in God's name has happened to you? You look like something out of hell.'

Hanna puts a hand on Katja's arm. The girl tries to keep her voice in control. 'Kahapa told you. We are here with him to find his wife.'

Many unarticulated feelings move like shadows across his blunt face. There is a difficult pause before he lets them past. The gun is shaking visibly in his ferocious grip.

At the front door Kahapa is talking to the women. They appear reluctant to comply with whatever he may be asking, and furtive glances are cast in the direction of the farmer with the gun. But in the end they lead him round the house. Hanna and Katja follow to the back, skirting the rocky top of the outcrop, and down the side of the rise, past two makeshift sheds, a few untidy enclosures of stacked branches, towards parched, dispirited fields.

Only now, out of earshot of the hovel, in angry spurts, do the women dare to inform Kahapa about what has happened. It is as he has feared. His wife was killed. And as Albert Gruber had refused to give permission for a funeral, which would interfere with the work on the farm, the dead woman was buried in the night, without any fire or light to betray the mourners. There was no time, and the soil was too hard, for a proper grave to be dug, so the body, rolled in an old blanket, was laid to rest in a shallow trench at the far end of the mealie land, among the stalks of the last failed harvest.

When the small procession comes to a standstill, Hanna and Katja remain a few yards away. In the full glare of the midday sun they take off their kappies and hold them against their breasts.

Kahapa is standing beside the small mound of the grave, staring down at it.

'Tell me what he do to her,' he asks the three women who have guided him to the place. He is speaking in his threadbare German, as if he wants to make sure that Hanna and Katja will understand.

They hear one of the black women protest, 'Hau! It is better not to ask.'

'I must know.'

For a while they stubbornly hold out, but when his attitude becomes threatening they relent. Retreating a few paces, as if scared that he might vent his anger on them, they take turns to tell the story, haltingly, drastically truncated. For it would indeed have been better not to know. How Albert Gruber kept on calling Kahapa's wife to his bed, and how she went on refusing, trying to persuade him by pointing to her swollen belly. She was five months pregnant. In the end he lost his temper and attacked her with his fists and beat her to the ground. When she went on resisting, he ordered two of his labourers to hold her down with force. Then he had his way with her. And afterwards he ordered the men to flog her in the 'German way', tied down on her back. They beat the child out of her. They didn't stop before every movement in the battered body had ceased.

Throughout the whole narrative Kahapa utters no sound. His face is contorted, but he does not speak. For a long time, minutes, perhaps half an hour, he stands beside the mound. Until, in the distance, from behind the derelict little dwelling, the figure of the farmer reappears, staring down towards them. Only then does Kahapa begin the long walk back, very slowly, moving his arms as if he is rowing upstream. As he comes past them, Hanna reaches out to touch his arm, but he shakes her off.

'Kahapa,' whispers Katja.

He does not even seem to hear.

They follow at a distance, their hands clenched together.

38

'WHAT DO YOU want?' demands the farmer as Kahapa comes up to him.

'I come for you,' says the dark giant.

'You know what you wanted to know, now get the hell off my farm.'

'You kill my woman dead,' says Kahapa. 'You try to kill me. Now I kill you.'

Albert Gruber raises his gun. There is outrage in his small eyes, but also – perhaps – a glint of fear. Above all incomprehension, for this is something that has never happened to him before, something beyond the reach of the possible.

The black man lunges at him. The white man tries to step aside but stumbles. Before he can get his rifle to his shoulder Kahapa grabs hold of the barrel. A furious tug of war begins. Kahapa is much taller, but he is still weak from his ordeal; and Gruber, though shorter, is heavy and stocky, he has the body of a primate, with hunched shoulders and long arms.

'You've got to help Kahapa,' pleads Katja, clutching Hanna's hand.

But Hanna pulls away. *This is the men's fight*, she gestures. *Let them be.*

They are like two fighting dogs, grunting and snarling, pulling, pushing, stumbling this way and that. But at last, managing to drag the white man off balance, Kahapa wrenches the gun from his grasp and flings it away. Now they have only their hands.

Using his slight advantage of higher ground, the farmer hurls himself down against Kahapa. They land on the ground, grappling, wrestling, hitting, tearing. They are covered in grit and dust. Both are bleeding. The white man manages to head-butt Kahapa in the face; there is a crunching sound. The black man bellows in rage and pain, rears up, digs his knee into his opponent's groin. He doubles up. Kahapa staggers to his feet, his face bleeding profusely. But seeing his chance he kicks the white man in the stomach. The farmer grabs him by the leg and tries to pull him down again. Then they are both on their feet again, thrashing about, stumbling up and down the incline in front of the hovel.

More figures appear in the background, hovering. Not just the three women who escorted Kahapa to the grave, but a small crowd of farm workers, dusty and dishevelled, ribbed like mongrels, clustered together in horrified eagerness, grunting and moaning as if they, too, are in the fight; but not daring to take sides.

At one stage the two wrestling men lurch through the front door into the house. There is a sound of breaking and splintering wood as they reel and stagger from the single room into the lean-to kitchen and back, then out into the fury of the sun again. Strip by strip their clothing is being torn from them. Soon they are naked, black and white, body against body, but both so covered with blood and grime and dust that the colour of their skins has become almost indistinguishable.

Hanna finds herself staring at the spectacle, transfixed, in a kind of awe, unable to turn away. Always in the past, when there was violence, she was involved in it, the victim, unable to watch from the outside. Now there is an urge to observe. She *has* to see, for this is what men do and she cannot deny or ignore it. She has to see *how* pain is inflicted, how it is made to hurt, what it does to the one who causes it as much as to the one who suffers it. *She must know.* She isn't even aware of Katja's nails digging into her arm as the girl keeps on repeating in a wail of distress, 'Just stop it, just stop it, Hanna, please make them stop . . .'

Kahapa shows the first signs of weakening. His breath comes gasping from his throat and he seems dazed, trying to wipe blood from his eyes, groaning deeply like some dying large animal.

'That man is going to kill him,' whimpers Katja. She is crying without realising it. Tears are making wet patterns through the red dust that covers her cheeks. 'He's going to kill him, Hanna, you've got to do something.'

And indeed the white man seems to be preparing for a final assault, going down low on his knees, then rearing up and grabbing Kahapa round the neck, his arms tightening, his muscles moving like moles under the skin. The black man is making choking sounds. His knees are buckling. On his forehead large veins bulge out, throbbing.

'For God's sake, Hanna!' sobs the girl, crouching on her knees now.

Kahapa's large body is going limp.

Only now does Hanna come forward. Katja hasn't even noticed that she has removed the Luger from her bundle. She cautiously steps up to the tangle of sweating, bleeding bodies, making sure she isn't drawn into the fray. For a while she has to step this way and that to avoid their thrashing. Then she presses the barrel against the back of the white man's head, and closes her eyes, turns her face away, and pulls the trigger.

The report is stunning. In the background the miserable spectators erupt in sound, but whether it is jubilation or jeering is impossible to make out.

There is a lot of blood.

The bodies remain locked together, twitching, jerking. But at last Kahapa shakes himself like a big dog coming from the water, and crawls away on all fours, squats down, his head buried in his arms.

The other body no longer moves.

'How did you do it?' asks Katja, gaping in awe.

It is only the first time that it is difficult, Hanna tries to say.

No one makes any sound or movement. They are waiting for Kahapa. After a long time he raises his face from his hands and looks at them. He gets up, swaying on his legs, walks down to where the dead farmer lies, prods him with a foot. The body rolls over. It is not an appetising sight. The face, where the bullet has come out, has been blown away.

'You do this for me,' says Kahapa, still panting. He looks at Hanna. 'Two times you save my life.' He nods towards the dead man as if to conclude an argument with himself. 'This is my man,' he says. 'Now we go find your man.'

39

No, SHE COULD never have thought that hate would be like this. So beautiful. So singular. So utterly pure. So abundantly full of life. It is as if she has always had an emptiness inside her — sometimes invaded temporarily by fear, by dread, by uncertainty and restlessness, occasionally even by a surge of love, all kinds of turbulent and opaque emotions, but mostly just empty — which is now filled with this resplendent hate. It's like a magnifying glass which forces together a great number of disparate light beams to focus with terrible precision on one spot only, setting it alight, and in one amazing moment giving direction and meaning to her whole life. Over so many years so many separate moments have prepared her, unknowingly, for it. Frau Agathe in the orphanage. Pastor Ulrich. The people she worked for, the men with their sordid needs, their power, their helplessness in her hands. The officer on the ship who denied her the right to her own name. The men on the train. Hauptmann Heinrich Böhlke. The blood spurting in her mouth and dripping down her chin on to her breasts. His subalterns in the crowded compartment taking off their studded belts. *When I fuck a woman.* That was the furthest she had ever been driven. But it was also the moment of ultimate emptiness. A space in which nothing could grow or move. Until the so-recent day when the army detachment came to Frauenstein with its wretched collection of prisoners. For the first time in all these years something stirred inside her when Colonel von Blixen drew Katja to him and said, 'I'll have this one.' Temporarily thwarted by Frau Knesebeck. But when he returned in the night and she found him beating the naked Katja, a flame was lit inside the darkest recess of herself. A flame as livid and dazzling as the sun. As if everything that had been gathering in her throughout her life had suddenly exploded. When she attacked him with the brass candlestick something broke free in her, an animal kept caged and tethered all its life. For the first time in the years since the train journey she could look at herself in the smudged and faded mirror. She looked, and she knew, everything she'd never even attempted to grasp. It was the beginning of hate, a liberation, an ecstasy she would never have dreamed possible. As if Herr Goethe himself was shouting inside her, *Herrlich wie am ersten Tag* . . . ! From that instant she has known where her life is heading for. She has light, she has fire, she has the will, a passion that can never be extinguished again. That is what has brought her here. And will take her from here, to where she knows, with such clarity, she must go. There is no haste or impatience in her. Everything is serene, all is transparent in that light. No love can possibly be as fulfilling and as good as this hate.

40

THEY ARE READY to set out on their way to the Rhenish mission station which, if Kahapa is to be believed, is five days from the farm, even if one travels by oxcart as they are doing.

So many things have shifted in the short time since they set foot on the farm. What Kahapa said on that first day, standing over the dead body of the man who had made his life hell and murdered his wife, has given a shape to her own thoughts: *This is my man. Now we go find your man.* Because this is what her hate is focused on, she now knows very clearly. It is not just an escape from Frauenstein, from living an immured existence, having the details of her life regulated and determined by others, being at the disposal of those who have assumed power over her. Nor is it just an attempt to forge a new kind of life for herself and Katja. It is, above all other things, a journey towards a confrontation with the man – the men – who turned her into what she is now. *You look like something out of hell.* Only when that has happened can her freedom acquire meaning and substance. And Kahapa is in it with her. There has been no need even to discuss it. She has helped him – not simply to take his revenge, for that notion, *revenge*, is too simple and too shallow; but to do what has to be done in order to be what he can be – and now he will help her. They are together.

Others have come with them. The labourers on the farm of Albert Gruber, thirteen men and women altogether (and any number of naked, snot-nosed children), ran amok after the death of their baas. Katja, shocked by the excesses of their rampage, wanted Hanna to intervene, but the woman shook her head. *Anyone who tries to interfere will be hacked to pieces*. And Kahapa agreed, though probably more from exhaustion and pain than conviction. There was no whole furniture left in the house when they were done. Not that there had been much to begin with: a carved wooden bedstead, presumably of German origin, some chests, a long table and eight chairs, all very roughly hammered together, a number of rickety shelves. The only object of value – fantastically out of place – was a dark rosewood piano, which collapsed under the blows of the frenzied labourers in an unbelievable cacophony of breaking strings. It must have belonged to the dead man's wife. Hanna remembered Kahapa's laconic account: *She make music. He beat her. She drink poison stuff.* A life in ten words.

Hanna intervened only after everything had been smashed, including doors and window frames, and the labourers prepared to set fire to the place. Pushing the still dazed Kahapa forward, she made him stop the plunder to salvage at least a number of utensils, some provisions (oil, sugar, salt, coffee, flour), a kaross and an old sheet from the broken bed, and all the guns and ammunition she could collect (seven guns in all, of various sizes and calibres, and ranging from an old-fashioned frontloader to Mausers and a Lee-Enfield). Then they stood back to watch the wretched place go up in flames until only a few blackened walls remained. After that the people quietened down. A strange calm beset them, almost a sense of melancholy, a *tristitia post coïtum*. Perhaps they were even, suddenly, inexplicably, too late, feeling ashamed of what they had done.

Without talking among themselves they went to a shed behind the house and emerged with picks and shovels to dig a shallow grave for the dead farmer, not to show him any consideration, merely to be rid of the carcass. Then some of the women took Kahapa away to wash him; water was drawn from a deep well a hundred yards downhill. (How many weeks, months had it taken how many men to dig it?) At long, long last, as dusk was already falling, they came to rest.

Kahapa engaged in conversation with them. To Hanna, he interpreted: 'They say who will be their baas now?'

Through Katja she responded: *For God's sake, they've just got rid of one, why should they want another?*

'They say who will look after them?'

Why can't they look after themselves? They are free now.

'They need food, they must work, they have families to look after.'

What did they do before they worked for Albert Gruber?

'They work for other white people.'

Hanna made a series of signs to Katja. And the girl interpreted, 'She stayed with a tribe of Namas once. They did not work for anyone.'

The people snorted and laughed dismissively. How could she presume to tell them what to do? A woman? One looking like that?

Then what will you do? asked Hanna through Katja.

That was when a man said, 'We must go the mission station. They will help us there.'

The following day, before they could begin to round up people and animals (twelve head of cattle apart from the two drawing oxen, a flock of bedraggled, foul-smelling goats, a few makeshift coops of chickens and muscovy ducks) two of the labourers announced that they had decided to set out on their own, with their families, to return to wherever they had once come from. All the others elected to accompany the oxcart, the men on foot, the women and children to take turns on the back of the jolting, swaying, creaking cart.

The entire small crowd is assembled on the *werf* at the back of the house watching the two families leave. Kahapa stands in the forefront, scowling into the sun. He is wearing Albert Gruber's clothes. The shirt is too short and too wide and Kahapa hasn't bothered to do up the buttons; the trousers, too, are ill-fitting. He doesn't care for shoes. But he is proud of the hat with the band of leopard skin around it, which he wears with a swagger. Like the others he follows with his brooding eyes the two men and their families as they move off with their paltry possessions balanced on the women's heads, and driving before them two of the cows and some goats. It seems an ordinary enough leavetaking. But it is interrupted in a completely unexpected way when, moving slightly to one side, Kahapa stretches out a hand to pick up one of the guns, the Lee-Enfield, from the back of the cart. He must have prepared everything beforehand, because without stopping to load, he raises the rifle to his shoulder and pulls the trigger. The sudden explosion is greeted with shouts and screams of dismay;

some of the children start hollering. Fifty yards away one of the two departing men falls down in a small cloud of dust, convulsing; the rest of the group appears to be in disarray. But before they can start scrambling out of the way, Kahapa ejects the spent shell, slips in a new cartridge, and lowers the hammer to repeat the action. This time Hanna comes running to him and grabs him by the arm, but it is too late: already the second man drops in his tracks.

'What are you doing?' screams Katja.

Hanna is shaking Kahapa this way and that in inarticulate rage.

He calmly frees himself from her grasp. 'That two men,' he says. 'They are the ones that hold my woman down for him to fuck. They are the ones that beat her dead.'

The children in the distance are scattering in all directions, screaming and howling with fear, as the women kneel down in the dust beside the killed men. There is much shouting and wailing on the *werf* too.

Hanna prepares to run after the others, but Kahapa holds her back.

'Leave them now,' he says. 'We go.'

She signals furiously to Katja; the girl says, 'But what about the women and children?'

'They bury their men. Their place is not with us.'

Katja hides her face in her hands.

In an uncharacteristic gesture of compassion Kahapa puts a hand on her shoulder. 'This is the way it must be,' he says.

In numbed silence they move away, without looking back again. The mission station will be only the first stop on the long road that lies ahead.

41

ALONG THE WAY, as Hanna walks on her own some distance from the oxcart, she finds the slough of a snake, long and thin and quite perfect, silvery against the reddish brown of the earth. When she squats down to pick it up it disintegrates into dust more insubstantial than ash at the touch of her finger. It leaves her unsettled. Once this skin was inhabited by something alive and quick, a feared shiver of lightning rippling through the scrub and stones. Now that life has moved on, leaving only this trace behind; and even the trace dissolves. There will be nothing left, nothing at all.

42

THE RHENISH MISSION station is a modest cluster of buildings set among low windblown makalani palms, held in the tight embrace of a high wall; from the entrance it juts out into the desert like a jetty into the sea, a resolutely straight line into the distance, a riddle which the eye cannot solve. In the middle of the tiny settlement is a small whitewashed church with a squat steeple and a freestanding bell-tower; there is a single long low house, also whitewashed, and a scattering of round huts. Someone must have sounded the alarm because in the deepening dusk quite a gathering awaits the travellers who all look the worse for wear. The group is led by a very tall, very thin, white man, his face burnt a fiery red by the sun, his long wiry arms covered in ginger hair. A step or two behind him is a woman who must be his wife, also very thin, with lanky blonde hair, a prominent beak-like nose, a long chintz dress. She is flanked by children, who at first sight seem like an innumerable brood, later distinguishable as eleven; all of them shockingly thin, and all of them girls – the youngest a baby in the mother's arms, the oldest trying to conceal, with self-consciously hunched shoulders, the first signs of budding breasts. They are all barefoot. So are the members of their congregation massed some distance behind the whites, a motley crowd that appears to represent a variety of types and tribes, from wiry ochre-coloured Namas to pitch-black Damaras and a number of Hereros and Ovambos in various shades of brown.

'Welcome to our vale of grace,' says the missionary in a booming voice much too large for his frame. 'God must have brought you here. To which purpose, we shall soon find out, I trust.'

Hanna pushes Katja forward with a series of quick hand-signs.

'These people are refugees from a farm,' explains Katja. 'The farmer died and they have nowhere to go. I am Katja Holtzhausen. My parents were traders, far from here, near Gobabis. Hanna here, and I, stayed at Frauenstein in the desert. This is Kahapa, our friend and guide who has brought us here.'

'You are most welcome, little sister,' says the man, extending a skeletal hand in a gesture of blessing. Yet there is something very severe in his attitude. He turns to Hanna, glances under the kappie, winces involuntarily in the reaction to which she has become accustomed. Then he continues in his studied, bookish way, as if he has memorised every phrase and trusts his audience to find it memorable too. 'God seems to have visited a terrible retribution on you, sister, for what vile sin I shall not presume to ask. But if ever you wish to discuss it, remember his mercy is infinite and as his servant I am at your disposal.' He looks round at his congregation and, in an unexpectedly stentorian tone, shouts a number of commands about preparing food, shelter and water for the white visitors. Only then does he summon the thin woman to his side. 'This is Gisela, whom God has appointed to care for me and support me in the performance of his work.' A mirthless and possessive smile: 'And these are the olive branches at our table. As you can see, we have been fulfilling his great command to be fruitful, and multiply and fill the earth. Amid the mass of dark heathens on this continent we try to form a small but growing source of light.' The line of girls blush and fumble and giggle until a withering look from their father imposes the fear of God on them. 'Now let us go forth to praise the Lord for his many blessings.'

Only after the many blessings have been duly – and individually - acknowledged in the swiftly darkening little church, does the Reverend Gottlieb Maier lead the way to the house for more earthly, and more needed, refreshment. Black women come in with large basins of warm water in which the feet of the visitors are washed. And then, at last, by the light of several crude home-made candles, they are seated at the very long, narrow dining table: the parents at the head, Hanna and Katja at the bottom, the girls on low benches at either side. They are served from a large dish of goat-meat with pumpkin and sweet potatoes, and bowls of milk. As the missionary seems temporarily to have forgotten about Kahapa, Katja – nudged by Hanna – has to remind the man of God that their guide, too, is in need of sustenance. To this end a Nama servant is summoned and ordered to serve the man some bread in the kitchen. The other visitors are, hopefully, looked after by members of the congregation in their huts.

A safari of kitchen-women has appeared to clear the table and wash the dishes (Hanna and Katja, who both rise to give a hand, are curtly instructed to resume their seats). It is followed by a session of reading from a huge bible. The children sit staring at the visitors in silent, breathless awe. After the reading each child except the youngest two or three is required to recite a verse from the passage read by the father. After a near-interminable prayer in which the visitors and their destinies are amply included, four of the children, who have botched their recitation, are summoned to be given cracking blows on their hands with a strap. One, who dares to succumb to tears, is punished with a second stroke. And then, at last, everybody may bed down. Ten of the children, as well as Hanna and Katja, will sleep on reed mats on the dung floor of the main room, while the parents and their baby retire to the small bedroom at the far end. Within a few minutes, while the house is still reeking of candle smoke, muffled rhythmic moaning sounds from next door signal the missionary's enthusiastic performance, undoubtedly to the greater glory of God, of his marital duties.

Hanna begins to feel nauseous; with a dozen breathing bodies gathered in the less than generous space of the front room and all doors and windows shut against the night, the interior is close and stifling. Rising from her mat which fortunately has been spread out right beside the front door, and moving cautiously so as not to wake the sleeping Katja, she unbars the door, pulls it open and slips outside into a night riddled with uncannily large stars. Even her fear of the dark subsides before this pale shimmering. It is as if a large, very dark blue moth-eaten cloth has been stretched across the earth, through the holes of which shines some distant cosmic fire.

Alone in the innocent night she stares up at the stars, trying to find the ones the Namas have named for her: the seven sisters of Khuseti, the bright eye of Khanous, the mighty hunter Heiseb striding towards the dark horizon. They seem like old friends. And yet, as a small shiver moves down her spine, she wonders whether it can all be really as innocent as it seems. What violence, what danger may lie behind it, lurking, looming, waiting?

The ground feels reassuring and cool under her bare feet. Nothing moves; there is no sound. She looks at the low steeple of the little church, pointing upward like a stubby finger. She thinks of the service, of the prayers that followed the supper, the pastor's laborious piety, the heavy hand with which he rules his family and his congregation. The words he spoke to her when he first looked at her. God's retribution for some vile sin she has committed. It is as if in her mind she is looking right through the shadow of his drawn, ascetic features at the fleshy face of Pastor Ulrich. How concerned they all are about her immortal soul. How enthusiastically they conspire to hasten it on its way to perdition.

But perhaps she is being unfair. The missionary has welcomed them generously enough. It must be her old suspicion of the subplots of religion which has prejudiced her. She should be grateful for this station on their violent road which has only just begun. Again she sees the half-clad body of the officer subsiding under the blow of her heavy candlestick. The two naked bodies, one black, one white, locked together outside the dilapidated farmhouse. Kahapa shooting the two labourers on their way into the desert. Blood, blood. Is there no other way at all? There *are* other worlds, she knows. She has entered them, however briefly: the stories from Fräulein Braunschweig's books. Simplicity, so powerful and so perfect. If only one's life could be like that. But that seems out of reach, a wholeness beyond her grasp except in dreams. And the only way, now, to move towards that is along this bright road of hate on which she has set out. At least, she tries to reassure herself, there is the brief respite in this place with its paltry palm trees.

A crunching sound makes her swing round with a small gasp of fright. A large dark figure is approaching. She tries to efface herself, but he must have seen her for he is coming directly towards her. The night is indeed no longer innocent.

Then she recognises Kahapa and breathes deeply in relief.

He stops. 'You must not walk alone,' he says, his voice a deep rumble in the silence. 'This is not a good place.'

But it's a mission station! she would like to counter. Then thinks: *Perhaps he knows more than I do, more than he will let on.*

'I cannot sleep,' he says, as if he has guessed her thoughts. 'I wonder if you are all right.'

She puts her hand on his shoulder and nods, not knowing whether he can even see it.

For a moment he hesitates as if he would like to say more, but then he grunts, and turns, and walks away again. She remains for a while, reassured by his appearance from the night, the knowledge that he is there, awake and wandering, keeping watch; but also perturbed by what he has said. *This is not a good place.* Has he, too, seen through the missionary's ostentatious piety?

She goes back to the low house, its stark whiteness a pale smudge against the night sky. As she opens the door she discovers a dark shape right in front of her, huddled over Katja's sleeping form. It is the Reverend Gottlieb Maier, dressed only in a nightshirt. As Hanna opens the door he recoils.

'Oh!' he exclaims, then drops his voice to a whisper. 'It is you.' He pauses. 'I was just hoping to find out from our little sister what had happened to you. I was worried. It is such an ungodly world and with all these heathens about . . .'

Katja wakes up. 'What is going on?' she mumbles, pushing herself up on her elbows.

'Nothing, nothing,' he whispers. 'I just came through to see if everybody was safely asleep. Good-night. God bless you.' To Hanna his explanation sounds more like a threat than a reassurance.

'Are you all right?' whispers Katja after he has left them.

Closing her eyes in the dark, Hanna nods. No need to upset the girl; not now. And she cannot use sign language in the dark.

After a while, from behind the curtain closing off the bedroom, the moaning sounds resume. God is truly being served assiduously tonight.

43

SHE IS HIDING, as she so often does, knowing she may be punished for it – not just for slipping out of the orphanage, but especially for coming to this ungodly, Catholic, place of worship – in a dark corner off the cathedral nave, to listen to the organist practising. Here she can be alone with the music which reverberates through the dark space of the high building, shuddering in the walls, trembling in the wood, causing the small flames of the votive candles to quiver as if caught in an invisible draught. Sometimes it almost dies down to a whisper, then gathers itself again and swells, increases, grows like a wave rearing up in an ocean without end, and breaks right over her again. The whole cathedral loses shape and substance, everything becomes pure sound, a vastness in which she completely loses herself, dissolving into music. And it is not just her ears which hear the sound: through every pore of her body it enters, permeating and transforming everything. All is sound, a booming, thundering roar too great to fathom, a terrible cleansing. And when at last it recedes, she is left shivering against the wall, her face wet with tears even though she never realised she was crying; and between her thighs another wetness she has never felt before, and which must come from the deepest secret places of herself. This, she knows, is the sound of which she can hear only a whisper in the silence of a shell. If this is God, she will believe in him.

44

THEY ARE TAKEN on a small tour of the mission station. Among other things, it clears up the mystery of the wall. It is a monument to Gottlieb Maier's belief in the redeeming power of work. For thirteen years now, he explains with evident pride, ever since he first arrived to take up his post at the station, the male members of his flock have been devoting all their physical energy – for they are a lazy, stupid, brutal breed in need of discipline – to the construction of this noble enterprise. Almost two metres high, it circles the small settlement and then heads into the desert, due north, dead straight as the narrow road to heaven. For kilometres on end it runs towards a horizon it will never reach, growing ever smaller in the distance, stone balanced upon stone, all of them collected by the labourers – initially, the missionary points out, lugged from the koppies in the immediate vicinity, but from farther and farther away as the work has progressed through the years. Big ones, medium-sized ones, small ones, no stone is left unturned; each finds its place in the large scheme of the thing. Every day a few centimetres are added in height or length; at the end of every week the progress is measured and compared to the achievements of the past. No man is spared, except the very old and sick; and even those are expected to contribute their slow and humble bit to the service of the Lord.

But why? Hanna asks him, through Katja. *What is it* **for**?

The missionary gives her a puzzled look. 'It keeps them busy,' he says.

I can understand the wall around the settlement . . . she perseveres.

'Indeed,' he interrupts approvingly. 'We must keep Africa out.'

. . . but this . . . ? She gestures into the distance.

'It is not for us to enquire into the mysterious ways of God,' he says with a touch of admonition.

But this is not God,' she protests. *It is* **you.**

'I am here to do his work,' he says, finality in his tone. 'Even more so in dangerous and difficult times like these.'

What news is there about the war? Hanna makes Katja ask.

'We are so far away from it all,' he says. 'Who can ever be sure? There are so many rumours. *Mischief shall come upon mischief, and rumour shall be upon rumour*, in the words of the prophet Ezekiel. Should you ask me about the end, I will tell you that it is nigh. These are for sure the last days, of which Saint Mark says, *For in those days shall be affliction, such as was not from the beginning of the creation which God created unto this time, neither shall be.'*

'But there must be news, from time to time,' says Katja.

'There are small military patrols who pass this way and that,' he agrees, 'and sometimes they bring us up to date. It seems that since General von Trotha took over the command two years ago from that well-meaning but weak man Leutwein, he destroyed the power of the Hereros in the north.'

'That much we know,' Katja interrupts.

But he launches forth as if he hasn't heard her. 'To my everlasting shame I must admit that many of my own brethren, misguided pastors of the Rhenish mission, took up the cause of the Hereros. But God soon showed which side he was really on. And then, as you may also know, the great man, von Trotha, like a scourge of heaven, moved south and broke the back of the Namas. You may have heard of the battles of Naris, and Gochas, and Vaalgras. Ever since that incarnation of Evil, Hendrik Witbooi, was killed last October, we have been making massive progress. Glory be to God. What a pity the uninformed authorities in Berlin decided to recall von Trotha before he could clean it all up. His successor, Dame, is not cut from the same stern cloth. As a result, there are still pockets of resistance and violence keeps flaring up here, there and everywhere; there are still agents of Satan abroad among the Namas, men like Cornelius and Fielding and Morenga. But with the help of God we are on the road to victory. Large parts of the country have already been pacified and more and more of the godless are rounded up in concentration camps.' He sighs. 'A sad, sad time, and we must remain vigilant. Did not Saint Luke tell us to watch therefore, and pray always, that we may be accounted worthy to escape all these things that shall come to pass, and to stand before the Son of man?'

'The country seemed a wasteland all the way we came,' says Katja. 'All the villages have been burnt down.'

'The army is doing the work of the Lord,' he assures her. 'That is not something a girl like you should be concerned about. Here in the desert we are safe.' His eyes rest probingly on her face; but then, as if he has caught himself in an indiscretion, he becomes agitated and businesslike, excusing himself in a hurry. 'I have to go. Some of the workers over there are malingering. They have to be seen to. The Lord does not brook shoddiness.'

In the meantime, in the church, as she does every day, Gisela Maier teaches the children. It goes on, they learn, all morning, a thankless, near-impossible task, as she tries to inculcate the elements of reading and writing into a hundred swarming, sweating children ranging in age from toddlers to youngsters of eighteen or twenty. The noise is enough to produce a permanent headache in whoever tries to control it. (From time to time the Reverend Maier does, unexpectedly, darken the doorway, randomly hauls out a few pupils, large, medium-sized and small, and thrashes the hell out of them by way of warning. But the ensuing silence seldom lasts long.)

In the afternoons, this time mercifully assisted by a few helpers who have already assimilated some skills, Gisela gathers the women together under the wide umbrella of a camel-thorn tree to teach them some useful industry: crocheting doilies, embroidering cloths, knitting tea-cosies. It is worse than Frauenstein, thinks Hanna. It makes her stomach turn. Katja can barely restrain a fit of giggles, but she composes herself very hurriedly when the missionary appears with the long stiff-legged strides of a *gompou*.

'Interesting?' he asks benignly. 'My wife has been working very diligently with these uncouth people, teaching them to perform their humble female skills in the service of the Almighty. It may not amount to much, it is of course not directly concerned with the saving of souls, but at least they keep the saved souls occupied. In its own small way, we believe, a woman's work is honourable in the eyes of the Lord.' Briefly, he puts a long bony hand on the girl's shoulder in what purports to be a fatherly gesture. Only for a moment is it perched there, a large pale spider; then, as if scared by what he sees, he hurriedly drops it, vigorously shaking the fingers as if to rid them of some invisible pollution.

Hanna is quick to notice. She doesn't understand what is happening inside her, this welter of suspicions ever since they arrived at the station, a possessiveness about Katja she has not felt before. She tries to persuade herself that the missionary can have no hidden motives, acts purely from altruism, concern and love; that the deviousness and perversity reside in her own mind. Whatever it is, she brusquely takes Katja by the arm and leads her elsewhere.

'What's the matter?' asks the girl.

I want you to be careful of that man.

'He reminds me of my father,' says Katja simply. 'This is so much like the place where I grew up, Hanna. It feels like home.'

Hanna tries to control the indignation she feels. *You don't understand,* she tells her. *I'm sure your father was different. You must keep your eyes open. You are so very young, Katja. For heaven's sake, be careful.*

'I don't think you're being fair,' protests the girl.

Are you with me, or with him?

'Why must I choose?' asks Katja. There is more rebelliousness in her than Hanna has encountered before; and it scares her. 'Of course I'm with you. You were the only one who cared about me when I came to Frauenstein.' She is pleading now. 'I ran away into the desert with you, remember. I don't even know where you're taking me, but it doesn't matter, I trust you. But what I feel about this place . . . Perhaps you cannot understand it, Hanna. Please try. For the first time since my parents and my brothers died, and Gertrud and I . . .' She stops, trembling. 'It really is like coming home again. Almost every single night since the killers came I've had nightmares. Blood everywhere. And men shouting and hacking people to pieces. Here I feel I can sleep again.'

All I'm trying to say . . . Hanna tries again, aware of a headache beginning to throb in her temples.

But they are interrupted. It is Gisela Maier. She approaches and sits down, unbidden, on a low pile of chopped wood.

'Do you mind if I talk to you?' she asks. Her face is wan. Loose strands of hair cling wetly to her cheeks; whether it is from sweat or tears is hard to make out.

You've had a busy day, says Hanna through Katja.

Gisela doesn't react.

'You're working even harder than we used to,' says Katja of her own accord. 'My father's trading post was also a place where people came for all kinds of help. They kept us busy all the time.'

Gisela casts a weary look at her. 'No wonder you ran away.'

'I did not run away! He was murdered. They killed all the men.'

For a moment Gisela does not respond. Then she asks, with flat, tired resentment in her voice, 'What possesses people to come to a place like this?'

'Answering the call of God?' suggests Katja.

'There is no God,' says Gisela flatly. It sounds, thinks Hanna, like someone saying to a begging child, There is no bread.

Then what are you doing here? Hanna prompts Katja to ask.

'Do I have a choice?' She makes an effort to control her voice. Quite unexpectedly a flood of words break out, as if they have been damming inside her for a long time. 'Gottlieb was a different kind of man when we first met in Dresden, fifteen years ago. It was only after his family was wiped out . . .' She pauses. 'They were on a boat on the Elbe. He and his parents and his two sisters. There was a storm, a sudden squall. I would have been there too, but my mother was ill and I stayed to look after her. And then the boat capsized and they were all gone. Gottlieb thought he was also going to drown. He started praying. He'd never been a particularly religious person. It was that experience that changed him. You see, he promised God that if he got out of it alive he'd devote the rest of his life to the work of the Lord. I was a teacher before we got married, I taught history, and when he said he would be going to Africa I was excited at first, I thought it could be interesting, I could find out things about the past . . .' She shakes her head slowly. 'But when we came here he didn't allow me to do anything except keep the house and look after the children. And anyway, the way we live here we're cut off from history, from *everything*. All that matters to him is to keep his vow.' A deep sigh. 'I suppose I cannot blame him.' She rests her chin on her two hands clenched together, stares into the monochrome distance. 'But I hate that God of his. Sometimes I hate him so much I almost think he must be real. But I'm not granted even that small satisfaction.' She takes a deep breath. 'For Gottlieb it is no problem. At least he had a choice. I was never given any.'

Not one of us has had much choice, Hanna reminds her through Katja. *Not me, not Katja either.*

'But now you are free to go as you wish.'

I am not yet free, Hanna conveys to her.

'What do you mean?'

Hanna just shakes her head.

'When are you leaving?' Gisela presses her.

As soon as we have rested.

'If only I could go away with you.' She shakes her head; the ends of her straggly hair swing past her chin. 'But what do I do with the children? If they stay with Gottlieb, God knows what will happen to them.'

'I'm sure he is a good father,' says Katja impulsively.

'What do you know?' Gisela says with listless reproach. 'If only they were not all girls. This is no land for women.'

It does not mean we can let the men have their way, Hanna makes Katja say. A difficult sentence to convey; but by now Katja knows how to round off with canny intuition the gaps of grammar.

'Anything must be better than staying here,' Gisela insists with a kind of numb stubbornness.

If you knew what we're going to do . . . Hanna shakes her head. *If we ourselves could tell* . . . She looks straight at Gisela, her fingers digging into Katja's arm with urgency. *For all we know there may be no end to the bloodshed.* There is the hint of a grim little smile around her misshapen mouth. *But at least no one will stop us.*

A long shadow falls over them; the pastor approaches with the sun directly behind him. They all look up, Hanna grimly, Katja with an energy of expectation, Gisela with apprehension.

'What are the ladies engaged in? Woman talk?' asks the Reverend Maier with as much dour lightness as he can muster. 'Well, enough of frivolity. Let our minds not wander too far from the things of the Lord. It is time for the service. Shall we go and set an example to the poor heathens?'

45

ONCE AGAIN HANNA slips outside into the night to escape the oppressive closeness of the thin house. This time, as a precaution, and suspecting that Katja is also lying awake, she takes the girl with her, taking care not to disturb any of the sleeping children. It is another night ablaze with stars. And again Kahapa looms up from the blackness; perhaps, it occurs to Hanna, he stays close to the house all the time to keep an eye on them. The thought is singularly reassuring.

'What are you doing here?' asks Katja, surprised.

'I wait for you.'

Hanna moves her fingers on Katja's forearm: *He thinks this is a bad place.*

'It is a good place!' Katja objects.

'You are white. For black people it is not good.' He adds with a vehemence he has not showed before: 'This land was a good place before the white people came. We lived everywhere, with all our cattle.'

'You said once your people also came from a far country,' Katja reminds him. 'And not all white people are the same, you know.'

He utters a guttural sound of contempt. Ignoring everything they have said so far, and with an eloquence he has seldom demonstrated before, he launches into a story. Long, long ago, he recalls, in the time when there were no people in the world, there was only the omumborumbonga tree in the middle of the world, at Okahandja. Then the god of the heavens, Njambi Karunga, came to the omumborumbonga tree and he called the first man and the first woman from the hollow of the tree. The man was Mukuru and the woman was Kamungundu. The cattle also came from that tree. Mukuru and Kamungundu slept together and they slept together, and all the Herero people came from them, the god's elect. And when their children grew up, they sacrificed an ox to the god. One of the women took the black liver of the ox for her family and from it came the other black people, the Ovambo and the Ovatyaona. And another woman took the blood of that ox, and from it came the Red People, the Nama. But the sheep and goats the god Njambi Karunga called from underneath a big flat rock. There was a bad Herero girl who ran away from her people and lay down on the flat rock to copulate with it, and from her cunt came the baboons and the Damaras.

Through the shimmering darkness Kahapa looks at them. 'So you see, there is no place for white people here. They come from another place and just make trouble for everybody.'

'This is not the same story you told us last time, about how your people came here,' Katja reminds him. 'About the two brothers at the big tree.'

Kahapa shrugs in the dark. 'We have many stories,' he says, unfazed. 'And they are all true. You must learn to listen right. What I tell you this time is about the trouble the white people bring. Even among themselves. Look what they do to Hanna. Look at that Albert Gruber. Look at the white people of this place.'

'There is nothing wrong with these people,' Katja protests.

'A father who only touch his children to beat them is a bad father,' he says calmly.

'Kahapa!' cries Katja, flustered and angry. 'How can you say a thing like that?'

'You do not see how unhappy his whole family is?'

Katja turns to Hanna: 'Tell him it isn't his fault, Hanna.'

I'm afraid I believe Kahapa, Hanna signals against the skin of her arm.

'You, Hanna,' says Kahapa. 'I understand what you must do in this land. You do what I do to the man that kill my woman. I walk with you. But when it is done you must go back to your home.'

Where is my home? Hanna asks through Katja. *I have no home, Katja has no home. We have only this land to live in. Together with the other people from your omumborumbonga tree.*

Kahapa shakes his head, but says nothing.

'You must go to sleep now,' Katja tells him. There is still hostility in her voice.

Hanna puts an arm around her shoulders. They remain there for a while, until Kahapa has disappeared behind the white blemish of the house on the smooth black skin of the night. Together they turn back.

When they slip through the front door, a black shape detaches itself from the darkness like an errant ghost and comes towards them. It is the missionary.

'I have just come to check that all is well,' he explains. 'You two really should not wander about in the dark.'

In an impulsive rush of emotion Katja throws herself against him, her arms around his neck. 'Thank God you're here to look after us,' she exclaims impulsively, her voice strangled with emotion. 'You are such a good man.'

He remains standing awkwardly, not knowing what to do with his hands. In the faint light from outside only Hanna can see his face. And what she reads there is unexpected: not pleasure, no hint of tenderness, but revulsion, as if he has been assaulted by something sordid and hideous.

'Take your hands off me, you little slut!' he hisses, so loudly that all the breathing in the dark room stops abruptly. 'I will have none of this lewdness. You are a child of the Devil.'

His reaction is so out of proportion to what has happened that it leaves both Katja and Hanna gasping with incomprehension.

Before they can recover he stalks away through the dark; they can hear him tearing open the curtain in the doorway as he rushes into the bedroom. Slowly, hesitantly, studiously, the breathing resumes around them.

Hanna pulls the front door shut. The two of them lie down together. Katja is shaking.

'I just wanted to . . .' she stammers. 'I thought . . . I never meant to . . . It was like hugging my father, but he . . . My God, Hanna, what is going on?'

All Hanna can do is to hold the girl very tightly against her, making low soothing sounds in her throat; but she is conscious of her own heart beating.

'He thought I . . .' Katja begins again. Hanna covers her mouth with her hand but she pushes it away. 'Hanna, I'm not like that! I'm not what he said . . . How could he . . .'

That's enough now, Hanna conveys to her with her fingers moving across her trembling face. *I know you're not like that.* A silence. *But to him it makes no difference.* She breathes in long and deeply. *I'm afraid he is just like those other men who came to Frauenstein. And the ones that punished me on the train.*

'I can't believe it. He always talks about God.'

He has to. Because he is scared of himself. Deep down he is no different.

Next door, beyond the thin curtain, the now familiar rhythms of the dark begin again.

46

HANNA CANNOT SHAKE off the memory of that German woman and her piano in the wilderness. Was she brought out, like Hanna herself, in expectation of a new life, a place to live, a place with palm trees? For a piano to survive the voyage by sea, the train journey, the trek through the desert – dear God, it must be almost more unlikely than for a woman. When she herself came out she had only her magic shell with her; and even that she's lost. Only the memory of a sound has lingered, like something dreamt. That woman, now lost too, buried in an unmarked grave, brought her sound with her. Now smashed to pieces. They would both of them have fared better with Opa's mute instrument. This terrible land.

47

IMAGINE HANNA SITTING in the narrow shade of the wall, staring out into the arrogant light which is beating down on the desert landscape as if it has the sole right to be there; as if no shade or darkness has a purchase on existence. In the distance the men of the settlement are toiling, as they do every goddamned day, heaving stone upon stone to add to the greater glory of God and his humble servant. Soon, she knows, she will have to move on. They could do with a few more days of rest – Kahapa, in particular, has not quite recovered his strength – but an uneasiness has been building up inside her, and in him. Katja, especially, has been showing signs of distress ever since the night she had the emotional encounter with Gottlieb Maier. At the same time there is a shadow of reluctance in Hanna's mind. If the missionary has whetted her resolve, honing the hate in her to an even keener steel, the knowledge of what lies ahead cannot but contain a sad fear as well. Not because of what awaits *her*, for she has been prepared to face it since they left Frauenstein, but for what it may demand of Katja.

It is not the violence as such that intimidates her, nor the pain it inflicts. It is rather the denial inherent to it: the threat it poses to whatever that strange, secret thing may be she would like to think of as 'human'. The horror perpetrated by that man – those men – on the train: yes, of course it cries out to be avenged. In the name of being human. But if she sets out to avenge that, is there anything in herself which is not placed in jeopardy? Is it possible to destroy another without destroying at least something in oneself? Can blood be redeemed by blood alone?

She has not heard Katja approaching and looks up, startled, when the girl comes up from behind, carrying a bible in her hand.

Hanna raises her hands in a gesture of questioning: *What are you doing here? I thought you were helping Gisela with her classes.*

'I couldn't take it any more. Do you know what that man had ordered her to teach the children today?' She opens the book where a pencil protrudes from the pages. 'The story of Noah and his sons. You know the bit about Ham, the father of Canaan, who sees the old man lying naked in a drunken stupor, and then telling his brothers about it, and then they walk backward into the tent to cover him up?'

Hanna shrugs, vaguely amused.

Katja starts reading in a voice quivering with rage, stabbing at the words with her pencil: *'And Noah awoke from his wine and knew what his younger son had done unto him. And he said, Cursed be Canaan: a servant of servants shall he be unto his brethren.'*

What is that to you? Hanna gesticulates.

'The pastor insisted that Gisela tell the children that because they're black they're the descendants of Ham or Canaan or whoever and that is why they've now got to slave for us. If you ask me, it's because a few of the men started complaining about working on this bloody wall. So now the wrath of God and all his angels have to be called in to keep them in their place. Even if he has to call in the Bible to help. I mean, where in this piece does it say that Ham was black? Suppose he was, how did Noah manage to have two white sons and one black? And who was the sinner anyway? The old drunken bastard or the son who just happened to find him snoring in his tent, covered in his own vomit, most likely? And if that really was supposed to be wrong, why not go for Ham himself? Why hit on Canaan who wasn't anywhere near, as far as I can make out?

Hanna reaches up to take the girl's hand. *Why should you let that upset you?* she wants to know, making small smooting motions with her fingers. *Just ignore it.*

'But Gisela is upset too,' Katja insists. 'And she has no choice.' She shakes her head. 'I suppose I should hve stayed to give her some support. But I just couldn't take it any more.' She makes an attempt to control herself. 'I don't know how she manages. She isn't strong. And all those children. Now her baby is sick too.'

You're working too hard.

'It's better to be busy.' She sits down next to Hanna and flings the black bible into the thin film of powdery grey dust which covers the rock-hard earth. 'Perhaps, you know, I'm trying to make up for all the times I didn't help my mother. Gertrud and I' – she seldom mentions her sister; there is obviously much she still has not come to terms with – 'we were both very disobedient, fractious. The trading post was such a lonely place for us.' A long silence. 'You know, my mother loved music. She had quite a good voice and would often sing to us. Hymns and things, mostly. But sometimes other songs, lighthearted and gay and sunshiny songs. I thought of her that day in the Grubers' farmhouse when they broke the piano: it was such an incredible sound. Like an explosion. As if all the sounds the piano had ever made, all the sounds it was capable of making, suddenly broke out together. And then the terrible silence afterwards. All that sound – gone. But where has it gone to? It must still be somewhere. If only one could find it. And Mother's singing too. All the music of our lives. I often lie awake at night thinking about it, wondering, and I understand nothing of it at all.'

I think you were forced to be a grownup much too soon.

'They did what they could. So did I.' Her voice is infused with a new passion. 'When we came to this place – I told you before – it was, in a way, like coming home. I remembered so many things from the time we were all together: Father, Mother, Gerhardt, Rolf, Gertrud and me. Mother's singing and everything. Mainly because this man, Reverend Maier, reminded me so strongly . . .' She chokes, takes time to compose herself. 'My father was such a gentle man, he meant everything to me, I loved him. Then the other night when I saw what the good missionary was really like . . . Hanna, it was as if all my deepest memories suddenly became lies. Suppose the father I knew was not the same man other people saw? Suppose he did the same things as the other traders the Hereros feared and hated so much – giving them credit and credit and credit, all the time, until they couldn't pay any more and then taking their cattle, their land . . . How will I ever know? All I know is that I cannot trust my own memories any more. Everything that used to be good, and important to me . . . Now there's nothing I can be sure of. And I'm just angry. I've never been so angry before. I want to do something. But what could I possibly do that would make any difference?'

Hanna looks hard at her. After a long time she starts moving her hands again to ask, *Are you sure you made the right choice when you came with me?*

Katja sniffs angrily, wipes tears across her scorched face. 'I couldn't stay in that place.'

But now that we have left it . . . ?

'Where are we going, Hanna?' Katja asks with sudden directness.

Hanna makes a gesture towards her scarred face, then lapses into silence again, trying to order her thoughts.

'You want to take revenge on the man who did that to you, I know. I understand that. But that was more than four years ago, wasn't it? What are the chances he'll still be in Windhoek? And even if he were . . . Once you've taken your revenge, what then? Will it be over? Will you have made peace with yourself?

Hanna puts her hand on Katja's to silence the girl. For a moment she looks round, searching, anxious to find a way out of her own muteness; then she sets to preparing a small square patch of ground, stroking and patting it with the palm of one hand. She finds a twig and starts scribbling hurriedly. But the cover of dust is too spare, the earth too hard, and the scratches remain near-indecipherable. In a rage of frustration she looks about her again, then notices the bible Katja has dropped on the ground and picks it up, puts it on her lap. In a fever of eagerness she takes out the pencil still stuck between the pages of Genesis and begins to flip through the heavy book, past the whole of the Old Testament with its bloody histories and its genealogies and its bleak curses and enhortations and imprecations, and past the New (which is not nearly as dog-eared and fingered and worn as the Old), past all the dire prophecies and visions of Revelations, to the blank pages at the very end. She glances up at Katja, and begins to write. I

Why do you keep on talking about revenge, Katja? It is not just revenge.

That too, of course. He cannot be allowed to get away with it. But it's so much more. You must believe me. You've seen for yourself, in Frauenstein, and even here in this place how many have been maimed. Not necessarily in the same way, not always so visible, but all of us harmed. Scarred. And for as long as we bear it in silence it will go on. There will always be new ones to suffer. There has been too much suffering already. There comes a time when one has got to say No. Someone has to stop it. And the world must know about it, they must learn what has been done to us, they must know our names.

She shoves the book across her knees for the girl to read. Her fingers are stiff and cramped, she is no longer used to writing. But she hasn't finished yet. When Katja looks up, opening her mouth to say something, Hanna grabs the book back, tears out a single page, and resumes on the next.

It's like what you said about the piano, remember? Those sounds are still somewhere. We are somewhere. And someone must find out about us and hear our sounds.

Katja has risen on her knees to read over her shoulder. Hanna stares out across the desert, makes a wide empty gesture towards it, and starts writing again, pressing so hard that the point of the pencil stabs holes in the paper.

Look at this desert, with its stones and its little bushes and its silences. It does not need me, it will be here long after I have gone. But I don't want it to forget about me. **I was here!** *You are here. I want this place to know about us. That is why we're going to Windhoek, don't you understand? And we must take with us all the others who have also suffered and who have also forgotten the need to say No.*

She drops the pencil and pauses to pick it up.

So you see, it is not just the one man we are looking for, she writes, the letters now thicker and smudgier than before as the point grows blunter. *Our hunt is on now. To find everybody who has joined forces with that man. Everybody who has made him possible.*

Incredulous, dazed, Katja moves her palm across the page as if to erase the words. 'How can you do that?' she asks, almost with awe. 'One woman – against the whole of the German Reich?' She shakes her head silently. 'Against the world?'

Hanna tears out the second page, coaxing the pencil stub into writing a few last words on the third: *If we move as an army against them*, she writes, *they will destroy us. But there is no need to fight an ordinary kind of war. We'll do it slowly, bit by bit. But in the end we shall prevail. Because I'm not alone. Never forget that. We are not alone.*

They sit in silence for a long time. Then Katja reaches for the bible to tear out the last page. She picks up the book.

Katja takes it from her. 'I must return this to the church,' she says. 'He will kill us if he finds out.'

Hanna crumples the pages she has torn out and stuffs them into the bodice of her dress; she will burn them later.

Katja makes to go, then comes back, and bends over, and presses her cheek against Hanna's. Perhaps she has understood after all. '

48

IN THE LATE afternoon they find themselves behind the stocky little church, where they have fled to escape the incessant wailing of the sick baby. Gottlieb Maier has refused the help they offered, arguing emphatically that one is expected to show fortitude in the face of adversity sent to test the faithful. 'It is probably something Gisela has eaten which has corrupted her milk,' he said, casting a reproachful glance at his wife. 'Now it is in the hands of God. I shall pray, and he will respond as he sees fit.' He has also turned away, much more testily, the Nama women who came to offer their arcane brews and philtres: 'Heathen superstition! Not only will they harm the child, but they'll offend the nostrils of the Lord.'

Hanna has to let off steam. *That man is a monster.*

But Katja is more pensive. 'You know,' she says cautiously, 'I've been thinking about what you said the other night. Why he is always so frantically busy. It's not just because it's his work. Or that he's scared of himself, as you said. I think it is worse. It's as if he's covering up, as if he's trying to make himself believe. Suppose, like Gisela, he doesn't really believe in God either. But because of his vow he's now got to spend the rest of his life in Africa. And perhaps he hates every moment of it. But there's no way he can ever get out of it.'

That is no reason to make others pay for it, Hanna reminds her. His wife. His children. Everybody. Perhaps that was why he needed the story of Noah to control his grumbling workers too.

Kahapa appears round the corner of the church to join them. There is a small group of people with him, nine or ten, men and women.

'I bring this people,' he says to Hanna. 'They want to go with us.'

Do they know where we are going?

'I tell them Windhoek. I tell them it is to fight, it is a hard thing to do.'

And why would they want to give up the life they have here to go with us?

Kahapa nudges the first of the group forward, a tall and somewhat surly young man. 'You tell her,' he instructs the man.

He doesn't have much to say, though. He comes from the far north, the Kaokoveld – the only moments when he waxes eloquent is when he starts talking about the great ana trees on the banks of the broad river on its way to the cold sea, and the wild hills and the dark patches of bush in the folds of the valleys, the magical spring of Kaoko Otavi where the elephants gather to drink in the moonlight; and his proud people who live there, the Ovahimbas, their tall bodies plastered with red ochre – but the ripple effects of the war these last ten years have disturbed the peaceful life his tribe had known for centuries, so some of them started trickling south, ever further, in search of employment; and unable to find anything stable or permanent (how could a proud man be content to work for strangers?), he ended up here at the mission station. But he dislikes the pastor and hates the work, and now he wants to go back to his own country. Windhoek will be a convenient stop on the long road home.

Tell him I'll think about it, announces Hanna. But as soon as the Ovahimba has left, she tells Kahapa through Katja, *No, this is not enough for us. He will go with us and then leave us when it suits him. We need people who will stay with us all the way.*

'I already tell him.' Kahapa nods approvingly. 'But he will not believe me.'

Several of the others are also turned down – among them a young woman whose main purpose is to find a husband in Windhoek; two pleasant and jocular Ovambos who have simply had enough of hard work; a middle-aged woman anxious to visit relatives in the north; a chronically smiling, very black Damara who can remember his father and grandfather meekly slaving for any master who came along, whether Ovambo, Herero, Nama or white, and who is willing to accept any new employment as long as he does not have to reason why; a beautiful muscular specimen of a man (though not quite as massive as Kahapa) who is eager to avenge a great number of atrocities in his past on the German occupiers. This sounds promising indeed, Hanna thinks. But then it turns out that while he will be happy to take orders from Kahapa, he will not defer to a woman. And that rules out his candidacy. In the end, after consulting with both Katja and Kahapa, Hanna accepts only three of the applicants.

The first is a Nama woman of uncertain age, wizened and emaciated, her breasts mere flaps of crumpled skin, flimsily covered with a tattered cloth imposed on her by the rigid religiosity of the place. Her name is Kamma, which, she says, means 'Water'. She is introduced by Kahapa as a medicine woman. Her tribe, Hanna learns, lives in a place called by the impossible and beautiful name of Otjihaenemaparero, where she built a reputation, like her mother and grandmother before her, as a healer. No one knows the herbs and secrets of the veld like she does. People used to come to her from as far as two or three full moons away. She healed them all. A few times, she assures them, and it is difficult to doubt her, she even brought back to life people who had already died. Then one day, about a year ago now, she – literally – got wind of a sick German *smous* stranded in the desert with his ox-wagon loaded with goods. He had been bitten by a snake and his whole body had swollen up so badly that he was close to death. But Kamma cut open the wound, sucked out the venom, and set to her task with potions and unguents and chanted incantations. And within a day the man could sit up and take his first food. He took her with him to Otjihaenemaparero on his wagon and distributed most of his merchandise among the tribe members.

Everybody was elated. Until he made it clear that he intended to take Kamma back to Windhoek with him. In the course of long deliberations that lasted through days and nights (the tribe's customary politeness practically prohibiting anyone to say no to a stranger) it transpired that he expected to become rich through Kamma's professional skills. Whereupon his offer was turned down. On learning this, the foreigner lost his temper and in an attempt to cut the Gordian knot he grabbed his guns and started firing at the tribe. They retaliated in their own way. Bristling with arrows like a porcupine the German fell down.

Kamma set about repairing as much of the damage as she could. But there was a sad end to it all. However much her services were needed by her people, the tribe could no longer afford to keep her. This kind of incident had a way of propagating itself, no doubt with the help of the wind; some time, sooner or later, they believed implicitly, a commando would be sent out from Windhoek to retaliate. Kamma had to be banished before that could happen. Amid loud lamenting from all sides she was expelled from the place with the magical name of Otjihaenemaparero. And after moons and moons of travelling, here she is. Safe, but burning with anger. All she wants now is revenge.

She will come with us, Hanna decides; and Katja and Kahapa concur without protest.

Then there is the Ovambo warrior, Himba. He, too, has a chequered career behind him. No longer a young man, he has, however, a formidable physique; his whole body bears the scars of innumerable battles and he walks with a slight limp, which Kahapa swears does not prevent him from travelling faster than most men can run, for days on end, without food or water. After the death of his father in a skirmish with a German patrol when he was still a youngster, he collected around him a band of hand-picked warriors and took an oath not to rest before the last foreigner had been driven from the land. But as the years went by he just saw more and more foreigners making their appearance – from the sea in the west, from the land of the Bechuana in the east, Boers from the south, occasionally even from Angola in the north. One by one his men disappeared from his side: most killed by the enemy, others falling prey to illness or predators, a few deserting to find an easier life elsewhere. Only when Himba was left behind on his own, did he grudgingly consent to retire. He took two young wives, fathered several children, and seemed at last to succumb to the easy pleasures of domesticity. But barely a year ago, soon after the outbreak of the new war which is still raging in the land, the remote settlement to which he had retired was overrun by the occupying army. They had no specific quarrel to pick with this village. But inspired by the merciless Lothar von Trotha the soldiers, heading towards the restive Nama armies in the south, sacked the small place of peace, killing everything that lived and breathed – dogs, chickens, pigs, cattle, goats and people – including Himba's wives and all his children. With only two companions he managed to get away on a moonless night. For weeks they wandered about, intent only on avoiding all enemies along the way. One of his companions was killed by a scorpion, the other was trampled by a solitary elephant bull at a water-hole. In the end Himba reached the mission station on his own. But this will be no more than a temporary halt, he assures them, an ancient fire smouldering in his throat. He is just waiting for the chance to go to war again. And this time only a knife, a bullet, or a bayonet will stop him.

He, too, is hired without more ado.

The third recruit elicits more discussion. He is a Nama. His name is Tookwi, which he explains means a thunderstorm. It seems he was born in a heavy downpour; and perhaps as a result he became the rainmaker of his tribe. A curious phenomenon, he tells them with evident pride, is that it often rained only on the spot where his people happened to find themselves at the time, nowhere else. So there would be drought and scorched earth for as far as the eye could see, and one small green patch in the middle of it all. There are many different ways of calling the rain, he explains to them. Small white pebbles can be buried in the veld with the chanting of special songs to the god of the Red Dawn, Tsui-Goab. Or the whole tribe can join in a rain dance under the full moon, singing the song of the girl Xurisib who defied Tsui-Goab. (The memory of the story she first heard in Xareb's tribe awakens a small pang of nostalgia in Hanna.) There are other remedies too, Tookwi says, but most of them are very secret.

For years he performed his rites for his tribe, and they prospered. But times grew worse. More and more of the young men moved away to work for white farmers – Boers who approached from the Cape Colony, or Germans on the Khomas Highland near Windhoek. They would still return to the tribe from time to time, but they were not the same people who had left. They brought new customs with them, new clothes, some got involved in gun-running. The young ones started jeering at Tookwi and persuaded others to abandon him too, calling his rites tomfoolery or superstition. And Tookwi found that, faced with their taunts, his magic would no longer work as potently as before. Browbeaten by a powerful faction of young men, the tribe expelled him. He started wandering through the desert on his own like an animal driven out by the herd. After years of loneliness he came to this place, in need of human company, even though he felt aggrieved by the customs and superstitions of the Christians. All this time his sadness has been nourished by anger: anger at the Germans who have changed the old way of life and driven him away from the only people with whom he belonged. That is why he now wants to join Hanna's little band.

Feeling genuine pity for the wiry little man, she is eager to accept him, but Katja is sceptical, Kahapa openly hostile. 'He will just be a nuisance,' he says. 'There's nothing he can really do to help us.'

Hanna puts her hand on Katja's arm in the old gesture of familiarity and resolution. *Tell him we feel pity for him. But we are not sure he can really be useful to us. Ask him what he can do to persuade us.*

'I can make rain for you,' Tookwi offers without hesitation.

'When?' asks Katja, unprompted.

'Tonight, if you wish,' says Tookwi.

Involuntarily they all look up. Above them, even at this hour of the afternoon, the sky is still white with rage, the sun like a blister in the shimmering expanse.

'The only thing is,' says Tookwi in a tone of warning, 'Tsui-Goab will not be mocked. He will send rain but he will also demand a sacrifice.'

'What will that be?' asks Kahapa.

'It is for him to decide.'

Hanna glances at the others, then nods.

'Then the rain will come tonight,' says Tookwi calmly, picking up the collection of little bags, tortoise shells and skins he has brought with him.

49

IT BEGINS AS another stifling night in the long narrow front room of the parsonage. The interminable wailing of the sick baby in the bedroom next door, behind the curtain, pierces the deepest darkest corners of mind and memory. The children are all awake, lying tense and straight on their thin reed mats, no one daring to utter a sound as they breathe and sweat in silence. There is no way of telling the time. At a given moment, quite unexpectedly, there is an angry outburst in the missionary's deep booming voice in the bedroom, followed by the unmistakable sound of a slap. The child starts screaming blue murder. Hanna can bear it no longer. She sits up on her mat and puts out a hand to open the door. She can feel all the children stiffening in the dark but pays no attention. There is no need to alert Katja: by the time Hanna steps barefoot on to the hard naked ground outside the girl is already with her.

The others are gathered behind the stern little church. Kahapa is there, and Tookwi of course, and their two new followers; but also the rest of the congregation, man, woman and child, it would seem. Whether they have been summoned, or whether the news has reached them by some occult nocturnal osmosis, is impossible to tell. There is a sense of subdued excitement: no distinct individual sound, even the children are quiet — only something like a bundled-up hush, as if the night itself has tensed its secret muscles as it contracts and waits.

Everybody seems to have been expecting Hanna and Katja to appear. They make way for the woman and the girl to find a place in the front row. Tookwi nods in their direction, and kneels in the small clearing left in the middle of the crowd, where he starts scraping away soil with what may be a flat shard of flint or a piece of tortoise shell. It takes a long time as the ground is as hard as stone. Everybody waits patiently. At last Tookwi appears to be satisfied with the long narrow hollow he has scooped out. Into it he drops a thin, limp object.

'Snake,' he explains briefly, as he catches Hanna's quizzical look. '*Geelslang.* A yellow cobra. I was lucky, I found it this afternoon.'

'Is it dead?' asks Katja cautiously, having glimpsed a tremor in the snake's long body.

'No, not quite. There must be some life left so it can call the rain.'

'Can you use any snake for it?' asks Katja.

'No, no, just the cobra. Because it is yellow like fire, like the lightning which is its sister. It must call the rain from up there down to the earth below.'

The cobra is stretched out full length on its back in the shallow trench. As he begins to cover it with the soil he has dug out, Tookwi intones in a low voice a long chant composed, it seems, exclusively of gutturals, sibilants and clicks. When he is done he looks up again and translates briefly:

'O Heiseb, our forefather!
Send good luck to me.
Give into my hand the rain of your sky.
Let us soon enjoy honeycomb and sweet roots
And I will sing your praise.
Are you not our father's father,
You who are Heiseb?'

It is, he explains, a hunting song adapted to the purposes of calling the rain. Then, falling silent again, all concentration, he takes from his bundle a long bow-shaped instrument which Hanna recognises from her stay with the Nama tribe: a *ghura,* a primitive wind-harp on which he blows as he plucks the single string to coax from it an endlessly repetitive hint of melody. In principle, if not in shape, she thinks with a touch of wry amusement, it is not far removed from the soundless instrument devised so many years ago by her gentle employer Opa.

Round and round the flattened mound where the cobra lies buried,

Tookwi moves, swaying gently on his reed-stalks of legs to the rhythm of his soporific melody.

'I hope he doesn't go on until the rain comes,' Katja whispers to Hanna, 'for then we'll be here for weeks.'

The rest of the crowd still waits in a hush, spellbound.

After some time Tookwi comes to a standstill astride the flattened mound. He looks at his audience.

'What I need now,' he says, 'is for a woman who has never known a man to piss on the grave.'

Everybody waits in earnest silence.

'I'll do it,' announces Katja suddenly.

Hanna tries to hold her back. *Not in front of all these people*, she signals. *You cannot humiliate yourself like that.*

'No one will even see,' says Katja. 'It is too dark.'

Shaking off Hanna's hand the girl steps forward towards old Tookwi.

'Now take off your clothes,' he says, his voice barely audible.

This makes Katja hesitate. But then she shrugs. It is indeed very dark; and there is no hint of lewdness in the procedure. On the contrary.

Still, Hanna tenses somewhat as she discerns from the vague movements in the darkness in front of her that Katja is indeed stripping off her dress, stepping out of her underclothes, untying her shoes. Without bidding, all the men in the crowd have silently turned their backs on her to show respect, while Tookwi has moved to one side. Katja squats over the cobra's grave. There is a slight hissing sound as her urine sprays the grave, a brief glint of wetness as the jet is caught in the faint light of the stars – the striding Hunter, the Southern Cross, the seven lights of Khuseti, Tsaob's arc of glimmering embers – a hint of frothiness on the black ground, before it is absorbed and disappears.

A very old memory stirs in Hanna's mind, bringing with it a pang of loss: that day on the narrow strip of beach along the river when the little girl from Ireland helped her to scoop a small dam from the sand so that she could pee in it; the day of the shell, the rustle of silence. And she knows, as she peers through the darkness at the squatting Katja, that she is still obsessed by the same silence; but at least, at last, she has now a clearer notion of where she is going, of being on the way there. To the end of her days that small person will give meaning to her life, a sense of direction.

Her pale body opalescent in the night, Katja gets up, stoops to retrieve her clothes, and returns to Hanna who helps her to get dressed again.

Now what? she wonders.

'Now we dance again,' announces Tookwi, as if he has read her thoughts. 'But we must do it very slowly, otherwise we wake up the rain-bull and that is not good. We must call the rain-cow who comes gently to soften the ground, so that it may be wet inside the earth, like the wetness of a woman who loves. If the bull wakes up it is too much noise.' He resumes his slow-motion dancing gait around the spot where the cobra has been buried, but this time he has a kind of flat tambourine in one hand – his *t'koi-t'koi*, no more than a hairless skin stretched tightly across a ring of bent wood or reeds – which he raps with the palm of the other, a slow rhythmic tam-tam, tam-tam, tam-tam, without variation, only growing steadily louder, more urgent. And the Namas in the congregation start murmuring, spontaneously, to the same cadence; the other people are drawn in as well, until even Katja and Hanna find themselves humming, tam-tam, tam-tam, tam-tam.

For how long it would have gone on is impossible to tell; but at some stage there is an unexpected interruption: a tall gaunt shadow taking shape from the night, a smudge of ink against the sky, blackest black on black. It is the Reverend Gottlieb Maier.

'What is going on here?' his deep voice booms in the background as he comes striding through the people, pushing them this way and that, until he is standing in the open spot right in the middle. Peering at the women, he asks in shock, 'You too, sister Hanna? Little sister Katja? What heathen ceremony are you taking part in, in a sacred place like this?'

'We are making rain,' says Katja is a quiet but steady voice.

'This is preposterous!' the missionary explodes. 'All these years I have been devoting my life to the struggle against the forces of superstition and evil among the black heathens. Now I must find that white women have joined the enemy.'

From all sides there are voices protesting from the assembled crowd; a few babies start crying. It has grown very dark indeed.

Kahapa pushes his way through the people who are beginning to edge away from the scene. He is barely visible in the night, only a sound thundering in their midst: 'Who are you to tell us what is good, what is bad?' He pauses; the silence is like rock walls caving in on them from all sides. 'You are a godless man.'

'God will smite you with his wrath!' shouts the pastor, beside himself.

At that moment, altogether unexpectedly, the rain begins to fall. It is hardly more than a drizzle, a rustling over the earth as if a large soft kaross is gently dragged across the dry surface.

For a moment the people are silent. Then there is an eruption of sound: shouts of fear and dread from some, jubilation and amazement from others.

'There is the rain,' pipes Tookwi in his small reedy voice.

No one seems in a hurry to find shelter. Instead, they respond to an atavistic and childlike urge in them to throw off their clothes, to soak up the unexpected wetness as the earth does, through their skins, deep into their bodies.

In the communal silence Katja says, prompted by Hanna, 'It is good. Tookwi, you will go with us.'

'I don't want to see any of your unchristian band defiling my station for one more day!' shouts Herr Maier. 'God himself is insulted by your presence.'

'We have brought you rain,' Katja reminds him. 'Is that not a sign that God has given us his blessing?'

The man of God stands heaving in the dark. The rain is coming down harder now. Instead of exploding again, as they all expect, the gaunt man gasps in a deep breath. 'It is not rain you have brought,' he hisses, 'but lewdness and ungodliness.' He turns on his heel and begins to stride back to the parsonage where a tentative rectangle of orange light spills through the open door.

For some reason Hanna and Katja follow him.

They are met by Gisela on the doorstep, clutching a small bundle in her arms.

'The child is dead,' she says.

50

IN A LARGELY ineffectual battle against the rock-hard earth (for the
rain penetrated no more than a few inches into that recalcitrant soil),
the men labour for nearly two days to make a dent in the form of
a shallow grave in the small enclosure reserved for white people,
away from the already overpopulated graveyard for members of the
congregation. It will be the first burial in that restricted place. Two
almost unbearable days spent mostly in prayer and droning readings
from Scripture. The children huddle dumbly in church or front
room, forbidden to indulge in any form of mourning, which the
father regards as signs of questioning the will of the Lord. Only
Gisela refuses to stir from the conjugal bed where she lies prostrate,
without eating or drinking, staring mutely at the beams that support
the roof of reeds and thatch.

She only gets up, as if sleepwalking, when she is summoned to the
funeral. The service is held in the church and lasts even longer than
usual; after the last melancholy wail of the hymn has been drawn
out for as long as it can be made to stretch without snapping,
the congregation proceeds to the grave. Gottlieb Maier leads the
procession outside, carrying the small coffin fashioned from a crate
in which flour was once delivered from Windhoek. The box is laid
in the shallow hole. There is, inevitably, another reading from the
Bible to which no one seems to be paying attention – something
from the Psalms, rejoicing in the wonders of the Lord – and another
prayer, followed by a thin hymn struggling to trail its way upward
like an ineffectual plume of smoke into the angry sky. There are the
immemorial words – *The Lord giveth, the Lord taketh away, blessed be the*

name of the Lord – and then the long body of the pastor stoops down to pick up a handful of earth and drop it into the grave. He waits for Gisela to follow suit, but she doesn't move, doesn't even seem to be aware of what is going on. He nudges her in the side. No reaction. Another nudge, this time so forceful that she loses her balance and nearly falls. She glances at him blankly. Muttering something under his breath he nods at the oldest girl to proceed, followed by all the others. Then the guests. Then the members of the congregation.

Disconsolate, they disperse under the sun. The clouds that brought the rain have long gone. Already the entire episode seems unreal.

The following day life at the station resumes its predestined course. The men go out again to work on the wall. But Gisela does not get up to teach the children and lead the women in their domestic drill; instead, her oldest daughter slips quietly into her place. The girl seems to have become, overnight, much older than her years, and her hunched shoulders and drawn face are, now, indicative more of age than of the embarrassments of adolescence.

Preparations for the departure of Hanna's trek begin in earnest; the missionary has reiterated his decision that their godless practices will not be tolerated in his vale of grace any longer. To remove any shadow of doubt about his attitude, from now on only a thin tasteless broth will be served to the visitors at mealtimes; they have come a long way from the abundance of that first supper. Trying to conceal from his febrile gaze their pangs of hunger they concentrate on the work at hand. Provisions are sorted, considered, loaded. The selection of recruits is finalised. In addition to the three chosen earlier, are a few new ones who presented themselves during the morning following Tookwi's rain. Two of them are refugees from Albert Gruber's farm – T'Kamkhab, 'rescued' years ago from certain death by the army in the desert where he had been left to die, one of twins, and then kept by the soldiers as a mascot, and given more beatings than food until he escaped many years later and ended up with Gruber; and his wife Nerina, whose spit is said to be more venomous than that of a puff-adder. In her youth she was abducted from her people by a police patrol who used her as their common whore; twice she forced abortions on herself to rid her of their offspring, and the second time was so bad that she could never have children again. The third new recruit is a woman who calls herself Koo, which means Death, and who drifted, half-crazed, to the mission after her only son had been abducted by soldiers when during a raid on her Nama village she'd refused to disclose to them the whereabouts of the men of her tribe. She knew they were going to kill the boy – the long terrible process had already begun before they left – and there has never been news of him again. But she will not rest, she swears in a sepulchral voice, before her eyes have seen his bones.

Now, at last, they are on their way, with their oxcart, into the desert. They have kept only the two oxen they need to pull it; the other cattle and goats and chickens they brought from Albert Gruber's farm have been left behind at the mission station; and the labourers not selected by Hanna, Katja and Kahapa will also remain there, prematurely stunned by the prospect of enforced salvation as members of the missionary's abject congregation.

As they are trekking due north, the early sun casts the dark shadow of the meaningless wall over them for the first lap of their journey. The whole settlement is assembled to see them off; in the forefront is the Reverend Gottlieb Maier and his skinny brood, silent, motionless. Occasionally some of the women and children from the congregation break into ululation, song or dance; here and there a wisp of coloured cloth flutters dispiritedly; the more morose figures of the men from time to time wave after them, their deep voices a rumble difficult to fathom. But at every new outbreak of sound or movement a single glance from the man of God is enough to impose order on the latent energies of the crowd.

Hanna is following the cart on foot, dragging one leg as is her wont, with Katja at her side. The rainmaker Tookwi leads the oxen; Kahapa marches beside them, brandishing a long whip. Abreast with him, on the other side of the small team, walks the battle-scarred warrior Himba. On the back of the cart sits the medicine woman Kamma. The others trundle along on either side of the cart. They do not look like an army.

Hanna is still brooding on the events of the last few days and how they have marked her, like everything that has happened since they left

Frauenstein. Unlike the snake skin she found in the desert, she thinks, she carries her sloughs with her, all her past lives, her accumulated deaths. What lies ahead, not even God knows.

But before they are very far from the mission station, the wall still on their right, there is a commotion behind them. There seems to be a scuffle going on just outside the gate. From the oxcart they can hear voices shouting in anger, the screams of a woman. And then, as they watch, the woman appears to break loose from the crowd and comes running towards the cart.

'It is Gisela!' Katja exclaims and darts off to meet her.

Far in the background another figure detaches himself from the churning group. It is the missionary himself. He is waving at them, shouting.

'Go to hell!' they can make out.

Gisela hurls herself against Katja. Her face is streaked with tears, in which the dust has formed smudges of dirt. Her breath comes in furious gasps.

Hanna brings an earthenware jar of water from the cart. Even then it takes some time before the agitated woman can speak. At last, looking imploringly at Hanna, she says, 'I want to come with you.'

'But your children?' protests Katja, shocked.

'My baby is dead. There's nothing I can do for the others anyway. He will not let me.'

In the distance the man of God is still standing, straight and tall, unmoving now, like a black scarecrow in the sun, one arm outstretched towards them in a silent apocalyptic curse.

Hanna puts her arm around Gisela's shoulders. *Let us go*, she motions. Thinking: *Let us all go to hell together. Hate will show us the way.*

51

THE SUDDENNESS OF seasons. The gentle rain – indeed, as Tookwi has foretold, a rain-cow rain that touched the earth with female moisture – has made a difference. Although only a few days have elapsed there is already a hint of green on the veld, and a myriad of flowers have sprung miraculously from the parched soil, in extravagant patches of yellow, orange, white and purple. The once unforgiving landscape appears less intractable. In the evenings there is already the slightest shiver of coolness in the air, and they find that they draw closer to the fire not just because it keeps predators and scavengers at bay (every night, as soon as the dark closes in, the maniacal cackling of jackals erupts) but because they have come to cherish the warmth.

It is the second night after they have left the mission station and Hanna is sitting in the thin circle of light surrounding the fire, but slightly apart from the rest. They are surrounded by emptiness. There seems to be no living creature left in this land under the sun or the moon.

One after the other she studies the faces in the erratic light of the flames. Katja, so achingly young, the smooth face framed in long blonde hair, as yet unmarked by what she has already experienced in her life. Gisela, old before her time, worn out by childbirth and the abuse of religion and her husband. The medicine woman Kamma, toothless and wise, little more than a small skull covered in wrinkled skin and tufts of hair, gimlet eyes staring grimly into the fire, where she seems to see what no one else can dream of. Old Tookwi, like a mantis absorbed in meditation. T'Kamkhab, who has come to look like the pert, angry monkey he was trained to be for the soldiers. His strong but bitter wife Nerina, her broad face quietly brooding over the rage she has sealed up inside her, with a lasting resentment against the world that has made her barren. And the woman of death, Koo, scowling at the memory of a son who disappeared without leaving a footprint or a bone behind. And then the two men who close the circle: the lame warrior Himba, his light-brown face scarred with ancient wounds; and the giant Kahapa, towering over all the others, his beautiful but stern face closed like a mask carved from very dark very smooth wood, wearing day and night the incongruous hat of the man who killed his wife and tried to kill him too. What on earth, she wonders with a small shudder, could have scooped up from the dregs and rejects of this godforsaken land such a disparate little band? Can it really be only hate? Or is there, behind the hate, something else, a smouldering force of life that refuses to be denied any longer? So many things, ultimately; and also the sound of the wind.

Lightly, lightly, it blows across the vast wilderness in which they find themselves, stirring in the dry grass, shivering like the breath of ghosts against their cheeks; and then moves on into what seems in the dark like emptiness but isn't. Past the fire and past the faces she stares into it, invisible but unavoidable. Such an ancient landscape, older than anything people could have thought up. And reassuring for that reason. It has its own memory; perhaps is memory itself, turned to stone. Bits of it may be shared by the Namas, the Hereros, the Ovambos, lurking in the stories she has heard. But most of it remains ungraspable, secret, remote. It teases and challenges – yet it instils a profound confidence precisely because nothing about it is easy or immediately accessible, however much it may seem reduced to elements and essentials.

How much of herself will be left behind in this place? What will it remember of her? Once again, as many times before, the thought brings a stirring of unease. She turns her head to look at Katja, whose face is obscured by the long hair that falls over it. *She* is the one who will have to carry and protect the memory. To make sure it does not entirely disappear.

As if Hanna's thoughts have summoned her, Katja moves away from her place in the thin circle next to Gisela to come and sit beside her. Kahapa, looking up as she comes past behind him, follows her. The others briefly glance at them, then lapse again into their own several silences.

'There are ten of us now,' says Kahapa after a moment. 'So where we go now? What we do?'

Hanna makes her rapid gestures to Katja; the girl interprets: *We are far away from the mission station now. Far away from anywhere. So we shall stay here for a few days. First of all, we must train everybody to use the weapons. You are the one to do that. After that, we can move on.*

'Ten people is not an army,' Kahapa objects. 'Even if I teach them to use the guns and do the things of war. The German army have hundreds and thousands of people.'

We won't be fighting them in a crowd, Hanna says through Katja, as she had explained to the girl before. *We must learn to be clever. Catch them one or two at a time.*

'For that we need more than guns,' says Kahapa. 'Gun make noise. To kill, the people must learn other ways. Very much more tough.'

Can you do it?

'I must have time.'

We shall give you time, Kahapa.

He nods with a grunt of satisfaction. 'We shall do that then,' he says. 'And then, if we die, we die. All of us together, but each one alone. Because a man cannot die of what another man eats.'

She knows this is facing the impossible. But they have left the world of the possible behind – the world of safety, of certainty, of calculation, of reason. Their domain, now, is the impossible. (*The whole German Reich*, Katja said once before. *The whole world.*) If this is madness, so be it. When sanity depends on the logic of violence her only choice is the kind of madness with which to oppose it. The day she and Katja left Frauenstein they set foot in that part of life from which there is no hope of returning.

She looks at Katja, intently; into the lambency of her eyes. That, she thinks, is how her own eyes must once have looked. The time of stories: the tale of the wretched creatures of Bremen, the ragtag band disowned and beaten and thrown out by their masters when they could no longer find any use for them; the history of Jeanne and her voices; the story of the little Gooseherd, of Bluebeard and his wives;

of young Werther as he wandered through the forest pining for his Lotte. All the stories she and her own Lotte used to tell each other in the dark. Lost, for ever with the loss of her tongue. This, now, what she has left, is no longer a story to be told. Her life itself is the only story she has been reduced to: and that cannot be told, it can only be endured.

She remembers the fury of frustration she suffered when she was with the Nama tribe and had to rely on her signs and what they knew of German: the hopelessness of not being able to speak their language (those clicks!). To speak at all. At least that rage has been assuaged. She need no longer look at words. Where she is moving – she, her whole band of dispossessed, her inglorious army – is a landscape beyond, or before, words. Meaning is different here. It resides in sand and stones, in the meagre and momentous events of the desert: a tortoise labouring past, the quick gliding of a snake, a whirlwind on the horizon, a hawk or a vulture overhead, every change of light, every flicker of movement far-reaching, unforeseeable in its consequences. Suffering, oh yes. Above all the suffering of everything discarded or lost on the way, everything that can no longer be, like children forever unborn. But suffering itself can become a kind of comfort, a reassurance about life.

Everything as simple and as profound as Kahapa's terse utterance. A man cannot die of what another man eats. *They* have eaten. Of the fruit of knowledge, of good and evil. They can face life. And if it comes to that, they will take charge of their own death.

52

HANNA SPENDS MUCH time with Gisela on the way. Conversation is difficult, because Katja has to be there to interpret; and Gisela does not yet feel at ease enough to talk freely in a young girl's presence. Occasionally she tells brief snatches from her life with the pastor – how she tried to keep faith, to support him in his covenant with a God she couldn't understand or accept; how, slowly, it was eroded by the daily and nightly proximity to his pettiness, his lust, his silent rages – but otherwise she tries to find neutral territory, or to turn away from her own life (which to her now seems utterly worthless, grey, without interest to anybody) to their present journey and its prospects.

'I don't know how you can hope to fight against evil,' she tells Hanna. 'It is too big, it has too many forms.'

I have no illusions, Hanna answers. *I know I cannot change the world I just want to do something. To show that it is possible to say No. I have started. I must go on. The important part still lies ahead.*

'But that is simply the way the world *is*,' counters Gisela. 'If we think it's different, or that it can be made to look different, or feel different, we're fooling ourselves.'

I'll tell you what the difference is, Hanna responds through Katja. *That is the only thing I can be sure of. All my life things have been happening to me. I cannot allow that to go on. From now on, whatever happens, I must be the one who **makes** it happen. Can you understand that?*

Gisela nods slowly. 'I think I do,' she says. 'But right now I'm simply too tired. I just want to go with you.'

But if you go with me you cannot stay out of anything. You must know that. There will be violence. If you are not ready to face that, I shall send you to Windhoek with one of the men.

Gisela only shrugs. After a while she says, 'All right. I shall go where you go. I have been passive long enough.' She gazes around her. 'But this land . . . It has been going on for so long, for centuries. You know, I once read – we were still in Dresden then, I told you I was a history teacher before we got married – I read about the first Portuguese explorers who came down the coast of Africa. Diego Cam. Bartolomeu Diaz. Well, they said that Diaz kidnapped four black women from the coast of Guinea to drop them at different spots. He thought they could make friends with the natives – of course in those days they believed everybody in Africa spoke the same language – and then he'd pick them up again on the way back. The first woman was set down at Angra Pequeña here on the coast of this land, and the second further down, I think they called the place Angra das Voltas. But then things went wrong, the little fleet was driven off course, and Diaz never came back for the women. Perhaps they never survived anyway. But what always shocked me was how they could just be used like that. No one thought of the families, the children, the lives they left behind. They were like markers, like the wooden crosses the men planted along the coast. Just because they were *women* anything could be done to them. And how often during the years I was married, I thought that, really, that was all I was to Gottlieb too. A beacon to mark his progress.'

That is why you must stay with us, insists Hanna, through Katja. *All these wooden crosses must rise up to say No.*

Gisela nods. Whether she is convinced remains to be seen.

53

WHAT WILL BE the turning point begins in an ordinary enough way. And although they have been preparing for just such an eventuality – days of strenuous weapons training, directed by Kahapa – a ripple of unease, even of fear, moves through the small company when, on the afternoon of the fourth or fifth day, he announces the news.

He has gone down on all fours, pressing his ear to the ground. 'There is people come this way,' he says. 'With horses and all.'

'How far?' asks Gisela, apprehension showing in her tightly drawn features.

'Still far.'

'How many?'

'I don't know,' says Kahapa. 'We must wait. More than five.' He holds up one hand, fingers spread wide.

'Good,' says Himba. 'We kill them all dead.'

'Not if there are too many,' Gisela objects.

If they are soldiers, Hanna gestures to Katja, *we must get ready. You know what to do.*

Gisela, it has been decided, will lie down on the cart pretending to be sick. (Not much pretence is needed; she is still in bad shape.) She will be the wife of a high official, who fell ill during a visit to the mission station and is being taken back to Windhoek for medical care. Over the past days they have rehearsed a number of possibilities; and Kahapa and Himba, sometimes the crafty and agile monkey man T'Kamkhab, have taken them through routines of attack and defence – with guns, with knives, with bows and arrows, with kieries, of which by now they have quite an assortment. But practising, Hanna knows only too well, is different from facing a real enemy. However, unlike the other women, she feels little fear. What makes the prickly hairs on the back of her neck stand up is excitement. At last, perhaps, at last something is going to happen.

It is a long wait, over two hours, before the dull thudding sounds Kahapa has picked up materialise into figures approaching from the horizon in the east. Eight of them.

'Too much men,' says Kahapa quietly. 'We are not ready for them. Not yet.'

We'll see, responds Hanna, her eyes revealing a determination which makes him feel slightly apprehensive.

The approaching figures resolve themselves into six soldiers on horseback; and two native batmen, presumably Namas, on mules. The soldiers are in uniform, the batmen in odds and ends of clothing, most of it too big for them. Each of these two holds a small figure in front of him on the saddle of his mule. They are young girls, Hanna discovers as they approach; naked but for the very small aprons worn by the barely nubile of their tribe. She feels herself tensing. And when the group dismounts and she sees the telltale thin streaks of blood on the thighs of the girls her mind is made up. Whatever reservations Kahapa may have, this will not be a peaceful encounter.

The six soldiers – five of them young men who have barely outgrown their adolescence, the sixth an officer of more mature years and rather stocky compared to the slender agility of the others – dismount very rapidly in a small cloud of powdery dust, their guns held in the crook of their arms. They seem prepared for trouble; and the sight of the three white women surrounded by blacks of various tribes and sizes clearly increases their tension.

'Who are you?' demands the officer. 'What are these natives doing here? Are you in danger?'

Hanna gestures to Katja, who takes over. 'There is no danger. These people are escorting us through the desert. The lady on the cart there, Frau Wunderlich of the Kolonialgesellschaft, was on a visit to Pastor Maier's mission station in the south when she fell ill. We are taking her to Windhoek to see a doctor.'

'What is the matter with this one?' asks the officer, trying to peer under Hanna's kappie and recoiling from what he dimly perceives in there.

'She is badly hurt,' says Katja. 'She cannot speak.'

'We heard gunfire earlier today,' says the officer. 'Were you involved in that? And what happened?'

For a fleeting moment Hanna feels worried: the soldiers must have heard, from afar, their shooting practice this morning. But Katja lies calmly: 'Just a band of robbers,' she says very quickly. 'Our escort managed to beat them off quite easily.'

The man glares suspiciously at Kahapa and his group. 'Which way did they flee?'

Katja makes a vague sweeping gesture towards the south. 'They'll be well out of reach by now, they got quite a scare.'

'We have to pursue them,' the officer says grimly. 'The whole desert is swarming with robbers and vagabonds dislodged by the war. It is not a safe place for women. Or anyone else, for that matter.'

'*We* haven't seen anybody,' Katja says pointedly. 'The few Nama settlements we found were all razed to the ground.'

There is a satisfied grin on the man's face. 'This is how General von Trotha taught us to make war,' he says. 'Leave nothing behind that can move or make a sound. Not even a chicken.' He seems unaware of the contradictions in his statements.

'Then you have nothing to fear, do you?' the girl comments.

For a second the officer examines her intently. Then he motions, once again, towards her companions. 'Are you quite sure this lot can be trusted?'

'They have been very loyal,' Katja assures him.

'You can never be too sure, Fräulein. They're like jackals, you know. You can tame them like a dog, but one day, when you least expect it, they suddenly bite your hand. Or go for your throat.'

'We've known these people for a long time, General.'

He gives a small smile, slightly embarrassed. 'Leutnant Auer, Fräulein. At your service.'

As if she has been born to it, Katja puts out her hand. He clicks his heels and bends over to brush her fingertips with his lips. Then he turns to his men. 'We must go off and track down those bastards before they get away.'

Hanna prods her with an elbow. 'It is so late already, Leutnant,' says Katja with her most beguiling smile, tossing back her long blonde hair. 'Why don't you and your men stay with us for the night? You must be exhausted. When last did you have a proper meal?' She makes a gesture towards Kahapa. 'This man shot a gemsbok today. We'll be only too happy . . .' And with a flutter of her eyelashes she offers the *coup de grâce*: 'We'll feel so much safer with you here.'

There is a murmur of approval from the eager young men behind him.

'Well, if it's a matter of a lady's safety.' He makes a brief, stiff bow and motions to his men. A series of staccato orders sends them scuttling in all directions to unsaddle the horses and pitch a camp and collect firewood for the night.

The two Nama batmen approach with some hesitation, shoving their scared young charges in front of them. Dust has caked on the drying blood on their legs. The tiny flaps of skin covering their genitals are trembling although there is no wind. Glancing at their bare bodies Hanna realises that they are even younger than she has first thought.

'What do we do with these two?' asks one of the batmen.

'Tie them to the back of the cart for now,' says the lieutenant curtly. 'We'll think of something later.'

Prompted by Hanna, Katja turns back to the officer. Her breath is shallower now. 'What are the girls doing with you?' she asks.

'Well.' For a moment he seems at a loss. Then, precipitately, he explains. 'We found them near our fort, when we set out yesterday morning.' He motions to the east. 'They were lost, their people must have abandoned them when they fled. We're trying to take them back to where they belong.'

'With their hands tied?'

'It is for their own protection,' he assures her, flustered.

'How very kind of you,' says Katja. 'I have no doubt you will look after them very well.'

He glances at her with narrowed eyes. 'This is not an easy time for anybody, Fräulein,' he says brusquely. 'Our men have been stationed in the desert for months now. Night and day, they cannot relax for a moment. Sometimes a fort is not much different from a prison. Can you imagine what it is like when you are young?'

'I know all about it,' says Katja.

He ignores the tartness in her voice. 'Every day patrols are sent out,' he continues. 'This way, that way, everywhere. To make sure the land is safe so that people like you can sleep peacefully.'

'I'm sure we are very grateful to you, Leutnant.'

He prepares to say something, then thinks better of it and turns away to oversee his men at their tasks.

Back at the oxcart Kahapa comes up to Hanna and Katja. He is clearly upset,

'You cannot do this,' he says. 'Six soldiers with guns and two others. It's too much for us. They kill us, Hanna.'

We cannot miss a chance like this, she says through Katja. *Can't you see?*

'I can see. That is why I want to stop it. This is big trouble.'

Leave it to me, she conveys to him. In transmitting the message, Katja's voice trembles with eagerness; but there is dread in it too.

Bring the medicine woman to me, Hanna signals. *She will help us.*

While Hanna and Katja confer with Kamma, the soldiers bustle about. They are still busy when the sun goes down; the west becomes gaudy with the approaching night. Then, gradually, the activity slows down. The men have made a huge fire. It must be visible all the way from the horizon, flaring up into the sky, the hard dry wood exploding from time to time, sending showers of sparks through the dark.

Overhead a shooting star briefly blazes through the sky.

'That is not a good sign,' mutters old Tookwi.

'Just wait, you'll see,' says Katja. She watches very closely as Hanna does the rounds dispensing roasted venison to the young blond men who sing her praises; they have not seen her without her kappie.

They are all grouped around the fire; only the two Nama batmen keep their distance. Himba has joined them, ostensibly to keep them company, though he clearly bears them no amicable feelings. ('They don't even have their Nama names any more,' he told Kahapa, who duly reported his sentiments to Hanna. 'They're Lukas and David now. That's white names. They have gone over to the other side.')

The women are trying to keep the conversation going. But behind the politeness of their efforts they are only waiting for Kamma's medicine to take effect.

Hanna sits with her chin resting on her drawn-up knees, staring not at the men but into the fire. Something lies in the hollow of her stomach like a heavy lump. Tonight it will happen. And tonight will decide whether they can go on. If anything goes wrong – and at this stage anything may – not all of them will see the sun rise from its own blood in the morning. For once she almost wishes there was someone, a God, a Jesus, a Mary, a star, the wind, to pray to. *Little Susan of the faraway beach*, she thinks, *if you are somewhere there, intercede for me; tell them what I have gone through, what blood I have waded through, to arrive at this dark still moment.*

Much sooner than she has expected the first of the soldiers start complaining of drowsiness, rise dully to their feet, stagger off towards where their batmen have unrolled their blankets on the far side of the fire. Two of them remain for longer, the lieutenant and one of the smiling youngsters. Without his military cap he looks like a boy.

Lieutenant Auer is the first of the two to get up. With determination on his face he starts walking stiff-legged towards the back of the cart. Hanna sits up, her body tensed, like a lioness preparing for the chase. But halfway to the cart he stops, yawns, stretches, grins sheepishly in the direction of the women, and then changes direction towards his blankets.

The young private is the only one to remain behind. He will be on sentry duty for the first quarter of the night. But already his head is lolling. Katja moves closer to his side and starts chatting to him, very gaily, seductively, her voice low and inviting. After a while he reaches clumsily towards her, half loses his balance, slumps against her.

She moves away. He rolls over like a bundle of washing.

'Kahapa,' the girl says, almost too softly for anyone to hear.

It happens with such amazing precision and swiftness that it seems like an unreal action taking place somewhere at a remove, from which they remain detached. A hallucination, a mirage in the dark, something they are dreaming. And yet they are involved in it, in the most immediate and urgent and bloody way. Looming up above the collapsed boy, larger than life in the flickering light, Kahapa brings down the heavy kierie he is clasping in both hands. The youngster utters something like a sigh, no more. In the same instant the others move to the positions Hanna has mapped out for them and communicated through Katja and Kahapa. The agile warrior Himba remains with the batmen to make sure they will not interfere or abscond. T'Kamkhab sets upon one of the sleeping young soldiers, old Tookwi on another. Koo and Nerina take charge of the third, Katja and old Kamma of the fourth. It has been decided that Hanna will dispense with the lieutenant on her own, but as she moves into position she discovers Gisela beside her. There is no stopping her.

It is over in barely a minute, two at most. It's been almost too easy. There is a sense of anticlimax when they gather at the fire afterwards. For a while they avoid each other's eyes. Hanna finds release in going to the back of the cart first to untie the thongs that bind the two scared Nama girls. Katja, glancing up as they approach, hurries away to fetch blankets for them.

Himba, joined by Kahapa, escorts the two trembling batmen to the fire. One has soiled his trousers; everybody else moves a few yards away.

'You stay with us now, or you want to go back to your fort?' asks Kahapa.

They seem to realise what the second choice will entail. 'Please, we want to be with you,' they plead in breaking voices, their legs collapsing. One grabs Kahapa's knees, the other Himba's. Both men impatiently kick them out of the way.

A deep silence, like a large black blanket, folds over them. The crackling of the long logs that feed the fire sounds like bursts of gunfire. As each looks at the others, one unspoken thought takes root in all: It may have been quick, but it wasn't clean. They are all spattered and smudged with blood – clothes, legs, hands, even faces.

'We've done it,' says Katja at last, a sob in her voice.

Hanna puts her arm around the girl, but only for a moment. Then she gesticulates; and Katja, regaining her composure, transmits the message to Gisela:

How did you manage to do it? We said you could stay out of it.

'But I wanted to. I *had* to.'

'I didn't think you had it in you,' says Katja.

Involuntarily, the thin woman raises her bloodstained hands and gazes uncomprehendingly at them. With a kind of wonder in her voice she says, 'Yes, I've done it. I just imagined it was my husband. Then it happened by itself.'

Hanna silently places a hand on Gisela's shoulder and presses it. She proceeds to Katja and repeats the gesture. And to each of the others in turn. They stare at her with new respect, some with awe. Slowly the tension subsides. In reaction, a few of the men become jocular. But Hanna rapidly puts an end to it.

Through Katja she says, *The place is a mess. We must clean up.*

'It can wait for tomorrow,' suggests Kahapa.

It will be done now. We don't want to attract predators. And we don't want anyone to know.

Reluctantly at first, but with increasing energy, they start digging a trench in the now accommodating earth. When it is big enough for the six bodies, Hanna orders them to strip the dead soldiers. They all help. Like six skinned animals the dead are piled into the trench.

That is when Kahapa wants to take over. The backs of the bodies must be broken, he says. The spines must be shattered into small pieces, otherwise their shadows will come back to haunt them and slay them in their dreams. But Hanna will not allow it. There is an angry argument between them, with Katja interpreting.

'You take no chances with enemies!' Kahapa argues.

Killing is enough, she counters. *We're not jackals or hyenas.*

'What you know of this land?' he challenges her. 'We have our own customs.'

Before we took on these soldiers you said we had no chance, she reminds him. *Was it I who said we must kill them, or was it not?*

'It was you,' he concedes, crestfallen.

Then you will now do as I say.

Kahapa hesitates for another moment, then shrugs and yields.

The burial resumes. The brass buttons and belt buckles torn from the uniforms and the belts are put in a canvas bag to be buried elsewhere, tomorrow, on Hanna's instructions. Even if the bodies are discovered it should be impossible for anyone to identify them.

Hanna notices Katja staring at the naked dead men in a troubled fascination she evidently finds it hard to conceal; and only when they are covered with earth does the girl turn away. The mound is covered with stones, and the huge fire is moved, log by log, to resume on top of the grave. The whole camp is swept with branches. Afterwards, when the fire is flaring up again, the uniforms are thrown into the flames. They give off an awful, suffocating, smoky smell; but after some time it dissipates in the stirring of the wind.

When it is all over they return to the fire, their faces blackened by smoke and streaked with sweat.

Kahapa takes off his hat with the leopard-skin band and violently dusts it with his free hand. 'You are a good fighter,' he says to Hanna, replacing the hat on his head. The others murmur in approval.

This is only the beginning, Hanna replies through Katja. *It will get harder as we go on.* She looks slowly from one to the other in the crazy light of the fire. *Is there anyone who would like to back out now? You will not have another chance.*

No one comes forward.

Old Tookwi glances up at the sky, half-obscured by the haphazard movement of the smoke. 'I still don't like that star,' he mumbles, more to himself than to them.

54

In the night, as usual, Hanna and Katja lie together, close to the fire. Hanna cannot sleep. She lies watching Kahapa's broad back as he sits keeping watch. She feels an urge to go and sit with him. But she senses that she cannot leave Katja. The girl is not sleeping either. Rigid, tense in every limb, she lies pressed against Hanna, her breath shallow and uneven. And later she starts shivering. It turns into an uncontrollable trembling; Hanna can hear her teeth chattering. She isn't crying, only shaking. Hanna holds her as tightly as she can. Once Katja utters a muffled moan. Hanna responds with an unarticulated sound in her throat, perhaps a question, perhaps a sound of soothing.

'They were all so young,' whispers Katja suddenly. 'They looked so innocent.'

Young, yes, answers Hanna with her fingers on the girl's body. *But not innocent. They brought the war here. You have seen the Nama villages they destroyed. You have seen those girls.*

Katja shivers. Hanna presses her open hand against the girl's mouth. For a moment Katja struggles against it, biting into the palm; but gradually she begins to relax. And now she is crying, but soundlessly. Then she drifts into sleep.

55

THEY HAVE TRAVELLED for a day and a half, on horseback and on the oxcart, and now they are approaching the fort from which the military patrol set out. The landscape is more uneven here and the fort remains obscured behind a series of high koppies. The two batmen, Lukas and David, have shown them the way. A few of the others in the group were reluctant, initially, about considering such a move. There used to be thirty men in the fort, according to the batmen, which means there will be twenty-four left. It sounds redoubtable, if not foolhardy. But Hanna is adamant. If the six soldiers do not return within a reasonable time their fellows are bound to go looking for them; and there may be a greater risk in encountering several patrols, probably coming from different directions, and unexpectedly, than having the whole garrison herded together, she argues. Besides, it is a challenge she cannot resist.

She spends many hours along the way, with Katja as her interpreter, interrogating Lukas and David on every detail that may in one way or another be relevant: the size and layout of the fort and its fortifications, the roster by which the guard is changed, by day, by night, the nature of its provisions and equipment, the extent of the arms and ammunition at its disposal, its supplies of fresh food and water (there is a well inside, she learns, and a vegetable garden; information which more or less rules out the possibility of a siege), its contacts with Windhoek (dispatches to and fro once a fortnight, the last having occurred just a day before the ill-fated patrol set out). She insists on hearing anything at all they can report – facts, anecdotes, gripes, suspicions, whatever – on the command structure, even on individual members of the garrison, their morale, their interaction in the barracks, their response to discipline, and the nature of that discipline, the length of their postings, their experience or inexperience in the army, their ages, the towns they come from, what they think about their enemies and how they treat prisoners. Sometimes David and Lukas can only shake their heads. Why, one can almost see them thinking, would this woman want to know whether the commander – Captain Weiss, a feared and respected man in his fifties – is reasonable or unreasonable in his demands and expectations of his men, whether he is married, and if so whether his wife lives in Windhoek or in Germany, and whether they think he misses her, whether he is a religious man, whether he reads before he goes to bed at night, whether he rises before his men in the morning or prefers to take it easy, whether he has a passion for his job or merely does his duty, whether he really cares for his soldiers or simply commands them . . . ? And then the second in command, Sergeant Vogel. And the third. For sure, she cannot be in her right mind.

After this inquisition, when they make their final halt among the koppies, Hanna beckons to Katja and Kahapa to follow her away from the others who are relieved to rest awhile in the shade of the thorn trees. She goes down on her haunches and starts drawing on a patch of sand with a long white thorn. Here is the fort with its garrison of twenty-four soldiers and three grooms for the horses. Here is their little company of ten, plus the two batmen whom she brackets separately, with a question mark beside them.

Right. Now look carefully. This is what we shall do . . . , she indicates to Katja.

'You can't be serious,' objects the girl. 'Hanna, this is not a stray patrol in the desert. It is an army garrison in a fortified place. They outnumber us almost three to one. They have months of warfare behind them. Some of them years.'

So much the better. I promise you I won't take unnecessary chances. But victory now will give our people all the confidence they need to face the tests that still lie ahead.

'We cannot just charge in!' Katja persists.

Absolutely not. That is why we're planning it all in advance. We have most of the information we need. Of course there are decisions we can only take once we're there. We have to leave room for improvisation. But we are not unprepared. And we have all the advantage of surprise on our side.

Kahapa observes in silence. Against her own better judgement, Katja is drawn into the passion of Hanna's convictions. With nothing less than awe she watches the woman elaborating her sketches and her scribblings on the sand. Hanna herself is conscious of an inexplicable deep contentment which has been dormant in her for years: that quiet, assured joy she used to feel on those distant evenings when she was huddled over the chessboard with Herr Ludwig in the dark amber light of the lamp in his study. This feels like the extension of the same game, although she is very deeply aware that it is infinitely more dangerous, and the stakes are higher. It is, in a very real way, a matter of life and death.

'How you are sure it will happen like this?' is all Kahapa asks when she has outlined her whole campaign to them. It requires old Tookwi and the six women to move ahead to the fort – Hanna and Katja and Gisela, the strong woman Nerina, the brooding Koo, the medicine crone Kamma – while Kahapa, Himba and T'Kamkhab will remain behind here among the koppies with the two batmen to prepare an ambush.

'But if they catch you in the fort?' he asks angrily. 'How can we help you then? You are six women, they are twenty-four men.'

The numbers are not everything, she insists. *We'll arrange for a dozen or more of them to go out on an expedition, perhaps two expeditions. With the others we can deal in ones and twos and threes. It is more important for you to be here, to set up your ambush, to wipe out the soldiers we send here.*

'And if you need me there? How I know you call me?'

There will be signals they can use, she assures him, and launches into a meticulous cataloguing of what she has in mind.

'You think of everything!' he exclaims, and this time there is a hint of real admiration in his voice.

First tell me where you think I'm wrong, she cautions. *Tell me how we can improve on it. We cannot go ahead before we've discussed all the possibilities.*

A new round of discussions begins. Kahapa and Katja go through every detail with her, come up with a few refinements, but finally approve of the whole campaign.

Katja is the one who, even after all the discussion, remains the most apprehensive. 'It looks fine here in your pictures on the sand,' she says. 'But what happens when there are real people involved? We simply cannot afford to risk too much too soon, Hanna!' she pleads.

We'll never know what we can do unless we try.

'But people may die. *We* can die.'

Trust me.

After a last brief hesitation, with the flicker of a wan smile, Katja concedes, 'All right. I trust you.'

Hanna leans over cautiously to obliterate her scrawls from the sand with the flat of her hand before they get up to return to the others. Once again the whole plan is presented, once again there is lengthy discussion. But at last they can move into action.

In final preparation for the approach to the fort they fire a large number of shots into the air, in irregular volleys, to create the impression of a skirmish. Now they are ready.

Lukas and David are left behind, still unarmed, among the koppies with Kahapa and his two men; they keep the horses with them.

Very slowly the oxcart begins to pick its way across the difficult terrain, accompanied by the women and the rainmaker. Once again Gisela has to bed down on the cart, this time under protest: she has undergone a quite startling transformation, as if in the violence of the encounter two nights ago she has found a passion and an energy of which there was little sign in her former lethargy. All the guns and ammunition won from the German commando are hidden under her bedclothes, because to avoid suspicion only four guns, three Mausers and a straight-pull Mannlicher, are openly in evidence on the cart.

It takes a good two hours to get through the hills. From there, at a distance of another few hours, they can make out the squat brown fort perched on a steep hilltop.

'They'll see us coming all the way,' warns Nerina.

That is the idea, Hanna makes Katja answer. *We don't want them to be surprised; that will make them feel threatened.*

There are sentries posted on the high front wall, watching them like falcons through binoculars as they approach. At a slow steady pace the two oxen trundle along, led by Tookwi. The women walk in two small groups, on either side.

When they are about a hundred metres from the gate it swings open and two soldiers on horseback come out, guns at the ready on the pommels in front of them. Hanna and Katja move to the front of their small company. The horsemen stop, scrutinising them, suspicious, apprehensive, challenging.

Katja tells them about Hanna's predicament and recounts the same story as before: the wife of the visiting dignitary stricken down by what seems to be a serious illness, their need to get her to a doctor. But this time she adds more elaborate explanation: on their way here, about half an hour beyond the hills over there, she says, they were overtaken by a band of armed Namas and lost two members of their escort before the attackers fled into the desert.

'A patrol from our fort was sent out in that direction several days ago,' says one of the horsemen. 'Did you not meet them on the way?'

Katja shakes her head. 'No. But we did hear a lot of shooting more to the west, two days ago. Perhaps they also ran into Namas.'

'Those vermin are everywhere,' says the soldier.

'The group that attacked us cannot have gone very far away,' Katja tells him. 'There were quite a few wounded with them and they moved very slowly.'

'You'd better talk to the captain,' the young man says, new eagerness lighting up his eyes. 'Bring your cart into the courtyard.'

Several other soldiers await them inside the gate. Despite the information provided by the batmen, the women find the courtyard less spacious than they expected; but the large stone well and the vegetable garden match their description in every detail. Apart from the barracks there are rows of stables and sheds, all according to their expectations. While the oxen are outspanned and the women are still taking stock of their surroundings, the commanding officer makes his appearance, summoned by two of the young men in the garrison. Captain Leopold Weiss is lean and middle-aged, exactly as the two batmen described him, with a bald head and penetrating eyes the colour of bayonet steel. With a stiff bow he introduces himself, then stands to attention to hear what they have to say. Katja repeats her story, trying to sound as urgent and agitated as she can. 'There is another group of women following us,' she says, inventing as she goes along. 'Seven of them, some already old. Relatives of the pastor at the mission station. They are exhausted, and quite unarmed, because the natives escorting them ran away one night and took all their food and guns. We trekked on ahead to look for help. Thank God we found you.'

'How far behind you are they?'

'Probably a full day by now,' says Katja. 'They were quite exhausted and we tried to move on as fast as we could.' Her voice becomes tearful. 'Please, Captain, for God's sake, they need your help, you must track down those robbers. It is just by the grace of the Lord that we escaped death.' A dramatic pause; she drops her voice. 'Or worse.' She clasps her hands in front of her breasts, a movement that elicits a pale glow from the captain's eyes. This, too, is what they have been led to expect, and it suits their scheme.

Captain Weiss glances up at the sky and makes a quick decision. 'We'll send out a commando immediately. With some luck they can find the marauders before dark, and then move on to rescue the women.' A few quick barks bring soldiers running from all sides. Hanna calculates that the whole remaining garrison in the small fort (including three grooms from the stables) must be assembled.

Six soldiers are dispatched. Hanna hoped that the captain could be persuaded to send as many as eight, but he will not be swayed. However, she does succeed in persuading him to send Koo with the detachment, on horseback and armed with one of the guns, to show them the way to where the skirmish with the fictitious band of hostile Namas took place. Her presence will make things much easier for Kahapa among the koppies.

The little commando canters off and in her mind Hanna crosses them out. That leaves eighteen soldiers and the grooms.

As if the old woman has read her thoughts, Kamma whispers to Hanna, 'There are too many soldiers for my medicine. I do not have enough for them all.'

'We do not need to poison all of them,' Katja reminds her on

Hanna's behalf. 'We only need to knock out a few to bring down the numbers.'

Once the heavy gate has been barricaded behind the departing commando, the rest of the men turn to their evening chores; the captain insists that his soldiers will entertain the ladies and make it a memorable night for them. A sumptuous meal is prepared – a goat is slaughtered, there is a thick broth, and fresh cabbage from the garden, and beetroot, and a great flow of beer. The atmosphere is heavy with festivity. Several toasts are drunk. The evening may yet turn into an uproarious event. But they have hardly finished the broth when there is a shout from the sentry outside on the wall, accompanied by a distant crackling of gunfire. In a turmoil of shouts and moving bodies soldiers from all sides start kicking out their chairs, grabbing their guns and running outside to the two heavy stone staircases that give access to the outside wall. The women follow. But there is nothing to be seen. The gunfire continues for a while, far away among the hills, falters, picks up again; then there are two brief final salvoes of four shots each, followed by a silence as absolute as the night.

Hanna nudges Katja with an elbow to acknowledge Kahapa's message: their small group has wiped out the enemy commando. They will have to wait for a full account later; but Hanna knows that if the encounter took place according to plan, Koo would have led the commando at a very slow pace through the narrow fold among the koppies where Kahapa and the others were lying in wait to pick off the one or two soldiers bringing up the rear; at the first shots Koo would have swung round to bring down the soldier closest to her, and then the rest of their band would close in. Their task completed, it is understood that they will remain among the koppies for a further decision to be taken in the morning.

Captain Weiss attaches a different interpretation to the shots. 'Got them,' he says, but his manner is rather less self-assured than his words. 'It was a long way off. They'll probably camp there and go in search of the women in the morning.' He turns to a subaltern. 'Hans, just for safety's sake, double the guard.'

In more orderly fashion everybody returns to the barracks, where the table has been set up on trestles. The room is long and low and rather gloomy in the light of torches mounted in brackets along the walls. No one seems quite as hungry as before.

'Another toast,' proposes the captain, raising his large mug. 'To His Imperial Majesty's victorious army.'

There is general, if somewhat forced, acclaim. In the hubbub no one notices that the two women do not drink.

The mugs are thumped down again on the heavy wooden table. The food is served by officious young men. One of them, a smooth-faced youth who seems barely seventeen, keeps on bustling about Katja, plying her with the choicest morsels, smiling and bowing and spilling until the captain curtly orders him over to the far side of the table. But not before the young man has slipped a clumsily scribbled note under the girl's serviette. She removes it, surreptitiously shares it with Hanna.

I must see you. You are so pretty. Werner.

Hanna grimaces. *Don't pay attention*, she advises. But she finds it slightly disturbing to see Katja blush. To direct the girl's attention to more pressing business she communicates an instruction which they have discussed earlier.

Katja, seated beside the captain, half rises from her chair with a becoming show of modesty, and curtsys in his direction. 'Is it possible,' she asks in her most dulcet tone, 'that someone can take Frau Wunderlich something to eat on the cart? A little broth perhaps?'

'By all means,' he agrees heartily, clearly determined to restore the earlier *gemütlichkeit*. 'But are you sure we should not bring her inside?'

'We don't want to risk moving her,' says Katja. 'And she is well looked after by our servants.' She sighs histrionically. 'She is very weak. We can only hope she will last the night.'

Without delay a soldier is sent out with a deep bowl of broth on a tray.

Hanna knows they will never see him again.

Now there are seventeen men. And four of these, including the captain, are beginning to show signs of severe discomfort. During the night, Hanna knows, they will start suffering from severe stomach cramps and bouts of vomiting. The men will not die, but with some luck they should remain incapacitated for a good twenty-four hours. By her calculations that should be enough.

56

THEY FIND IT difficult to sleep that night. It is uncomfortable with the body of the young man stabbed and throttled by Gisela and Nerina and who now lies rolled in a blanket among bundles and packages under the hood of the oxcart. Also, they are concerned about the next day. Even if Kahapa's group has taken care of the six soldiers sent out to them, have they not been too ambitious in their calculations? Will the garrison not become suspicious about the women's purpose in their midst? For Katja there are other irritations too: three times in the night a young soldier steals out into the courtyard, creeps like a shadow to the open hood of the cart and tries to attract her attention. Twice it is the fond young man from the dinner table, Werner; once someone else. On Hanna's instructions she feigns sleep. It is Gisela who rises to send the amorous youths scuttling back to the barracks. In different circumstances it might have been amusing; not now.

They also have to consult old Tookwi. Questioned by Katja on Hanna's behalf, he proudly presents a chameleon he has found on their trek across the plains on their way down from the koppies. The little creature looks half-paralysed, but according to Tookwi it is as fine a specimen as he requires. 'He is stronger than a snake,' he assures them. 'You just tell me when you want the rain.'

After this they can have a few hours of restless sleep. But well before sunrise they are awakened by a hurrying and scurrying of soldiers inside the walls of the fort. The disappearance of the young man who took Gisela her supper has been confirmed and an intensive search is launched. No nook or corner is left unexplored. Several soldiers are sent outside to scour the surroundings of the fort. But there is no sign of the missing private. Gisela is also questioned. Still feigning weakness, she assures them that he had indeed brought her food – there is the plate, the mug, the cutlery – but then left her alone.

'Desert sickness,' the captain comments angrily. He looks deadly pale and can barely walk for the cramps. 'It seems to be happening to more and more of the men posted out here. But it is unforgivable. Lack of self-discipline.' He doubles over in agony.

Through Katja, Hanna expresses her sympathy and informs him that she, too, has been suffering from contractions in the night. So, in fact, has Gisela. Which suggests that there must have been something wrong with the broth. She urges him to take to his bed. Surely, however much she admires his fortitude, there is no need for him to remain vigilant. There are enough able-bodied men about; some time soon his commando will be back in the full flush of their triumph.

Just then, at the moment of sunrise, the discussion is interrupted by another crackling of gunfire in the distance. The women count the reports in a low hum of half-whispered voices which sounds like an orison. One – two – three – and a quick four-five. It is a confirmation from Kahapa: he will be waiting for news or orders from them.

But all around them there is great agitation. The most urgent problem for the garrison to resolve is whether the gunshots spell good or bad news, friendly fire or enemy retaliation. Should they all wait here, standing by for action; or must another commando be sent out in case the first group has met with unexpected resistance or some mishap?

The captain, in the throes of severe convulsions, is not in a fit state to issue instructions. While he is being escorted to the barracks by two of the remaining soldiers, the second in command, Sergeant Vogel, takes charge. He orders the heliograph to be brought. One of the amorous youths of the night before – not the stricken young Werner but the other, a corporal, whose name they learn is Günther – starts sending an urgent message towards the distant hills. There is no response. Once again the message is flashed across the landscape which is gradually gaining definition in the light. And yet again. Still no signal from the distance.

'We really cannot afford to wait,' says young Günther, clearly in a state of serious agitation. 'We *have* to do something.'

'I shall be the judge of that.' Sergeant Vogel, blowing himself up like a bull frog, brings him up short with a stare that would wither a thorn tree. 'Already our numbers are reduced. We cannot leave the fort undermanned. Remember, there are only eighteen of us.' He checks himself, looks round, frowns severely. 'Or seventeen, if the missing Carl does not turn up. And several of them unwell. It is most vexing.'

Hanna pushes Katja forward, prompting her. The girl curtsys like before. 'Please, Sergeant,' she says, trying to exploit all the drama in the situation. 'The men out there may be in great danger. Perhaps those Namas came back with reinforcements. Or perhaps they found the women we left behind and now *they* are in danger . . .'

'We shall take every possible precaution, Fräulein,' he says irritably. 'You may leave that to me. Thank you.'

I'm sure you will do the right thing, Hanna responds through Katja. *It is just that if I think of those poor women, and here you are with seventeen – or eighteen – well-armed men all safe in a redoubt like this . . .*

Sergeant Vogel, who at the best of times has a flushed appearance, is scarlet with the effort of trying to make up his mind. Under a commander as strong and overbearing as Captain Weiss, there has never been much need for the subalterns to take charge. (Hanna, informed of this by the batmen along the way, shows no surprise.) He makes a laborious calculation. 'We shall send out six men,' he announces, turning to the young Günther. 'Corporal, you will pick five volunteers and depart in ten minutes.' Turning sharply on his heel he marches off at a pace rather too energetic for his short, corpulent figure.

Minutes later the great gate is swung open and Günther rides out with his small band of hand-picked men. Hanna nods at the other women. She, Katja and Nerina each grabs one of the guns which have been lying in readiness on the oxcart. Their three shots are fired in rapid succession, followed by a pause, and then another three shots *New commando on its way*, they signal to the distant Kahapa.

Sergeant Vogel comes running back from the barracks. 'What

the hell was that?' he shouts breathlessly. 'What do you think you're doing?'

'I'm sorry, Sergeant,' apologises Katja with her most seductive smile. (From the background young Werner gapes at her in open adoration.) 'But we thought we ought to honour your brave men with a few shots. Don't you think they deserve it?' She inclines her head. 'I'm sorry, Sergeant. I suppose when all is said and done, we're only women. We are not so used to controlling our emotions as you are. Please forgive us. We owe so much to you.'

'Well . . .' he mumbles. 'All right then. I appreciate your sentiments. But I'd prefer you to leave all shooting to the men who are trained to do it. We wouldn't like an accident in our midst.'

Together they stand looking after the departing soldiers who, after a sudden halt upon hearing the shots behind them, have resumed their brisk canter.

Auf Wiedersehen, thinks Hanna. *With some luck this will be the end of you.*

That leaves eleven soldiers in the fort, four of them temporarily out of action. And the three grooms.

57

THE NEXT MOVE is up to Katja. It is one of the many things they have discussed overnight. The girl has to persuade one of the soldiers to accompany her outside, ostensibly to point out the route the women will follow on their next lap to Windhoek. Once they are out of sight – and by going down the rocky eastern slope of the koppie at the back of the fort, this need not be very far at all – she will dispose of him. No one will notice the weapons concealed under her wide skirt.

She is free to choose anyone. But in the light of recent events the obvious victim, Hanna now points out, should be young Werner. Katja blanches visibly.

'But wouldn't it be better to find someone else . . . ?' she stammers. 'He is so very young, Hanna. What has he done?'

It is not what he has done, but what he is.

'If only this wasn't necessary.' Her breath catches in her throat.

I wish the same. But you know what we have to do. And above all, why. She shakes her head. I really don't know what is the matter with you lately. I realise just how hard it is. But he's playing right into your hands, Katja. There can be no better choice.

'Is it only killing and death you can think of now?' Katja asks with a vehemence Hanna has not seen in her before. 'Don't you have feelings any more?'

All I can still allow myself to feel is hate. This word she has to spell out letter by letter; she has no shorthand sign for it as yet. *There isn't room for anything else.*

'It will destroy you.'

On the contrary, it's the only thing that keeps me alive.

'Hate is hideous.'

I wish you could understand how clear and bright it can be.

'You must be out of your mind to say a thing like that.'

You think this land has space for anything else?

'It must have space for me too. And I cannot hate the way you do. I don't *want* to.'

You may not realise it, but you've already begun.

'I can still feel. I don't ever want to stop feeling.'

We cannot, cannot allow ourselves to have feelings, Katja. One day, perhaps. But not now.

'But then we're not human any more, Hanna!' Tears are running down her cheeks now. 'Then we're as despicable as the men we are fighting.'

The need to be violent — that, too, has been forced on us.

'No, we chose that. It wasn't forced.'

What other way did they ever leave open to us, Katja? Either we do something now to stop it, or we allow the world to go on like before. And that we will no longer accept.

'Whatever the cost?'

It depends on what we are fighting for, answers Hanna, struggling against her own emotion. In a quick, jerky movement she tears the kappie from her head, her face turned up to the sun. *Have you forgotten what they have done to us? To you? That night in Frauenstein . . . ?*

'Not all of them,' whispers Katja. 'Not Werner.'

If that is true, then you'll be saving him from becoming like the others.

'I can't believe that you can be so cynical, Hanna. Not you, of all people.'

Hanna places her hands on the girl's shoulders, then pulls Katja's face against her own shoulder. The blonde hair brushes against her burning cheeks. *It is myself I am condemning*, she thinks.

Katja turns away abruptly and goes towards the barracks where soldiers are cleaning and polishing and sweeping. Half an hour later Hanna sees the girl, very tense and pale, going to the stables with young Werner. When they come out again, both are on horseback. Near the gate she sees them talking to the sentry. There is a fair deal of discussion before the gate is drawn open. Slowly the young couple ride out. Hanna goes up to the rear wall to watch. They go down the rough hillside. They appear to be rapt in eager discussion. From the bottom of the koppie they cover a few hundred metres of open, even terrain. Then they move into a thicket. She does not see them emerge again at the far side. No one else appears to have noticed.

Hanna waits. It is taking longer than she expected. Could anything have gone wrong? Anxiety is trembling in her guts. If something were to happen to Katja she would be to blame, no one else. (But is it really Katja she is anxious about – or the possibility of one of her moves going wrong? The idea hits her like a stab in the chest.)

Then at last there is further movement below. Katja comes galloping back from the thicket. She is alone.

Hanna is at the front gate to greet her when it is opened. The girl is in a state, her hair dishevelled, tangled, her clothes crumpled. She has been crying; she is still crying.

Did you kill him?

Katja nods furiously, too emotional to speak. Soldiers are approaching, attracted by the noise of her return. And to Hanna's vast relief, and her astonishment, Katja manages to play her role to perfection in spite of the turbulence inside her. Unless that, too, is part of it?

'Someone must come quickly,' the girl gasps to her audience. 'A snake. There was a snake. Werner was bitten on the leg. Please send someone back with me or he'll die.'

There are several volunteers, but the sergeant designates only one of them.

Hanna grabs the bridle of Katja's horse and gesticulates urgently. *Let Nerina go with you too.*

Within minutes the three horses canter off. Hanna returns to the parapet, with the soldiers. A wave of anxiety tears through the fort. The horses disappear into the thicket. For a while everything is very quiet. Then a shot rings out. It is received with shouts and much running about along the wall, exclamations of dismay and shock. At last there is movement again below on the plain. The two women are on their way back, very slowly this time, on foot. They are leading the three horses.

'What is going on?' shouts Sergeant Vogel at the gate. 'Where's Werner? Where's Lionel?'

Katja is sobbing. It looks real enough. 'The snake came back. Werner tried to shoot it, although he was already very weak. It was too fast. He missed, and hit his friend. Now they are both dead.'

Nine left, thinks Hanna. Four of them incapacitated. This is becoming more manageable.

58

THE DAY IS not yet over. The bodies have been brought in. (Katja is not there to see; she has withdrawn under the hood of the oxcart.) Gloom has settled on the brown fort against the high koppie.

Towards noon there is a chattering of gunfire in the distance, from the hills. It continues for quite a while, fiercely, erratically; to those in the fort, men and women alike, it is nerve-racking. But at last it dies down. The pause that follows is even more worrying. Then comes a conclusion, a repeat of last night's volley: two brief series of three shots each. The women can breathe again: Kahapa's men have evidently finished off the second commando. But the soldiers in the fort are approaching a state of mutinous agitation: something has to be done, someone has to go and find out what has happened, it cannot go on like this. There is a curse on this place.

Sergeant Vogel has the heliograph mounted on the front wall again and tries several times to beam a message to the distant hills, but there is no response. He has more and more difficulty keeping his drastically diminished garrison under control. The three grooms, who seem beside themselves with fear, are confined to the stables. All four remaining able men are posted on the walls, while the sergeant scuttles to and fro between them and the suffering soldiers in the barracks. From time to time Hanna sends old Kamma to offer help with what remains of her potions. The sergeant is only too grateful for the assistance, which will ensure that the sick soldiers continue to suffer. The captain, who is the most seriously afflicted, is drifting in and out of delirium most of the time.

At lunchtime, through Katja, who is still almost too disturbed to react, Hanna asks one of the soldiers to take another bowl of soup to the desperately sick woman on the oxcart. He, too, does not return; but so unobtrusive has been his exit and such is the raging consternation in the fort, that no one registers it. Gisela's pile of bedding is growing steadily.

Eight soldiers left, only half of them fit to do battle.

In the mid-afternoon there is another salvo of shots from the koppies, the morning's pattern repeated – one, two, three, four-five – but although all the available men are falling over one another as they scramble to the front wall with their binoculars to scour the emptiness ahead it is doubtful whether anyone but the female visitors has recognised the repetition.

Hanna realises that a response is needed: Kahapa is now waiting for instructions. After the sergeant's reaction to the morning's parting volley she knows the risk involved; but the time for the endgame has come.

She hurries to the cart where Katja is lying on a bundle of blankets behind Gisela. The girl barely moves when Hanna arrives, staring fixedly at the canvas hood above her.

I'm calling Kahapa and the others back, Hanna informs her.

Katja shows no reaction.

Hanna grabs one of their guns and motions to Gisela and Nerina to do the same. With four fingers pressed together and her thumb held separate she orders them to fire their responding salvo: four shots in quick succession, a brief pause, then a single. *Come back.*

Katja stares listlessly at them; she seems unable to comprehend their urgency, even when Hanna grabs her by the shoulders to shake her.

The sentries come running towards them from the front wall; the thickset sergeant misses the bottom step of the stone staircase and approaches on all fours, his face a deep purple.

Hanna nudges Katja. But it is Gisela who calmly takes over, to the manner born.

'Your men needed some sign of reassurance from the fort, Sergeant, don't you think? It seemed to us the least we could do was just to let them know we're still all right in here. Whatever may have been happening to them out there.' She pauses briefly. 'We can but hope and pray that all went well.'

Sergeant Vogel makes an effort to control himself. He half-heartedly tries to brush dust from his khaki trousers before he stretches himself to his full, not very considerable, height. 'I do not want you women to get involved with any military matters again. However well-meaning your attempts may be. Otherwise I shall have to confiscate your guns. Is that understood? This is an order.'

'We are very, very sorry,' says Gisela with an air of genuine contrition. 'It's just . . . Our lives depend on you and your men, in here and out there. And we really thought – it was quite spontaneous – that some sign of support . . . It is all such a nightmare to us.' She breaks into tears.

'All right, all right.' He starts fumbling. 'I understand. But don't – please don't ever – try to interfere again.' Perturbed by her sobs, he raises his arms in a gesture of futility, and rounds up his men again to return to their sentry posts on the wall.

Hanna nods in satisfaction and pats Gisela on the shoulder. Then she turns back to Katja.

We don't have much time, she signals to the girl. *I'm going to fetch Tookwi. He's been keeping an eye on the grooms, but now we need him here. And you must interpret to him. Will you do that?*

Katja does not react.

Hanna shakes her again, gently this time. *Katja. Please.*

Still no reaction.

Hanna is conscious of a small tug of panic in her guts. This is the one eventuality she has not planned for. With Katja out of the equation she herself is plunged into silence, which will reduce her to near-impotence.

A shout goes up from a sentry on the wall with binoculars pressed, it seems, permanently to his eyes as if he is some strange man-sized mantis. 'They're coming back!'

The binoculars are passed from one pair of hands to the next.

'They're our soldiers indeed,' acknowledges the sergeant. 'I rec-ognise the uniforms. But there seem to be only four of them.'

'The rest must have gone on to find the other women.'

'Must have.'

No one dares to speak of an alternative.

Nudged by Hanna, Nerina and Kamma hurry to the staircase to join the soldiers on the wall. Gisela urgently leans over Katja to add her entreaties to Hanna's; but Hanna motions at her to leave her alone with the girl.

She presses down on Katja's shoulders. *Please. You must pull yourself together.*

'I have done enough. I'm not doing anything more.' The girl sounds too weary even to cry.

Katja. Fighting with every fibre to restrain her agitation, Hanna sits down beside the girl. In this moment everything is at stake. It may be more important than the battle which is still to come. *You knew it was not going to be easy. You chose to come with me.*

'Not for what we are doing now.'

Oh yes. For that and whatever still lies ahead. This thing is bigger than you and me.

'Nothing is bigger than life.'

Meine Liebe. It is the first time she has ever said this to Katja. *My darling. It is precisely for the sake of life that we have to do this*

After an agonising pause Katja turns her head. She takes a deep breath. For a long time she remains silent, struggling to regain her self-control. At last she says in a small voice, 'I'm sorry, Hanna. I didn't mean to be so weak. You must despise me very much.'

I admire you very much.

'I need you to help me.'

*I shall give you all the help I can. But right now I need **you**. If I bring Tookwi, will you tell him what to do?*

After a moment Katja nods. Without wasting another moment — every minute is infinitely precious right now — Hanna hurries off to the stables, where she finds Tookwi, as instructed, still in conversation with the three grooms, all of them visibly unsettled by what has been happening in and around the fort. Followed by the old man who looks like a praying mantis, she returns to the cart.

Katja is now sitting up, waiting for them. Hanna proceeds to give her quick, clear instructions to convey to the eager old man, and without delay he gets busy with his elaborate preparations behind the oxcart, clawing a small hollow into the ground, placing the chameleon – limp, but still feebly wriggling – on its back inside, covering it with earth, mumbling his invocations.

'I'm not going to pee again,' Katja says quickly, looking around as if she's scared someone may try to intervene. 'Not in front of these people.'

'Is all right,' Tookwi reassures her. 'This is not a snake, it is *gurutsi-kubib*, the chameleon. He comes straight from Tsui-Goab, goes straight back to him. He needs no girl's piss. This time we want the rain-bull, not the cow.' He makes a series of clicks, cocking his head. 'The only thing is we cannot hurry Tsui-Goab. It will make him angry.'

This time you **must** *ask him to hurry*, Hanna urges him through Katja.

Tookwi mumbles something incomprehensible. 'He will make us pay bad. But you say we hurry, so we hurry.'

We need the rain quickly, otherwise everything could go wrong with Kahapa and the others.

He resumes. But there is an interruption. Sergeant Vogel comes round the oxcart and stops to stare at them with grave suspicion on his perspiring face.

'What is this going on?' he demands to know.

Katja puts a finger to her lips. 'Shhh. He is praying to his ancestors. To bless your company and give them what they so richly deserve.'

The thickset man snorts, gazes down at them for another moment, then goes off.

They turn back to Tookwi's intricate performance, watching intently, half intrigued, half sceptical. Gisela, too, is leaning on one elbow over the edge of the cart. Nerina and Kamma complete the little gathering. They are all spellbound. But it is unlikely that any one of them really expects a result. Most certainly not the spectacular outbreak of a thunderstorm from a nearly empty sky barely fifteen minutes later, which sends everybody in the courtyard and on the walls scurrying for cover.

This is exactly what they are most in need of: a cataract of rain washing down in massive grey sheets, obscuring the surroundings of the fort so effectively that no one can see clearly any more. There are only brief glimpses of the approaching group; one can make out a huddle of horses, figures in dark uniforms, but no more. They have to take on trust that it is the patrol returning; and everybody is too overwhelmed by the suddenness of the event to think clearly. All the soldiers know is that they are in need of relief, which – almost literally in a flash – now seems at hand.

Without waiting for orders from Sergeant Vogel the sentries throw open the gates. There is a thin chorus of cheers. Which is drowned very quickly when Kahapa, Himba, Koo and the batman David come storming in among them. They are joined immediately by old Tookwi and the women from the oxcart. With guns and kieries and clubs they set upon the remains of the drastically depleted garrison.

The sick men come staggering from the barracks, too weak and bewildered to help and causing more of a hindrance than anything else. Within less than ten minutes there is no soldier left standing. Here and there one is still moaning in agony but Kahapa and Himba are doing the rounds with bayonets to administer the *coup de grâce*.

The rain continues to pour down for some time. Only the thin wet sounds of small, separate leaks and trickles along the stone walls continue. These, too, abate. And then there is only silence. The fort is taken.

59

LATER IN THE evening they are all gathered in the barracks around a new fire which Kahapa has made. The interior is thick with smoke, in which their faces drift eerily, ghost-like, lit by the torches which are flickering in the draughts from outside. In spite of the victory there is little exuberance. They are conscious of the bodies stacked like logs of firewood in the farthest, darkest corner. And of their own losses. Kahapa's group lost the sad monkey-man T'Kamkhab in their ambush of the first expedition sent from the fort the night before, while Himba has an ugly wound in the left shoulder. The two young Nama girls, the soldiers' whores, forced to stay behind with Kahapa in order to avoid suspicion at the fort, got caught in crossfire when, scared out of their wits by the fighting, they darted off blindly like hares in a hunt. In the second ambush, this morning, one of the two batmen who had accompanied them from the very first encounter on the plains had to be shot by Kahapa when he tried to escape. During the final battle in the fort itself, David was killed and old Tookwi badly trampled by a horse; it remains to be seen whether Kamma's medicine can pull him through.

The old man already seems to have resigned himself to death. 'It is the sacrifice of Tsui-Goab,' he mumbles whenever someone tries to encourage him. 'He is angry because I was in too much of a hurry to bring this rain. We already saw the sign when he sent the shooting star the other night.' Which wounds Hanna with a pang of guilt and remorse; but there is nothing to be done about it now, except urge Kamma to do her utmost.

Something else has happened to disturb her. The three grooms in the stable have been shot, but it is not clear by whom. Hanna is outraged. For a long time she confers intently with Katja, whose eyes appear unnaturally large and shiny in the torchlight and who seems, still, on the verge of hysteria.

If they were killed by someone from our side, Hanna instructs Katja to tell them, *this is the last time a thing like that will be tolerated. We kill in fighting, when we must, but we do not murder. Anyone who does this will be shot, even if I have to do it myself.*

'We cannot take risks with people who can be traitors,' Kahapa objects gruffly.

We cannot kill them before we have first made sure. Those three men could have been useful to us.

'One of the two batmen want to betray us,' Kahapa reminds her. 'That Lukas. All the time we think they are on our side, then the fight come and he go over to the soldiers. So I kill him.'

That was different. These grooms had no chance to show which side they were on.

'You are a woman,' grumbles Kahapa. 'What you know about men and war?'

It is my war, she responds, in a rage. *I shall decide what we do, and when, and how. If you don't like that you can go now.*

He is clearly taken aback. But for the moment he refuses to yield. 'You need me,' he retorts defiantly. 'If I am not here you can do nothing.'

And if I did not save your life you would not have been here at all.

The dense silence weighs on them like a burden almost too heavy to bear. Hanna has removed her kappie to expose the terrifying reality of her appearance. Unmoving, they stare at each other, watched by all the others. Their faces appear like blotches in the treacherous light.

After a long time Kahapa slowly inclines his head. 'You give me my life,' he says, his voice like a very subdued roll of thunder. 'I stay with you.'

60

MUCH LATER, WHEN Hanna and Katja lie close together on the oxcart
— all the others have chosen to bed down inside the barracks — the
girl whispers, 'You took a risk with Kahapa.'

I had to make sure. In his heart he is a man.

'He is no longer a man,' Katja reminds her. 'Don't you remember
what they'd done to him?'

It is not that thing alone that makes a man.

There is a silence. Overhead, so close they can almost be heard,
the stars are shining in a sky washed luminous and black. Then Katja
says, 'I have never lived a day like this.'

I am proud of you. Hanna holds the girl tightly against her, a
mother's comforting, possessive clutch. *For everything you've done.
Especially this morning.*

'You don't know what happened.'

You did what you had to do. That is all that matters.

'It wasn't just the killing,' says Katja in a drained voice, beyond
distress or fear or hurt. 'Before I killed him, he . . .' She breathes
in. 'I let him take me.'

Hanna feels her whole body go rigid. *What do you mean, 'take
you'?*

'That is why I could not have peed on Tookwi's chameleon
even if he'd asked me. I am no longer a girl who has never been
with a man.'

Hanna shakes her furiously. *I don't want to hear about it!*

'He was very gentle,' says Katja. Clearly she has to speak now,
nothing can silence her. 'Perhaps he was more afraid than I was. But

I made sure he wouldn't stop. I was in such a hurry I didn't even take off my shoes. I didn't want to waste time, because then he might have given up. And I had to go through with it. It was the only way in which I could forgive myself for what I had to do. Perhaps it makes no sense. Perhaps, where we are now, nothing makes sense. It is a madness. You yourself said so before. I'm not sure I understood what you meant then. But now I understand, and I believe you.' This time the silence lasts so long that Hanna asssumes she has said all she could. But then Katja asks in a wavering voice, 'Is this what it means to be a woman?'

Hanna shakes her head very decisively. *No. No. No, it doesn't. I think it has very little to do with it.*

'Still,' Katja persists, 'I know I had to do it. There was no other way. I had to find out what it is like.'

It could have waited.

'No. It was the right time. The only time. When we rode out from here I didn't think of it happening at all. But when we got there I knew it was the only way I could do it.' Another silence tense with the unspoken; the unspeakable. 'And when it was over, he was still lying on me, I killed him. Because that was what you expected of me. The first part was for me, the second for you.'

61

Is THIS WHAT she has become – an avenging demon? Nothing but this? In the dark silence, long after Katja has gone to sleep, Hanna remains looking up at the night. Words cannot reach where she wants to go. Only sounds and images remain. The sound of a piano broken apart, all its strings exploding, releasing the pent-up sound of years, lifetimes, darknesses. And behind the sound, the shadow of a woman she will never know and has never met, yet who will haunt her for ever, the shadow of whatever has remained unrealised in herself. *The second part is for you.*

62

I CAN IMAGINE how difficult it will be for Hanna to fall asleep that night. And listening to Katja's breathing – disturbed at intervals by anxious gasping, and once a bout of soundless crying – unsettles Hanna so much that at last, in some small hour into which no sound can reach, she rolls off the mattress and slips from the oxcart. It is a curious sensation to wander, barefoot, soundless, through the silent fort which until so recently teemed with life.

In the barracks she visits the quiet dead. But she does not stay long, because old Tookwi's moans suggest that he is awake and may awaken others too. Outside, she creeps up the stone staircase to the top of the walls where the sentries used to be posted. Her eyes move across the moonlit plains, trying to pick out the dark thicket into which Katja rode with her young suitor, the trip from which she returned alone. *I was in such a hurry I didn't even take off my shoes.* No, she must not think of that. But she cannot restrain her thoughts. Too much has happened over the past two days. It has gone so well. As such things go. And she, who has all her life been so clumsy in everything she attempted, has passed this test with so much confidence and efficacy that it would seem as if it she's always been destined for it. But is this really what she has foreseen? Is this what was supposed to happen? And for how long, how far, must it go on? Until they reach Windhoek, she imagines. And then . . . ?

Throughout this day, and through everything that has led up to it, she has had to contain herself, keep a tight, tight rein on her feelings. But now, at last, alone in the vastness of the night, she can feel a tremor building up inside. She still tries to control it. She must not, dare not, give way. She must keep the end in sight, otherwise nothing can be justified.

A slight moan escapes her. She tries to stifle it. At that moment a hand touches her shoulder from behind. The shock is so great that her whole body contracts; she would have fallen had two enormously strong arms not taken hold of her.

'Is me,' says Kahapa, so softly that it feels like a rumbling in the earth itself. 'I watch for you.'

As at the mission station. As everywehere. As always. *I watch for you.*

This is too much for her. She collapses against his massive shoulder. He sits down with her, his broad back supported against the high parapet, his arms holding her.

'If you want, you cry,' he tells her.

She doesn't know for how long she keeps shaking, her body sheltered against his, his hands holding her, making long stroking movements over her shoulders, her arms, her scarred face.

'You cry,' he says again.

It is an animal sound that comes from her, a sound from the depths of her being, the accumulated crying of a lifetime in which all her pain and bitterness, the lack of understanding, the futile gropings, the emptiness, the hope against all hope, the disappointments, the agonies, break out. And it takes a long time to subside. But he is patient, there is no irritation or haste or urgency in him, he has all the time in the world, she feels.

Spent, exhausted, she sinks into silence. Now she needs to talk, more urgently than ever since the night she lost her tongue. And yet she knows that even if she had a tongue tonight there would be no words for what she so desperately wants to say.

Perhaps he senses it. What he says, at last, without interrupting the slow rocking of her body cradled against him, is, 'I talk now?'

She nods her head against him in the dark.

'You tell me it is your war,' he says. 'I understand. But you must know it is my war too. It is the war of all of us. And you cannot fight, fight, all the time. You rest now. It is better like that. You understand?'

She nods. She is too tired to do more. She hears his voice rumbling in his chest again, but she can no longer make the effort to listen. She slides into sleep. For how long it lasts she cannot tell. But when she wakes up he is still holding her. Early light washes across his face which looms dark and peaceful above her.

I watch for you.

Empty, yet at the same time inexplicably fulfilled, she moves to her feet. Hesitates. Then bends down and presses her mouth against his forehead. Before she returns to the oxcart in the courtyard below.

63

AFTER THAT, I know, there will be other battles, skirmishes, encounters, other forts, other encampments on the veld which seems without
end. Behind them they leave the spectacle – in due course the memory
– of their conquered fort exploding, clad in flames, an unforgettable
display: having loaded as much of arms and ammunition on their cart
as the oxen can haul, everything else was taken to the barracks. Drums
of fuel kept for lamps, many bags of gunpowder, piles of thatch, stacks
of roughly made furniture, were all heaped up, and once everybody
had vacated the enclosure Hanna and Kahapa lit the torches and hurled
them inside. There was an ungodly explosion, and the place burned
for hours while they began to move on, almost reluctantly.

They have kept a few of the horses. All the others – and this
was an almost unbearable thing to do – had to be shot, as they
would either die if turned loose, or arouse suspicion should they
find their way back to wherever they came from. The two oxen
will be slaughtered along the way for food, and replaced by the
salvaged horses. What happens to these, will be determined when the
time comes by balancing their usefulness against their requirements
of fodder and, especially, water.

The small trek zigzags across the plains, trying to track what
Katja remembers of the directions young Werner had mapped
out for her before she killed him: from one well to the other,
the wells constructed a good time ago by von Trotha's troops to
make his war possible, to keep his army supplied as they trekked
through the untamed land to subdue and destroy Ovambos, Hereros,
Damaras, Namas, wherever there was still resistance to the might of

the imperial homeland. Sometimes they meet a lonely *smous* in his wagon; then time must be spent to establish the side he's on, and whether he is prepared to take them seriously or will treat them with derision. Depending on this, his life will be forfeited or spared. The same happens when they reach a farm, a small or extended family in the remoteness of the semi-desert. *You are either for us or against us*. To this immemorial formula everything is reduced. Life or death. It is so simple. When they espy a detachment of soldiers on some errand – and the powers of Kahapa, Himba and old Tookwi (still suffering from his injuries, often delirious) in detecting them never cease to stupefy Hanna and Katja and Gisela – they usually try to set up an ambush. They will use bows and arrows to pick off the last soldier in a straggling line, then the next, then the next; so that enough are eliminated by the time the vanguard discovers that something is amiss behind them. Only then will they resort to open battle.

Forts are often avoided, depending on how well-manned they appear to be. It is not necessary, or wise, to lay waste the whole land. And if a garrison is too large, and the opposing forces involved in open violence too uneven, and stealth and subterfuge too risky, they prefer to move on. They do not want news of their movements, their slow inexorable advance, to precede them.

More and more clearly, as they proceed, as one obstacle after the other is removed, their destination comes into focus. It may take months; late summer will be, abruptly, replaced by the translucent shivers of winter: but that is where they are heading for, and where the trek will end.

Windhoek.

64

ALL HER LIFE she has lived on the fringe of her own story, she thinks. Now at last she is taking charge of it herself. She makes it happen. She also *sees* it happen. Sees how through the last months of their wandering through the memory of the desert, as they move from ridge to ridge, from one armed patrol to the next, from well to well and fort to fort, their numbers increase. In the beginning, when she left Frauenstein, only Katja was with her. Then they found Kahapa, the man as massive as the omumborumbongo tree. From the farm of Albert Gruber they brought the monkey man T'Kamkhab who is no longer with them, and his strong wife Nerina enraged by her barrenness. At the mission station the woman of death, Koo, joined them, burnt up inside by the urge to find the bones of her child. And the medicine woman Kamma. And the warrior Himba, now still recovering from his wound. The rainmaker Tookwi. And Gisela, who has finally begun to avenge a lifetime of bitterness at the hands of her husband by killing men.

In the first fort every living soul was annihilated. But from the next they recruited five more followers; from the one after that, twenty; then thirty, then more. Whole garrisons who have somehow learned – from the wind, avers Kahapa – of their advance, come over to their side. Young men in the prime of their life, with the bloom of youth and arrogant innocence still on them. Whole Nama villages through which they pass, abandon their huts and goats and pots and mats to follow them. Travellers, *smouse*, farm labourers trekking in search of grazing, explorers, prospectors lured by tales of fabulous treasure waiting to be discovered, gun-runners, once the entire population of an unlikely brothel flourishing in the wilderness – everybody comes flocking towards them.

A day's journey from Windhoek they reach one of the vast concentration camps von Trotha has had constructed before his departure to contain the hundreds and thousands of indigenous people rounded up as a protective measure in the war: the populations of whole villages are siphoned into them, women and men and children indiscriminately, to ensure the safety of the hinterland. At the approach of Hanna's army the garrison in charge surrenders without firing a shot. Eight thousand detainees flood through the gates, famished and wasted but jubilant, to join the new army. Stretching from horizon to horizon, they move on, triumphant before they have even engaged in battle.

And not only the living, but the dead as well, come flocking to Hanna's standard of buckram and silk, in blue and silver and gold. Graves open as they pass and yield up their humble occupants, some still with skin and dried flesh on them, others skeletons with rattling bones and invincible grimaces. The numerous ghosts from the corridors and empty spaces of Frauenstein return to Hanna to show their solidarity. A host of ghosts, from all over the country, from the distant south where the great Gariep runs into the Atlantic and washes out its diamonds on the sand to the far north where the Kunene winds its tortuous way through mountains and forests, spilling over its banks to leave whole plains inundated, brilliant in the moving sun. And still they come, from all times, all layers of time. The black women stolen by Diaz from the coast of Guinea, the hordes of slaves gathered in the House of the Dead on the isle of Gorée off the coast of Senegal and who died even before they boarded the ships for the New World, all the innumerable ghosts of the wastelands on the great continent. The *hei nun*, as the Nama people call them, the grey-feet; the *sobo khoin*, the people of the shadows. Throbbing and thriving, grim and grey, they advance from all sides to clamour for their liberation, at last, God, at last. A horde so great that not even the light of the sun can penetrate them. Like a vast cloud they come sweeping across the landscape, a shadow of death claiming the life they have been deprived of, over centuries and centuries. Moving with Hanna and her host, an army like no one has ever seen or dreamed of, growing, ever growing, like a silence trapped inside a shell suddenly starting to swell into a whisper, a drone, a boom, an exultant triumphant roar that demolishes everything before it, a huge wave breaking over the ruined land to bring hope, and life, and life, and life.

This is what she sees, what she dreams of.

In a mirage the trees are always upside down.

65

WHAT REALLY HAPPENS in the desert is very different. In retrospect, the moment of their great triumph in the fort seems more and more to have been also the beginning of a decline, an entry into darkness and adversity. It begins with the death of old Tookwi. In spite of all Kamma's remedies (or because of them, Katja dares to suspect) the old rainmaker never gets well again; and eight days after they have blown up the fort they wake up to find he has quietly died in the night.

'It is Tsui-Goab,' says Kamma with a knowing nod; as if they needed the reminder.

And not even a week later they lose Nerina as well. The death of T'Kamkhab in the ambush among the koppies has hit her harder than they would have expected from someone as strong and angry as Nerina. Often she has seemed more of a mother than a wife to him; as if in looking after a man brought up to be the fool of others she could express all the dammed-up love left in her after being compelled to accept the fact of her own barrenness. She seemed, Hanna sometimes thought, condemned to continue looking in the desert for the children she'd lost by aborting them when she couldn't face the idea of bringing into the world the babies of German soldiers. As if for the rest of her life she wouldn't be left in peace by their shadows. And now she is gone. One morning when they wake up she is no longer there. Hanna is stricken. Her first thought is that a predator may have come in among them in the night and carried her off. But there are no tracks; and there were no sounds.

It is Kahapa who tries to explain the inexplicable: 'T'Kamkhab is dead. Her children is gone. She must go too.'

'But she has nowhere to go!' protests Katja.

'So that is where she go. Nowhere. To find what she has not lost.'

'How can we go on like this?' asks Katja, a hint of despair in her voice. 'There were ten of us. Now we're only seven.'

It is not a matter of numbers but of will, Hanna gently reminds her.

But she thinks: We are all in search of what we have not had, are we not? The children, the dreams, everything that was never allowed to become what might have been. Everything which diminishes what *we* are capable of and now will never know. But for that very reason we cannot stop. The going itself is more important than loss or gain. We are here because we must go on. We will go on because we are here. As long as those of us who remain can stay together we shall not give up.

She studies the others when they are not looking. Her army, her sad menagerie. Katja, the gazelle girl, her early sprightliness beginning to fade. Gisela, a pale beaked stork, withdrawing more and more into herself. The toothless Kamma, a shrivelled little baboon, mumbling over her herbs and smelly tufts of hair and bits of skin. Koo, the owl-woman, whose eyes are ever on the distance where she imagines the bones of her lost son. Kahapa the lonely elephant bull. Himba the wounded buffalo. And she herself, the morose marabou. They can make it. They must. They will.

Then comes their most calamitous day.

66

THEY SEE THE little fort from quite a long way off, set on a low rise above a plain covered in thorn trees. There are too few of them now to work out the kind of battle plan that worked so well at the first fort: not knowing how many soldiers are housed inside they would be foolhardy to mount an ambush with only two or three of their own; and the thorn trees provide less shelter than the rocky outcrops they were able to use as a hideout the first time. So all they can do is to approach as openly as possible and hope to devise something once they arrive; if the odds are too big, as they have been on a few other more recent occasions, they will simply feign innocence and ask for shelter overnight.

Their approach is closely watched from high up on the front wall of the little fort: they can make out at least eight men, later ten, several of them with binoculars, all armed with rifles. Hanna leads her group on a relaxed trot so as to allay suspicion. As by this time they have only five horses left, apart from the two pulling the cart, Katja and Gisela share one mare, Kamma and Koo another. Kahapa and Himba each has his own gelding; so does Hanna, as befits a commander.

Six soldiers in uniform emerge from the wide front gate when they draw up outside. Hanna reins in her horse. Her troops follow suit.

'Who are you?' shouts the commanding officer, a man with bright red hair and a red moustache. 'What do you want?'

By this time they all know the story by heart, so Katja replies without prompting, 'We come from the mission station of Pastor Maier. This is his wife. We're on our way to Windhoek. Can you put us up for the night?'

'What are these natives doing with you?'

'They're escorting us for our protection. They are all members of Reverend Maier's congregation.'

'You three white women can come in.'

'What about our two domestic servants?'

The officer confers with his men. 'All right then,' he announces, clearly reluctant. 'But the men must be locked up until you leave. We can't take any risks.' He shrugs. 'I'm sorry, but I'm sure you will understand.'

'Can't the men camp outside?'

'No.'

If some of us are not allowed inside, we'll all stay outside, Hanna angrily prompts Katja. But Gisela interrupts her. They need a proper rest. And who knows, once they're inside . . .

After a moment Hanna consents. Kahapa and Himba withdraw into themselves in sullen anger. They are disarmed by the soldiers and roughly marched to a small dark cubicle attached to the barracks inside the enclosure; clearly some kind of detention cell. In the tussle Kahapa's hat is knocked from his head. This so enrages him that for a moment Hanna fears that he will break loose and attack his captors, which will endanger them all.

She urgently jabs Katja in the side and the girl calls out, 'Please, Kahapa! Don't!'

In the brief silence that follows Hanna rushes forward, picks up the hat, dusts it, and presses it against her chest in a protective and reassuring gesture. Several of the soldiers look at her in open disapproval, if not disgust. The big man makes an effort to restrain himself before he is bundled into the cell. From the low heavy door he briefly looks back, smouldering.

Hanna waves at him with the hat. *It won't be for long*, she tries to signal; but whether he understands she does not know.

The door is locked, the key pocketed by the lieutenant.

The cart, with Gisela on it, is pulled into the courtyard and left in the care of Koo and Kamma, while the other women are offered a corner in the barracks. A couple of soldiers rig up a curtain to offer them some privacy. But from the way in which they eye Katja it does not seem as if much store can be set by that.

It is not a happy place. The fifteen soldiers who man it have not been relieved for months, their commander's discipline is strict, their food supplies are running as low as their morale.

I'm sure we can win some of them over to our side, Hanna tells Katja while the red-haired Lieutenant Müller, flanked by two orderlies, takes them on a tour of the fort.

'We don't have time,' the girl whispers anxiously. 'For God's sake, don't try anything rash.'

We cannot let them get away with what they've done to Kahapa and Himba.

'This is just a small stop on our way,' Katja reminds her. 'We still have far to go. Please don't risk everything now.'

We shall see. The square set of her jaw alarms Katja even more than what she has said in her sign language.

But Katja has to reconsider when in the late afternoon they are invited, with a suspect show of generosity, to attend a session of 'target practice' behind the fort. With the exception of two sentries left on the walls, the whole garrison is in attendance. In what looks like a cattle kraal a number of Nama prisoners, about thirty or forty of them, are kept shackled together. They are in a shocking state. It is obvious they haven't been fed in days, and in the open kraal, exposed to the blaze of the sun by day and the fierce desert cold by night, they are clearly in the last stages of deprivation.

Six of the prisoners are unshackled and dragged outside and ordered to run. Only two or three make the effort to stagger to their feet, the rest remain sprawling on the ground. Lieutenant Müller makes a curt gesture with his head to his men. They need no further instruction. Surging forward, they set upon the prisoners with sjamboks and the butts of their rifles to beat them to their feet. The Namas break into a pitiful imitation of jogging. That is when the target practice starts.

'Stop them!' shouts Gisela, grabbing the lieutenant by the arm. 'For God's sake, you can't do that!'

'My men need to stay in shape,' he answers with a pinched grin like the cut of a knife across his face. 'You must try to understand. It is the only diversion we can offer them to keep them happy.'

Without waiting to see any more the women hurry back round the walls of the fort to the entrance. Behind them the shooting and the shouting continue. Both Gisela and Katja have to stop along the way to vomit. Hanna doesn't, but tears are running down her cheeks. She makes no sound.

You see, we have no choice, she tells Katja once they are back at their cart inside the enclosure. *These men have no right to live. Do you agree?*

Katja sits with her knees drawn up, hiding her face in her arms. 'They will kill us all,' she says. She looks up. 'But you're right. We have no choice.'

With strange detachment Hanna discusses her strategy with them. It is desperate; but they cannot come up with anything better. Koo and Kamma are brought into the discussion; Kamma silently starts working on her potions. Before the men return Katja goes to the heavy door of the detention cell to talk to Kahapa inside.

Shortly before supper, the sun already down, the men return. The sullenness they have shown during the day seems to have lifted; but there is a kind of desperation in their exaggerated jocularity. It is, Katja whispers to Hanna, like singing an obscene song at a funeral.

Unlike the copious meals they have been served by garrisons elsewhere, this supper is frugal. And not very well prepared. Not one of the women is in a mood for talking, but they grimly try to swallow their hostility, although Hanna offsets it in a gesture of dangerous defiance by taking Kahapa's hat with her to the mess and putting it on the table next to her place.

The lieutenant tries to ignore it. 'It seems the ladies were too delicate to enjoy our target practice?' he sneers.

They remain silent.

'You must not try to compare it to life on a mission station,' he persists. 'It is not souls we are trying to save but our country.'

'Perhaps there are other ways,' says Gisela icily.

'We are at war,' he points out. 'Don't forget that.'

'In all the time we have been trekking through the desert,' says Gisela with a hard edge to her voice, 'we have heard many soldiers talking about the dangers of this war. But we have never seen it. We have only seen peace and quiet.'

'You are women,' he says in a patronising voice. 'You do not know what to look for. I cannot expect you to understand the world of men.'

'There you are quite right,' snaps Gisela.

The evening seems headed for disaster. But then, to the surprise of the others, Katja turns to the lieutenant, her eyes unnaturally bright. 'I think it takes a very brave man to survive in conditions like these,' she says. 'Of course we were shocked this afternoon. But it is because we cannot hope to understand what you have to put up with. Without men like you there would be no Germans left in Africa.'

It seems amazing that he should fall for this. But for the rest of the meal he ignores Hanna and Gisela to focus all his attention on the young woman. And long after the table has been cleared and the soldiers have withdrawn to their sleeping quarters he is still in earnest conversation with Katja. Which gives her ample opportunity unobtrusively to lace his beer with old Kamma's concoction. He must be far gone, she thinks derisively, not to notice the bitter taste. But she puts away all thought and feeling, hardly even glancing towards Hanna and Gisela in the shadows on the far side of the table, as she concentrates only on what is at hand, on the flow of this conversation.

More and more unevenly it moves on as the men on their bunks begin to snore. The officer is turning maudlin, telling Katja about his family, his wife, his three adorable children – just look, here I have a photograph of them, don't you think they're beautiful? I cannot wait to see them again. To get out of this goddamned place, back to civilisation, to decent people, musical evenings, bands playing in the park of a Sunday, visits to good friends, green green trees and manicured gardens. Gardens. Children. Gardens. So green, so green. And then he is gone.

Katja feels nauseous again. But this is not the time.

From the breast pocket of his uniform she retrieves the key to the detention cell. In a minute the two prisoners are free. The hat with the band of leopard skin is restored to Kahapa.

There is a near-full naked moon. Which helps them. But it will also help the two sentries on the front and back walls.

Like shadows they flit across the courtyard. Kahapa and Himba creep up the stairs to the sentry posts. With surprising ease – but they are so used to this by now – they garrotte the two guards and throw the bodies over the wall. Now the women can move about more easily. They open the stable doors and begin to lead out the horses, two by two; their own and those of the garrison. To make sure they cannot be pursued later. Down in the valley below the horses are tethered to the thorn trees.

Afterwards, the Nama prisoners in the kraal behind the fort are freed. Later, Hanna may find it difficult to explain this impulsive decision. Everything else she has done has been so lucidly planned and executed; whence, then, this one moment of rashness? It can only have been prompted by the excess of rage stirred up in her by the treatment of the prisoners at the hands of their captors that afternoon. And even when they are set free the wretched Namas are in such a state that they seem incapable of realising what is happening; most of them simply cower, trying to cover their heads against the blows they take for granted. Some do not even move. Only a few of the strongest seem to grasp the unbelievable and stagger to their feet in the dull moonlight.

They do not have too much time. What they are waiting for is the relief of the guard at midnight; this information, with everything else they need to know, Hanna has elicited, through Katja, from the lieutenant on their first conducted tour. With the two new sentries out of the way, the garrison will be down to thirteen. Still an uncomfortable disproportion, but the risk will be lessened.

Once all the horses are outside, they pull the cart to the entrance. This will allow only one or two persons at a time to go past. And none at all if Hanna's strategy succeeds.

Kahapa, Himba and Hanna return to the sentry posts on the wall. They are all armed with guns and pistols now. As soon as the new guards have been killed, Himba will go down to join the other women in the courtyard below.

But that is where it all goes wrong. Just before the new sentries are to come on duty the silence of the night is rent by noises from behind the fort. As the reality of their release has begun to dawn on more and more of the prisoners in the kraal, shouts of surprise and jubilation grow from a series of low uncertain separate murmurs into a chorus of amazement and celebration. Soldiers, befuddled with sleep, some naked, some partly clothed, come stumbling and tumbling from their quarters, spilling into the courtyard, not knowing what the hell is going on.

Hanna's depleted troops are caught just as unprepared. From her post on the wall she sees Kahapa jump down the outside of the wall to join the others at the gate.

She knows that she has to follow. But the wall is much too high. Still, the only alternative is to be caught. She closes her eyes, and jumps into the darkness, to her certain death.

67

Koo, who is supposed to watch in the courtyard for a signal from Hanna, panics in the sudden confusion that engulfs the fort and rushes forward to put the cart to the torch. Immediately the whole load of gunpowder explodes, taking her with it. Not a shred of clothing, not a bone of her body, will be left. The night turns a furious red as if Gaunab, the god of darkness, has come down from the sky.

Hanna does not meet her death. Inexplicably, perhaps miraculously, she lands on her feet outside the wall, and goes down on hands and knees the moment the cart explodes in the courtyard. Purely by instinct she starts running. Kahapa, she assumes, will be doing the same.

But the angry giant has landed, swearing and cursing and bellowing, on a heap of loose stones, and has broken his hip, collapsing in agony. At the front entrance Himba and the others are thrown back by the impact of the explosion, but manage to scramble to their feet to shoot wildly at anyone who tries to break past the burning cart through the gates of hell.

When at last they reach the thorn trees where the horses are supposed to wait, they find that most have snapped their reins and bolted, obviously terrified by the explosion. Two others have half strangled themselves and broken their legs; they have to be shot at close range. On the remaining three Hanna and Katja and Gisela, Himba and Kamma succeed in making their escape. At least they cannot be pursued with any effect. But they have no idea if it has been defeat or victory.

From a safe distance, shaking with shock and rage, they watch for a long time the fire blazing in the night, eclipsing the tentative stars.

We have to go back, Hanna urges Katja. *We must find Kahapa, we cannot leave him there.*

But they may all be killed if they do. Both Katja and Gisela physically hold her back. Even so she might have broken free; but Himba joins them in restraining her, leaving her sobbing with rage and frustration.

Throughout the long day that follows they have to wait in the distance, hidden among trees. There are still signs of life at the fort, a few soldiers moving about, appearing on the walls to scour the veld through binoculars, emerging from the front, setting to work on mending the gate and a caved-in portion of the wall before dark.

Katja is anxious to continue on their way while they can; even if the fort has not been wiped out, they must have decimated the garrison. There is reason to be content. But Hanna refuses. They will not budge until Kahapa has been found, she insists with quiet fury. They have never seen her in such a state. No one dares to counter her. And through the long hours of the winter's day, white with piercing light, they wait for night to fall.

As it turns out, they have no problem finding Kahapa. Though it is not easy to recognise the man they used to know so well. The body has been thrown out, like garbage, right in front of the gate. It seems barely human, more like a large slaughtered animal. Because it has been flayed. Not a tatter of skin remains on the bloody mess of flesh and sinews and bones, the eyes gouged out.

And then the shooting starts. Surely they should have been alert to that. The body has been thrown out as bait to lure them close. But the discovery of Kahapa is so terrible that for some time they can do nothing but stand and stare. It can only be the treachery of the moonlight, or the excessive eagerness and rage of the few attackers on the walls, that prevents the total, swift annihilation of Hanna's army. All around them bullets thud and zing past, ricocheting, sounding from close by like angry bees. But they do get away.

Except for Himba, who refuses to mount his horse. Making no attempt at all to hide, or even to duck, he storms the gate on his own and takes up position right in front of it, his chest heaving, his legs planted into the earth like tree stumps, his gun pressed against his barely healed shoulder. It is likely that he brings two or even three of his attackers down from their high perch on the wall (there is no time to make sure). But then, inevitably, with a smothered groan, he himself goes down.

Before the end of the night Kamma disappears. No one has seen her go. It is as if she has simply vanished, without sign or sound, leaving nothing at all behind. The desert has reclaimed her.

And the following morning Gisela takes what has remained of the potion prepared for Lieutenant Müller, and dies very peacefully.

Only Hanna and Katja remain.

68

KATJA NO LONGER bleeds. She is pregnant.

69

THE VULTURES ARE the first sign of life they see as they approach the hills above the town. In intricate, interwoven spirals they descend to the rubbish dumps on the far side of the hollow in which the small, tidy town with its four thoroughfares is set.

And then the palms. Palms everywhere. Along the axis of the main street – the Kaiser Wilhelmstrasse, Katja informs Hanna, with an unexpected catch in her throat – and in small clusters among the sprinkling of homes, around the fort and the few sprawling administrative buildings on the opposite hillside, and on the outskirts. An emerald oasis in the harsh brown landscape. It could be a place of dreams, nestled deep in the whorl of a shell.

'How strange,' says Katja. 'I almost cannot believe that it has taken us so long to get here.'

The Israelites took forty years to cross the desert from Egypt to Canaan.

'You think this is our Promised Land?'

It has palm trees.

'Shall we go down now?'

Hanna nods quietly.

They tether the horses to a tree and start the descent on foot. Now that at last they have arrived, they are reluctant about covering the final lap. It takes a long time to climb down.

Hanna remembers, wryly, her childhood dream of leading a procession through the streets, a woman arrayed in purple and scarlet colour and sitting on a scarlet coloured beast, with seven heads and ten horns. It was supposed to be Bremen then, certainly a larger town than this Windhoek.

The place is bustling like a broken anthill. After the silence of the desert even a normal day here would have been bewildering; but this is clearly not a normal day. Judging from the number of carts and carriages and wagons of all descriptions cluttering the streets (there are even a few motor cars) many of the people must have arrived from elsewhere in the colony. Perhaps there is a fair? The crowd gets more and more dense as they approach what Katja recognises as the railway station. In this turmoil no one pays any attention to the two women.

Katja stops a man in lederhosen to ask about the crowds.

A train has just arrived from Swakopmund, he tells them, so eager to move on that half of what he says is spoken over his shoulder. They're bringing in passengers from a ship that landed four days ago. A new consignment of women, he explains, his face glowing with excitement.

Hanna feels her guts contract. For a moment she wants to turn around and head for the desert again.

Katja, sensing her distress, reaches for her hand. 'We needn't do this,' she says. 'We can go round the crowd.'

No, I have to see it.

Of course she has no recollection at all of her own arrival. She was dead.

From the station building, obscured by the crowd, they can hear the deep farting of a brass band, oompah-oompah.

Troubled but fascinated, unable to move — because of the crowd, because of the leadenness in their own limbs — they stare ahead. The people are shuffling laboriously out of the way to let the new arrivals pass. The two sides are lined by soldiers in uniform, staring stiffly ahead, as if they are not even aware of the passengers they are allowing through, a thin band straggling through a parted sea, heading towards some as yet unseen tract of land promised by the Lord of hosts. Oompah-oompah, the band goes. It is like the Rathausplatz in Bremen on a Sunday afternoon. *Deutschland, Deutschland über alles.*

The newly disembarked passengers approach, two by two, like animals from an ark, one couple after another, man and woman, man and woman, a seemingly endlessly procession. Most are holding hands, some walk in a tight embrace; others simply stride stiffly beside each other, not exchanging looks, not saying anything. Many of the men are red-faced, several openly drunk; a few have to be dragged along by cronies, with embarrassed women shuffling after them. There are pale and haggard faces among the women, but most have a determined look about them, as if to defy the world. They *are* happy, goddamnit. They *are* in a new land of opportunity. They *are* going to make a success of it. They will get married. They will have many children to populate the empty land and ensure a future for civilisation, christianity, the German Reich. Oh God have mercy.

After the couples there follows a large and rumbustious crowd of men, uproariously drunk, shouting obscenities, collapsing with mirth, lurching forward to vomit, singing songs from the distant fatherland. Occasionally soldiers intervene to remove some of the more obnoxious elements. Right at the back, like a small bundle of sheep somehow cut off from the flock, follow a group of women. They are the ones not chosen, the outcasts, unwanted by man or beast. They look dishevelled and unwashed, crumpled like dirty laundry, lank hair hanging tattily over their wan faces. They are not crying, but it is only, one surmises, because they have no tears left. They are way beyond all that. Clearly they have all been used on the four-day journey from the coast. And thrown away, like snotty handkerchiefs. They are covered in filth, grime, spittle, semen. And even as they stumble along people in the crowd hurl peel and eggs and tomatoes at them, jeer at them, spit at them. Drunken men tear open their flies to piss on them, then collapse with laughter. At the far end of the tunnel through which they pass, two ox-wagons are waiting. Most likely they will take the discarded women through the desert to that out-of-reach place everyone has heard about but no one wants to see, the prison, the nunnery, the brothel, the shithouse, Frauenstein.

On moonless nights, Hanna remembers – a quite irrelevant memory – the huge house, the ship stranded in the desert, breaking away from its moorings, straining against gravity, and soaring up into sky, a magical journey, beyond the reach of the world, its load of grey ghosts intact.

The two women do not cry, they do not speak. They just stand there.

'We must go on,' Katja says at last, gently tugging Hanna by the arm. 'We still have a lot to do today.' This may be the completion of a circle, but it is not yet their destination.

I need some time on my own.

Katja breathes in slowly, quietly, and nods. She knows this is not the moment to protest. And there is no need to discuss what remains to be done: they have gone over it so many times already.

'I'll do my best to find him,' she says. 'Take care. I shall be back.'

70

THE STATION IS deserted by now. The people have dispersed in the wake of the procession, the band has packed up and left, the last few drunks have staggered to their feet from their puddles of piss and vomit. Only their litter remains behind. Hanna instals herself on a corner of the wide stoep, her back resting against a pillar. Vacantly she stares ahead. This moment, she knows with a sense of sadness, but also of deep satisfaction, is perhaps the most necessary of her life. A life that suddenly feels immeasurably longer than it has been. Behind the anxiety and the tumult of her emotions is an awareness of the inevitable. She cannot have too much longer to go on. And there are still so many memories to sort out.

Leaning back, she looks up at the fronds of the high palms in front of the brown sandstone building with its red roof. At last she is where she has wanted to be, even if it is so very different from her dreams. She remembers the first picture of palm trees she saw in the Children's Bible in the orphanage, and how it enthralled her, transported her to places as yet without names, long before in her sessions with Fräulein Braunschweig the names began to sound in her mind like a memory of bells. Guadalquivir, Macchu Pichu, Smolensk, Barbezieux, Parramatta, Ondangua, Omaruru, Otjiwarongo. How they soothed and comforted her in the dark hole in which they locked her up when she was a child, when she fell ill and died and led her army of rats up the stairs to sweep into the room where Frau Agathe was waiting, all in black. Her own glorious, victorious army, from Chinon to Poitiers to Orléans to Rheims. Closing her eyes, she can still hear the soft droning of Fräulein Braunschweig's voice reading and reciting. The stories of Jeanne, of young Werther, of Bluebeard, of Cinderella, of the little Goatherd, of the poor outcast Musicians of Bremen who took their revenge on an unaccommodating world. A voice that imperceptibly becomes smaller, speaking now with an accent that must be Irish. Susan with the little mole below her navel, peeing frothily in the dam they have made in the sand, holding against her ear the shell that will change her life, a shell that reaches out, far beyond all silence, to what lies forever beyond, like a world without end. There are the sounds of her voices, some stern and damning, others sugary with evil (*Stand closer, child, let us see where you are trying to hide your sins — Now take off your shirt, I promise not to touch . . .*), the shrill giggly whispers of Trixie, Spixie and Finny, speaking from the far side of the Little Children of Jesus, deep within her dreams, the screeching of cicadas, the call of a hadedah in the twilight, the explosion of a piano smashed to pieces.

Not only sounds does she recall. Smells too. The smells of the orphanage — sauerkraut, leeks, potatoes, fish heads steaming in a pot. So much later, the smells of the sea, of Lotte's hair, of Lotte's love. The tobacco and stale sweat in the office at Swakopmund. The cellary smells of Frauenstein, of mustiness and ghosts and dry rot, of women menstruating. And then the smells of Africa, its dryness and its acrid shrubs, its bitter aloes, its veldfire smoke, the sudden generosity of its rain, Tookwi's rain, the good god Tsui-Goab's rain, sometimes female and gentle, sometimes fierce and devastating and male.

And tastes and smells. Carrots stolen from the orphanage garden, small gritty lumps of mud still clinging to them. Stew in Fräulein Braunschweig's cosy kitchen. Kässler ribs with Opa and Oma. Salted pork on the ship, and the tang of sea-spray on the equator. The bitter, healing concoctions of the wise old woman Taras. The thin broth of the parsonage at the mission station. The taste of rain, of an ostrich egg, of a strip of roasted springbok meat, a locust.

Yes, and textures. The polished wood of the desk in the Herrenzimmer. The pockmarked column against which she presses her face when she hides in the cathedral to listen to the organ. The smoothness of a chess piece, ebony or ivory, between her fingers. The stone bannisters in Frauenstein. The eroded surface of the rock formation in the shape of a woman trying forever to look back. The coarseness of desert sand, the silkiness of an aloe leaf. The powdery dust of a skin shed by a snake.

Sight, then. The beads of perspiration on Pastor Ulrich's upper lip. Frau Agathe's sewed-on button eyes. Frau Knesebeck's fowl-arse mouth. Cobblestones in Bremen glistening in the rain. A bleeding sunset. The pale wash of the squat little church at the mission. The hat perched on Kahapa's head. The skinny girls of the missionary. A fort erupting spectacularly in flames. The slow, unstoppable progress of a tortoise in the veld. The smooth porcelain of a chipped figurine – a donkey, a dog, a cat and a rooster – displayed on a crude matchbox dresser at the church *Messe*.

All the memories subsumed in her many deaths. The vaguely remembered blackness from which she first awoke in the Hutfilterstrasse, knowing there must have been something before it, without ever retrieving more than ragged ends trailing off, back into the dark. The peat-cellar below the orphanage. The bitter pills she took after old Opa's quiet death. Lotte changing places with herself. The night on the train, watching the buckled belts come off. Her fall – her jump? – from the wagon on the road to Frauenstein. Succumbing to exposure in the desert. Hurling herself from the wall of the fort. Followed every time by a return to life, because there was still unifinished business to assume.

Her years in the Little Children of Jesus: wetting her bed, caught out on lies or her many 'stories', running back to her imaginary friends, to the moon or the place where the wind comes from; beatings, beatings, beatings. Her first bleeding, *I think you're growing into a woman*, says Fräulein Braunschweig who gives her cloths and books. *Die Leiden des jungen Werther*. Her years in service: Herr Dieter depositing the small pile of coins on the corner of his desk, the list of sins in Frau Hildegarde's spidery handwriting. Herr Ludwig's face in the light of the lamp. Opa's fabulous instrument that makes no sound. Frau Sprandel behind the long table with the dusty light from behind: *As long as you don't expect too much of your palm trees*. And the sea voyage with the silvery flying fishes and the phosphorescent water and the swell sighing in its equatorial sleep, and Lotte's breathing in her ear, her body wrapped in canvas and tipped into the black waves. The man to whom she is assigned in the drab office at Swakopmund, his narrow head, his broad hands, his rasping voice: *All it takes is a little firmness. There are ways and means.* Then the men with the knives and the belts and the rough wedge of wood. The swaying and jolting of the wagon. Waking up among the Namas with their herbs and stories. A whole land, a whole continent of stories. The beautiful vain woman Xurisib, the Milky Way of Tsui-Goab. The omumborumbonga tree from which the first man and the first woman emerged. Frauenstein with its hidden fountain where a body lies hidden, restored to bone by now. Frauenstein with its ribbed dunes of sand invading the lower rooms, its mottled mirrors and dark empty spaces, its barren women. Her attempts to write her story for Frau Knesebeck, to find someone who will read it, going up in flames. So much has gone up in flames these last months. And then that night after the clamour and cavorting of the military men had died down, the thud-thud-thud of a head dragged down the stone stairs. Katja cowering naked in a corner. The truth of her own face, her body, for the first time in years, in the mirror, by candlelight. This once she must look and not avoid anything. Then out towards the emptiness outside, and the voice behind her saying, *Where are you going?* Oh God, little Katja. Could you ever have suspected what would happen? Those early days, living on *tsammas* and tortoises and roots and sometimes honey. The vultures circling over the anthill with Kahapa's mutilated body. *The German way.* The rage of Albert Gruber, the unmarked grave enclosing the bones of a woman who once played the piano. The pitiful little oasis of the mission station, the prayers in the church, the stifling nights in the parsonage, the tiny coffin deposited in the much-too-shallow grave.

She reviews her troops. The mighty Kahapa who feared no man and held her in his arms and then was flayed alive. Himba the wounded warrior who stormed a fort on his own and drew all the fire on himself. Kamma who dispensed life and death with her potions. The sad monkey T'Kamkhab and his smouldering wife, playthings of an occupying army. Tookwi who brought rain when they needed it, a merciful rain-cow followed by the mad rage of a rain-bull. The woman of death, Koo, who never found the bones of her child and did not even leave her own behind. And Gisela with her beaked face, her dead eyes, briefly thriving on violence before it all became too much for her.

Leaving only Katja with her. Katja who was smitten with her beautiful Werner and made love to him with her shoes on, and killed him, and now bears his child. Oh my Katja, my little girl, my resurrected Lotte, my own young long-haired self. 'How far do we go on? Until what happens?' *Until we know what is on the other side.* 'Suppose it never ends?' *Then at least we'll know the desert.*

All of it, all this life, written on her body, in her blood, all of it gathered around a hate that is perhaps no longer adequate, reduced to – what? Her silent self sitting here on the corner of a wide stoep deserted of people, a stoep across which generations of women have passed towards their own versions of palm trees in the sun. Who will ever know about them? Who knows about her? One woman against the whole German Reich, against the world. Katja, Katja. Will you ever understand? Will I ever understand? To be mad in this place is the only sanity.

71

SHE IS STILL sitting there when Katja returns in the late afternoon.

'We must go and find something to eat,' says the young woman. 'You must be exhausted.'

She just shakes her head. The grimace of her slashed mouth shows that she is smiling.

Did you find out something?

Katja is silent. Hanna knows what the answer will be: *The man returned to Germany years ago.* Or perhaps: *No one remembers him any more. When I ask about Hauptmann Heinrich Böhlke they just shake their heads.*

But that is not what Katja says. She sits down next to Hanna and takes one of her hands in both of hers, and says, 'Yes. I found him. I spoke to him. He will see you tomorrow.'

How in God's name did you do that?

Katja shrugs. 'I spoke to some soldiers. They sent me to others, to higher officers. In the end I was taken to the military headquarters. I told them I'm the daughter of Hauptmann Böhlke's sister, I've just arrived from Hamburg, I have a message for him.'

But how come they believed you?

'Men are so gullible, especially I think in a dry land,' Katja says simply. And then tosses her long hair back, and smiles. In spite of the paleness of her face, her hollow cheeks, there is a radiance about her which hits Hanna like a stab. She has seen it before, she has lived with this young person for so long now, they have shared so much; and yet she continues to be surprised by her.

And you say tomorrow . . . ?

'In the morning. At ten o' clock. I told him I'd bring someone with me. A woman he hasn't seen for years and who has travelled a very long way to see him. You can't imagine how intrigued he was.'

As Katja puts out her hands to pull Hanna up from the stoep a man approaches. He is pushing a rickety wheelbarrow piled high with dried animal skins. A small vervet monkey with an ancient wizened black face is perched on top. When the man notices the women he stops to raise a jaunty little Tyrolean hat from his unkempt grey hair, an incongruous sight in the late dusty glare of the African sun.

'Guten Tag, meine Damen.'

Katja gives a diffident nod; Hanna does not respond. She just takes Katja's arm and prepares to stalk off.

'You must have been walking a long way,' he remarks, wiping sweat from his face with a cuff. His face looks tired, his clothes tidy but worn – wide moleskin trousers, corduroy jacket – but in contrast with his hangdog appearance his brown boots are immaculately polished, and there is an almost boyish twinkle in the eyes set deeply under the very bushy eyebrows.

Hanna tugs at Katja, but the young woman, clearly intrigued by the man's appearance, stops to challenge him: 'What makes you think we've been walking far?'

Replacing his merry little hat, he points: 'Your shoes. They look terrible.'

'You're very observant,' says Katja.

'It's my job. I'm a shoemaker. The best in Windhoek.'

'You seem very sure of yourself.'

'It's because I'm the only one around, that's why.' He takes off his hat again and makes a bow before them. 'Siggi Fischer,' he says, 'at your ladies' service.'

Hanna rapidly conveys something to Katja, who translates, 'Thank you, Herr Fischer, but we have to go.'

'Do you have a place to stay?' he asks.

'No, but . . . ,' begins Katja, but Hanna pulls her away.

'You both look tired, if I may say so,' interposes Siggi Fischer. 'Why don't you come to my house? You are no doubt used to more comfort, but it is clean and you can have a bed and a bath. I often put up people who have nowhere else to go. And it's very close.' An almost impish grin. 'Of course, in Windhoek everything is close. We have only four streets.'

We have a busy day tomorrow, Hanna curtly conveys through Katja. *We have an appointment with an important person at ten o' clock. And we still have to get back to our horses. They have been tied up all day.*

'Where are your horses?'

Up there on the ridge, among the trees.

'Poor beasts.' He closes one eye and displaces his hat to scratch his head. 'May I make a proposal? You can come to my house and rest there while I bring down your horses. After that I can make you some supper – nothing special, I should warn you, I'm not a rich man – and tonight while you sleep I can repair your shoes. They really are in a sorry state.'

'We have no money to pay you,' says Katja quickly, but she evidently finds it hard to suppress the sudden desire for some basic comfort he has stirred up in her.

'Have I asked you for money?' he counters with a show of indignation.

Why should you go to so much trouble? asks Hanna through Katja. *You don't even know us.*

'That is why,' says Siggi Fischer raising his hands in a theatrical gesture. 'We see so few new people here. Except the military, of course, who come and go, but they mostly keep to themselves. And just as well, if you ask me.'

He is too talkative, Hanna signals to Katja. *We need our rest tonight.*

'It will be a very long night if it's just the two of us,' the young woman answers in a low voice.

'Is she ill?' asks the shoemaker, gesturing towards Hanna. 'Why doesn't she speak?'

'She's had an accident,' says Katja. 'She lost her tongue.'

'Tsk, tsk.' He shakes his head. Then he resumes in a matter-of-fact tone: 'I'll tell you what. You can have a bath at my house while I fetch the horses. And when I come back you tell me if you want to stay or not.'

At that moment the little monkey leaves his perch on the wheel-barrow and jumps on Katja's shoulder. For a moment, uttering a small cry, she contracts in fright, then realises that it is hugging her, uttering small baby sounds.

'You see, Bismarck likes you,' says Siggi.

That appears to settle the matter. Hanna is still not placated at all, but she grudgingly agrees to stay behind in the small sheet-iron house on the outskirts of the town while the shoemaker goes off to find their horses. Katja stokes the copper geyser in the kitchen and prepares a bath. There is a tin tub on the kitchen floor. Hanna goes first, while Katja makes coffee. It is the first time, she realises, that she has seen Hanna naked and it is shocking. Not the ancient disfigurements and cuts and sutures so much, however atrocious they are – the lines and ridges across her belly and breasts, the scar tissue where her nipples used to be – as the skeletal appearance of her body, the way the skin clings to the bones, the patterns of her ribcage and her hips, the protuberance of her matted sex. Hanna makes no attempt to cover up. As she washes with the coarse soap Siggi has put out for them, she appears almost deliberately to display herself – *See, see, this is me* – and then remains standing for Katja to sluice clean hot water over her. She stands with her eyes closed, head thrown back, feet apart, to let it run over her body, an immersion and a cleansing, the closest perhaps she has come to a feeling of voluptuousness in years.

Then, still naked, she takes her turn to wash Katja. The girlish body has begun to fill out, anticipating a more matronly heaviness around the hips, her breasts are fuller than they were, the areolae large and dark, the belly showing the early swelling of pregnancy.

For a moment she instinctively, self-consciously covers her breasts with her hands. 'I've changed a lot,' she says, her face flushed. 'I no longer look the way I used to.'

You are beautiful.

'No, I am not beautiful,' says Katja. 'I'm just a woman.'

Hanna pursues the bathing ritual, the rites of cleansing, a careful and almost loving long caress. They are mother and child, they are woman and woman, each acknowledging in the other the mortality of the self. In a way it is a lingering leavetaking, because beyond tomorrow there is only the darkness of the unknown. They have come so far; there is only a short last lap to complete, and this is their preparation for it.

They are so clean, so new and liquid, that it is almost a pity to put on their dusty and crumpled old clothes again. But they remain barefoot, feeling guilty about the shoes after what the shoemaker has said about them.

Together they clean up the kitchen and mop up the floor, then set about exploring the house. It is indeed very small. Apart from the kitchen there is only a long narrow room which clearly serves as sitting room and dining room and work room combined; and, at the far end, a tiny bedroom. The front room is cluttered with the signs of their host's trade: lasts and anvils, hammers, awls and other tools of many shapes and sizes, a large work bench much the worse for wear, which shows evidence of also serving as a dining table, shelves with finished and half-finished shoes, hooks on the wall from which harnesses and saddles and bridles are suspended, piles and bundles of skins and hides on the floor, everything pervaded with the smell of leather and linseed oil and wax.

Most of the bedroom is occupied by the huge bedstead of dark polished wood. The curtain around the canopy is dusty, but the bedclothes look surprisingly crisp; and the mattress must be stuffed with feathers as it bulges so hugely. Next to the bed is a small cradle, stacked with books and newspapers. On the wall opposite is a single picture, a foxed engraving of what looks like the Alps. On the bedside table is a yellowed photograph in a too-heavy wooden frame, showing the face of a woman, her features faded into a blur.

It is all so ordinary. But it is the very ordinariness of it that shocks them. It is too unreal, too ludicrous, too preposterous in its ordinariness, belonging to a world that must have gone its own way while their lives have been unwinding in another dimension altogether. The same thought may strike them: That this is the first time in God knows how many months that they find themselves in a space where they will not have to plot the death of their host.

For Hanna it is too much. *As soon as he comes back, we must go*, she signals to Katja. *We cannot stay here. It is not right.*

That is when she notices the single object that changes everything, though it is hardly any less ordinary than the rest. In the corner near the door stands a small rickety table with a single chair pulled up to it; and on the chequered surface are set out the figures of a crudely carved chess set. The game seems to be still in progress as several pieces lie overturned on one side, and the rest are set up in broken formation. Across the years, like the memory of a once-loved voice, a sound trapped in a shell, comes the image of Herr Ludwig's face moulded in the lamplight – the aquiline nose, the sad, gentle mouth, the firm-set chin, the bird-tracks around the eyes – as he stares down at her hand hovering over the board with a black bishop between her fingers; moving it, not towards the checkmating of his king, but on a tangent. She hears the distant echo of his voice, asking, 'What have you done?' And her own, controlled and quiet, answering, 'You win.'

Hanna is still fingering a discarded black rook from Siggi Fischer's chess set, smooth from much handling, when she is distracted by a sound. The wiry shoemaker enters from the kitchen and comes towards them through the happy mess of the living room. His monkey is perched on his shoulder, but it leaps to Katja's when he arrives in the doorway to the bedroom.

Hanna's first thought is that she has not yet covered her face; involuntarily she moves her hands up to shield herself. But he seems not to have noticed anything untoward.

'I've watered the horses,' says Siggi. He looks at the rook in her hand. 'I see you've found the chess set. Do you play?'

Hanna half turns away, shaking her head, panicky with embarrassment. She signals to Katja to explain, *You must excuse me, I must put on my kappie.*

'You don't need it indoors, do you?'

Surprised, Hanna glances at him, but he shows no sign at all that her appearance has unsettled him.

As if he has trapped her in a petty theft she hands him the rook. *I'm sorry. I didn't mean to disturb your setting. It looks as if your game was interrupted.*

'I only play with myself.' He smiles. 'And I always lose. Perhaps you will join me after supper.' A pause. 'I hope you have decided to stay.' He looks from one to the other.

'Where will you sleep if we do?' asks Katja.

'I make a bed on my work bench. I always do when there are visitors. Not that I get many of them.'

'We shall be happy to stay,' says Katja without consulting Hanna. She feels the woman stiffening momentarily beside her, then relaxing with what may be a sigh of resignation.

'Good.' He lovingly rubs the rook between thumb and forefinger. 'Not exactly a masterpiece, but it does the job.'

'Did you carve it?'

'No, it was my wife. She was an Ovambo woman. She died three years ago.'

'I'm sorry to hear that.'

He shrugs. 'One gets used to loneliness. One gets used to everything. Only in the beginning it was hard. But it's good to have visitors. Even though I have always been something of a loner.'

He came from Bavaria over twenty years ago, they learn. A small village in the mountains, Bayerisch Zell. He was eager to see the world and there was much talk at the time, the mid-1880s, of the exotic wilderness of German South-West Africa and its untold treasures. The reality turned out to be rather different. Still he fell under the spell of the place, its spaces, its spareness, its unexpected explosions of extravagant beauty in sunsets, desert flowers, shifting red dunes, migrating herds of antelope. After prospecting for a few years he acquired a farm near Tsumeb in the north. The final decision was really taken out of his hands when the fiancée he'd left behind in Bavaria and who was to have followed him to Africa as soon as he'd settled, wrote a letter (which only caught up with him four months later) to tell him that she'd married someone else. It is her photograph, there on the bedside table.

While he is talking, with all the eagerness of a man who hasn't had a chance to unburden for months, they move to the cluttered living room, and later to the kitchen, where they help him to prepare Knödel for supper.

'And when did you meet your wife?' asks Katja.

'Kaguti?' he asks, beginning to stir his pot on the open hearth very vigorously. 'She was a headman's daughter. I bought the farm from him. From the first moment I set eyes on her I was in love. But she was not so easily persuaded. Nor was her father. I had to work for him for many years. At last she came to live with me, it was a big feast. The problem was that my white neighbours shunned us. And some of her people didn't accept it either. It got worse after her father died. Our farm was raided and on several occasions we lost all our cattle, sometimes to the Ovambos, sometimes to the Germans. This land is so big but it had no place for us. In the end we decided to come down here to Windhoek. We were still outcasts, but we made a few friends. And people bought my shoes and saddles and bridles. Kaguti took in washing and carved figurines from wood, like the chess set. We used to play in the evenings, she was very good. But then she died.'

'What happened to your children?' asks Katja.

'We had no children.'

'And the cradle in the bedroom?'

'It was always empty.' For a moment it seems as if he wishes to say more, but then changes his mind.

The food is ready, but Hanna wants to feed the horses first. Siggi has some oats which he assures them he keeps specially for such occasions. Afterwards they go in for their supper; a section of the work bench has been cleared for it.

Katja wants to serve Siggi first, but he refuses, highly indignant: 'I always serve myself last, even when I'm alone.'

The Knödel are sticky and not very good, but they have not eaten all day; and the food is served with such enthusiasm that it feels like a celebration. They only stop when there is nothing left.

After they have done the dishes Siggi brings the chess table into the living room. He sets up the pieces and looks at Hanna.

'Shall we play?'

Katja can feel the gathering anxiety in her. Something in Hanna wants to hold back, to refuse outright; at the same time she feels a desire she has not been aware of for years. In the end, without a sound, she sits down. She knows her hands are shaking.

I have forgotten most of it, she tries to say, through Katja.

Siggi looks down at her, then brings a chair up for himself. 'It will soon come back,' he says encouragingly.

She realises that she still hasn't put her kappie on. Now it is too late. But she does feel very exposed as she makes the first move. Plan it, Herr Ludwig used to say, like a military campaign. But she cannot concentrate properly. And something inside her revolts against the idea of a campaign, any campaign, right now; she has had too much of it and is no longer sure of where it has brought her. Yet the urge to play must be as passionate as, in others, perhaps, at times, the urge to make love. Her face is burning. But she cannot focus properly. Nor can she withdraw, now that she has begun.

Katja watches from the work bench, sensing the terrible tension mounting in Hanna, but unable to understand exactly what is happening.

Before they have gone very far – it is not even an hour since they started – it is obvious to Hanna that her situation is hopeless. She is going to lose, and she no longer has the skill to extricate herself.

Katja can see her getting more and more agitated, claustrophobic. And suddenly, with a vehement shake of her head, Hanna jumps up.

I'm not going on, she signals to Katja, who conveys it to Siggi.

'Then we stop,' he says affably, dropping his long hands to his sides. 'I'm sure you must be very tired. It was inconsiderate of me.' The monkey, back on his shoulder, is chattering eagerly in his ear. He puts a hand on Hanna's shoulder, pretending not to notice how she shrinks back. 'There is no need for anyone to win or lose,' he says.

Hanna clenches her teeth so tightly that it hurts. She makes a brief gesture with her head towards the bedroom and hurries out.

Katja glances at Siggi. 'Let me help you make your bed,' she offers.

But he shakes his head. 'I still have work to do,' he reminds her, stooping to pick up the two pairs of worn shoes he has left just inside the doorway to the kitchen.

'You cannot do that now!' she protests.

'I work best at night,' he assures her. 'Now off you go.' He turns up the lamp. The monkey finds a perch on a pile of lasts. The two of them are clearly used to their routine.

Katja closes the bedroom door behind her. For a moment she leans her forehead against the cool hardness of the wall, feeling the full weight of her tiredness pressing down on her. 'I feel safe here,' she whispers.

Hanna makes no reply. She is already in the big bed, in her petticoat, deeply snuggled into the feather mattress under the eiderdown.

Katja takes off her dress and creeps in beside her. She leans over to kiss the woman, overcome by thoughts she has not even been conscious of. Hanna responds briefly. Her closed eyes are trembling. But she makes no attempt to communicate. Katja blows out the candle. The long day, the many months, fall from them. The dark space is invaded by everything that cannot, dare not, be spoken. Not yet, or not any more.

There are small sounds coming from the living room. Shuffling, tapping, scraping, rustling sounds. Occasionally something mumbled in Siggi's voice, a small chattering from the monkey in response. Katja's breathing deepens into sleep. Hanna lies awake.

Beyond the silence of the house she remains conscious of the living, moving sounds of the town. After the months in the desert there is a constant awareness of many things happening below the threshold of hearing. From time to time this uneven, indistinct hum is broken by sharper sounds. The squalling of two mating cats in the backyard. A dog barking. In the distance, so help me God, even the braying of a donkey. Only the rooster is missing, thinks Hanna, feeling a wry smile form around her wounded mouth, before the band of musicians will be complete.

The last time they slept in a house was in the parsonage at the Rhenish mission. But this is so different. There is reason to believe, as Katja said, that they are safe here.

Later the dull sounds in the living room drain away too. The thin line of light under the door goes dark. The house itself is sinking into sleep, muttering occasionally, a creaking of iron sheets and heavy beams, a scuttling perhaps of mice. If not of secret elves who come in the dark to complete the shoemaker's work for him.

A whole life drawing itself in around her, as close now as the body of the sleeping Katja. How lovely she was, standing up in the small bath. *I am not beautiful. I'm just a woman.* She too, once, who knows. She did not always look this.

But everything is now drawing to a close. Only this night, and then tomorrow. Hauptmann Heinrich Böhlke. He promised he'd be there. At ten. To meet the woman who has travelled a very long way to see him.

What did the spindly little shoemaker say? *There is no need for anyone to win.* She pushes it away, almost angrily. What does he know about her life?

And yet he has been suffering too, even if only glimpses of it showed around the edges of his words. The fiancée whose faded little portrait still stands here beside the bed. The raids on his farm, all the cattle stolen, sometimes by Ovambos, sometimes by Germans. He and his wife, ostracised by all, and then she died. How? Why? Leaving him so lonely that he takes in any stranger that comes around. With a small black-faced monkey named Bismarck as his only company.

She is still awake when the cocks begin to crow (there they are now!) and daylight comes, but she does not want to wake Katja. She may well need all her energy for what lies ahead and what she doesn't even know yet. This silence is so deeply peaceful. But it will not last.

When they get up, breakfast is already waiting. Dark bread and goat's milk cheese. Mugs of coffee. Bismarck is chattering excitedly.

On the edge of the work bench sit their shoes, with smooth new soles, the edges finely stitched, the torn flaps mended. Bright with polish.

'If you have important business today as you told me,' says Siggi, beaming with pride, 'at least you will be well appointed. With a pair of good shoes you need not be afraid of anything.'

72

ALL THOSE DOCUMENTS, the old copies of *Afrika Post*, the correspondence, the registers from Frauenstein, the police records; and yet armed with no more than a name only half released by history – Hanna X – what is there to conclude? Had there been a court case to round it off, everything would have spilled into recorded history. But as I explained at the beginning of this account, the unfortunate option chosen by the German officer pre-empted a trial, and after that the machinations of power kept it from public notice in the interests of protecting the honour of the Empire. As a consequence all my enquiries – begun in Windhoek, pursued in Bremen and Hamburg, afterwards resumed in Namibia – could only end in conjecture. But having come so far, I cannot now turn back or abandon the quest. Having followed Hanna and Katja to Windhoek I have little choice but to imagine the rest. A narrative accumulates its own weight and demands its own conclusion. And so they will leave the humble home of the shoemaker Siggie Fischer early that Friday morning in November 1906 to keep what has become an appointment with destiny. Before Hanna X is restored to the silence from which she emerged, there has to be a final chapter, which will of necessity take place in the sprawling sandstone building of the army headquarters where Katja met Hauptmann Heinrich Böhlke the day before.

73

He is a small dry man with a monocle, seated in a large leather-upholstered chair behind an enormous desk at the far end of the long, low-ceilinged room. He is nearly bald, he has a thin moustache, his face is tanned although a sickly pallor shows through it. When the women are escorted in he rises and comes stiffly towards them, waves the orderly away, gives instructions to be left alone with his visitors.

In front of Katja he makes a formal bow, takes her hand, offers a kiss without touching her with his lips. Perhaps he doesn't like touching people.

'Fräulein.'

Then he turns to Hanna. Hidden by the long beak of her kappie her face is invisible, so he gives only a perfunctory nod.

'I believe we met before?'

'She cannot speak,' says Katja. 'Perhaps I forgot to mention that?'

'Indeed?' He seems disappointed. 'I cannot recall that you did.'

'I'm sure you must remember her,' Katja goes on.

He motions them towards two large easy chairs, also upholstered in dark red leather. They do not move.

'May I ask, Fräulein . . . ?' He sounds perplexed. For the first time a hint of suspicion enters his voice which is slightly hoarse, perhaps from too many years of barking orders.

That is when Hanna unties her kappie, and removes it, and drops it on the floor as if discarding it.

He stares at her, takes a step back. There is, however, no sign of recognition yet; how can he be expected to remember?

'Hauptmann Böhlke,' says Katja, bending over and pulling up her long skirt. He stares in disbelief. Even more so when she whips a Luger from under her clothes and points it at him. When he turns towards Hanna she has done the same.

'Now listen . . .'

'Shut up,' says Katja quietly. 'If you make a sound we shall kill you.'

'I don't understand.'

Hanna makes a brief gesture towards Katja.

'Turn round,' Katja orders him. 'Put your hands behind your back. We have to tie you up.'

'But . . .'

Hanna moves very quickly, like a snake striking. The butt of the Luger crashes against the side of his face. In a reflex action he pulls back his arm, his fist clenched.

'Don't try that,' snaps Katja.

He has dropped his monocle. His eyes, suddenly naked, are burning on the gun in her hand as he reluctantly moves his hands behind his back. Hanna has a length of rope wound about her waist under her dress. It does not take very long to tie him up. Then she gags him.

'Why don't we just shoot him and have done with it?' asks Katja, breathing heavily.

Hanna shakes her head and grimaces again. *We are not in a hurry.* She picks up the gun she has left on the chair while she was tying his arms together. *Take off his clothes.*

'What are you going to do now?' asks Katja, shocked. They have never discussed this part of the plan before.

Take off his clothes. Use your knife if you have to.

Dumbfounded, Katja does not dare disobey. Another two minutes and Hauptmann Heinrich Böhlke is standing naked before them. His feet are very white. His toenails are yellow. Strange what one notices in a moment like this. He has a small pot-belly, which does not go well with his delicate bony frame. She gazes openly at his penis, a mangled, blackened little stub of a thing. It looks, she thinks, like the remains of her tongue. Can this really be all? Is this miserable little appendix all it has been about? All the suffering, all the agony, all the hell, these years and years. For this. *When I . . .* No, it does not bear repetition; it is too pathetic.

Perhaps Katja senses her confusion. 'What do we do now?' she asks, very pale.

You must now leave him to me, Hanna gestures.

'Where shall I wait for you?' the young woman asks, hesitant, dubious, worried.

I shall not see you again, Katja. You must go away. Make sure no one — no one, understand? — finds you. Go to Siggie, he will help you. Cut off your hair, tie it up, put on man's clothes, do something. Anything. Just make sure you get away.

'I don't understand!'

This is not for understanding. Just do it. Please. It is now all up to you.

It feels like for ever before Katja, stunned and fighting back her tears, makes a move to leave. She tries to come up to Hanna, to say goodbye, to kiss her, just to touch her one last time. But Hanna shakes her head. No, no. There was a time for this. Not now.

For an incalculable time Hanna waits inside with her hostage. The first few minutes she stands listening very intently, but there is no sound from outside. Katja probably told whatever military personnel she encountered that the Hauptmann has requested to be left alone with his lady visitor. Perhaps she winked at them. They would have put two and two together. Reassured, Hanna moves in behind the desk, facing the little man. She never noticed, on the train, how small he was.

Putting the gun down on the smooth polished wood in front of her she removes a sheet of paper from a pile on the corner and selects a pen from a row meticulously arranged beside the large blotter like a phalanx of soldiers on parade. Leaning over, she dips it in the inkwell and starts writing in large block letters. The nib makes a scratching sound in the silence. One or two of the words are marred by blots. The officer stares fixedly at her moving hand as if expecting something unusual to happen.

She shifts the paper across the desk for him to read. Wary about approaching too closely he stretches his scrawny neck like a chicken preparing to drink. There is only one line:

WHEN I FUCK A WOMAN SHE STAYS FUCKED.

Even now it takes some time before he understands. But as the meaning slowly filters into his mind she sees recognition spreading across his face.

He looks up slowly to gawk at her. Hanna nods.

A few drops come dribbling from the tip of his pathetic member.

Hanna is very calm now. She stands back and begins to undo the buttons of her dress one by one, her gaze very steady on the officer's face. She is in no hurry. As she did once before, in front of that dark mirror in Frauenstein, she bares her body, not to herself this time, but to this quaking little man. He must see it all. The ravages he has wrought, the horror he has visited on her. Once she has removed all her clothes, hideously naked, she again picks up the gun, comes round the desk towards him, and lowers herself on the edge, not removing her eyes from him for an instant. He has backed a few metres away, well out of reach. She is taking no chances. Not that there seems to be much likelihood of his lunging at her. He stands shivering, his teeth chattering, yet it is not cold. From close up she can see the ceaseless, rotating motion of the skin on his wrinkled, purple scrotum, like a small vulnerable animal trying to shrink away, to shrivel up, yet never quite succeeding. Through the cloth that gags his mouth he utters plaintive, whining, moaning sounds. She does not really hear him. It is not that her thoughts are elsewhere. They are nowhere. Nowhere at all.

Only when she is quite sure that Katja is well out of the way does Hanna get up from the desk. There is a slow, almost imperceptible change in the expression with which she looks at him. It is as if the thoughts are siphoned into her from very far away. Hate? Oh yes, the hate is still there, the hate which has made it possible for her to survive. All these years it has kept her alive, it has driven her on, even before she had learned to give it a name. Waiting. Waiting for this. For this moment. To redeem it all. Then why does it now seem so paltry, so insignificant? To kill him, to carve him up the way he once maimed her, to make him writhe in agony, to make it last and linger – what would that mean? Only that she has become, as Katja once said, as despicable as he? There was that night after they had taken the first fort, when she and Katja lay talking and the girl – she was still a girl then – told her about making love to her young soldier before she killed him. *The first part was for me, the second for you.* That was when she first began to wonder: perhaps hate is not enough. If her whole life had to remain trapped in hate it would mean that she could never get beyond this moment of standing opposite this wretched little person.

The years fall away. She is facing, once again, Herr Ludwig in his study, the smooth black bishop in her hand. And with an extraordinary sense of liberation she thinks: No. No, she will not kill him. It is no longer necessary. It is not worth it. Killing him cannot undo the world that has made him possible. She need not stoop to that. It is too simple. And there has been blood enough. All she needs is to make sure the world will take note That passionate message scrawled on a hot morning on the blank pages from a bible dropped in the dust. So that it cannot be shut away in a drawer again as Frau Knesebeck once did. She sighs deeply. And puts on her clothes again with fastidious care.

When she has finished, she motions towards the door. Leaving a thin trail of urine on the carpet, he starts moving. She opens the door for him, then hesitates and looks back: Should she put on her kappie again? No. Not this time. She will not make it easier for others, or for herself. She follows him outside. The corridor is empty. So is the staircase.

On the ground floor they encounter the first soldiers. There are shouts, loud vacant orders, confused outcries. Hanna presses the pistol into the man's naked back. His backbone is studded like a belt. She can count his pointed vertebrae. He is blubbering more loudly now, but the sounds remain muffled in the cloth that gags him.

Many soldiers follow in their wake, but at a safe distance, overcome by the suddenness, the preposterousness, of this thing that is happening before their eyes.

As they move from the large sandstone building into the palm-lined street, downhill, towards the Kaiser Wilhelmstrasse, more and more people gather to watch them. The news must be spreading very rapidly. Kahapa would have believed it was done by the wind. Soon there is a crowd.

Once or twice Hauptmann Heinrich Böhlke stumbles and falls on his knees, but a quick stab with the barrel of the pistol sends him scrambling wretchedly to his feet again. On one occasion, when people threaten to come too close, Hanna fires a shot into the ground right next to him. The people tumble out of the way, allowing her and her prisoner to pass unhindered among them. The shot also causes the man to lose control of his sphincter. Watery shit dribbles down the backs of his thin hairy legs. There are titters in the crowd. They are beginning to enjoy it.

It cannot of course go on for very long. It is hard to say whether it comes as a surprise when two pairs of arms in khaki uniform suddenly clutch her from behind.

This time, she thinks, she will not die. This time it may be worse.

Yet she does not offer any resistance; to those closest to her she seems even, vaguely, content. Perhaps, if one may use the word, serene. At least, she thinks, there is nothing she regrets. No pain, no agony, no fear, no darkness, no extremity or outrage.

What she sees will not be the people in the crowd, but the grave face of a small girl on a distant beach. Knowing that this is why she is still here today, and will not kill. For the sake of that tiny image. And what she hears will not be the shouts and cries and curses or even the tumult of applause, but the very quiet sibilance within the confines of a shell. And if she smiles, if what she shows can be interpreted as a smile, it is because now, at last, Hanna X has reached the other side.

Acknowledgements

FOR TWENTY YEARS or more the title *The Other Side of Silence* has been waiting patiently in my mind for the right story to come along. At last it has happened. It was George Weideman who first told me about the shiploads of women transported to the colony of German South-West Africa in the early years of the twentieth-century, and supplied me with hundreds of pages of archive documents. I first dipped into the material for the history of the Landman family in *An Act of Terror* (1991), but the story continued to haunt me and demanded a book on its own. This is it.

It was also George who first told me about Frauenstein, where the rejects among the immigrant women were housed. But the Frauenstein of my story exists only in my imagination, as does most of the life of Hanna X. I am, however, deeply indebted to Rainer Loose, as well as Susanne Pfeiffer, Gabriele Hoffmann and Günter Garbrecht, who have provided me with information about Bremen at the end of the nineteenth century, and about the German shipping lines to southern Africa. In some respects I have departed from their facts to serve the needs of my story, as in the depiction of the Little Children of Jesus, which is a fictitious institution; and in the description of conditions in the third-class section of the *Hans Woermann*.

For the historical background to German South-West Africa a number of books proved most useful; they include Olga Levinson: *The Ageless Land* (Cape Town: Tafelberg Publishers, 1961), Heinrich Vedder: *Das alte Südwestafrika* (Berlin: Martin Warneck, 1934), Helmut Bley: *South-West Africa under German Rule* (London etc.

Heinemann, 1971), Horst Drechsler: *Südwestafrika unter Deutscher Kolonialherrschaft* (Berlin: Akademie Verlag, 1966) and *Die Dagboek van Hendrik Witbooi* (Cape Town: Van Riebeeck Society, 1929).

Much of the information about Jeanne d'Arc, who has remained a luminous shadow in my memory since she figured in *On the Contrary* (1993), comes from Lucien Fabre's *Jeanne d'Arc* (Paris: Le Club du Livre, 1948), Marina Warner's *Joan of Arc* (London: Vintage, 1991) and Vita Sackville West's *Saint Joan of Arc* (London: Cobdan-Sanderson, 1936); from this book comes the remark in Chapter 15: 'She makes us think and she makes us question. She uncovers the dark places into which we may fear to look.'

Myths and folk tales of Namas and Hereros were gleaned from many sources, among them I. Schapera's *The Khoisan Peoples of South Africa* (London: Routledge & Kegan Paul, 1930), Penny Miller's *Myths and Legends of Southern Africa* (Cape Town: T. V. Bulpin, 1979), Thomas A. Nevin's *The Quivering Spear* (Johannesburg: QS Partners in Publishing, 1996) and Friedrich von der Leyen's *Märchen aus Namibia* (Eugen Diederichs Verlag, n.d.).

The rain song of the Namas in Chapter 12 has been translated from 'Die dans van die reën' by Eugène Marais (although only published in 1921 one can safely assume that it is based on a much earlier version in the vernacular). Hanna's pact with God in Chapter 17 was signalled by Nancy Huston in her beautiful introduction to the French translation of Göran Tunström's *Un prosateur à New York* (Arles: Actes Sud, 2001); the remark in Chapter 51 about setting foot in a life from which no return is possible comes from Dante's *La vita nuova*, XIV).

Glossary

[Nama words are indicated with (N), Afrikaans words with (A)]

aruma (N) – edible thorny succulent
ati (N) – reed flutes

baas (A) – master
bossie (A) – small shrub

geelslang (A) – Cape cobra
gemsbok (A) – large antelope, oryx
ghura (N) – stringed instrument
gli root (N) – root used in a concoction that induces sleep and
    numbness
gompou (A) – kori bustard
gurutsi-kubib (N) – chameleon

Heiseb (N) – hunter-trickster god who is constantly reborn
hei nun (N) – grey-feet, ghosts

kappie (A) – large-hooded bonnet
kaross (N) – blanket or cloak made of skins
Khanous (N) – evening/morning star, Venus
khurob (N) – tortoise
Khuseti (N) – Pleiades
kierie (N) – stick
koo (N) – death

koppie (A) – small rocky hill

kukemakranka (N) – edible, bulbaceous plant with sweet-smelling
   orange pods

meerkat (A) – ground squirrel

meid (A) – black woman (pejorative)

nawas (N) – rhinoceros

nerina (N) – flower

norra (N) – sweet edible root

sam-sam (N) – peace

sarês (N) – dust devil (inhabited by evil spirit)

smous (A) – itinerant trader

sobo khoin (N) – people of the shadows, ghosts

stoep (A) – veranda

t'kanna (N) – eland

t'kaoop (N) – buffalo

t'koi-t'koi (N) – primitive drum

t'kwu (N) – springbok

torob (N) – war

tsamma (N) – wild melon

Tsaob (N) – 'Embers', the Milky Way

werf (A) – (farm)yard